D1117867

Elizabeth's War

A Novel of the First Seminole War

By

John and Mary Lou Missall

Elizabeth's War

A Novel of the First Seminole War

Cover art: *The Americans at Barrancas: American General Andrew Jackson invades Pensacola, Spanish Florida, 1818* by Jackson Walker ©2005. Cover design by Jackson Walker Studios ©2015.

"This project is sponsored in part by the Department of State, Division of Cultural Affairs, the Florida Council of Arts and Culture and the State of Florida." (Section 286.25, Florida Statutes).

ISBN: 978-1-886104-83-9

The Florida Historical Society Press
435 Brevard Avenue
Cocoa, FL 32922
http://myfloridahistory.org/fhspress

Publisher's Note

Established in 1856, the Florida Historical Society (FHS) is an independent not-for-profit organization dedicated to educating the public about the rich history and culture of our diverse state. Publishing is at the heart of the Florida Historical Society's mission. The Florida Historical Society began publishing our outstanding academic journal the *Florida Historical Quarterly* in 1908. Since 1925, the Florida Historical Society has been publishing books, beginning with *The History of Jacksonville, Florida and Vicinity* by Frederick T. Davis. For 78 years, FHS only occasionally published books, but in 2003, the decision was made to establish a more active and regular publication schedule. Today, the Florida Historical Society Press is publishing between five and ten books per year.

The Florida Historical Society Press preserves Florida's past through the publication of books on a wide variety of topics relating to our state's diverse history and culture. We publish non-fiction books, of course, and our goal of disseminating Florida history to the widest possible audience is also well served by the publication of novels firmly based upon scholarly research. Teachers and students alike find that our high quality fictionalized accounts of Florida history bring the past to life and make historic events, people, and places more accessible and "real." We also publish books focusing on creative expressions of Florida history and culture such as painting, cooking, and photography.

Elizabeth's War: A Novel of the First Seminole War by John and Mary Lou Missall is a work of fiction based on actual people and situations. At the end of the book, the authors separate fact from fiction and identify their sources. As writers and historians who specialize in the Seminole Wars, John and Mary Lou Missall are particularly qualified to engage in the educated supposition required to "fill in the blanks" of the historical record. *Elizabeth's War* serves as a prequel to the Missall's book *Hollow Victory: A Novel of the Second Seminole War,* which is also published by FHS Press.

Thanks are owed to artist Jackson Walker for the use of his painting *The Americans at Barrancas: American General Andrew Jackson invades Pensacola, Spanish Florida, 1818,* and to Jackson Walker Studios for the design of the book cover. Thanks to Jon White for realizing that design for publication. Thanks also to Paul Pruett for his assistance with layout and design of the text.

Thanks to copy editor Chris Gallaway for her careful attention to detail.

This project is sponsored in part by the Department of State, Division of Cultural Affairs, the Florida Council of Arts and Culture, and the State of Florida. Their support is much appreciated.

Dr. Ben Brotemarkle
Executive Director
Florida Historical Society

1

8th November 1814
Pensacola, West Florida

To:
His Ex'cy James Madison
Pres't of the United States
Washington City

Your Excellency:

I have the pleasure to report that I have, this day, forced the cowardly British occupiers of Spanish West Florida to flee Pensacola. Upon our approach they took to their ships, delaying only long enough to spike the cannon at the Barrancas. Artillery personnel are, at this moment, attempting repairs, and we shall have the battery operational in a matter of days. This will put an end to British efforts in this quarter to recruit the disaffected savages and runaway negroes to their cause.

As to the disposition of the Spanish Gov'nr and other officials, they are at present confined to quarters and shall remain so until I receive further instructions. They continue to claim neutrality and insist our two governments are at peace. It is a diplomatic nicety I refuse to accept. They cannot claim to be the ally of Great Britain against the French, but not the ally of Great Britain in the war against the U. States. Nor can the Gov'nr give adequate explanation for his allowing the British to occupy this city, other than a general lack of military force to prevent the act. Such may be the case, but I shall not accept it as an excuse. If the Spaniards are unable to fulfill their treaty obligations, I see no reason why the United States should not retain this colony until such time as Spain can properly garrison her posts and indemnify us for our losses.

As to the army's next move, I cannot yet say with certainty. That the British intend to invade the Southern States through the Gulf of Mexico is not to be doubted, but where they shall land is the question that remains unanswered. Of one thing you may be assured, sir: Although they may set foot on American soil, I shall not, as long as life is within me, permit them to long remain.

I am, sir,
Your Most Obedient Servant
Andrew Jackson,
Maj. Genl. U. States Army

Andrew Jackson paced the parapet of Fort Barrancas, the bastion guarding the entrance to Pensacola Bay. It was a perfect fall day, not so hot that he felt his heavy woolen coat a burden to wear, nor cold enough to make him feel he really needed it. Before him was an especially tranquil, lovely scene, with the low, sandy dunes of Santa Rosa Island just across the channel and the sparkling Gulf of Mexico beyond it. Yet as beautiful as it was, the scenery was wasted on Jackson. In his mind he saw large wooden warships with broadsides blazing, intent on forcing their way past Fort Barrancas and a sister fort on Santa Rosa. It was all in his imagination, of course, but as a military man, it was the sort of thing he thought about. There was little doubt in his mind that Florida would one day be an American possession, and the deep, spacious harbor would be the perfect place for a naval base.

Jackson knew he wasn't supposed to be in Pensacola. His instructions from the War Department had reminded him that the United States was at war with England, not Spain. The implication was that he was free to fight the British wherever he found them, but he was not to molest the Spaniards. Having found the British in possession of the capital of Spanish West Florida, Jackson had entered the city and driven them out. Of course, now that he had possession of Pensacola, he had no intention of just marching away, no matter what the orders said. He was a general, not a politician, and was quite willing to let the diplomats work out the details. Not that Pensacola was any great prize. One of his officers had quipped that one good broadside from a man-of-war would thoroughly demolish the dilapidated town. Jackson tended to agree.

He looked out toward the Gulf of Mexico, straining to see something that wasn't there. *Paul Revere*. The name flashed through his mind. *Well, I don't need Paul Revere to tell me the British are coming, I just need to know where the hell they're going to come ashore.* Somewhere out in the Gulf was a large British fleet carrying thousands of Redcoat troops intent on invading the southern United States. Jackson knew they were coming; he just didn't know where the fleet would drop anchor.

There were three possibilities: Pensacola, Mobile, or New Orleans. The small force he had just sent packing were nothing more than troublemakers attempting to rally the Indians and runaway slaves to the British cause. The main invasion force would be much harder to get rid of, but for the moment, Pensacola seemed secure. The entrance to the harbor was well defended, and the English were now aware that thousands of American soldiers were on hand to contest any landing. Mobile was another matter. Portions of this same British fleet had attempted to enter Mobile Bay in September, but had been repulsed at Fort Bowyer with the loss of one ship. Despite that, Mobile was still a viable target. A large naval flotilla, carrying thousands of troops, might be able to force its way past the fort and into the bay. Once in control of Mobile Bay, the British would be almost impossible to dislodge. From there they could march inland or take boats upriver and unite with disgruntled Indian tribes eager to regain land lost to the Americans. With strong Indian allies, they could strike the thinly settled frontier before moving on to wreak havoc on the plantations of Georgia, the Carolinas, and Tennessee, freeing thousands of vengeful slaves in the process. It was Jackson's worst nightmare.

Then there was New Orleans. The Crescent City was the key to the entire western United States. Stored in the city's warehouses were millions of dollars worth of agricultural products from the western states. If the British were to gain control of New Orleans, they would also gain control of the Mississippi, and with that they could strangle the American economy. New Orleans also had the advantage of being more accessible to the British. For the most part, there was only one way into either Pensacola or Mobile Bays. New Orleans, surrounded by water, could be approached from any number of directions. Jackson might be able to defend the city of New Orleans, but he couldn't stop the British from landing nearby. If it were he, Jackson would have gone for Mobile. Better to strike swiftly, cause as much destruction as possible, and force your enemy to sue for peace. But the British, he knew, didn't think that way. They were building a world empire and wanted another foothold in North America. If the English held New Orleans at the end of the war they would keep it, and America's westward expansion would be stifled. It was a situation Jackson could not allow.

And that's what was so frustrating. He was hundreds of miles from New Orleans, and there was no way to get there quickly. The Royal Navy controlled the Gulf of Mexico, so the normal water route was out of the question. On the other hand, there were no good roads between Pensacola and Louisiana; the path would be through almost total wilderness. It would take weeks to march his army to New Orleans, yet there was no other choice. He was not going to let his nation's future die without a fight.

For seventeen-year-old Jack Dill the war was proving an exciting adventure, despite the fact that he was frequently hungry and most of his time was spent marching through thick forests or constructing roads and bridges. The son of a shopkeeper from Charleston, Dill had answered his nation's call to take up arms against the hated English, just as his father had done in the Revolution. He had assumed he'd be helping defend South Carolina from a possible British invasion, but the war and the army had need of him elsewhere, and he soon found himself marching through the Georgia wilderness to fight Creek Indians who were allied with the English. By the time his company had arrived on the scene, Jackson had defeated the Creeks, so there was little to do but make camp and stand guard duty. Then word was received that large numbers of Indian refugees and the British were in Pensacola, so the army moved south.

The capture of Pensacola had been a relatively bloodless affair, but thrilling nonetheless. Jackson's army of about 3,000 men had arrived on November 6, and on the following day the general called for the city's surrender. Spanish Governor Mateo Manrique, expecting support from the five British warships in the harbor, refused to give up his post without a fight. Unfortunately, as dawn broke on the morning of the 8th, he saw the English fleet hoist their anchors and sail out of the harbor. Left with only a few hundred men to defend the city, Manrique hastily prepared a defensive line at the town's northern edge and waited for the attack.

Jackson didn't give him long to wait. Although the Spanish had a few small cannon to bolster their defenses, the weapons did little to intimidate the Americans. When the bugle sounded the charge, Dill and his compatriots shouted at the top of their lungs, pointed their bayonets forward, and ran towards the Spaniards. The defenders fired several volleys and a number of Americans fell, but the advancing line was not going to be stopped. As the attackers began to climb the barricades, the Spanish defenders fell back into the town. Dill, one of the first over the wall, shouted at the fleeing soldiers, urging them to stand and fight.

Relative quiet fell as the Americans consolidated their position and turned the captured Spanish cannons toward the town. Before they could be fired or a fresh assault launched, someone noticed a white flag waving from a doorway. The white cloth continued to wave for a few seconds, and then a Spanish soldier carefully stepped into the street, still waving his flag. When it was obvious the Americans weren't going to shoot anyone, Governor Manrique and another officer joined the soldier. The battle was over.

Dill was proud of himself. He had faced the enemy guns and had survived. Like all soldiers experiencing their first taste of battle he had been nervous and a bit frightened, but once the charge had been sounded, all fear left him, and he ran as hard toward the Spanish line as anyone. Part of his confidence had come from the fact that he knew the odds were in his favor. The Spanish were outnumbered at least ten to one, so his chances of being hit were at worst one in ten. Of course few of the Spanish musket balls would actually hit anyone, and not all wounds were fatal, so Dill reasoned he had little to worry about. It was an odd way to look at a possibly mortal situation, but Dill found comfort in the logic, and in this instance he had been proven correct.

As soon as Pensacola was safely under the control of an American garrison, the army, more than two thousand strong, began its march to New Orleans, driven forward by the will of Andrew Jackson. Choctaw Indian guides led them along ancient pathways that ran indirectly from Pensacola to New Orleans, through dense woods and seemingly impenetrable swamps. Most of the way the path was no wider than what would allow a horse to pass. At times like these, the pioneers would break out the axes and saws to clear the way, making the path wide enough for the baggage wagons to negotiate. Rafts were constructed to cross the rivers, crude bridges were built over large streams, and small creeks were forded. Causeways were built through wetlands, and logs were laid to make corduroy roads through the bogs. The terrain slowed them, the cold nights made them shiver, and the rain soaked them to the skin, but nothing would stop them.

Food began to run out two weeks into the trek. The men had already been on half rations for a week, and now the daily allotment was reduced even further. Not only were the rations small, the quality was far from pleasing. The biscuits were moldy and worm-eaten, the bacon was rancid, and the coffee was not much stronger than the swamp water it was brewed from. Yet no one grumbled, at least not within earshot of the general, who kept pressing the men on, all the while extolling the storied riches and comforts of New Orleans. When they reached their destination, he promised, all their wants, be it food, drink, or the pleasure of a lady's bed, would be theirs for the asking.

In his own way, private Dill was as purposeful as General Jackson. Though driven more by hunger than thoughts of glory, he was as determined as anyone to reach New Orleans in the shortest possible amount of time. If trees needed to be felled, he was the first to pick up an axe and was the man who swung it the hardest. If a bridge needed to be built, he would be the first one in the water. If the other soldiers were tired and slow to get moving, he was the first to shout encouragement. As the days and the miles fell behind, the officers began to notice the young man's efforts. Good leaders were hard to find; Jack Dill was the sort of man they needed.

Confusion was the reigning king when Jackson's army arrived at New Orleans. Some officials were prepared to surrender the city, while others vowed to burn it to the ground before breaching the levees and letting the Mississippi flood everything in sight. Merchants frantically scoured the docks, looking for boats to transport themselves and their goods safely upriver. Some warehouse operators were in a panic, selling whatever they could for anything they could get. Speculators bought up whatever was available at the lowest price they could get, assuming the British would be happy to buy anything available. No one, it seemed, thought the British could be stopped.

All that changed with the arrival of Andrew Jackson. Within twenty-four hours, the very thought of allowing the British into New Orleans seemed to disappear. Yet as Jackson gathered his army, even his supporters must have had their doubts. True, there were about 4,000 men available, but it was a motley crew. There were perhaps a thousand soldiers from the regular army. Some of them had come with Jackson, while others had already been stationed in Louisiana or the Mississippi Territory. They were well-disciplined men and better equipped than anyone else in the defending force, but there were simply too few of them.

Most of the fighters were state or territorial militia or volunteer units, and their potential effectiveness varied. The militia was a conscripted force, poorly motivated, led, trained, and equipped. Jackson would give them the motivation, a portion of the leadership, and provide what training he could, but it was up to the War Department to get them the proper equipment in time for the upcoming battle. Jackson didn't expect much from that quarter.

The volunteer units posed a different set of problems, but motivation certainly wasn't one of them. These men had willingly answered the nation's call, forming their own companies and electing their own leaders. The largest contingent was from Jackson's home state of Tennessee. To these men Jackson was one step removed from God, and they were happy to be part of his cult. The biggest problem with the volunteers was their independent attitude. Generally recruited from the middle and upper classes of frontier society, they considered themselves a cut above the common soldiers and lower class militiamen, and were quick to question orders or someone's military expertise. For some generals, it was a situation that might lead to difficulties. For

Jackson, it was of little concern. No one acted independently when Andrew Jackson was in charge.

The most questionable parts of the fighting force were the convicts, slaves, drifters, and outlaws who had signed on for any number or reasons, some noble, most self-serving. In addition, there were Jean Lafitte's Baratarian pirates. Some Louisiana officials had protested against the inclusion of such men and even Jackson had been reluctant, but the pirates' fighting experience and local knowledge could not be ignored, and Jackson certainly didn't want them fighting on the side of the British. For the most part, it was an undisciplined, unmilitary-looking army, and the British spies in New Orleans must have been pleased with what they saw.

Jackson immediately began to organize his forces, shifting men from overstaffed companies to those that had too few men. There was also a lack of experienced officers, both commissioned and noncommissioned. Volunteer Captain George Vashon, a native of Baton Rouge, had recruited a company of riflemen and had found some of the best marksmen in Louisiana to fill his ranks. Unfortunately, most of them were backwoodsmen with little military experience. Vashon needed help in turning the men into a proper fighting force and requested the aid of a seasoned noncommissioned officer. The best Jackson could do was promote Jack Dill to corporal and assign him to Vashon's command.

The following morning, as Dill approached the camp occupied by Vashon's command, he shook his head. *Not a soldier among them,* he thought. The most conspicuous man in the group appeared to be an officer, judging from the fact that he was carrying a rusty old sword and would occasionally issue an order that might or might not be obeyed. The young man was no older than Dill, wore stylish civilian clothes, and had a short, deformed left arm. Dill continued to watch everyone from a distance for a few minutes, sizing things up. He noticed a tall, handsome young man with a casual attitude who appeared to have some authority.

Dill approached the man, extended his hand, and said, "Corporal Jack Dill. I've been assigned to Captain Vashon's company. Do you know where I might find the captain?" Pointing to the man with the withered arm, Dill asked, "Is that him?"

The other man extended his hand and replied, "John Stuart's m' name. Company sergeant. Glad to have you." He then raised his voice loud enough for the surrounding soldiers to hear. "Glad to have anybody that can help make fighting men out of these worthless louts." The soldiers laughed, knowing the spirit in which the remark had been made. Stuart then glanced at the man with the deformed arm and smiled. "Would that fellow be Captain Vashon? God, no. He's the captain's son, Robert. He's our lieutenant, I suppose. No one elected him, but no one else wants the job, so I guess he's it. Still, he'll fight alongside the rest of us as best he can, if the damn Brits ever get close enough for him to use that old blade of his granddaddy's." He winked and wiggled his left arm, as if it were as useless as the young Vashon's. "Not much good with a musket, but a good man to sit down and enjoy a bit of rum with." He then motioned toward a tent. Dill could see a pair of feet hanging off the end of a cot. "You'll have to wait awhile to see the captain. He's still in his tent sleeping off last night's revelry. That's why Robert's running around giving out the orders. The old man's headache doesn't usually go away until late morning."

Dill was beginning to wonder what sort of company he'd been sent to. A carefree sergeant, a crippled officer who wasn't really an officer, and a drunken captain. If this was the best Jackson could find, the British flag might soon be flying over New Orleans. Yet as he looked around, he saw things that were encouraging. Robert was forming the men into squads and running them through the manual of arms, or at least attempting to. Stuart turned to a nearby soldier who was tinkering with his rifle and said, "This isn't turkey shooting, Jimmy. You don't take one good shot, pick up the bird, and go home. It's one shot after another, and after a dozen or so the gun's gonna get fouled. Take the wire pick and clean out the touchhole, use the brush to clean out the pan, then point the rifle straight down and tap the muzzle on the ground to get the burnt powder out. That'll be good enough until the battle's over, when you can give it a proper cleaning. If you're still alive."

The pair walked over to where Robert was drilling the soldiers. After Sergeant Stuart made the introductions, Robert extended his hand. "My pleasure, Dill. Welcome to the company." Looking about, he said, "We're a bit short of tents. . . . Well, we're a bit short of everything, but the flints and powder won't be a problem until the Redcoats pay a visit. Anyway, you can bunk with Stuart, here. He doesn't snore too badly. I'll move in with Father. Seen any fighting?"

Dill nodded. "Pensacola and some skirmishes with the Creeks."

"Well, any experience is more than what these boys have. Get yourself settled in and by then Father might be up and about." Robert smiled and turned back to his men. "All right, lads, back to it! You may be the best marksmen in the army, but you're a far cry from being soldiers. I want you to shoot the damn Redcoats, not make them think you're trying out for the position of King George's Jester."

Whatever confidence Jackson had been able to instill in the citizens of New Orleans began to erode on December 14. Two days earlier the British fleet, with 8,000 soldiers and sailors aboard, had anchored near the entrance to Lake Borgne, east of New Orleans. Barring their way was a small flotilla of American gunboats, which the British immediately attacked. Overwhelmed by hundreds of Redcoats converging on them in more than forty small boats, the gunboats were soon lost. The Royal Navy was now free to enter Lake Borgne, and when news reached the city, people once again began to panic. Fearing desertions and a loss of public support, Jackson declared martial law. All of a sudden, publicly expressing one's doubts about the general's ability to protect the city could land a person in jail.

That didn't stop people from worrying, but the conversations were kept private. The morning after the announcement, Captain Vashon and the other leaders of the company met outside his tent to plan the day's training. Talk soon drifted to the subject of Jackson's declaration. Sergeant Stuart had reservations about the necessity of martial law. "I don't much like the idea that the general can just throw a man in jail for simply speaking his mind. Having an opinion and supporting the British are two different things. Mind you, I know the circumstances warrant a firm hand, but it worries me a bit. Does he really have the authority?"

Captain Vashon shrugged. "Personally, I'll withhold judgment until after the battle. He's the man in charge and has to do what he feels is necessary to protect the city. Anyway, right now martial law is the least of our concerns." He turned to Dill. "Are the men ready to take on the Redcoats, Corporal?"

Dill thought for a moment, and then answered, "Depends on the situation, sir. Behind a strong defensive barrier, I'd have to say they are, but just barely. Out in the open, face to face against a disciplined, seasoned line of professional soldiers, I'd be a bit concerned. Let's just hope the general constructs a good defense and the Brits oblige us by attacking it."

Stuart added, "They're good, brave men, sir, and will fight with all they've got within 'em, but they need a bit more time to learn to trust themselves and the men next to them. They also need ammunition."

Vashon winked. "The general says it's coming."

His son Robert quipped, "So are the Redcoats. Do you think Mother and Elizabeth are safe in Baton Rouge?"

"Fear not, son. Your mother knows what to do should New Orleans fall. Even if the British are successful, I doubt they'll bother with Baton Rouge. They'll already have control of the Mississippi, and the farther they send their troops inland, the more vulnerable they become." That may have been true, but Vashon knew that only by defeating the British at New Orleans would his wife and daughter be truly secure. "If we all do our jobs, then all our loved ones will be safe." Robert's concerns mirrored those of many of the soldiers. The announcement of martial law had increased apprehension within the ranks, as the men began to realize the seriousness of their situation. Perhaps it was time to shift the conversation away from purely military matters and dwell on something more personal. Looking to Stuart, he asked, "Who are you fighting for, Sergeant?"

Stuart shook his head. "Don't know, sir. Other than my uncle, who I'm not that close to, I don't really have any family. I guess it's a bit selfish, sir, but I suppose I'm fighting for myself, meaning my freedom. I'm my own man, and I'll be no subject to a king, if I can help it. If I have to have a reason to fight, I believe that's as good a reason as any."

Vashon nodded. "It is in my book. You have your whole future ahead of you in a nation that puts no limitations on a man. Don't let the English take that away from you. What about you, Corporal Dill? It's hard to protect your kinfolk in South Carolina way out here in Louisiana."

"Aye, sir, it does bother me a bit. For all I know, the British could be burning Charleston right now, just like they burnt Washington City. I don't worry about my father too much; he's strong as an ox, but my mother's always been a bit sickly. I don't think she could take having to flee the city."

Vashon tried to be reassuring, saying, "I wouldn't worry too much, son. The Redcoats are coming here, not Charleston. Save New Orleans, and you save everyone's home."

"Thank you, sir. That's what I intend to do." Dill appreciated the captain's concern. Most of the regular army officers he'd met considered themselves socially superior to the enlisted men and treated them accordingly. It annoyed the young corporal, who believed it when Jefferson said all men were created equal. At the same time, he understood the need for discipline. In contrast, Vashon, as a volunteer captain, was a civilian and possessed civilian attitudes. When the war was over he would go back to his previous life and the men under his command would once again be his neighbors. Regular officers seemed to view leadership as a right and privilege. Vashon looked upon it as a responsibility.

While his company leaders were in a philosophical mood, Vashon needed to make a point. "Gentlemen, we are the leaders of these men, and besides seeing to their welfare, competency, and supply, we must see to their moral strength. General Jackson can only do so much. He cannot talk to each individual soldier. He cannot bolster the courage of every man who will face a British musket. That is our job. Fortify your own resolve to carry this through to victory, and pass that confidence on to the men. If every man believes in our eventual triumph, we shall not fail."

On the morning of December 23, the British landed about fifteen miles east of New Orleans, where they quickly established a camp containing about 1,800 soldiers. Incensed that the British had landed on American soil, Jackson immediately called a council of war. Senior officers filed into what had been the mayor's office, now Jackson's headquarters. Pacing back and forth, the general fumed. "By the Eternal, they shall not sleep peacefully upon our soil!"

Tennessee Volunteer Colonel John Coffee, a close friend of Jackson's, noted, "They could march right up the River Road to the gates of the city. We're simply not ready yet."

Jackson shook his head. "Neither are they. They won't move until the rest of their troops are landed. If we strike them now, we can drive them back into the sea." Murmurs could be heard among the officers, but Jackson ignored them. "Would you rather wait until they have 10,000 men ashore? Defeat them now, and they'll think twice about attacking New Orleans."

Nearly every officer in the room wanted to protest that their men were unprepared to take on the British in open battle, but no one spoke up. They knew Jackson's mind was made up and it would be a waste of breath. One of the militia colonels offered, "Even if we do drive them back to their ships, they'll simply come back stronger. In the meantime, we've used up precious ammunition and risk losing a good many men." Seeing the scowl on Jackson's face, he added, "Not that I'm speaking against the plan, sir, but is it our best option?"

If there were any other options, Jackson didn't ask to hear them. "We need to show them what we're made of, gentlemen. We need to bloody their noses and make them nervous. If we accomplish nothing else, we gain the time necessary to complete our defenses. Prepare your men. We attack tonight!"

By the time of the British landing, Corporal Dill had changed his opinion about the military nature of Captain Vashon and his company. The biggest surprise had been the captain. Although Vashon enjoyed his share of liquor in the evening, it never seemed to interfere with his duties. True, if there was no good reason to get up early he might sleep in, but when he did rise, he was all business. He was a strict but congenial commander, concerned more with battlefield preparedness than with mindless discipline, a slightly rotund man with thinning hair and a long, pointed nose. He had also, in an amazingly short amount of time, earned the respect of Andrew Jackson. Although Vashon was a volunteer, the general saw in him the qualities of a true soldier. He was the sort of man Jackson had faith in.

Both Vashon and Jackson intended for the company to be something special, made up of the best marksmen using the best weapons. To that end, the men had been supplied with Kentucky long rifles, some of the most accurate guns available. The majority of the troops in the army were using the standard smoothbore muskets, which were less accurate and had a much shorter range than the rifles. In the hands of a disciplined marksman, the Kentucky rifles could be a potent weapon against the British invaders.

Vashon's company had been assigned to Colonel Coffee, Jackson's most trusted officer. Their task would be to hold the flank of the British camp, forcing the enemy into a position between the main body of the American force and the cannon of the warship *Carolina*, anchored in the river. It was the most extended, exposed position the American forces would occupy, and a measure of the faith Jackson placed in both Coffee and Vashon.

In the cold, damp midnight hours, the American force moved silently to within a half mile of the British camp. Colonel Coffee, in the lead, took his division to the left and set up position in a dry cypress swamp to the north of the camp. The British sentries, distracted by *Carolina* maneuvering into position in the river, remained unaware of the encirclement. Meanwhile, Vashon and his men took cover in back of the trees or behind large cypress knees. There they waited for the battle to begin.

A few hours before dawn, *Carolina* opened fire. It wasn't a deafening broadside, but rather one cannon at a time firing soon after the noise of the previous shot faded away. The British cannon responded, but they were short-range howitzers, which only served to keep the American vessel out in the center of the river. Then, as the English soldiers began to crawl out of their tents, the rice fields to the west of their camp erupted with gunfire and the shouts of advancing American soldiers.

The well-disciplined Redcoats formed into companies and prepared to repel the attack, but until their officers could assess the situation, they would not move. The British officers, for their part, were unsure if they were under full attack or just being harassed. Only a portion of their army had landed, and they had no way of knowing if they were outnumbered or not. Should they take up defensive positions or counterattack? In the end, it was decided the main force would dig in while a smaller force would circle to the right and attack the American flank from the dry cypress swamp to the north.

Dill and Stuart watched as the Redcoats slowly approached, unaware the Americans were in the swamp and waiting for them. Captain Vashon came up and whispered, "Make sure we hold our fire until the general gives the order." Dill and Stuart moved from man to man and relayed the order. Each man steadied his gun against a tree and chose a target.

Suddenly there was a shout, and the woods to their right erupted in a volley of gunfire. Dill and Stuart, knowing the order had been given, shouted for their men to open fire. Redcoats fell, but the line only stopped to fire a well-ordered volley, then continued its steady advance.

Dill watched as his men kept up a steady fire on the British line. Even through the darkness and the fog of gun smoke, the enemy soldiers could be seen in the moonlight. Half their line would advance a few steps, raise their muskets, aim, and fire. The other half would immediately step forward to replace the first, who quickly reloaded. Killed or wounded comrades were ignored, left to suffer until the battle was over. It was a mechanical, soulless operation that Dill found fascinating.

He was less impressed with his own men. Although they were excellent marksmen and were holding their ground, they shouted and laughed as they went about their business, and seemed all too casual in their attitude. They wasted time loading, bragging to one another, or worrying about someone who might have been wounded. To Dill, the situation was like a mathematical equation. Time wasted meant fewer shots per man. Fewer shots per man meant fewer enemy killed. In a perverse way, they were making the enemy stronger. At present, protected by the trees, the

Americans were at an advantage, and it was of less importance. On an open battlefield, they would have been slaughtered.

Unfortunately, one of the worst offenders was Sergeant Stuart. Dill noticed that Stuart was uncommonly slow at reloading the rifle. The sergeant would set the butt on the ground, blow at the smoke coming out of the barrel, and then fumble around in his cartridge box, seeming to select the finest one. Dill couldn't believe it. All the cartridges were the same, and Stuart would eventually fire them all. Why waste time choosing one? Stuart would then bring the paper-wrapped cartridge up to his teeth, carefully tear the end off, then precisely measure the amount of powder needed for the pan. He then slowly poured the remaining powder into the barrel, neatly wrapped the paper around the lead ball, and gently pushed it into place with the ramrod. Dill could fire two rounds in the time it took Stuart to reload from one.

Yet what Stuart lacked in speed, he made up for in accuracy. Having finally reloaded, the sergeant took careful aim at a Redcoat and slowly squeezed the trigger. In an instant, flint scraped against iron, causing a spark to fly into the pan filled with gunpowder, creating a small explosion that sent a miniature jet of flame through the tiny hole in the barrel. This ignited the powder charge and sent the ball hurtling out of the rifle, followed by flame and a cloud of smoke. Never did he miss. As the Redcoat fell, Stuart would give a short victory yell, make some comment to the men nearby, and then set the rifle butt on the ground in preparation to load it.

Exasperated at the inefficiency, Dill grabbed the weapon and handed Stuart his own gun. "Give me that thing! My grandmother could load faster than you." Stuart shrugged and took Dill's rifle. By the time he had selected his target and fired, Dill had already loaded the other gun. They kept up the process, Stuart shooting and Dill loading. The other soldiers began to notice. Dill was like a machine. His hands moved swiftly, and there were no wasted motions. He kept his eyes focused on the gun and never looked up to see where the Redcoats were. Robert Vashon came up and shook his head in admiration. The two were a perfect team.

Then the fog rolled in. Suddenly, there was no one to take aim at. The gunners on *Carolina,* unsure of their targets, ceased fire. Dill could hear the British officers shouting orders, organizing their men into ranks, preparing to make a bayonet charge. Stuart rested his rifle on a tree limb, listening for any sound he could take a bearing on. Robert Vashon stepped over and whispered, "Word from the general: Fall back in an orderly fashion. We've done our job." By the time the sun rose over New Orleans, Jackson and his army were back at their camp. No, they hadn't defeated the British, but they had certainly purchased some precious time.

That evening, Stuart and Dill sat before the campfire in front of their tent, blankets pulled tight around their bodies to ward off the chill. Stuart chuckled and remarked, "You don't like the way I load my gun."

Dill shook his head. "You don't load it, you dance with it."

Stuart smiled. "I do sort of dally about, don't I?"

"I could skin a skunk and a skink in the time it takes you to charge your weapon."

"Even so, I can shoot with the best of them, can't I?"

Dill nodded. "Aye, and you shot twice as many Redcoats when I was doing the loading, didn't you?"

Stuart laughed as a thought came to mind. "If the army had a man who could shoot as good as me and load as fast as you, they'd make him a general."

"No they wouldn't. They'd keep him a private, just to make sure he always had a rifle in his hands."

They sat silently for a few minutes, until Stuart asked, "Were you scared out there?"

"Never even crossed my mind. Too many other things to think about."

Stuart looked intensely at the fire. "I was, at least until the shooting started. I could say I was shivering from the cold, but I know better. I've been with Captain Vashon for six months now, but this is the first fighting I've seen."

Dill appreciated his friend's honesty. "Look: The men did well, and you did a good job out there. They just need more discipline, and we're the ones who have to give it to them. The next time we meet the British, we may not have trees to hide behind. Do you honestly think our men could stand up to those Redcoats line to line?"

Stuart knew the answer and also knew it was up to him to change things. "All of a sudden, sergeant isn't such a fun job. I suppose I'll have to start cracking the whip a bit."

Dill was curious. "I'm not saying you aren't the best man for the job, but how'd you make sergeant so fast?"

An impish smile crossed Stuart's face. "Captain Vashon likes me. Thinks I'll make a good soldier someday. How'd you make corporal so quick?"

"General Jackson likes me. Thinks I'll take his place someday." The two young men laughed. They couldn't have been more different in their personalities, yet they complemented each other perfectly. Both of them knew they had found a lifelong friend.

The British made probing attacks on the twenty-eighth, more to test the American defenses than with any hope of defeating the defenders. On New Year's Day, their artillery was moved into position and began a bombardment of the American earthworks. Dill and Stuart watched from a distance, General Jackson having ordered only artillery crews to remain on the line. Up until this time, the only cannon fire they had seen had been directed against the British. Now those cannonballs and exploding shells were pointed at them. Both men were awed by the destructive power. A bullet wound might be survived; being struck by a cannonball would certainly be fatal.

The barrage lasted for several hours before a welcome silence returned to the fields east of New Orleans. Although some of the American cannon were temporarily taken out of action and the earthworks slightly damaged, it was a wasted effort. If the British wanted to take New Orleans, they would first have to take Jackson's line of defense.

By the time the British attacked on January 8, 1815, General Jackson was ready. He had set up his defensive line behind the Rodriguez Canal and had fortified it surprisingly well. The British would first have to march across an open killing field, then wade the canal, climb the defensive wall, and overrun four thousand determined Americans. Still, the British force was close to eight thousand strong. People on both sides knew that no matter who carried the day, it was going to be a bloody affair.

Jack Dill watched as the Redcoats moved forward. They were in perfect line, their muskets on their shoulders, bayonets fixed. Bugles blared, drums pounded, and bagpipes wailed. It was a magnificent, frightening sight. When the enemy was within one hundred yards, Colonel Coffee nodded. Captain Vashon rode behind the line, calmly issuing orders. "Let them have it, lads. Pick your targets well." This time there was no fog to obscure the view, only the smoke of expended gunpowder. Once again, Stuart did the shooting while Dill did the loading. By the time the battle was over, Robert would name them "Jack and Johnny's Patented Redcoat Killing Machine."

As was his habit, Stuart took time to select each target. He wasn't sure why; one dead Redcoat was as good as another. He looked for the most determined British soldier he could see, the man most intent on killing Americans, the sort of man who would consider it glorious to die on the field of battle. In a way, Stuart was giving the man what he wanted. Dill, on the other hand, never saw a Redcoat fall. Fully focused on the rifle he was loading, Dill rarely looked up, and when he did, it was to check on the men in his company. The British were simply a distraction.

Yet for every Redcoat Stuart shot, two more seemed to step over the body and continue the march. Even as the enemy line thinned, it did not stop. Some of the soldiers made it across the canal, but could only huddle beneath the earthen wall. Someone, it seemed, had forgotten the scaling ladders.

The slaughter continued. In the canal below were the bodies of Scottish highlanders who had reached the American line but had been unable to scale the wall. Fully exposed and too proud to retreat, they had given their lives for the empire. Realizing the futility of their efforts, individual British units slowed then stopped their advance, but continued to keep up a steady rate of fire, even as their ranks thinned. It was a dangerous situation. They were no longer moving targets, and the dead and wounded could no longer be stepped over and momentarily put out of mind. Yet with most of the British generals either killed or wounded, no one seemed to be in charge. No one was pushing the men forward; no one sounded the retreat. Finally, from the back of the British line a bugle could be heard, calling for the withdrawal. Slowly, without turning their back to the Americans, the British fell back and the battle ended.

After the cease-fire was called and the smoke blew away, Stuart looked out over the Chalmette Plain and felt a tear run down his cheek. Hundreds, perhaps thousands, of Redcoats lay dead or wounded, some screaming in agony, some trying to attract the attention of anyone who could help them. The victory was astounding. Only a handful of Americans had been slain or wounded. Among the wounded was Robert Vashon, yet as far as he was concerned, the wound was a wonderful thing. He ran up to Stuart, dancing and yelling, exalting in the victory. Waving his bandaged, shrunken left arm, Robert shouted, "My badge of honor, boys! I'll no longer have to tell everyone that my mother popped me out of the oven half baked. I can say I was wounded at New Orleans. I'll be a damned hero!"

The British army remained at their camp while the Royal Navy tried to reach New Orleans via the Mississippi. For ten days they bombarded Fort St. Phillip, but the bastion held. On the night of the eighteenth, the British boarded their ships and sailed off into the Gulf of Mexico.

As news of the departure reached New Orleans, the city erupted in celebration, unlike anything it had ever seen. Inside the meeting hall the officers, politicians, and well-to-do folks of Louisiana danced their cotillions, while on the outside the soldiers and common folk set their feet in motion to simple jigs and reels. Among them were Jack Dill, John Stuart, and Robert Vashon.

People milled about, looking for food, drink, or someone to spend the night with. Occasionally someone would wander up to the trio, pat them on the back, or congratulate them on a job well done. About half the people who approached them were obviously drunk, but no one was obnoxious or belligerent. It was a night to celebrate, and as Robert had observed, even the suspected British spies were enjoying themselves.

From within the crowd Captain Vashon emerged, a woman on each arm. Robert called out, "Ah, the boat from Baton Rouge has safely come to port! What better way to celebrate our triumph than in the presence of my two favorite ladies!"

One of the women was a petite lady, elegantly dressed in bright blue. The other was a girl in her early teens, wearing a high-waisted green silk dress trimmed in gold. Yet the most eye-catching feature about her was the bright red hair. Stuart stood transfixed by it.

Robert quickly made the introductions. "Sergeant Stuart, Corporal Dill: This is my mother, Madam Vashon, and my sister, Elizabeth."

Dill looked to the mother and made a slight, very proper bow. "It is an honor, Mrs. Vashon."

Stuart kept his eyes on Elizabeth. Unlike Dill, he made a sweeping bow, and then took the girl's hand and kissed it. Smiling broadly, he said, "It is more than a pleasure to make your acquaintance, Miss Elizabeth."

Elizabeth blushed. "It is an honor, Mr. Stuart. Father has often spoken well of you and Mr. Dill." She immediately liked the man. He was outgoing and warm, and quite handsome. He was tall but not ungainly, appeared strong but not muscular. The light brown hair looked soft and had a slight curl to it. She could see why father had chosen him as one of the company's leaders.

She then turned to Dill. The corporal stiffened slightly, tilted his head, and tipped his hat. "I am at your service, Miss Elizabeth."

"Thank you, Corporal. I am most appreciative of your attention." She had a difficult time assessing Dill. He was more reserved, and therefore harder to get an immediate sense of. He was certainly not cold or standoffish, yet his smile seemed forced, almost as if he couldn't allow himself the pleasure of meeting her. He was shorter than Stuart, but more solidly built. There was obvious strength in his arms and an intensity in his eyes. The somewhat square face was topped by dark, curly hair. No, he wasn't especially handsome, but he was not displeasing to the eye. At any rate, if he was a friend of Robert's, he would certainly be a friend of hers.

Captain Vashon took a deep breath. He'd heard there was an especially fine keg of whiskey inside the meeting house and was anxious to sample it. "I, for one, would like to go inside and partake of the refreshments. Robert, would you care to join us or would you prefer to remain outside with your friends?"

Robert laughed. "If it's all the same, sir, I'll remain out here with the men. I don't do well around generals and governors and the such. They keep wanting to shake my hand, which doesn't leave me a free one to hold m' drink."

Mrs. Vashon shook her head and smiled. "The father's son, to be sure."

Elizabeth asked, "Mother, may I remain with Robert? There is naught but old people in there."

"Your father and I are old?"

The Captain, concerned for his daughter's safety, mentioned, "There will be a lot of drinking and carousing. Perhaps it would be better if you remained with us."

Elizabeth was not so easily swayed. "I'll have Robert, Corporal Dill, and Sergeant Stuart to watch over me. Could I be any safer?"

Vashon sighed. He knew he was in a losing battle, but like a good soldier, he fought on. "My dear, they are the ones who will be doing all the drinking and carousing."

Drawing close to her brother, she announced, "Then I shall keep a close watch over them all to see they do not get too intoxicated or boisterous."

Mrs. Vashon reminded her that, "Perhaps they *want* to get intoxicated and boisterous."

Stuart stepped forward and said, "It shall be our duty and our pleasure to watch over the young lady, ma'am."

Dill added, "She shall be safe with us, Mrs. Vashon."

She stared at her son. "You'll keep a very close eye on her, Robert?"

"Yes, ma'am."

Captain Vashon gave in to the inevitable. Like his wife, Elizabeth was not an easy person to deny. "Very well. We've survived the British, and I'm sure we'll survive one night of revelry." Taking his wife's arm, he said, "Come, my dear, the entertainments await us."

When Captain and Mrs. Vashon were out of earshot, Robert put his arm around Stuart's shoulder. He'd noticed how the sergeant had been captivated by Elizabeth. "Now mind you, Johnny, she's my sister, and she's but fourteen years of age."

Elizabeth interrupted, "I'm nearly fifteen."

Robert shook his head and returned to his lecture. "If you sully her reputation I'll have to challenge you to a duel, and what with my grievously wounded arm and all, I'd have to have Jack here stand in for me. We all know how horrid a shot he is. You certainly wouldn't want that on your conscience."

Elizabeth giggled and stepped between Stuart and Dill, offering each an arm. "Rarely has a lady had such a gallant escort. Shall we stroll, gentlemen?"

The evening passed wonderfully, the four of them moving about the crowd for hours, laughing and joking, reveling in their victory over the English. They spoke of the battle, of the British, and of their futures. Dill announced that now that he'd seen the frontier, there was no going back to Charleston. When his enlistment was up he was going to find some newly formed town and become a prosperous merchant. Stuart wasn't sure what he was going to do. There was a war to win first, and for the moment, he was perfectly happy serving under Captain Vashon. Robert said, "Well, my plans are made. Uncle Paul wants me to go to St. Louis and open a warehouse for him. As soon as the war is over, I'll be on my way upriver."

It was well past midnight by the time Jack and Johnny departed for their tent, leaving Robert and Elizabeth to find their parents. All of them walked quietly, lost in their own thoughts. Jack Dill was thinking of the battle and all the fallen Redcoats. Robert Vashon had his mind on his impending trip upriver to St. Louis. John Stuart and Elizabeth Vashon were thinking of each other.

June 15, 1816
Baton Rouge

To:
Mr. Robert Vashon
St. Louis, Missouri Territory

Dearest Robert,

If it be in your power, I beseech you to repair to this city with all possible haste. Mother is very ill and, I fear, near death. She was taken with the fever last week and did not at first appear to be in great danger. The night before last, however, she suddenly took a turn for the worse, and the doctor holds little hope for her recovery. I pray she lasts until your arrival. She is resting fitfully as I write, asleep, though drenched in her own perspiration. I give what care the doctor recommends, but can see no benefit. I feed her water and a light broth when she can take it, but little stays down, and what does, quickly passes through. Her skin has lost all color, and she appears to have lost some weight, which is alarming in one who was so petite to begin with. While I pray you are able to see her before her passing, I know it would cause you much pain to see Mother in this condition. She asks for you often.

I have written to Uncle Paul and Aunt Mae in New Orleans and expect them today. As you know, Father and the company have been sent to the wilds of Georgia, and it will take weeks for word to reach him. He will be devastated by the news and, I fear, feel the guilt of not having been here with Mother. Our friends here at Baton Rouge have been most caring and attentive, but I long for family. Sgt. Stuart and a squad are also expected to return here shortly, having been sent to Natchez as escort for the paymaster shortly before Father received orders to report to Georgia. Dear Robert, I feel so alone, please come.

You loving sister,
Elizabeth

Elizabeth Vashon sat in the parlor of her home, staring at the pattern formed on the wall by the morning sunlight passing through the lace curtains. It was an elegant home, furnished in the latest fashion and situated in one of Baton Rouge's better neighborhoods. Her mother had been proud of the place, a symbol of Captain Vashon's status in the community, both as a lawyer before the war and now as a military leader.

Elizabeth covered her face with her hands, lowered her head, and quietly sobbed. For the first time in her sixteen years of life, she felt totally alone. The undertaker had removed her mother's body, and Uncle Paul had gone with him to make final arrangements. Aunt Mae was meeting with the wives of friends and fellow officers, making the necessary plans for the food and refreshments that would be served after the funeral. The house was quiet and seemingly devoid of life.

Changes had taken place in the year and a half since the Battle of New Orleans, and up until this point, most had seemed good. The most important change had been that her father had received a commission as a captain in the regular army. At first he had been reluctant to accept the position, afraid that he would be stationed far away from Baton Rouge and his law practice. General Jackson, however, had been persuasive. He wanted people he could trust in the New Orleans area, and Vashon was one of them. Vashon would be assigned to the Fourth Infantry, which was headquartered in Baton Rouge. True, there might be the occasional temporary assignment when the situation warranted it, but as long as Old Hickory was in command, Vashon's permanent home would be Louisiana. Satisfied, Vashon had made only one further request: If John Stuart was willing, could he be enlisted in the regular army as Vashon's Master Sergeant, and could Jack Dill also be assigned to the company? Jackson made it happen.

At first, it had seemed odd to Elizabeth that her father would even consider the proposal. A captain's pay was small compared to what he could earn as a lawyer. What she didn't appreciate was the prestige that went with the position. As a well-known veteran of the Battle of New Orleans and commanding officer of the small garrison at Baton Rouge, he was one of the most respected members of the community. In addition, his military duties were minimal, leaving him ample time to practice law, and though his clients were now fewer in number, they were more prominent in Louisiana society. In the end, she had to admit it had been a very good move.

In recent months, Elizabeth had come to appreciate how easily her mother had adapted to life as an army wife. When Father was around, Mother had been the loving, demure helpmate, always standing quietly in her husband's shadow. When he was away on duty, she was the commander-in-chief. No problem existed that she could not handle. No decision was beyond her reasoning. The odd part was that she seemed to enjoy having it both ways. She had once said, "I could survive without your father, but I couldn't live without him." Elizabeth now realized that she felt the same way about her mother.

Elizabeth knew that she should get out of the chair, that she should *do* something. But what? She wasn't hungry or thirsty. Her studies seemed meaningless, and she did not want to play the piano. It would remind her too much of her mother. The floor could be swept, but the floor could wait. The only thing she knew that required attention was the one thing she couldn't bring herself to do: mend her black dress. In truth, the only thing she wanted to do was stare at the wall and contemplate life without her mother.

It was not an easy task. How could she start her day without her mother's sweet voice calling her to breakfast? How could she—why should she?—study French without her mother to converse with? How could she sew a new dress without Mother to help pick out the pattern and material? How could she prepare supper for her father without Mother to guide her through the market and butcher shop and show her how to cook and bake? Every activity she thought of included a vision of Mother by her side.

Her thoughts were interrupted by the sound of footsteps on the front porch stairway. It was probably Aunt Mae. Then there was a soft knock at the door. She got up slowly. It was odd: As lonely as she felt, she didn't really care to see anyone. She walked to the door and reluctantly opened it. There, with an unsure look on his face, was John Stuart. Removing the tall, cylindrical uniform hat and placing it under his arm, he said, "I heard about your mother. Is there anything I or the men can do?"

She didn't say a word. She just stood there, closed her eyes, and began to cry. Stuart wasn't sure how to respond. His instincts were to enfold her protectively in his arms, but in such a public place, it would not be seen as proper. The best he could do was place one hand on her shoulder and offer her a handkerchief. For some minutes they stood there, until she finally composed herself, straightened up, and stepped back. Running a hand through her red hair, she said, "Would you care to sit down, Sergeant?" She motioned toward a pair of chairs on the porch and they both took a seat.

They had come into contact many times since the end of the war, but rarely for extended periods of time. It occurred most often when Elizabeth would accompany her father to the fort, but the conversations never went much further than a quick greeting.

The exception was when Robert was in town. As planned, Robert had gone to St. Louis to open and manage his uncle's warehouse. He had returned home several times and would invariably get together with "Jack and Johnny." Whenever that happened, Elizabeth would insist on going along. Robert could tell that Johnny and Elizabeth were attracted to each other and was happy to provide the opportunity for them to get better acquainted. He considered Stuart one of his best friends and would have been perfectly happy if a romance evolved. Unfortunately, with Jack and Robert along, the couple could do little more than talk and stare at each other, unable to express their feelings and unsure of how the other felt.

During that year and a half, Johnny had watched Elizabeth mature, and his attraction to her had continued to grow. Both her demeanor and physical features were more adult-like, and she no longer looked like a child. Her figure was well proportioned, her height was average, and while it had been the bright red hair that had first caught Johnny's eye, it was the face that captivated him. It was round, with cheeks that seemed to glow when she smiled. Her eyes were extraordinarily expressive: dark and piercing when angered or skeptical, wide and bright when surprised or happy. He could read every emotion in that face, but no matter how often he looked at it, he could never discover how she felt about him.

Yet all those things were forgotten for the moment. Almost pleading but knowing there was no good answer, Elizabeth asked, "What am I going to do, Johnny?"

He smoothed his hair, rubbed his chin, scratched his ear, and tried to think of something to tell her. Here she was, the only woman he had ever been romantically inclined toward, desperately in need of his support, and he was tongue-tied. He'd never known his own mother or father, so he couldn't fathom her loss. He had been raised by an uncle who had dutifully seen to his education but had shown him little love. The simple fact was that for the past two years, Captain Vashon had been more of a father to him than anyone else had ever been. He wasn't sure why; it was just one of those things. Maybe Vashon had seen a bright young man in need of direction. At any rate, Stuart felt like part of the captain's family. Looking at Elizabeth, he felt that perhaps someday he actually would be.

As to solving Elizabeth's present problems, he could only relate to his own experience, and it simply wasn't adequate. "Will your aunt and uncle care for you until your father returns? The troubles in Florida shouldn't last long. He'll be back soon."

She nodded, but it wasn't the short term she was thinking about or simply having a roof over her head. For sixteen years her mother had been there, directing her studies, conducting her social life, teaching her what it would take to be a good wife and mother. She felt horribly adrift, like a sailing ship that had lost its masts. Her father, as loving as he was, would have no idea how to care for a daughter. Indeed, he wouldn't know how to care for himself. "My future is all on me now, Johnny, and I don't feel ready for it."

"It's never that bad, Miss Elizabeth. Family and friends will always come through when you need them. You just can't see it yet." Stuart leaned back, stretched out his legs, and thought about the possible options. "The way I see it, you have three choices: You can stay here in Baton Rouge and maintain your father's house, or you could go to New Orleans and live with your aunt and uncle. Your other choice would be to go to St. Louis with Robert."

For the first time that day, she actually laughed. "Go with Robert? He lives in the loft of his warehouse! I shan't even be able to climb the ladder with any modesty. A fine place for a lady."

"Well, it *would* have a civilizing influence upon him."

"It would take a better woman than I to civilize Robert." She gazed at Stuart warmly. He was making her smile. Half an hour earlier, she wasn't sure if she would ever be able to do that again.

For another hour they sat there, talking and laughing, sharing stories about themselves, Jack, Robert, and others they knew. When Aunt Mae returned, she was surprised to see the sergeant with Elizabeth, but she was also pleased. She had feared the girl would not be able to rise above her grief. Somehow, this young soldier had gotten Elizabeth through her most difficult hours.

By the time Stuart rose to leave, Elizabeth had decided upon her future. She would stay in Baton Rouge with her father. He would need her, and she was now the lady of the house. Beyond that, however, was the realization that eventually she needed to be wherever John Stuart was.

Sailing Master Jarius Loomis looked at Sergeant Stuart and his ten soldiers, most of whom were leaning over the gunboat's rail. *Ah, it's going to be a long week,* he thought. The fleet of four small ships had left New Orleans on July 5, and everyone was still a bit groggy from the previous night's Independence Day celebrations. The trip across Lakes Pontchartrain and Borgne had been easy on the landlubbers, with calm waters and an easy breeze. Once in the Gulf, however, the breeze remained the same, but the waves grew larger. They were, in fact, the perfect type of wave to make someone sick: gently rolling, coming from slightly abeam of the starboard quarter, with the boat making little headway. Even one or two of Loomis's seasoned sailors looked a bit green, though he suspected it had more to do with the liquor in them than the liquid under them.

The soldiers were on board the gunboat because it seemed the quickest way to reunite them with their unit. Stuart and his men had been inadvertently left behind when their company was ordered to Fort Scott, located near the border separating Georgia and Spanish Florida, deep within the territory of the Creek Indians. Because the fort was situated on the remote Georgia frontier, General Gaines, the army's commander along the Gulf Coast, had deemed it most expedient to resupply the post from New Orleans via the Apalachicola River. Two transport vessels, *General Pike* and *Semilante,* had been loaded with military stores and were being escorted by two navy gunboats, numbers 149 and 154. Loomis commanded number 149, while Sailing Master Bassett was captain of number 154 and had overall command of the fleet.

As they cleared Cat Island, Loomis turned to his second-in-command. "Mr. Luffborough, you have the deck. Hold her eas'-sou'-east as long as the wind allows and try not to lose sight of the other vessels." He yawned. "I feel a solid sleep coming on." Loomis was lucky to have Midshipman Luffborough on board. The young man had already turned in his resignation but had happily agreed to stay on for this one last cruise. The lad would have been a good officer if he'd remained in the navy, but a well-paying position ashore and the love of a pretty young lady had lured him away. Loomis was sorry to lose the man, but didn't blame him in the least. At times he wished that he too had fallen in love with a woman instead of the ocean.

If the wind remained constant, it would take three or four days to reach Apalachicola Bay. Most of the crew assumed they were on a simple supply mission, but Loomis knew otherwise. To get to Fort Scott they would have to ascend the Apalachicola River through Spanish Florida. Along the way the little convoy would have to pass under the guns of a large fort built by the British during the last war. Instead of simply abandoning the fort at war's end, the British had stocked it with massive quantities of munitions and turned it over to the escaped slaves who resided in the area. To the residents of Georgia and the Mississippi Territory, the stronghold had become known as the "Negro Fort."

Although the fort was in Spanish territory, it was proving a nuisance to the Americans. Slaveholders in the southern states viewed it as a beacon, luring runaways with the promise of freedom if they somehow managed to make it across the border. Worse than that, the slave owners feared the armed blacks would return to the plantations and incite a slave rebellion. It was the sort of thought that kept Southerners awake at night. In theory, removing the fort should have been a Spanish responsibility, but the old empire was crumbling and the Spanish authorities lacked the military strength to deal with the situation. Without intervention, the population of the Negro Fort and the surrounding villages would continue to grow.

Southern residents had expressed their fears to their representatives in Washington, who then voiced those concerns to President Madison. The War Department relayed the messages to General Jackson, who in turn ordered General Gaines to do something about the Negro Fort. In response, Gaines had authorized the construction of Fort Scott. He assumed the runaways at the Negro Fort would challenge the passage of the supply ships. When they did, Gaines would feel justified in destroying the fort, seizing the runaways, and returning them to their owners. Slaveholders were a powerful political force. Sailing Master Loomis had been in the South long enough to know they almost always got their way.

The tall, muscular black man was dressed in a colorful assortment of clothes, the whole outfit adorned by garish gold and silver ornaments and a saber that hung from a wide leather belt. Standing behind the wall of the fortification, he cast his gaze down the Apalachicola River. It was a wide, slow-moving stream, about a hundred yards across, with thick vegetation on the opposite shore. The fort itself stood on a low bluff overlooking the river and was surrounded by marshland. A small stream flowed to the north. It was a large fort, with earthen walls topped by a wooden palisade. Cannon were mounted at strategic positions along the wall, some of them aimed at the river, some of them pointed inland toward the most likely paths an aggressor might take. Should the American boats that were reportedly in the bay decide to attack, they would find the fort a formidable obstacle.

He didn't know when the Americans were coming, and he wasn't sure why they were waiting at the mouth of the river. Some of his men believed those ships would be met by an army coming from the north. He looked around the fort and at the parade ground where the men from the outlying villages and their families were starting to gather. Since news of the ships' arrival had reached the fort, there had been a steady stream of refugees coming in for protection. Nearly all of them were runaway slaves, many from Spanish plantations in Florida. Many of the American runaways had elected to move farther south, away from the slave catchers that would no doubt be following the army. Most of the Indians had also departed. They put more faith in distance and concealment than in the walls of a fort.

As the fort's headman, he was confident he could repel the American attack. They had been gathering food for days, and the British had left ample weaponry. If the American gunboats were foolish enough to pass in front of his fort, he would send them to the bottom of the river. Whatever the outcome of any battle that might be fought, he knew that neither he nor his people would surrender. To a man, they would rather die fighting for their freedom than be returned to slavery.

Hearing a voice behind him, he turned and saw a black man with his wrists tied, accompanied by two Seminole warriors. Looking coldly down at the bound man, he asked the same question he asked of all runaways who found their way to the Negro Fort: "I am Garçon, a free man. Who are you, and where are you from?"

The runaway was nervous. He had heard the Negro Fort was a place of sanctuary, but so far, the reception had been less than welcoming. He had been found by the Indians, wandering through the Florida wilds, lost and hungry. The Indians had bound him, given him a small amount of food and water, and taken him to this place. Everyone had stared at him as he was led inside the fort, and the commander, if that's what he was, was eyeing him with suspicion. He swallowed hard and gave his answer. "My name be Burrell, and I's belong to Mr. Yancy up in Georgia."

The words were barely out of his mouth before Garçon's hand flew out and slapped him hard across the face. "If you belong to Mr. Yancy, then you'd best go back to him. We have no slaves here. Are you property, or are you your own man?"

"I's runaway and I ain'ts goin' back, so I guess I's my own man. I jes' wants t' be free, Massa."

Once again, the hand of Garçon slammed against Burrell's cheek. "There is no 'Massa' here, you fool! You don't *want* to be free, you *are* free! Act like a free man, and we will give you a home. Act like a slave, and we will consider you a spy, slit your throat, and throw you in the river. Take him away!"

One of the Indians took hold of Burrell's left arm and began to lead him away. After a few steps, Burrell stopped, tearing his arm away from the Indian's grip. He turned and looked hard at Garçon. "Cut my bindings. A free man walks free."

Garçon smiled and nodded to the Indian. Slavery was a hard habit to break.

Colonel Duncan Clinch stepped off the small keelboat and onto the landing below Fort Scott. *Good location,* he thought. *Nice high bluff overlooking the river, open pine forest all around, no way for anybody to sneak up on the place once the trees are cut down. Perfect.* Greeting him on the landing was his second-in-command, Major William Wooster. *Now there's a man with a future,* Clinch thought. *Young, energetic, confident, and with friends in high places.* Wooster was a favorite of Generals Edmund Gaines and Winfield Scott, two of the brightest stars to emerge from the war with England. The major's only drawback was that he wasn't too fast on his feet, having received a serious wound to his thigh at the Battle of Fort Erie. With any luck, Wooster would make general someday.

As they climbed the long, winding path to the top of the bluff, Clinch decided he needed to lose some weight. He'd been living well lately, posted at the quiet little town of Savannah, courting the lovely young daughter of a wealthy Georgia planter. He was approaching thirty, and he'd reached a somewhat senior position in the army. It was time to start thinking of a more settled life. In truth, this transfer to the wilderness at the far western side of the state was a welcome change of pace. It would provide some exercise and adventure, give him combat experience, and, if things went well, furnish a boost to his career.

When he and Wooster reached the top of the bluff, Clinch was able to take a closer look at the fort. It always amazed him what a hundred soldiers, two dozen axes, and a variety of saws could accomplish. Still, to call it a "fort" was being generous. The installation was built on what had once been a thin pine forest, a portion of which had been cleared. All that remained were the stumps of the fallen trees from which the men had erected three buildings in a rectangular layout. The largest stood parallel to the river bluff, facing inwards, and was the men's barracks. On opposite ends, also facing inwards, were the officers' quarters on the right and a storehouse on the left. There was no defensive picket work and no tall guard tower. Fort Scott was intended as a temporary installation, constructed only as a pretext for destroying the Negro Fort. Once that target was eliminated, Fort Scott would no longer have a purpose and would be abandoned.

The army may have considered the fort temporary, but Wooster had designed the layout with an eye toward possible permanence. The back walls of the buildings could serve as the outer walls of an enclosed fort, and the buildings had been placed so that it would take a minimum of work to enclose the entire compound, either with a well-constructed picket work and blockhouses, or a hastily-thrown-together breastwork. Both Clinch and Wooster knew this was the frontier. Before long, settlers would be staking their claims to Indian land, and disputes would arise. There was also the matter of the hostile Seminoles in Florida. The fort's location was only a few miles from the Spanish border, on the northwest side of the Flint River. Seven miles farther downstream, the Flint combined with the Chattahoochee to form the Apalachicola. Above the confluence it was United States Territory. Below that, on the Apalachicola, was Spanish Florida.

As Clinch entered the open compound, the other officers at Fort Scott came out to greet him. Most of them he knew well, they having been sent from Savannah or Charleston. The only one he wasn't familiar with was Captain Vashon, who had recently arrived from Baton Rouge. Reports indicated he was a good battlefield officer, though a lax disciplinarian. Rumor also mentioned a drinking problem. *Well,* Clinch thought, *that puts him equal with about half the officers at this post.*

After greeting the officers, Clinch inspected the troops. For the most part they looked like good men. Many were veterans of the war, waiting for their five-year enlistments to run out. Clinch was going to need good men. To destroy the Negro Fort, Clinch would take his force south, meet up with a pair of navy gunboats, reduce the fort to submission, and then return the slaves to their owners. As a slaveholder himself, he understood the necessity of removing the Negro Fort. Without slaves, the Southern economy could not exist, and protecting the American way of life was something he was sworn to do.

The task sounded straightforward, but Clinch was beginning to doubt whether he had sufficient resources to do the job. Indian spies were painting a rather formidable picture of the Negro Fort. He did not have a large number of men, at the most three hundred. Half of those were Creek Indian volunteers. If the gunboats couldn't reduce the fort quickly or if the defenders managed to sink the gunboats, he might not be able to take the fort. If that happened, it would effectively end his military career.

As Clinch casually surveyed Fort Scott, two of the leaders from the Creek volunteers approached him. One of them was an important headman by the name of William McIntosh. Both his name and his features showed him to be of mixed heritage. Except for the traditional Indian turban and feathers that adorned his head, he wore the same clothes that any well-to-do white civilian might. When in battle, however, "General" McIntosh would wear the dress of a Creek warrior. He was truly a man of two cultures. The young man by his side, Tom Woodward, was also a man of two cultures, but in a different way. An educated man from a good family, he had given up the white world and taken up residence among the Indians. He dressed like a native, spoke their language fluently, and, if not for his wavy brown hair and facial features, could easily be mistaken for an Indian. Such was life on the frontier.

McIntosh stepped forward with his hand extended. "It is good to see you again, Colonel. My people welcome you to our land." It was a subtle reminder of an unsettled issue. Three years earlier there had been a civil war between the Upper and Lower factions of the Creek Nation. The Upper Creeks, known as "Red Sticks," generally lived to the west of the Chattahoochee, in the Mississippi Territory, and were opposed to the encroachment of the white men and the imposition of their ways. The Lower Creeks of Georgia, McIntosh among them, were more accustomed to the white ways and had little sympathy for a war against their white neighbors. The differences continued to grow until violence broke out and the Lower Creeks found themselves under attack from the Red Sticks. The Americans became embroiled in the conflict, leading to the defeat of the Red Sticks by Andrew Jackson at the Battle of Horseshoe Bend. After the war, many of the Upper Creeks fled south and sought refuge with the Seminoles in Florida, where they plotted their revenge.

In the treaty that ended the war, Jackson had forced the cession of millions of acres of Creek land, from both the Upper and the Lower Creeks. The Lower Creeks were understandably upset with the treaty, and McIntosh's greeting was simply a way of reminding Clinch of that fact. For the time being, his people were friendly and willing, for a fee, to fight their common enemies, the

Red Sticks and the Seminoles. A large influx of white settlers into Creek land might change all that.

Clinch took the chief's hand and shook it warmly. "And it is good to see you again, my friend. Are your warriors ready for the march?"

"We await but your command. Within three days of receiving the word, I shall gather 150 warriors at the joining of the rivers. My men are eager for the bounty and the many trophies we will take." Clinch knew what he was referring to. The government had authorized a bounty of fifty dollars for each captured slave. As for the trophies, those would be in the form of scalps lifted from the slain. Clinch wasn't sure which was more important to the Indians.

"We march in five days. The transport ships and the gunboats should be arriving at the mouth of the Apalachicola most any day now."

McIntosh nodded. "It is good. My warriors' knives are sharp, and they are ready to use them."

Sailing Master Loomis was getting impatient. They had been in Apalachicola Bay for four days, and he was ready to move upstream. Sailing Master Basset, in command of the flotilla, was hesitant to proceed upriver until he received word from Colonel Clinch that the army was in position. Basset knew that once he had committed the ships to entering the river, there could be no turning back. In the meantime, the crew had used nearly all the fresh water on board. The last barrel was almost dry, and he needed to fill at least one of them. To that end, Loomis ordered Midshipman Luffborough to take a launch upstream until he reached fresh water and could fill one of the barrels.

Both men were concerned about an Indian attack, but the lookouts had seen no sign of Indians since the ships had entered the bay, so they felt the risk was low. Just to be sure, Loomis sent a guard of six men, two of them soldiers from Sergeant Stuart's detachment. If Luffborough moved quickly, he could fill the barrel and return before the Indians could do anything, even if they were spotted.

When all was ready, the launch pushed off from the gunboat and began to row upriver. It was a warm, clear morning with little breeze, and the boat moved easily against the light current coming from the river. They had gone about a mile upriver when Luffborough spotted a large stream pouring into the main flow. Hopefully they wouldn't have to row far up the stream to reach fresh water.

When they had gone about a hundred yards upstream the midshipman reached over the side, dipped his hand into the water, and then brought it to his lips. He smiled. "Bring her ashore on that little beach there, boys. Tastes sweet enough to me." After beaching the boat, Lopez and Daniels, the two soldiers from Stuart's detachment, stepped out and assumed the watch. Daniels walked a bit farther upstream while Lopez worked his way toward the river. The four sailors rolled the barrel out of the boat and into the water. When the mud that had been kicked up by their feet settled, they pulled the stopper, dipped the hole below the surface, and the water began to run in. Feeling exposed, three of the sailors went back to the boat to retrieve their muskets.

It was a prudent move, but before they could reach their guns, two warriors ran out from behind a wall of tall marsh grass and wrestled Daniels to the ground. About ten others rose up and quickly fired at the sailors and Lopez, who was nearly at the mouth of the stream. Luffborough and three of his men fell instantly. One of the sailors, Burroughs, was wounded but was able to run toward the end of the stream. Realizing he was vastly outnumbered, Lopez fired off a shot, dropped his musket, and ran for open water. Burroughs followed close behind, clutching at the wound in his side.

Lopez stopped for a moment, giving the wounded sailor a chance to catch up. Putting his arm around him, the soldier helped Burroughs run toward the river. "C'mon, sailor, we'll make it. We can swim out to the sandbar." The Indians fired again, missed, but did not pursue the two men. The pair reached the edge of the river and waded in. Suddenly Burroughs went limp. Lopez looked down at the man. He was dead. Pushing the body into the stream, Lopez dove into the water and began to swim for a sandbar that was less than two hundred yards away. After about twenty feet he stopped and tore off his heavy uniform coat. Continuing on, he finally stumbled out of the water and onto the bar. Sitting on the sand, breathing hard, he looked out to sea. A launch was coming from the other gunboat. He lowered his head and wept softly. He could hear Daniels screaming.

Garçon stood on the wall of the Negro Fort and looked north toward the thick forest. Somewhere out there, just out of cannon range, the American army was waiting. They had been there for three days. The white commander had sent an Indian to the fort under a white flag, demanding that the occupants surrender. Garçon had sent the Indian away, telling him that he would never surrender, that he would blow the fort up first. The people within the fort had all cheered. They would not return to slavery.

He assumed the army was waiting for the gunboats to come up from the bay. Spies had told him there were about 150 soldiers and maybe as many Creek warriors. Garçon had less than two hundred men and over a hundred women and children. They had plenty of food, water, and ammunition, and could hold out for weeks against such a small force, especially if the enemy didn't have any cannon. He assumed that's why they were waiting on the gunboats. He had sent a runner to the Mikasuki towns, asking for help. If Indian forces arrived before the gunboats did, the Americans might be driven off. If he could sink the gunboats, the small American force could be defeated. Garçon was confident, but he was also worried.

Sailing Master Bassett shook his head slowly. He didn't trust the Indian. The warrior was telling him that the American army was waiting at the Negro Fort and that he should proceed upriver. There was a problem, however: The Indian runner said he couldn't remember the name of the American commanding officer. Ever since the killing of Midshipman Luffborough and his men, Bassett had decided to be overcautious. He had no way of knowing if this Indian was telling the truth or was leading him into a trap. He told the runner to return to the army and come back either with a handwritten note or a white officer.

Clinch was exasperated. Why was Bassett being so timid? The Indian, not willing to admit he'd forgotten the commander's name, could offer no explanation. Clinch picked up a piece of paper and hastily scrawled "Bassett: Proceed upriver. Clinch." He then turned to Tom Woodward, the young white man who was serving with the Creek forces. "Go with this runner and deliver this to Bassett. Tell him to proceed with all haste. We need his cannon, and for all we know, a large Seminole and Red Stick force might be moving against us any day. Be careful, but don't waste time. We may not have it."

Garçon watched as the gunboats approached, the two transports staying well behind. For two days, the American soldiers on shore had been shooting at the fort, but had inflicted no damage or serious injuries. Now, however, things were about to change. The first of the two gunboats turned toward the opposite side of the river, then eased up alongside the trees and dropped its sail. The second one took place behind it. Garçon shook his head. Were the whites stupid enough to tie up right in front of his guns?

Sailing Master Loomis paced the deck, shouting orders. "Make her fast to the trees, lads. I want her as steady as that fort over there. Riflemen to the gunnels! Choose your targets carefully. Sergeant Stuart, get your men up there, too. No use wasting a good marksman. Mr. Peavey, stoke the furnace, start warming one up!" Suddenly, he saw a flash of fire from the fort followed by the boom of a cannon. He watched a cannonball smash into the trees behind the other gunboat. "Don't worry, lads, they'll have to be better gunners than that if they hope to send us to the bottom of the river." Another cannon fired, and a shot splashed into the water well in front of the boat. Loomis walked up behind one of the gunboat's two large cannon. "A bit more elevation, lads, a bit less charge." He watched as the crew finished loading the gun. He checked the aim one last time, and then nodded to the gunner, who lowered his match to the fuse. The gun roared and recoiled. He watched the shot arc toward the fort and land in the parade ground. He could see dirt flying, but couldn't tell if the massive thirty-two-pound iron ball had caused any serious damage.

The riflemen at the rail opened fire, attempting to pick off anyone who showed himself around the fort's cannon. The fort fired again, but the ball passed harmlessly through a bit of sail hanging from the boom. Suddenly there was a roar from the other gunboat. Loomis watched as the ball slammed into the fort's wall, sending dirt and wood flying. The damage, however, was minimal. It would take a lot more shots like that to reduce the fort to rubble. Loomis had a better idea.

Garçon screamed at his men. Some had fled their posts, seeking shelter behind the wall. Others were fumbling with the cannon, unsure of how to handle it. They had trained with the guns a little, but he now realized it had not been enough. He watched two of his men argue. One wanted to increase the gun's elevation, the other wanted to use more powder. It was obvious that neither one knew what he was doing. They would have to learn fast, or the gunboats would destroy the walls, allowing the soldiers waiting in the woods to overrun the fort. Suddenly, one of the men screamed and wheeled around, blood streaming down his face. The man he had been arguing with simply stood there in silence, watching the other man die. Garçon ran up, shoved the dying man aside, and shouted at the other one to finish loading the cannon.

Loomis stood behind the gunboat's cannon, eyeing the alignment carefully. "A wee bit lower, lad, and a degree or so to the left. Aye, that's it." Satisfied, he nodded to the gunner, and the cannon boomed. Through the smoke, Loomis saw wood fly near the center of the fort. He smiled and patted the gunner on the back. "We got her now, lad." Once again, the fort's cannon fired. The gunboat shook slightly, and there was the sound of breaking wood. Loomis shouted to one of the men at the rail. "Where'd he get us?"

"About a foot above the waterline, sir!"

"Well, run below and stuff something in the hole. We can do a proper patch later. As long as it's above the line it won't bother us any." He turned to one of the sailors standing nearby. "How's the hot shot, Mr. Peavey?"

"Red as a baby's cheek, sir."

"Load her up, then, lad." As the gunners loaded a powder bag into the cannon, Peavey and another sailor picked up a round metal cradle with long handles on it. Near the center of the ship was an open furnace, and in the fire was a cannon ball, glowing red-hot from sitting in the coals. The ball was rolled into the cradle, and Peavey and the other man carried it over to the gun. Loomis checked the aim one last time and nodded. Peavey and his companion lifted the cradle to the muzzle of the cannon and tilted it, allowing the ball to roll into the barrel. Quickly dropping the cradle, the men stepped back, covering their ears. The gun roared as the hot ball came into contact with the powder.

Although it only took an instant to reach its target, the ball seemed to hang in the air before smashing into a small wooden building at the center of the fort. Everyone ducked behind the railing. Suddenly there was a deafening roar, and the boat shook. Mud and wood began to rain down on the vessel. Then someone noticed a black arm on the deck.

Jack Dill slowly stood up, brushed the dirt off his uniform, and looked at the Negro Fort. For all practical purposes, it no longer existed, thoroughly destroyed after the hot shot had slammed into the powder magaine. The fort's wooden walls were blown outward, and no one was moving within the compound. Scores of bodies lay strewn about, and he caught sight of a child's body hanging lifeless in a tree. He took a few steps forward and stopped beside Major Wooster, who was standing still, staring at the ground. On the dirt in front of them was the naked form of a young black woman with a lovely face and perfectly formed breasts. Dill then realized there was nothing else to see. The lower half of her body was missing. She had been torn apart at the waist by the force of the blast.

Wooster shuddered for a moment and turned away. He remembered the battle at Fort Erie, where he had been wounded fighting the British. He recalled the look on a dying friend's face. Like his friend, this woman had paid the price of freedom.

Dill forced himself to look away from the dead girl. "My god, Major, there must have been tons of powder in that magazine. What a lucky shot!"

Wooster shook his head. He had been watching the gunboats do their work. Every shot had gotten closer to its mark. Whoever the commander of that gunboat was, he had done precisely what he had intended to do. "The battle's over, Corporal. Have Captain Vashon gather his men, and have them tend to the survivors, if there are any. I don't think the Creeks will be too happy. Won't be many bounties to collect out of this batch of runaways."

As the American soldiers moved slowly toward the remains of the fort, Wooster saw Colonel Clinch in the distance, conferring with some junior officers. He walked in the colonel's direction, occasionally telling a dazed soldier to get to the fort and look for survivors. Clinch looked visibly shaken. The colonel wiped a tear from his eye as Wooster approached. "One weeps for the loss, Major, especially the women and children. Yet you can see the hand of the Almighty at work, chastising the murderous banditti and savages." Wooster kept silent. God had nothing to do with it.

Garçon staggered through the mud in disbelief, blood trickling from his ears. How could he be alive? The last thing he remembered was standing atop the wall, urging his gunners to take better aim at the gunboat. Then he had seen one of the shots arc straight into the powder magazine. The blast must have knocked him from the wall and into the marsh below. Suddenly he felt strong hands grip his arms. He looked around and saw a Creek warrior on either side of him. Still dazed, he could offer no resistance. As he was led away from the fort, he began to struggle. One of the Indians swung a war club into his stomach. He screamed and doubled over. His captors forced him to his feet and marched him toward a cluster of warriors. When they reached the group, another Indian came behind him and tied his wrists together. He tried to struggle, but it was no use. They forced him onto his knees.

A man walked up to him, obviously a chief. He heard one of the warriors address the chief as "McIntosh." Garçon looked up into his eyes. McIntosh looked down and saw complete defiance. He turned to one of the warriors. "Forget your bounty. This man will never be a slave." Garçon smiled weakly. The proud smile stayed on his face until the war club smashed into his skull.

John Stuart stepped from the gunboat's launch and onto the dirt in front of the obliterated fort. He couldn't believe his eyes. He climbed the wall and looked down into the parade ground. Bodies, wood, and weapons were everywhere. On the other side of the compound he saw Captain Vashon and Jack Dill. He walked toward the men slowly, studying Vashon's face. Occasionally, the captain would smile. Stuart took a deep breath; Vashon didn't know about his wife.

3

November 11, 1816
Baton Rouge

To:
Mr. Robert Vashon
St. Louis, Missouri Territory

Dearest Robert,

I hope this finds you well and the business thriving. I am writing to tell you that we are soon to be on the move. Father has received word that the company is to report to Fort Montgomery in the Mississippi Territory, somewhere north of Mobile Bay. Unlike the assignment to Fort Scott, which was temporary in nature, this appears to be a more permanent posting. There is some talk of dividing Mississippi into two Territories, an eastern half to be known as Alabama and a western half that will retain the present name. The boundaries for the Creek cession from Genl. Jackson's treaty also need to be run, so Father feels there will be much work to be done escorting the surveyors and cutting roads through the Indian lands. It goes without saying that the Creeks and Choctaws will not be happy with all this activity in their homelands. Father is also concerned that with the formation of a new Territory, settlers will commence pouring into the land, which will no doubt cause trouble with the savages.

The house here in Baton Rouge is to be rented out, and Uncle Paul and Aunt Mae will keep watch over it as best they can from New Orleans. They have implored me to stay with them instead of going off into the wilderness with Father, but I feel he needs me. I tell you this in the strictest confidence, Robert, but I am worried about Father. The loss of Mother weighs heavily upon him, more than I thought at first. He has completely withdrawn from his law practice, having turned most of his clients over to other lawyers and declining any new ones. The governor had talked of appointing him as a judge here in Baton Rouge, but he let it be known he did not wish such a position. The only thing that seems to interest him is his military duty. He goes down to the fort every morning, stays the entire day, only to return in time for supper. What he does there all day, I cannot imagine, and no one can tell me, other than that he spends most of his time in his office.

It is in the evening that I notice the biggest difference, as his two or three small glasses of whiskey have now become four or five. Before Mother's passing, he would drink in the company of friends or his fellow officers, always laughing and in good spirits, but now he spends his evenings alone, quiet, and in a melancholy mood. He is never angry or hurtful toward me or anyone else, so I feel in no personal apprehension, but I am concerned for his health and his career. Perhaps the move to the new posting will restore his peace of mind.

I actually look forward to living in the wilderness. Since the passing of Mother, Louisiana holds little joy for me. Besides Father, Uncle Paul and Aunt Mae, the people I am closest to are our old friends Jack and Johnny, and the women of the company. Father, of course, says the frontier is no place for a sixteen-year-old young lady, but I know of many a girl my age who is already married and with children who do quite well in the wilds. Besides, I shall have the whole company to watch over me.

I shall close for now, dear brother, with the promise to send you more detailed information when I have it. We have not received precise orders yet, only a "warning" from Genl. Gaines. For the moment, everyone is packing and storing, trying to prepare for the journey. Take care, and give our best to Anna Lynn and her family. If there is to be a wedding, please give us sufficient advance notice so that we may at least attempt the journey.

Your loving sister,
Elizabeth

Captain Vashon's Company G, Fourth Infantry, left Louisiana by boat in late November and arrived in Mobile a few days later.

They were soon joined by Captain Allison's Company J from New Orleans, and when all was in readiness, the two companies and their dependents boarded smaller boats for the trip into the interior. The group, made up of 103 men, about two dozen women, and perhaps half that number of children, traveled upriver about thirty miles until they reached a small landing at the edge of a surrounding cypress swamp. They then marched inland for another three miles, through a forested wilderness punctuated by the occasional abandoned homestead. Upon reaching their destination they found the remains of Camp Montgomery, a temporary fort that had been built during the Creek War. This was to be their new home.

It wasn't much, and it was certainly the most isolated spot Elizabeth could imagine. In truth, it was nothing more than a cleared field in a vast pine forest that looked to stretch endlessly to the east. To their west was a lowland hardwood forest that extended to the cypress swamps bordering the river. The original fort's location had been chosen as a matter of convenience. It was close to the river for supply and communications purposes, elevated enough to be free of flooding, and close to the tall, straight pine trees needed for construction. Near the center of the clearing were the remains of a simple log breastwork and no buildings, the previous occupants having lived in their tents. Until new buildings were constructed, the newcomers would be doing the same.

The group had reached the campsite shortly after noon, and the entire force immediately went to work setting up camp. Some men began to clear weeds and brush from within the breastwork, while others followed behind them, setting up tents. A few worked at digging a latrine, while others cleaned out the water well. In one corner of the enclosure the women toiled at the task of setting up the kitchen facilities and preparing the food. Everyone had eaten a minimum of a midday meal, knowing that hot food would be waiting when the day's work was done.

Over the next few weeks, a small village began to take shape. With winter approaching, the first priority was to construct the dwelling structures. No one wanted to stay in the tents any longer than necessary. Axe men went to work, felling trees and removing limbs, while other men removed the bark and smoothed the logs. A saw pit was set up for cutting logs into planks for the floors or shingles for the roofs. The more experienced woodworkers cut up smaller trees to make simple furniture. In an amazingly short amount of time they constructed a barracks building, an officers' quarters, and a storehouse. When those were completed, work began on a cookhouse and a blacksmith's shop, all of which were presently operating under canvas.

The entire compound was enclosed in a picket work of vertical logs stacked close together. Watchtowers were erected at each corner where a sentry kept constant watch. This was Indian territory, and ownership of the land was very much in dispute. Everyone was aware that only a few miles away and a few years earlier, the Red Stick Creeks had attacked Fort Mims, a small, weakly fortified homestead where hundreds of settlers had taken refuge at the beginning of the Creek War. Forcing their way in, the Red Stick marauders had slaughtered everyone they could find, be it man, woman, child, slave, or mixed-blood Indian. Andrew Jackson had crushed the Red Sticks months later, but the peace was tenuous. Settlers had been slow to return to the area, and suspicious Indians were constantly lurking about. The occupants of Fort Montgomery, be they soldiers, women, or children, knew they were in a dangerous place, far from any assistance.

There were other small cabins being built in the area around the fort, not officially part of the military installation, but integral to it. The two dozen or so women who had accompanied the troops were wives to some of the soldiers, though few were legally married. Until the fort was completed, families were forced to live in tents, just like the common soldier. As work on the fort's structures slackened, the men were able to devote time to constructing cabins for the married men and their dependents. Some were built close to the fort for protection, while others were erected at some distance, usually on an especially favorable piece of land. These men and women were willing to take the chance of losing their homes, even their lives, to stake out a homestead. When their enlistments expired they would leave the army, but not the area. Families were helping to push back the frontier, just as much as muskets, bayonets, and treaties.

Alexander Arbuthnot leaned on the railing of the small sailing vessel anchored near the mouth of the Suwannee River. The Scotsman was close to seventy now, weathered, with white hair and a grin that showed more than a few gaps in his dental work. His schooner *Chance* was about half that age, badly in need of paint and some good carpentry. The sails and rigging were in good shape, however, and her hull was sound. As he often told friends, "She ain't much to look at, but she always gets me home."

Arbuthnot couldn't remember the number of times he'd sailed *Chance* from his Bahamian home in Nassau to the west coast of Spanish Florida. Somehow, in all those years, he'd managed to avoid the threatening storms, dangerous reefs, and plundering pirates that had taken so many of the ships and sailors who braved the coasts and keys of Florida. For the most part, he enjoyed the trip. He was never in a hurry and always steered clear of unfamiliar waterways. He didn't need to make the runs for financial reasons, having saved enough to allow him to live comfortably for whatever years were remaining to him. He did it because he liked the sailing, the trading, and the Indians. Why stop?

Arbuthnot smiled as he saw an Indian canoe leave shore, occupied by three people. One was just a child, a boy maybe six or seven years old. Just behind the boy was a middle-aged Indian by the name of Bolek, someone Arbuthnot knew well. The other man was a young runaway slave called Abraham. Arbuthnot had only met him a few times but had been impressed by the black man's intelligence and wit. He had quickly learned that negotiating prices with Abraham was tricky business.

The canoe gently bumped into the side of *Chance,* and Arbuthnot tossed down a rope ladder to Bolek. The chief tied a line to the ladder, then took hold of the boy and held him aloft. A tall, black sailor reached over the side of the schooner and swung the laughing boy onto the deck. Then Bolek climbed the ladder, followed by Abraham. As soon as Bolek had steadied himself on deck, Arbuthnot stepped forward and the two embraced warmly. Arbuthnot smiled and said, "It does me heart good to see you again, old friend."

Bolek answered as best his poor command of English would allow. "Me happy see you, friend." He then put his hand on the boy's shoulder. "My sister-son, Holata. He want see big canoe."

Arbuthnot smiled and walked over to a wooden chest. Opening it, he sifted through the contents, and then pulled out a small Spanish coin with a thin leather thong attached. He placed it over the boy's head and let the coin rest against his chest. "Someday this will rest over the heart of a great chief." Holata smiled as Abraham interpreted. Arbuthnot was knowledgeable enough in the Seminole tongue to know that the interpreter had embellished things a bit, adding something about the boy being a fearless warrior who would collect many trophies. The Scotsman turned back to the chest and brought forth an exquisite tomahawk with a carved, red-stained handle and an engraved bronze blade. Bolek's eyes widened when he saw it. Arbuthnot always brought presents, but this was better than expected. Finally, the trader handed Abraham an ostrich feather and a large kerchief trimmed with bright green fringe. "You look like you could use a new turban, my friend, and with it a fine feather from your African homeland."

Abraham smiled. "Cap'n Alexander always treats the Seminole good, I says. Me and the chief and the boy thanks you kindly, sir."

Two other men, having finished the task of stowing the sails, approached the group. One was a young man, less than twenty, and the other was about twice that age. Arbuthnot motioned toward the older man. "Chief Bolek, you remember my son, Jonathan?" Bolek nodded and extended his hand. "Jonathan has just returned from Edinburgh and London with some fine hunting rifles to make your warriors proud, and some beautiful cloth to make your women squeal." Arbuthnot then introduced the younger man. "And this is Peter Cook. He'll be working as a clerk for me here." Abraham eyed Cook, noticing how the man's gaze shifted about, as if he were sizing everything up, making plans of some sort. Instinctively, Abraham didn't trust the young Bahamian.

Arbuthnot smiled and gave a nod to Cook, who ran below deck. "I've brought some fine Irish whiskey and some sweet Virginia tobacco, my friends. Shall we have a seat on deck and talk of things that have passed since last we saw each other?" There would be time enough for business discussions later. For the moment, he just wanted to enjoy the company. Cook soon appeared on deck carrying a large bottle, a ceremonial pipe, and a small leather pouch. Arbuthnot took the bottle, pulled the stopper, then held it aloft, sort of as an offering to the Great Spirit, God, or whatever entity was watching over them. He then handed the bottle to Bolek for the first sip. As the chief took a good swallow, Arbuthnot packed the pipe and then lit it.

After the bottle and the pipe had made one round, Arbuthnot asked, "So what news does Bolek have for his British friends?"

Bolek nodded to Abraham, who knew the reports as well as anyone and could more easily convey them. "Same old stuff, Cap. Damn 'mericans think they own everthin', 'specially since they blowed up the fort on the Apalach'. Thievin' raiders come down from Georgia, steal cattle and horses, catch runaways, even kill an Injun once-awhile. Bolek here and the other chiefs complain to the agent, an' he says, 'Sho, we do somethin' about it,' but they never does. Gonna be big war someday. Injun ain't gonna put up with it forever, you know."

Arbuthnot understood. The Spanish authorities in St. Augustine and Pensacola were simply too weak to stop the cross-border incursions of the lawless squatters in Georgia, nor were they able to halt retaliatory raids by the Seminoles. The Americans, if they cared to, might have been able to control their own citizens, but showed little inclination to do so. Sooner or later, something was bound to happen that would ignite a war.

Bolek added, "We wait for help from Big King in London. He promise to remember his red brothers." Arbuthnot was also waiting for support from the British government. During the war with the Americans, British officers had landed in Florida, promising aid to the Indians and runaways if they would join the cause against the United States. Many had answered the call, and many had lost their lives during the Creek Civil War. When the war ended, the British departed, leaving nothing but the Negro Fort and solemn assurances that they would not abandon their red brethren to the aggressive Americans. So far, few, if any, of those promises had been kept. On paper, at least, the English had done one major thing: In the treaty that had ended the War of 1812, they'd inserted a clause stipulating that all Indian land occupied at war's end was to be returned to its rightful owners. As far as Arbuthnot and many of his British friends were concerned, that included all the land forfeited at the end of the Creek War. The Americans, predictably, insisted that Jackson's treaty with the Creeks had nothing to do with the Treaty of Ghent. Arbuthnot and those who were sympathetic to the plight of their Indian friends expected the British government to put pressure on the Americans to return the land. They also knew it wasn't likely to happen.

While there was nothing the old Scotsman could do about the situation directly, he did want to help. These people were his friends, and he felt the crown should honor its commitments. "Lord Cameron, the Governor of the Bahamas, is a friend of mine. With his aid, I shall write, on your behalf, to the Foreign Office in London and to the British Ambassador in Washington. They will tell the Americans to return the stolen land and to stop their people from coming into Florida to steal your livestock and hurt your people. What the King promises, he must deliver."

Abraham nodded approvingly. Arbuthnot was a good man and would do everything he could. The interpreter had less faith, however, in the faraway King of England. It was much easier to make false promises when you didn't have to look a man in the eye.

By January 1817, life at Fort Montgomery had settled into a routine. For the most part, these routines were beneficial. The buildings were erected and maintained, the men trained and disciplined, and the neighboring Indians kept under surveillance. When things ran smoothly, Captain Vashon, as the post's commanding officer, was happy.

Routines were meant to be broken, however, especially on the frontier, where isolation and hostile neighbors put everyone on edge. Most troublesome for Vashon and the other officers were the domestic disputes that seemed to occur on a regular basis. It was an inevitable part of camp life. Many of the soldiers had wives and families with them, and not all the relationships were stable and loving. It was no different than anywhere else, but the demands of military life often put unbearable pressures on the men and women of Fort Montgomery. Generally, these disturbances were more of an annoyance than a problem. Infidelity and abusiveness were to be expected, and situations needed to be dealt with when they disrupted orderly camp life. Stern warnings to the women and punishments to the offending soldiers usually took care of the problem. Yet everyone knew such matters could easily get out of hand. Jealousy and drunkenness might lead to serious injury or even murder. It was the responsibility of the officers to see things never went that far.

By mid-January, one such situation appeared to have become a crisis. Polly Brewer, a ragged, toothless woman with a dirt-covered toddler continually gripping her skirt, had accused one of the other women, Lacey Moore, of trying to steal her husband. In response, Lacey's husband had accused Private Brewer of making unwanted advances toward Lacey. The accusations were becoming a regular occurrence, were getting more heated, and the officers were tired of dealing with it. Vashon decided the matter needed to be settled once and for all and ordered all the officers to gather at the Officers' Mess. At one end of the table sat Captain Vashon, with Allison opposite him. To Vashon's left was his company's second-in-command, First Lieutenant Clinch, the younger brother of Colonel Clinch. Next to Allison were Ross and Leftwich, his first and second lieutenants, respectively. Vashon was still waiting on a new second lieutenant.

Also sitting at the table was Elizabeth, who had become the unofficial representative of the fort's women and children. She hadn't asked for the position, didn't really want it, but had found she couldn't avoid it. The enlisted soldiers' wives, not being an official part of the army, couldn't bring their complaints directly to the officers. They needed an intermediary, and as the commanding officer's daughter and the only female in camp associated with the other officers, Elizabeth ended up being the person they came to.

Captain Allison seemed especially annoyed with having to deal with another domestic quarrel. "We ought to just send all the women back to New Orleans." He then remembered Elizabeth was at the table, but didn't sound totally sincere in his apology. "Present company excepted, of course."

Captain Vashon didn't agree with Allison's idea. "Aye, and have a mutiny on our hands when the cooking, cleaning, and laundry aren't done. Not to mention a few desertions. Like it or not, gentlemen, the ladies are part of our community. Even the War Department accedes to their presence, or else they wouldn't allow them rations or provide what little funding they do for the hard work these wives perform."

Allison scowled. "To call them wives is being generous. Few of these unions have been sanctified by God or are sanctioned by the law. Most of these women are nothing more than common trollops, especially the one in question. With so many unattached soldiers in camp, can we expect anything but trouble? What happens if we come under attack? How many of these men are going to desert their posts to fly to the aid of their women and children? Let the men do their own cooking and cleaning. They would have to do it in time of war."

Elizabeth quickly came to the women's defense, saying, "I should strongly disagree, Captain. While some of these ladies may have once led a sordid life, none of them do so now. All of them work harder than their husbands, many suffer abuse at the hands of those who are supposed to care for them, and when they do complain, it is usually with good cause and as a last resort. Few are drunkards, which is more than you can say for the men at this post, and all give more to the army than the army gives to them."

Vashon smiled. His daughter had no hesitation in speaking her mind, especially if she felt an injustice had been done. Still, he didn't want the conversation to degenerate into an argument over the value of the camp followers. "We are arguing a moot point, I fear. Whether or not the women and children should be here is not the question before us. Lieutenant Ross, has Lacey Moore been plying her old trade?"

Ross, who was the post's quartermaster and commissary officer, dealt with the families on a regular basis and knew them better than anyone except Elizabeth. "As far as I can tell, sir, no."

Clinch, whose family owned a large number of slaves, had a simple solution. "Send the nigger wench back to New Orleans, where she belongs."

Ross shot back, "Damn it, Clinch, she's no such thing."

"Well, she's certainly not white."

Vashon raised his voice slightly. "Gentlemen, the woman's ancestry is not the question before us." Lacey Moore was one of the many Louisiana residents whose ethnic background was impossible to determine. There was certainly black blood in her veins, but there was also plenty of Spanish, French, and Indian blood there, too. Whatever the mixture, it had given her an enchanting face and a lustrous mane of wavy black hair. An attractive figure and a certain manner of walking guaranteed that she caught the eye of every man she came across. As Lieutenant Leftwich had remarked, "Trouble doesn't come in any prettier a package."

Clinch's mind was still made up. "I still say she's a strumpet and should be sent back to New Orleans."

This time it was Elizabeth who took exception to his comments. "She is not a strumpet! She may have been a fallen woman at one time, but she has left that life behind and is a faithful wife to Corporal Moore, even to the point of having been married in the church."

Clinch huffed, "Catholic church, no doubt. Damn Papists will allow anything."

Ross sighed. "We all know what the problem is, and please excuse my bluntness, Miss Elizabeth, but every man at this post desires Lacey Moore. It doesn't matter what she wants or how she acts. They see her, and they want her. We also know that Polly Brewer is a woman who has little faith in her man, and probably with good reason. Polly thinks every woman is out to steal her husband, and knows full well that he'd take whatever opportunity was offered. Not that I can imagine anyone who would have him, and certainly not Lacey. On the other hand, Corporal Moore knows how enticing Lacey is and fears every soldier in camp is ready to take his place. They all see what they fear, real or not."

Elizabeth nodded in agreement. "Lacey has a pure heart, but her habits of expression do seem to lead the men's minds in an unsavory direction. Perhaps it was her upbringing. I assume it was not the most wholesome."

Leftwich laughed. "Quite the opposite, I would think."

Vashon felt the conversation was getting a bit risqué for his daughter's ears and decided to move it in another direction. "Very well, gentlemen, I believe we have identified the problem. Now what shall we do about it?"

Clinch hadn't changed his mind. "I still say we should send her back to New Orleans."

Ross protested, "On what grounds? You cannot punish her if she has done no wrong."

Clinch responded, "She's a threat to good order and discipline."

Allison added, "And a threat to the moral cleanliness of our troops."

Leftwich laughed. "Aye, there's a righteous lot, if ever I saw one." Allison and Clinch gave him a cold stare, but the others were inclined to smile.

Once again, Vashon was forced to keep the conversation within bounds. "Gentlemen, I shall not punish Corporal Moore or his wife simply for convenience or out of fear of what others might do. At the same time, I realize few of our soldiers are familiar with the 'lead us not into temptation' part of the Lord's Prayer, and that the lovely Mrs. Moore is quite a temptation. Now, can we please come to some practical solution?"

Ross shook his head, saying, "How do you keep her from being an enticement to the troops without banishing her, which would be an undeserved punishment for Corporal Moore? He's a good soldier; one of our best men."

No one seemed to have an answer. Had Captain Allison been in command, he would simply have sent the woman away. Clinch tended to agree, while Ross and Leftwich were sympathetic to the lady. Vashon had hoped for some usable advice from his junior officers but wasn't getting any. By default, the decision was up to him.

Allison felt he had the only answer. "Like it or not, you have to get rid of the source of the problem."

Elizabeth didn't like the captain's attitude. "Lacey isn't the problem. She's perfectly innocent, yet somehow it's the woman who gets the blame. It's your lecherous soldiers who are at fault."

Leftwich stifled a laugh and said in a low voice, "Banish all the lecherous soldiers and we won't have an army."

A thoughtful silence fell over the group as they tried to think of a solution. Then Elizabeth's eyes brightened, and she smiled. "Banish Lacey from the fort itself, not the surrounding camp. At the same time, place the Moore's cabin off-limits to the men. Keep everyone separated, and you eliminate the problem."

Ross had a quizzical look on his face as he considered the possibilities. "It might work. We'd have to restrict her from coming within perhaps a hundred feet of the fort, but I see no problem there. Her primary reason for coming here is to pick up laundry. Have her pick it up at one of the other cabins not too far from the fort. She has friends among the women who would gather it for her. As for making the Moore cabin off-limits, that isn't a problem either. They're well out of sight of the fort, and there isn't much reason for any of the men to be near there anyway. If the men don't see her, they won't be lusting after her."

Elizabeth still felt Lacey was being unfairly singled out, but understood the practical considerations. The best protest she could make was, "You could always tell the men to start acting like gentlemen."

Leftwich noted that, "Of course once we set Moore's cabin off-limits, everyone will consider it a challenge to sneak over there."

Vashon understood the truth of the statement, but wasn't bothered by it. "At least it will be a definite offense with a definite punishment." Turning to his daughter, he said, "I will give you the task of explaining to Corporal Moore that banishing Lacey from the fort is somehow doing them a favor." He was proud of the girl. When all his well-trained and experienced officers were stymied, she had come up with the solution. He thought, *I need more men like her.*

Elizabeth stopped peeling the potato and looked at her friend Nellie Crump. They were an unlikely pair, looking more like a mother and daughter sitting on the front step of the small cabin than simple companions. The wife of Private Reason Crump, Nellie was twice the age and weight of Elizabeth, illiterate, and far from ladylike. Although Elizabeth was considered the families' liaison to the officers, Nellie was their leader. She was the sort of woman who took charge and got things done. She had also become Elizabeth's closest confidant, especially when it came to personal matters. It was Nellie who had made her feel a part of the "ladies' camp."

When they'd first arrived at Fort Montgomery, Elizabeth had felt isolated and useless. There was little for her to do besides set up her and her father's quarters. As the commanding officer's daughter, no one thought of her doing anything strenuous, such as the laundry or planting the garden. She had no real aversion to hard work, and often felt guilty that other women were working so hard while she enjoyed a life of relative leisure. Whether she liked it or not, she was viewed as someone of a higher social class, and there were certain tasks a young lady of her class simply did not perform. It was Nellie who had taken her aside and told her what to do. "Don't just do your father's sewing and mending, offer to do it for all the officers. Don't expect Private Wall to feed your father and the other officers a decent meal. You do it. I'll show you how it's done." It was all so obvious, yet Elizabeth's awkwardness had prevented her from seeing it.

The two women did most of their talking while preparing the afternoon meal. Part of the conversation was gossip, part of it unofficial administration. On this particular occasion, Elizabeth asked, "How is Polly Brewer?" Separating the woman from Lacey Moore had solved one problem, but another had gotten worse.

Nellie didn't look up from the dough she was kneading. "She'll be all right. The jaw's not broken, but if she'd have had any teeth, she'd have lost a few. My man Reason and Sergeant Jack went over and had words—so to speak—with her man David. Can't say that it will stop him from beating on the poor woman whenever he gets drunk, but at least he knows he'll get his due the next day."

Nellie had said "whenever he gets drunk" as if it were a rare occasion. In truth, it was a daily event. Drunkenness was the scourge of the army, and everyone knew it. Even Elizabeth's father had a drinking problem, which had only gotten worse since the death of her mother. Elizabeth had hoped leaving Baton Rouge would distance him from the memories and improve his spirits. To some extent it had, but the habit of three or four glasses of whiskey every night was too strong to be broken. Still, as Johnny had said, "He's a happy drunk," and Elizabeth had to admit that the worst effect the liquor seemed to have was to make it very difficult to awaken her father every morning.

She had also hoped that being on the frontier would make the whiskey harder to come by. In Baton Rouge, it was as plentiful as water, but on the frontier, good whiskey was less easily acquired. Bad whiskey, on the other hand, was quite easily found. No sooner had the troops arrived at the remains of old Camp Montgomery than a ragged old man had appeared dragging a battered cart laden with earthenware jugs full of the worst liquor anyone had ever tasted. Within an hour, his entire stock was sold. Once established, "Whiskey Joe" proved impossible to remove.

Captain Allison, a pious man who never touched the stuff, tried to run Joe off, but succeeded in sending him no farther than around the nearest bend in the road, from where he continued to run a thriving trade.

Elizabeth remarked, "If only Father could get rid of Whiskey Joe."

Nellie laughed. "And where do you think your Papa gets his whiskey, Lizzy? He may run Joe off once in awhile, but he ain't gonna run him far. Anyway, if he ran Joe off, there'd just be some other old whiskey seller hangin' 'round the next day. If there's soldiers, there's drink, and blaming it on the whiskey seller don't get to the root of the matter, does it?"

Elizabeth couldn't disagree. The only thing she could do was ask, "Why do men drink, Nellie?"

"The same reason women drink, Lizzy. It's either in the blood or it's somethin' weighin' heavy on the mind. In your Papa, I'd say it's both. For someone like my Reason, it ain't neither. He's happy with his daily ration the army gives him and don't need no more. I'm not saying anything bad about your Papa, but you need to find a man like my Reason. Someone who cares more about you than about his drink."

Elizabeth laughed. "Well, let me know if you see one, Nellie."

Nellie stopped kneading the dough and set it aside. She gave Elizabeth a wink and said, "That good-looking Sergeant Stuart is right sweet on you, if I know anything about men."

Elizabeth blushed. "Oh, don't be silly, Nellie! Johnny is naught but a friend, just like Jack." She may have been acting as if she were dismissing the notion, but in her mind, she knew better. In her private hours, her mind was filled with visions of the future, and in every vision Johnny was by her side. She could see them in their own small cabin, just starting out, with an infant in her arms. At other times, they were in a house like her own in Baton Rouge, with small children scurrying about, laughter and contented looks passing between her and Johnny. Every now and then she envisioned them a bit older, living in a large house with a dozen liveried slaves in attendance, hosting large parties with the most fashionable guests and important visitors. Yet no matter what the vision, Johnny was always close at hand.

She told no one of her feelings, however, not even Nellie. The reason for her silence was simple: She was the daughter of an officer, and Johnny was an enlisted man. The officers and enlisted men were two distinct classes and rarely socialized. Elizabeth knew that a romance with Johnny would most likely lead to trouble. For the moment, until she was older or his enlistment ran out, it was best that she keep her feelings to herself. It was proving a difficult thing to do.

It was a deserted place, a stretch of beach overlooking the Gulf of Mexico with no visible structure except a crude lean-to fashioned from branches and covered with thatch. Anchored offshore was a single-masted sailing vessel, and pulled up on the beach was a small rowboat. Sitting on the sand inside the lean-to were three men, two of them Indians. One, Hillishadjo, looked weathered and weary. His companion, Homathlemico, was strong and intense. The other person was a young white man dressed in a British officer's uniform.

Hillishadjo had a right to feel weary. He was no longer a young man and had just returned from a long and arduous journey to England. His old friend Colonel Nicolls of the Royal Marines had taken him there, promising that the Big King in London would see him and give the Creek people protection from the Americans. In the end, it had been a difficult and wasted trip. He had spent weeks traveling over the endless ocean, sick from the motion of the ship and eating food that was fit only for the many rats that lived in the stench at the bottom of the vessel. Unfortunately, when they finally arrived in London, no one wanted to talk to them, especially the Big King. Even the King's advisors refused to see them. Colonel Nicolls said it would take time and that the King and his men were busy, but eventually they would get an audience.

At first, Hillishadjo was awestruck by the size of the city and all that was in it. After many months spent waiting to talk to people who wanted nothing to do with him, he was simply disgusted by it. London was filthy, the people were rude, and he missed the forest. Most of all, he missed his people. London was no place for an Indian. Finally, after countless meetings with little men who promised to do "their best" but did nothing, a meeting was arranged with someone called the Foreign Secretary. The meeting was cordial, but short and to the point: The Big King and the British people had made peace with the Americans, and the Indians should do likewise. The Foreign Secretary then handed him an especially fine tomahawk and some other presents, saying they were from the Big King. Hillishadjo doubted that the Big King even knew there was an Indian in London.

Worst of all, Hillishadjo felt trapped in a net of his own making. Years earlier he had listened intently as the great warrior Tecumseh spoke eloquently about the necessity of the Indian peoples to unite against the encroachments of the white man. He had been moved by the words of Tecumseh's brother, the Shawnee Prophet, and the message of a better life ahead if the native people would only return to the ways of their elders. As a powerful medicine man, Hillishadjo took up the cause, became known as a Prophet, and extolled the virtues of the Indian way of life, while pointing out the evils of the white man's ways. Fired by his own enthusiasm, Hillishadjo urged his people to make war on the Americans and any Indians who supported them. Those who gathered around him became known as Red Sticks, and their numbers grew with each village Hillishadjo visited. The British, at war with the Americans, had come to Florida with promises of aid and weaponry. They had brought shiploads of guns, knives, and tomahawks. They had built a big fort on the Apalachicola and convinced the many runaway slaves to join in the fight. Hillishadjo had begun to dream of the day when the Americans would be driven back to the sea.

Then came the devil called Andrew Jackson. With thousands of soldiers he marched from the north and slaughtered the Red Sticks and drove the British from Florida and New Orleans. Farther north, up near the Big Lakes, Tecumseh was killed in battle and the Shawnee Prophet driven into hiding. Hillishadjo had barely escaped with his life, fleeing to the wilds of Spanish Florida with nothing more than his daughter Milly by his side. He had been a fool to believe he could stop the Americans, a dreamer to think his people would give up the white ways to live as the ancestors had. Those days, and the days of Creek power, were gone forever.

The Red Sticks may have been defeated, but they were not totally destroyed. They had fled to Florida, living among the various native tribes before separating and forming their own villages. The arrival of these refugees added yet another shade to the colorful mixture of Indians living in Florida. To most whites, an Indian was an Indian, and few distinctions were applied. As far as the British, Spanish, and Americans were concerned, all the Indians in Florida were Seminoles. The natives themselves saw no such homogeneity. Most of the true Seminoles lived in the center of the peninsula, around the Alachua Prairie and the Withlacoochee River area. Then there were the Mikasukis, the most independent group, who generally lived around Lake Miccosukee just south of the Georgia border, but had also migrated into the St. Johns River area and had villages north of the border. There were also smaller bands, such as the Uchees, Tallahassees, Apalachicolas, and others. Add to that the hundreds of runaway blacks who had taken up the Seminole way of life, and it was little wonder the whites called them all by one name.

For the Red Sticks, the dream of driving the Americans from their land did not die. New leaders, such as Homathlemico, vowed to continue the fight. Unfortunately, they still looked to Hillishadjo for spiritual guidance. The old man wished the past could be forgotten, and that he and Milly could move deep into Florida and live in peace, but it was not to be. His people looked up to him, and he could not turn away from them. To keep their spirits alive, his people needed the dream of someday returning to their homeland. And now there was another Englishman among them, telling them the hope was still alive and that the British would once again come to their aid. Hillishadjo knew better, but held his tongue. He could not destroy the only hope his people had.

The third man in the shelter, Robert Chrystie Ambrister, was excited to once again be in Florida. He felt himself part of some great adventure, a lead player in some important enterprise. He was a trim, handsome youth, proud to be wearing the red uniform of the British Colonial Marines. The fact that his mission to Florida was not officially sanctioned by the Crown was a necessary deceit. The Indians were impressed by uniforms and the military manner, and if he didn't look official, they wouldn't listen to him. Although only twenty years of age, he was a man of some experience and good connections. In the recent wars against France and America, he had been a midshipman in the Royal Navy, and had made the acquaintance of Colonel Nicolls of the Royal Marines. After the war he had left the service, returning to his home in Nassau in the Bahamas. No longer part of the navy, he still longed for a military career and had good reasons to believe he could find one: His father was a senior officer in Colonial Militia, and his uncle was Governor of the Bahamas. True to expectations, he soon found himself commissioned as a lieutenant in the Colonial Marines.

Unfortunately, with no war going on, it was an inactive, largely unpaid position. The young man needed something to do, something to fatten his purse. Once again, old connections provided an opportunity. There were a large number of unemployed soldiers and sailors milling about Nassau, and one of them was George Woodbine, another former Royal Marine officer who had served under Colonel Nicolls. During the war, both Woodbine and Ambrister had been sent to the Apalachicola to recruit, train, and arm the Indians and runaway slaves to fight against the Americans. While there they had observed that the Scottish firm of Forbes & Co., who held the lucrative Spanish monopoly on trade with the southern Indians, were finding it difficult to provide the quality goods the Indians demanded. Woodbine and Governor Cameron both saw an opportunity to displace the Scottish merchants. All they needed was to reestablish good relations with the Creeks and the Seminoles. At least that's what they told Ambrister.

And so it came to be that Ambrister found himself back along the shore of the Gulf of Mexico, holding a meeting with two of the most influential Creek leaders. What he was telling them was certainly not a lie, but it was far from the whole truth. He told them their friends the British were once again going to send arms and other supplies. He was careful, however, not to say it was the British *government*. He told them his friends would soon open new trading houses with a wonderful variety of low-cost, high-quality British goods. He didn't tell them these would be unlicensed traders that the Spanish might try to run off and that the Indians would have to defend. Above all, he reminded them of the article in the Treaty of Ghent that stipulated the Americans must return all Indian land that had been taken during the war, including the massive cession Jackson had forced the Indians to give up at the end of the Creek War. What he didn't tell them was that the Americans had a different interpretation of the article and that the British government had no intention of making the Americans return the land.

Listening intently to all this, with joy in his heart, was Homathlemico, one of the principal war leaders of the Red Sticks. He was around thirty years of age and in the prime of life, both physically and mentally. He had lost his family and many friends during the Creek War and was burning with the hope of revenge against the Americans. He wouldn't have cared if the promised guns came from the British government or a few British subjects. It didn't matter to him whether the traders were licensed or not; he only wanted the gunpowder they would sell him. More than anything, he wanted his homeland back. Anyone who would give him the means to kill the Americans and force them from Creek land was a friend to Homathlemico.

The gates of Fort Montgomery opened slowly, swinging heavily on their wrought-iron hinges. Through the portal came a fully laden wagon, followed by a dozen men on horseback. Most of the riders were soldiers who immediately dismounted and began to lead their mounts toward the stable. From the seat of the wagon Jack Dill and another soldier jumped to the ground and began to loosen the canvas that covered the bed of the wagon. The other four riders, an officer and three civilians, also dismounted and handed the reins to waiting soldiers.

It was a pleasant spring day and people began to gather in the fort's parade ground, anxious to see who and what had just arrived. For the most part, the enlisted men and some of the women collected around the wagon, some to help unload it, others to see what was in Sergeant Dill's trunk. Dill smiled and held up his hands, acting as if he were protecting the trunk. "Now, now, lads and lassies, we are not open for business yet. Not a person feasts their eyes upon the contents of this treasure chest until the coins grace my palms. There is, of course, one exception . . ." He turned and pulled a small basket from behind the chest and handed it to Nellie Crump. "For the good Lady Crump, a peck of the finest pecans to be had in Mobile."

The woman beamed. "Oh! Thank ye, Sergeant Jack. You know what I shall be doin' wi' these."

Dill winked at the woman and spoke as if he were relaying a secret. "I think I can prevail upon the captain to issue a few extra rations of flour and sugar so that you might provide the garrison with a round of those wonderful pecan dainties you make."

"Oh! That I shall!" Happy as a child at Christmas, she bounded off toward the storehouse, her basket of pecans tightly in hand.

As Nellie moved off, others pressed closer, voicing a disorganized chorus of "Did ya get . . .?"

Dill nodded. "If I don't have it here, then it wasn't to be had in Mobile. Ladies, there are threads and needles aplenty, a bolt of sturdy cotton cloth, a few yards of ribbon, a cook pot or two, and a kettle if someone needs it. Mr. Gravit, I have your boot black, and Sissom, I have your shoe leather, an awl, and a last so that you may open up your cobbler's shop. Asbury, I have those playing cards you requested, so that I may once again lose what little I have gained from the sale of these items, and Mrs. Fail, I did not fail to find you a lovely bonnet. Now, if someone would kindly help me carry this trunk to my quarters, the emporium shall soon be open."

No one was quite sure how Dill had managed to become the post's sutler. The army supplied only the basic necessities of life for its troops, and for those other items that made life in the military bearable, the soldiers and their families turned to the camp sutler. The regiment's official sutler had remained in Baton Rouge, leaving a vacancy at Fort Montgomery that needed to be filled. A good businessman could make a tidy profit as a sutler, and no one had doubts that Jack Dill was a good businessman. What no one could figure out was where he had gotten the money to start his business or who had given him the authority.

Meanwhile, on the porch of the officers' quarters, a group of men had gathered, making introductions. The officer who had ridden in with Dill presented a folded piece of paper to Captain

Vashon and saluted. "Brevet First Lieutenant Richard W. Scott, reporting as ordered, sir."

Vashon looked the officer over. He was of ordinary height and build with light brown hair and a face that was very unremarkable. He spoke with the accent of a Virginia planter, proud and aloof, but his manner belied his put-on confidence. Vashon could sense an uneasiness in the man and saw a look in the lieutenant's eye that begged for acceptance. Still, Vashon was not one to make snap judgments. He smiled warmly and said, "Welcome to Fort Montgomery, Lieutenant. Where were your previous postings?"

"Baltimore, sir, and Washington City."

Vashon nodded. That could easily explain the uneasiness. This was obviously the young man's first trip into the wilderness. "Well, you'll find things much less formal and a bit more dangerous out here, Mr. Scott. Still, no one's lost their hair yet, so I wouldn't be too worried." Vashon then looked to the three civilians. "Introduce us to your friends, Mr. Scott."

The civilians were surveyors who had come to lay out the boundaries of the Creek land cession. As the introductions were concluding, Vashon saw Elizabeth approaching. "Ah, here comes the Queen of Fort Montgomery."

The gentlemen moved aside to allow Elizabeth to step onto the platform. Vashon beamed and made the introductions. "Gentlemen, my daughter Elizabeth." The surveyors greeted her politely and gently shook her hand.

Scott, determined to be the Southern gentleman, removed his hat and bowed deeply. Then, instead of shaking her hand, he kissed it. "Will the lovely lady grace the officers' mess this afternoon?" Behind him, Lieutenant Leftwich smiled and poked a finger into Ross's side.

Elizabeth was taken slightly aback. She was much too familiar with the other officers to expect any deferential treatment. "It is my habit to dine with Father's fellow officers, Mr. Scott, but 'grace' is a word I would reserve for the before-meal prayer." If there was one thing she didn't like, it was to be treated specially, and Scott had certainly gotten off on the wrong foot.

Jack and Johnny stood in the watchtower on a clear May evening, gazing at the waxing moon as it drifted toward the horizon. Dill put a reassuring hand on his friend's shoulder. "There's no cure for the thirst, Johnny, but to take a deep draught."

"If only I could, Jack."

"And why can't you?"

Johnny shook his head. "She'd never have me, Jack, and on top of that, she's an officer's daughter."

"She'd have you in a minute, Johnny, if only you'd ask."

"Do you really think so? I can't see it."

"You can't see it because you're afraid it isn't there. She loves you, my friend, and I have no doubt about it."

"Her father would never agree to it, Jack. I'm just an enlisted man, I've got no family, and I certainly have no money. He'd not let her live the drudgery of an enlisted man's wife."

"Two more years, Johnny, and we'll be enlisted no more. We'll find us a growing town, open a store, and be as respectable as a judge. One man's as good as the next on the frontier, you know. You'll make Elizabeth a fine husband, and the captain knows it."

Johnny sighed. For the past two and a half years, many things had crossed his mind, but the one constant had been Elizabeth. In his mind's eye he could see her on his arm, walking down the docks at New Orleans, catching a boat upriver. Maybe they would spend time in St. Louis with Robert. Maybe her father would retire from the army and join them. He would truly be part of the family then. Perhaps after a few years in St. Louis they would ascend the Missouri and settle for awhile in the next frontier boom town. The nation was expanding westward, and he and Elizabeth would help lead the way.

Yet still, he had his doubts. If Jack saw something in her manner or actions that indicated some special affection for him, Johnny was missing it. She treated him no differently than she did anyone else, spent no extra time with him, and never seemed to mention him to anyone, other than in an official manner. For his part, he had done nothing to encourage her, and went out of his way to treat her with the proper respect his commanding officer's daughter deserved. "She can't be loving me, Jack. No man could be that lucky."

It was in early June, 1817, when Elizabeth realized she was faced with a serious problem. Perhaps it had something to do with her having recently turned seventeen. Maybe it was simply the delightful weather. Most likely, it was that she just hadn't noticed. She had been quite busy for some time, having taken on numerous tasks just to keep herself occupied. Elizabeth had many close relationships at the fort, and she felt comfortable with nearly everyone. Foremost in her heart, of course, was John Stuart, though she still took pains not to reveal those feelings. She also considered Jack Dill one of her dearest friends, though there were no romantic feelings toward him whatsoever. Among the enlisted men there were some she favored over others, but none who were really close to her. Most of her time was spent among the six officers, and it was there that she felt most at home. Captain Allison and Lieutenant Clinch were nearly as paternal toward her as her own father, while Lieutenants Ross and Leftwich treated her much like a sister. Both were handsome young men, but both had sweethearts they were totally devoted to. The only officer she did not feel comfortable with was Lieutenant Scott.

The problem wasn't that Scott was impolite to her. If anything, he was too polite, to the point of being condescending. It wasn't that she didn't trust him, it was just that she never knew which of his fantastic stories to believe. Had he really been the one who saved that "Star Spangled Banner" from falling at Fort McHenry? Did he really know every member of President Monroe's Cabinet? Had his father really been a close friend of General Washington, and was the family plantation actually larger than Mount Vernon and Monticello combined? It all sounded ridiculous and very plausible at the same time. Elizabeth had no idea what sort of man Lieutenant Scott was because he was always trying to be someone else.

Having never shown any interest in the man, Elizabeth was completely taken by surprise when Scott informed everyone he intended to start courting her. It occurred as she and the officers were finishing their afternoon meal. Scott cleared his throat, which everyone recognized as his way of indicating that he had an important announcement to make. Turning to Vashon he said, "Captain, I would consider it a high honor if you would grant permission for me to court your daughter." Elizabeth turned white.

Vashon sat there for a moment, a faintly amused look on his face. Then he nodded slightly and said, "Good luck, Lieutenant." Everyone else at the table understood the response as a sarcastic warning, an indication that Vashon thought Scott had little chance of success. Scott, on the other hand, took it as an encouragement. It never occurred to him that his pursuit might prove unsuccessful.

Later that evening, alone in their room, Elizabeth cornered her father and gave him an angry look. Knowing Scott might be in the next room, she whispered, "I do not wish to be courted!"

Vashon poured a glass of whiskey, sat down at the table, and smiled. He still missed his wife tremendously, but the presence of his daughter had served to soothe the pain. It was simply impossible to be melancholy when she was in the room. In previous years, he had always looked forward to the time he would spend with his wife, especially as they grew older. Now he looked forward to watching Elizabeth grow into adulthood and start her own family. It was something to live for. He winked and said, "It will be a good experience. You'll have to go courting sooner or later; might as well consider this as training."

"But what if he asks me to marry him?"

"Say, 'No.'"

"What if he asks *you* for my hand?"

Vashon smiled broadly. He was enjoying his daughter's discomfort. "Maybe I'll say, 'Yes.'"

As with everything else he did, Lieutenant Scott was very proper in his method of courting. At about half an hour before sunset he would change into a clean uniform, strap on his sword, and knock on Elizabeth's door. Taking the arm that was offered, Elizabeth would accompany the lieutenant on a stroll around and outside the fort. Whenever they left the confines of the fort, Elizabeth would insist on a chaperon. If Scott was going to be perfectly proper, so was she. Most of the time, the chaperon was Nellie Crump and her husband, Reason. As the oldest woman at the camp and Elizabeth's closest confidant, Nellie seemed the obvious choice.

On occasion, however, Elizabeth called on Jack and Johnny to provide the escort, especially if they were walking far from the fort. Dill found it all very amusing; Stuart found it frustrating.

The whole affair was proving equally frustrating for Elizabeth. She quickly tired of hearing about Scott's family plantation, his numerous slaves, and his accomplishments in the war with England. She also began to realize that the lieutenant did not love her. He "thought highly" of her, held "deep affection" for her, and "cherished" her company. There was not, however, any passion or conviction in his words. He wanted her for practical reasons, and most of those reasons were about him. Once married (if her father would be so kind as to entertain the proposition), they would be a "handsome couple," she would "look exquisite" on his arm, and her "lustrous crimson locks" would be a "beacon for the envious eyes" of his Virginia neighbors. Worst of all was the notion that she would be a "fitting mother" for his many children, a necessity to preserve his refined bloodline. More than once she had wanted to blurt out, "I'm a woman, not a mare you keep for breeding!" but held her tongue.

Dealing with Johnny was another matter. She wanted to let him know that she had no interest in Lieutenant Scott, but that would imply there was some reason for Stuart to actually care. One evening she saw him standing alone in the storehouse and decided it would be a good time to talk. Strolling in as casually as possible, she stood next to him as he looked through an assortment of iron hardware. "I do thank you for escorting the lieutenant and me to the pond this afternoon. I always feel safer when you and Jack are nearby."

Johnny tried not to sound sarcastic, but it didn't come out that way. "The illustrious Lieutenant Scott and his flashing saber aren't protection enough?"

She looked down at the floor, embarrassed. She knew his feelings were hurt. Scott's courting had been going on for weeks, and she should have put a stop to it before now. Then a thought occurred to her: *Why should Johnny's feelings be hurt? Why should he care if Lieutenant Scott is interested in marrying me? If the lieutenant's attentions are bothering Johnny, then . . .* She didn't need to finish her thought.

Her next move was completely impulsive. She reached out and took Johnny's hand, then leaned over and placed a kiss on his cheek. She had no intention of saying anything and didn't expect him to say anything. She just wanted to send the message, then leave.

"Unhand the lady, you rogue!" Both Elizabeth and Johnny spun around. Standing in the doorway was Lieutenant Scott. The officer quickly stepped into the storehouse, took Elizabeth's free hand, and began to lead her outside.

"Unhand *me*, sir!" She jerked her hand out of his and looked at him defiantly.

Scott wheeled around and stepped quickly to the door. "Guard!" Elizabeth stepped back and once again took Johnny's hand.

In a matter of moments, half the fort's occupants were standing outside the storehouse. One of the last to show up was Captain Vashon. He'd already poured the third glass of the evening's whiskey and was not going to be rushed. As he approached the storehouse step, the surrounding soldiers stepped aside. Scott's chest puffed as he pointed into the building. "I found the sergeant making improper advances toward your daughter, sir. I demand that he be punished. Confinement and lashes would be most appropriate. Were he a gentleman, I would insist that the matter be settled on the field of honor."

"Father!" Elizabeth started to protest, but a raised finger from her father stopped her.

Vashon sighed and slowly shook his head. "Mr. Scott, I'm not blind. Those two have been *advancing* toward each other for the past two years, even if they didn't know it themselves." A muted chuckle ran through the gathered soldiers. Vashon turned and looked at Johnny. "Sergeant, do you mean to do right by my daughter and marry her?"

Johnny's eyes widened. He looked at Elizabeth and saw the excitement in her expression. "Uh . . . Yes, sir, in time."

"Well, Sergeant, I think the time has come."

June 29, 1817
Fort Montgomery, Alabama Territory

To:
Mr. Robert Vashon
St. Louis, Missouri Territory

Dearest Robert,

There is so much news, I know not where to begin. First of all, Father and I send our most heartfelt and loving congratulations on your marriage to Anna Lynn. We regret not being able to attend, but the situation here would not allow Father to leave the post. There is, however, a gift for you making its way up the Mississippi, carefully placed in the hands of an officer who has been assigned to St. Louis. We hope you and Anna Lynn enjoy it.

Do not, however, think you are the only one in the family to feel the joy of wedded life. Just yesterday, Johnny and I were married! So much has happened in the past few weeks, you should not believe it. As you know, I was suffering through the courtship of that boorish Lt. Scott, terrified that he might actually ask Father for my hand. One evening he saw Johnny and me together (in not the least compromising situation, I must add) and began to raise the greatest commotion about it, demanding Johnny be flogged and confined and otherwise punished for taking liberties with his "intended." He even went so far as to suggest he might challenge Johnny to a duel! Of course Father was there, and I was dreadfully mortified for what might happen to Johnny. Much to my surprise, Father simply brushed the Lt. aside and asked Johnny if he intended to marry me!

And now I must admit to being the fool. Everyone, it seems, knew how Johnny and I felt about each other except us! Father said he knew it soon after the Battle of New Orleans. In truth, I suspect Mother knew it and told him. He would never have noticed such a thing on his own. Jack knew it, of course, as did most of the other officers and many of the camp's ladies, including Nellie Crump. The only one who seemed not to know was poor Scott, who rarely sees farther than the mirror anyway. How could Johnny and I have been so unaware? By far the biggest surprise was that Father and Jack had already been making plans for our eventual marriage. I mentioned to you before that Jack had taken on the duties of sutler for the post, but that no one could imagine where he had gotten the money to begin the enterprise. I just assumed it was money he had put aside. He is very conservative that way, you know.

I can now tell the secret: It was Father who put up the money. He said there were three things he was sure of: That Johnny and I would be married, that Jack had a sense for business, and that Jack and Johnny would stay together after their enlistments were over and start some sort of enterprise. So Father set Jack up as sutler and has set aside his half of the profits as a dowry. I should never have believed it! Not only am I wedded to the most handsome sergeant in the army, I am the wife of a partner, of sorts, in a profitable business!

The ceremony itself was as magnificent as could be held at a frontier outpost. Judge Toulmin came to officiate, accompanied by several officers from Mobile. All the officers donned their dress uniforms for the occasion, even the "aggrieved" Lt. Scott, who seems to have reconciled himself to his loss. The soldiers formed two lines for us to proceed through, and the camp ladies cooked the most wonderful feast. Dear Nellie, of course, baked the cake and fussed over me as much as if I were her own daughter. I do wish Mother could have been here to see it all. The wedding presents were varied, as one might expect on the frontier. Most were simple and practical, while a few were ordered sight unseen from Mobile. Father gave us a beautiful gold locket on a chain, in which I am to place a lock of my hair that Johnny will carry with him forever. The ever-practical Jack gave us the finest set of cookery he could procure. We are living in a cabin outside the fort, a gift of sorts from Pvt. Darbey, who moved back into the barracks after his wife ran off with a deserter.

The ceremony was much larger than I would have expected, due to the arrival last week of several more companies of the regiment. Indeed, the *place is quite crowded. It is well that Johnny and I have moved outside the fort. With all the new officers to accommodate, Capt. Allison has moved in with Father, and the lieutenants are now sleeping in their tents. Father, alas, is no longer the commanding officer here, being outranked by Majors Wooster and Muhlenberg. The situation, however, is temporary and brings me to the sad news that must accompany the good news that I have related. We are soon to leave this post, bound for Georgia and the border with Florida. General Gaines has ordered Major Wooster to take half the companies here at Fort Montgomery and use them to reactivate Fort Scott on the Flint, just north of the border. Sadly, one of those companies is Father's. It seems there have been increasing troubles with the Seminoles, who have been incited by English adventurers, so the General feels a need to position forces in the area. The most distressing news is that the women and children are not to be allowed to accompany the troops on the march. Instead, we will have to wait here until the fort is rebuilt and habitable, <u>then</u> await transport by water, up the Apalachicola River. Knowing the speed at which the army moves, it may be months before Johnny and I are reunited. I already begin to feel like a widow.*

For now, there is not much else that is new. The ceremony yesterday was simply a respite from the preparations for the march. I'm afraid I must rely on Nellie and the other women to show me how to prepare for such a long voyage, one that necessitates us packing all that we have, for we most likely will not be returning to this post. Rumor has it that the company will remain in Georgia for quite some time, guarding against the Indians and helping establish new towns. Perhaps, when Jack and Johnny's enlistments are up, we'll settle somewhere in Georgia. But listen to me! One day married and already making grand plans for the future.

I shall close for now. Johnny will be off duty soon, and I must tend to the cooking and getting the cabin in order, if, indeed, he gives me time to do it!

Your loving sister,
<u>Mrs. John Stuart</u>

It was a cloudy, rain-threatened morning in mid-July as Elizabeth stood in the doorway of her cabin and watched the soldiers form into ranks. Standing alongside Company G, Jack and Johnny shouted commands, getting the men positioned properly and making sure everything was in order. At the head of the line were a standard bearer and a drummer, followed by two neat rows of soldiers, arranged from the tallest to the shortest, their muskets slung over their shoulders and pointing straight up. Their uniforms were as clean as they were going to be, the cross belts for their bayonets and cartridge boxes as white as they were likely to be, and their round, flat-topped hats as shiny and black as polishing could make them. Elizabeth would have liked to have credited the company's fine military appearance to Johnny, but she knew better. It was all Jack's doing. Dill was an orderly, precise sergeant, and liked his men to look good. This was odd, because his own appearance, even at its finest, always appeared a little frayed and unkempt. Johnny, though very careful of how he personally looked, was more of the opinion that while the men needed to look reasonably sharp, at the end of a two-week, two-hundred-mile march, everything and everyone would be equally ragged and filthy.

Elizabeth and Johnny had made love early in the morning, knowing it would be the last time they felt each other's warmth for at least several months. She smiled and closed her eyes; she could still feel him. *Strange,* she thought, *I've gone seventeen years without a man, now I can't go seventeen hours without having him. How will I do without him for the next few months?*

Elizabeth never really understood why the army did things the way they did. Company A of the Fourth Infantry and Companies B and F of the Seventh had been brought to Fort Montgomery from farther west. Vashon and Allison's Companies G and J were then to proceed to Fort Scott in Georgia. Why didn't the three new companies just go to Fort Scott and leave Vashon and Allison at Fort Montgomery? It would have saved a lot of people the trouble of pulling up stakes and moving, and, most important, it would have prevented Elizabeth and Johnny from separating only two weeks after having been married. Like a lot of other things the army did, it just didn't make sense.

It was going to be difficult to be alone, with both her father and Johnny so far away. She would have gladly gone on the march with the men, but General Gaines's orders had been specific, and Major Muhlenberg, the senior officer, had no intention of ignoring them. It especially bothered her that there were so many strange men around. Although she knew most of the officers and all had promised her father they would look after her, it did little to help relieve the anxiety. She had seen the new soldiers eyeing the women, sizing them up, trying to determine which ones might be available after their husbands and lovers left. Indeed, the flirting had already commenced. One or two had tried to make veiled advances toward Elizabeth, but she had given them nothing but a cold look for their trouble. When word got around that she was Captain Vashon's daughter and Sergeant Stuart's wife, the flirting quickly ceased. She wondered if it would resume once her father and Johnny were gone.

Still, not every familiar face was going away. First of all there were the other women of the camp and their children, and foremost among those was Nellie Crump. As soon as it had become official that Captain Vashon and Johnny would be assigned to Fort Scott, Nellie had announced that Elizabeth would be moving in with her. She also made it known that she kept a loaded shotgun by the door, and any soldier found skulking within fifty feet of her cabin would soon find out that she knew how to use it.

The other familiar face that was remaining at Fort Montgomery was Jack Dill. Because the two companies were leaving a large amount of personal belongings behind that would later be shipped to Fort Scott, someone had to stay to watch over it and see that it made it safely aboard the transport vessels. Both Elizabeth and her father would have preferred to have had Johnny stay behind, but it would have appeared too much as favoritism, and Vashon had never suggested it. Dill, as the agent for the regimental sutler, had been the logical choice. There would almost certainly be items needed to complete the work of restoring Fort Scott and make it habitable, and Dill would know how and where to get those things.

As the soldiers stood in their ranks they shuffled about, waiting for the officers to arrive so they could commence the march. Elizabeth saw a horse stride out the fort's gate, the beginning of a small procession made up of seven officers and half a dozen wagons. The lead officer was Major Wooster, followed by Captains Vashon and Allison, then their lieutenants. At the sight of the officers the men came to attention, ready to commence the journey. Jack and Johnny shook hands, said a few words to each other, then Jack stepped back, giving the men one last examination. Shaking his head, he stepped forward and adjusted Private Gray's hat. The private showed only the slightest sign of annoyance. Both he and Dill knew that once the column was out of sight, the hat would be moved back into a more comfortable position.

When everyone was ready, Wooster gave the command to march. The drummers began to beat the cadence, and the men stepped forward, each one hesitating slightly before taking a step so the ranks would open up, allowing them to move at an easier gait. Elizabeth saw Johnny turn toward her, smile and wink, and then turn his eyes straight forward again. Within five minutes he was out of sight.

The three young Seminoles chatted easily among themselves as they prepared their camp for the night. Otulke, the tallest of the trio, laughed as he washed out the small cast iron pot. The handle of the pot had obviously been replaced; a bent, tortured strip of slender iron rod now substituted for what had once been a graceful curve of metal. "Chitto, did you make the handle for this pot? What did you bend it with, your teeth? If you curve a bow like this, you had better watch out that the arrow does not fly around and stick you in the ass!"

Halpatter, a powerful, compact youth, stirred the campfire and quipped, "It is a big target and would be easy to hit."

Chitto, with a round face and a stomach to match, unrolled his blanket and spread it on the ground. "Not near so large as Growing Moon's."

Halpatter was instantly on his feet and charging toward Chitto. The pair grappled and fell to the ground, laughing and swearing as they wrestled in the dirt. As the two playfully tussled, Otulke smiled. It was not wise to make fun of Halpatter's girl. Walking up to the fighters, he threw the dirty water from the pot onto them. "Enough of that. You'll frighten the cattle. Then we shall be in trouble."

The three young men were all about the same age, not yet warriors, but no longer children. The clan had deemed them responsible enough to stand watch over more than fifty head of cattle, and they were doing as good a job as boys their age were likely to. As the two combatants rose to their feet and dusted themselves off, they could see the animals milling about and hear the occasional lowing. It was going to be a warm, clear night, a good night to gaze at the stars, tell stories, and talk about battles they would fight in, the great warriors they would become, and the girls they would conquer. As far as they could tell, life would only get better.

Otulke set the pot down and began to unroll his own blanket. Halpatter went back to tending the fire while Chitto went over to the small stream to wash his face. Their campsite was in the middle of open range land, part of the large Alachua Prairie where the Seminole people had lived for nearly a hundred years. As the last bit of sunlight faded, the three young men lay back, picking out stars as they appeared in the growing darkness, and calling them out by name. They talked for awhile, and then one by one they nodded off to sleep.

Otulke awoke with a start. Something wasn't right. He looked up. He could tell by the position of the stars how much time had passed. Rising to his feet, he looked out at the cattle, saw they were still there, and relaxed. Then he heard a laugh. "Mornin', boys." Suddenly the night exploded. Otulke gripped his chest and fell to the ground. Halpatter screamed and doubled up in pain as blood ran from his abdomen. Chitto did nothing. His face had been blown away. Halpatter tried to rise and crawl away, but a tall, thin white man slowly walked up and kicked the young Indian onto his back. He then put a foot on Halpatter's chest to hold him down. The youth's eyes opened wide as he saw the man produce a large knife, then he screamed as he felt the blade cut a circle around his skull and the skin being ripped from his head. Then he felt the blade slash across his throat.

Four more white men approached the campfire. Two of them lifted the scalps from Otulke and Chitto while the others shuffled around the campsite, looking for any valuables the three young Indians might have had. One picked up the pot with the misshapen handle. The man who had killed Halpatter said, "What ya takin' that fer, Lucius?"

"Aw, the damn missus been bitchin' she needs a new one. Reckon this'll do."

The other man shook his head and began to walk off. "Let's go, boys. We need to get them cattle back to Georgia before them damn Injuns find out we done took 'em."

Through the night and into the next day, the rustlers drove the cattle northward. If they were being pursued, they never knew it, and when the cattle were safely sold, they split up and headed back to their homes. Somewhere on the road to St. Marys, the old pot fell from Lucius's pack horse. He never missed it.

Jack Dill smiled as he lay in the bed, the warm female form close by his side. *It was good to be with a woman,* he thought, *a damn sight better than sleeping alone.* He had been surprised how fast she had come on to him after the company was gone. Did it bother him that she belonged to another man? Yes, but not as much as he thought it would. It was a little like business: She needed someone to supply her wants, and he had the ability to deliver the goods. Would there be repercussions later on? Probably, but he had convinced himself he could handle them. Having her in his bed for the next few months would be well worth the price.

The first two days of the march from Fort Montgomery to Fort Scott had been relatively easy. Their first destination was Camp Crawford on the Conecuh River, just above the Florida border, north of Pensacola. The road was hard packed and well traveled, it being the main supply route for the fort. It would have been easier to supply the fort by water via Pensacola, but General Gaines had run into problems with the Spanish governor and refused to pay the duties the Spaniard demanded. It was a proud but expensive stance the general had taken. To avoid the twelve percent duty, Gaines was forced to hire wagons and teamsters at a rate that was more than double the value of the goods they carried. For Gaines and a lot of other people, it was just another reason to kick the Spanish out of Florida. If only the people in Washington would see it that way.

Beyond Camp Crawford, the progress was slower. The third day's travel wasn't too bad, mainly because the fort's garrison had cleared some roads in the fort's vicinity. After that, it was either an old Indian trail or an abandoned military road, neither of which were easily traversed. When the path narrowed to the point where the wagons couldn't get through, the pioneers went forward with their axes, saws, shovels, and spades, and built a minimal road. It all took time, but there was nothing else they could do. It was hot work, toiling under the late July sun, and more than one man passed out from the heat. There was never enough water, and certainly not enough food and rest.

Major Wooster had hired a half-blooded Choctaw guide by the name of Sammy Powell, but the farther they got from his home in Mississippi, the less sure of the route he became. Although they were traveling through the newly-created Territory of Alabama, this was Creek land, and few whites had ventured into it. It was rumored that many of those who did were never heard from again. Wooster laughed it off. Rumors about the ferocity of the Indians were always exaggerated, he said. A good show of force by the army would overawe them every time.

Wooster's assurances were of little comfort to most of the soldiers. Their force of only ninety-seven men was not going to overawe any Indian nation. They also knew they were being watched. The Creek warriors were rarely seen but often heard, especially at night. Again, Wooster shrugged it off. Indians only attacked from ambush, he said. As long as you knew they were out there, you were safe. Most of the younger soldiers were not convinced.

Confident as he was, Wooster was not a fool. As the army marched, they followed time-honored rules to prevent an ambush. An advance guard walked ahead of the main body of troops, and an equally strong rear guard followed some distance behind the wagons. Whenever the surrounding brush was thick enough to conceal an Indian war party, a few soldiers would be sent out as flankers to beat the bushes and look for hostiles. It was dangerous work, but it was the only way to prevent an ambush.

No one could truly relax. Even when they stopped to eat or rest, sentries were sent out to patrol the surroundings. Every soldier's musket was loaded, and as every man marched, he kept an eye out for a tree or boulder to take cover behind. At night, the men were even more on their guard. Sentry fires were built some distance away from the camp, making it difficult for any skulking warriors to approach unseen. Each man slept with his loaded musket by his side, ready to repel an attack at a moment's notice. The army had learned past lessons well: They might be attacked, but they would not be caught unawares.

The Creeks certainly had reason to be unfriendly. Andrew Jackson had taken most of their land in 1814, leaving many of them destitute and homeless. Whites, having caught what many called "Alabama Fever," were streaming into the new territory in record numbers, often paying little attention to what land had been ceded and what had not, or what parcels of land had been set aside for Creeks who were actually friendly to the United States. If a piece of land looked fertile and well watered or if it looked perfect for a future settlement, sooner or later some white man and his family would set up a homestead on it. There was simply no stopping it. The Creeks could complain to their agent or to the army, but nothing was ever done. The only way to remove a white man was to send a war party to drive him off, but that would lead to a swift reprisal from the government. Still, there were times when an Indian could no longer stand the insults, and violence seemed the only answer.

Wooster and his men were being sent to Fort Scott to quell such violence, but it was not from the Creeks in Georgia and Alabama. Instead, it was from the displaced Red Stick Creeks who had fled to Florida, their friends the Seminoles and Mikasukis, and the runaway slaves who lived among them. The border between Spanish Florida and the United States was a long, thinly populated line running from the Atlantic to Mobile Bay, and anyone, from white outlaws to Indian war parties, could cross it with impunity. Fort Scott would be a small plug in a large hole, but at least it was something. The real plug would be the thousands of settlers who would soon inhabit the area, forcing the Indians further into the wilderness. In this respect, establishing a fort was like planting a cutting from a fast-growing vine: It was a point from where clawing tendrils of civilization would spread, eventually covering every bit of land in sight.

Few of the men in Captain Vashon's command thought about the implications of their work. They were simply doing their job, cutting down trees, building forts, and protecting settlers who had pushed the frontier just a little too far. When not performing his tasks, John Stuart could think of little more than his young bride. Was she safe among so many strangers? Did she miss him? Who would she turn to if there were problems? Most important, would she be with child when next he saw her? Heaven knows, he had certainly planted enough seeds to get the process started.

He could take some consolation in knowing that Jack was still at Fort Montgomery, but even that knowledge could be a bit troubling. With himself and her father gone, Jack would be one of the few men Elizabeth would socialize with. Although he had no reason to distrust either of them, he could not keep the suspicion from entering his mind. He had seen it plenty of times with other soldiers' wives. As soon as the men left camp, there was always a woman or two looking for a new companion. Would Elizabeth be looking, too? Would her gaze fall upon Jack?

The farther he got from Fort Montgomery, the more plausible the idea seemed. In the two short weeks they had been married, Johnny had found Elizabeth to be a very passionate woman. Could she simply turn that passion off until they were reunited? The more he thought about it, the less likely it seemed. And what about Jack? Although he might never intend to step into Johnny's place, could he resist the temptation if it were offered? He knew Jack to be a very practical man, at least as far as business was concerned. If a commercial opportunity presented itself, he would take it. Would the same reasoning apply if a woman presented herself? How loyal would either of them be as time passed and the memory of the friend and husband faded? The more he dwelled on the matter, the more his imagination began to feed on itself, and the more distracted he became.

Sooner or later, someone was bound to notice the change in Johnny's demeanor. One evening, deep in the Alabama woods,

Reason Crump decided it was time to ease Johnny's mind. The private was a bear of a man, and, some would say, not much more talkative than one. At forty-two, he was the oldest man in the company and one of the steadiest. The same could be said of his wife, Nellie. The pair were dependable, both as individuals and as a team. Their devotion to each other was remarkable. Neither one was attractive in any way, but for each other they were perfect. Without the subject even being brought up, Crump got right to the heart of the matter. "Don't worry 'bout Miss Elizabeth, Sarge. She's with Nellie, and there ain't no safer place for a young girl to be. She'll keep any rovin' soldiers away, and she sure won't let Miss Elizabeth go lookin', not that she would anyway. She ain't never had eyes for anyone but you, and you knows it."

It was not something Johnny cared to discuss in front of half a dozen soldiers, and he tried to brush it off. "Never crossed my mind."

Sitting next to Crump was Private Jonathan Driver, who shook his head and laughed. "Like Washington never crossed the Delaware. If I had as fine a woman as Miss Elizabeth, I wouldn't think of anything else."

Johnny tried once again to deflect the conversation and said, "You've got Annie."

With that, everyone in front of the tent let out a laugh. When he ceased laughing, Driver corrected the sergeant, telling him, "I *had* Annie, but we all know that was over the day we marched out of Fort Montgomery. Me and her, we'd run our course, and we both knew it. Anyway, Annie's had her eye on Jack for some time now. She no doubt had him in her bed before we reached Camp Crawford." Both Johnny and Reason Crump nodded; Annie's behavior was both predictable and expected. As someone had pointed out, it couldn't be called infidelity, because she'd never promised to be faithful. Exactly who or what she was seemed a bit of a mystery. No one was sure where and when she'd taken up with the army, and no one had any idea what her real name was.

When meeting someone, she would just say her name was Annie, and if pressed for a surname, she would give the name of the man she was currently with. She was rather plain and ordinary in size and appearance, yet she could be very alluring when she wanted to be. A certain smile, a somewhat open bodice, or a slightly exposed lower leg went a long way in an isolated outpost full of lonely soldiers. At the same time, no one could call her overly promiscuous. When she took up with a man she was his alone, at least until they grew tired of each other and decided it would be best to go their separate ways. Then, after a few days of being on her own, Annie would suddenly be with someone else. Yet she would never make plans for the future, never say she loved someone, and would always remind her lover that she was "just seeing how good he fit."

Johnny had to admit that both Driver and Crump were probably right, but nothing they said could entirely ease his doubts. Yes, Nellie would keep watch over Elizabeth like a mother hen, but what if something were to happen to Nellie? Yes, Jack was a true friend and had never shown the least bit of romantic interest in Elizabeth, but the pair had rarely been in each other's company without Johnny being there too. It would be several months before he saw either one of them again. A lot of things could happen in such a long amount of time. There were so many factors to consider, and nothing he could do about any of them.

It was a cool September morning and Fanny Garrett was in the process of fastening her dress after feeding the baby when she heard a noise outside the cabin. Placing the infant in its cradle, she moved cautiously toward the door. She always felt vulnerable when her husband wasn't home, especially with all the rumors about Indian attacks. Every month, it seemed, she heard news of another raid, though most proved false or were at best questionable. Everyone knew the cause. Cattle thieves and slave catchers crossed into Florida, intent on taking whatever they could find. If an Indian happened to get in their way, a murder would be committed. The Seminoles, in turn, would take revenge upon any whites they suspected of having some connection to the crime. It was a back-and-forth butchery, with both sides blaming the other.

The Garrett cabin was in an isolated spot, about ten miles from St. Marys in Georgia, and not far from the Okefenokee Swamp. The location was beautiful and the land fertile, but Fanny just didn't feel safe there. She was always friendly to any Indian that came by, but never felt comfortable in their presence. They might smile and thank her for the hospitality, but she never knew if they were being sincere, or simply taking stock of what could be stolen at a later date.

As she reached for the cabin door, she suddenly heard her four-year-old son Obed yell from somewhere near the cow pen. "Mama! Mama! Injuns! There's Injuns out here!" She flung open the door, took a step outside, and came face to face with a fiercely-painted warrior.

She screamed, "Run, Obed! Run and get your Papa! Run, boy!" The warrior calmly placed his hands on her shoulders and pushed her back into the cabin. Terrified, she ran and stood protectively in front of the cradle. Without saying a word, the warrior stepped in and stood still, giving her a cold stare. Through the open door she could see other warriors looking at the cattle, checking the brands and other markings. Another warrior had Obed by the wrist and was dragging him toward the cabin. Once inside, he shoved the boy toward his mother. The child then cowered next to her, clinging to her skirt.

"What you want?" she said, but neither Indian answered. Instead, one kept an eye on her while the other began to rummage through the cabin. "Let me know what you want. I'll give it to you!" she pleaded, but the warriors said nothing. As the one warrior continued his search, he began to throw things around, frustrated at finding nothing of interest. Fanny started to sob, saying, "Please don't hurt my babies."

For a moment it appeared as if the Indians might leave her and the children unharmed, not having found anything of interest. Suddenly the warrior who was guarding her let out a yell and pointed to a small iron cook pot that his companion had just thrown on the floor. The two Indians exchanged a few words, and then the one who had been going through the belongings picked up the pot and shook it in front of Fanny's face, screaming questions in a language she didn't understand.

She answered as best she could, desperation in her voice, knowing they couldn't understand her. "You want that old pot? You can have it. I don't even like it! My husband just picked it up alongside the road. Take it, take it! Just go away and don't hurt us." She saw rage in the Indian's eyes, and couldn't imagine what the pot had to do with it. All she could do was give out a long, mournful, "Please."

Suddenly the Indian threw the pot onto the floor, drew his knife, and plunged it deep into her stomach. She screamed and fell back against the wall. She watched helplessly as the warrior reached into the cradle, took the infant by the ankles, and swung it violently against the wall, smashing the baby's fragile skull. He then casually tossed the lifeless body out an open window.

Obed suddenly bolted for the door. Instead of reaching for the boy, the warrior who had been watching Fanny picked up his rifle, calmly took aim, and fired. Obed's back arched, and he fell to the ground. Letting out a victory cry, the warrior stepped out the door, drew his knife, and removed the boy's scalp. Stuffing the bloody trophy under his waist sash, he stepped back into the cabin.

Fanny, sitting with her back to the wall and clutching the bleeding wound in her stomach, stared at the blood soaking into her dress. She looked up as the warrior who had stabbed her took a step toward her, knife in hand. "No, please, no," she begged weakly, putting one hand atop her head, clutching her hair. The first warrior reached out a hand and put it on the other man's shoulder, stopping him. He then picked up his companion's rifle and aimed it at her chest. The gun fired, Fanny lurched, and then slid to the floor. The last thing her dying eyes saw was the old cook pot with the misshapen handle.

Elizabeth was ecstatic. Finally, after nearly three months, she would be on her way to her father and Johnny. As she and Nellie packed the last blanket into the chest, she heard a knock and saw Jack at the open door, accompanied by a pair of soldiers. "Time to go, ladies. Your elegant coach awaits you." The soldiers stepped in, took the chest, carried it out the door, and loaded it into a battered old wagon. Nellie took a last look around and wiped away a tear. There was so much she had to leave behind. The furniture, simple as it was, held fond memories. A few household goods were being left behind, she having failed to find room in the chest. For the most part she had been able to sell them, though not for a very good price. The cabin, however, was another matter. A soldier from Company B with a wife, three children, and only two months left on his enlistment had bought it for a very fine price. She almost squealed when she thought of the look she would see on Reason's face when she handed him the money.

Elizabeth was leaving nothing behind. She and Johnny had lived in Private Darbey's cabin for only two weeks and had little in the way of belongings. In addition, as Captain Vashon's daughter and a close friend of Sergeant Dill, the sutler's agent, she was able to secure more room on the wagons. After all, she was bringing the captain's personal belongings as well as her own.

As the soldiers formed their column and the wagons fell in behind, the scene reminded Elizabeth of the day Johnny had left for Fort Scott. Fortunately, she and the others would not be marching through two hundred miles of wilderness, but only three miles to the boat landing on the Alabama River. Yet even for that short distance, the march would be conducted in a military manner. The Creeks were still unhappy with the white man's presence.

At the head of the column rode Major Peter Muhlenberg, the senior officer present and captain of Company A of the Fourth Infantry. Elizabeth wasn't sure whether she liked him or not. He was always very courteous and proper, but he was never warm or considerate. His father had been a general in the Revolution, and the major seemed to be trying to live up to his father's reputation. It would be a difficult thing to do: The elder Muhlenberg had been a pastor when the Revolution began, but had famously thrown off his preacher's gown while in the pulpit to reveal a Continental Army uniform. He then delivered a stirring patriotic sermon before leaving to fight the war. How the junior Muhlenberg could surpass such a legend was beyond Elizabeth's imagination.

The walk to the landing was pleasant enough, the October air cool, the wind light, and the sky clear. An officer had offered Elizabeth a seat on one of the wagons, but she had politely declined, saying, "I am the wife of a common soldier, Lieutenant, I shall walk with my friends." In the months since Johnny's departure, it was a distinction she had worked on. When she had been living with her father, certain privileges had naturally been extended to her. Now that she was no longer living among the officers, she didn't care to be treated as one of their social class. It wasn't that she felt one was any better than the other, it was just an acknowledgement of her change in status. She was a wife now, not a daughter.

For the most part, the other women had taken her in as one of their own. She did her best to fit in, doing everything Nellie did, from cooking, to laundry, to making soap. She cleaned and maintained the cabin and tended the little garden. It was hard work, but she enjoyed it. The other women saw her at work and appreciated her efforts. Most of them had become close friends, especially Annie, who was now almost inseparable from Jack. In a way, the closeness was easy to understand. They all faced many of the same hardships, from inadequate rations to the demands the army placed on their husbands. Elizabeth began to appreciate people like Nellie, who had spent their whole married life following their soldier husbands. Townspeople often looked down on them, even going so far as to call them whores, but Elizabeth knew better. Most of the women truly loved their husbands and were willing to make the sacrifices necessary to be with them, and others, like Annie, hung around because in their own way they wanted to be with the army, even if the army didn't want them.

The column, consisting of about eighty men and perhaps two dozen women and children, arrived at the landing a little before noon. From her place at the back of the column Elizabeth could hear loud voices and see some sort of commotion taking place at the front of the line. Slowly the news filtered back: There was only one boat, not the five that had been arranged for. She could easily imagine Muhlenberg's anger. He had been given orders to be at Fort Scott no later than November 10. It was already October 21.

After some minutes of confusion, the order came down to set up camp. The remaining boats would be arriving in a day or two, and in the meantime there was nothing to do but unload the wagons and sit and wait. As the men began to remove the baggage from the wagons, the women went to work setting up a temporary kitchen. All of the women seemed to know what to do with little direction from Nellie, who, as usual, seemed to be in charge. The two women with infants found a seat out of the way and took on the task of watching over the toddlers. Older children were dispatched to gather firewood, while those in their early teens helped their mothers. Some of the boys, not wanting to be seen doing "women's work," decided to help the soldiers unload the wagons. No one was without something to do.

As Nellie began to mix dough, Elizabeth found a large board and sprinkled flour over it. Taking some of the dough, she broke off small balls and patted them into biscuits. Off to their side, Annie and some of the other women were building the fires, hanging Dutch ovens over them, or putting frying pans by the side, ready to place on the coals when the fires were hot enough. Other women were slicing dried beef and salt pork or cutting up greens and other vegetables they had harvested from their gardens before leaving. It would take half the afternoon to cook the meal, fifteen minutes for the men to devour it, and the rest of the afternoon to clean up and pack everything away again. The women were working harder than any soldier, but only the soldiers were being paid.

Later, as the sun reddened and approached the horizon, the soldiers and the women and children sat around campfires, discussing matters of little importance. They were all a little annoyed at having to sit and wait. The women were especially unhappy at the delay, nearly all of them being anxious to be reunited with their husbands. Finally, as a drummer beat tattoo, the last of the coffee was thrown onto the campfires, and everyone made their way to their tents. As Elizabeth and Nellie crawled into the standard army tent they would share for the night, they both let out a deep sigh. They were exhausted. The marching, the unloading of the kitchen gear, the cooking, the cleaning, and the packing away had all made for a hard day's work. Elizabeth lay on one blanket, covered herself with another and let the sounds of the night lull her to sleep. On one side she heard Nellie softly snoring and on the other side, in the next tent, she heard Jack and Annie making love. She smiled and began a dream of Johnny. *If he were here,* she thought, *we'd give those two some competition.*

The remaining boats arrived late on the second day, and the soldiers worked well into the evening placing all the baggage aboard. By six o'clock the next morning the boats had cast off their lines and were making their way down the Alabama River toward Mobile Bay. It was a confusing, twisting channel, and Elizabeth could only hope the boats' crews knew where they were going. A few miles below the landing the Tombigbee joined the Alabama River to become the Tensaw. Several miles below that the river split again as it entered the delta, with the Mobile River on the west, the Tensaw on the east, and a host of small streams, lakes, and islands in between. Major Muhlenberg, in the lead vessel, wanted to continue down the narrower Mobile, but the boatmen, pointing out how heavily laden the boats were, insisted on taking the wider and deeper Tensaw. It was probably a wise move, but the decision had its price: The Mobile emptied right into the town of Mobile, while the Tensaw emptied into the opposite side of Mobile Bay. Taking the Tensaw might possibly add another day to the trip. In the end, the boatmen won the argument. Muhlenberg had only hired the boats. He didn't own them.

As the major had predicted, taking the Tensaw cost them a day's time. It was late afternoon when they reached the town of Blakeley, several miles from the bay. Muhlenberg wanted to press on, but the boatmen refused to cross Mobile Bay in the dark. Once again it was no doubt a wise decision, but Muhlenberg was worried about the cost, both in time and money. The boats had been hired by the day, and the major was convinced that every argument the boatmen made was motivated by profit, not by concerns for the safety of the boats or their passengers.

Blakeley was a boom town of sorts, a place where settlers arrived before proceeding upriver to stake out a homestead in the newly opened Alabama wilderness. Indeed, so many vessels were tied up to the docks that the boatmen had a difficult time finding a place to secure their boats. They finally found a spot at the far end of the dock, next to a coastal schooner called *Phoebe Ann*. Elizabeth, Nellie, and Annie were thrilled to be able to wander through a general store, fingering the colorful fabrics, examining the cooking utensils, and admiring the many useful and frivolous items on display. The soldiers, of course, were drawn to the many taverns.

Morning found them back on the river, heading south toward the bay. While in the river with the current to their backs, progress was good, and they reached the edge of the bay within two hours. From there, the trip became much more tedious. These were small boats, no more than thirty feet long, shallow drafted, with rounded bottoms. In the river they had glided smoothly, pulled along by a few sets of oars. Once in the bay, the boats were faced with choppy water, a condition they were ill suited for. Small sails were hoisted, but the breeze was light and headway was minimal. As the boats pitched and rolled, most of the men, women, and children became seasick. There were precious few places to sit comfortably and absolutely nowhere to lie down.

The fifteen-mile trip took most of the day. By late afternoon, when the boats tied up in Mobile, everyone was tired, thirsty, and hungry. Hardtack, dried beef, and water were passed around, and everyone wandered about the dock, waiting while Major Muhlenberg went to the shipping office to determine which ships the cargo and passengers would be loaded onto.

As the major entered the shipping office, a short, bespectacled man stepped from behind a desk and held out his hand. "Major Muhlenberg, I presume?"

"Mr. Tankersley? Pleasure to meet you." If there was any real pleasure, there wasn't a smile to show it.

After shaking hands, Tankersley motioned towards a chair. "Please be seated. I've been expecting you for a few days."

Muhlenberg grumbled, "Damn boatmen can always find some excuse to cause delay at twenty dollars a day. Are my ships ready?"

The shipping agent smiled, but there was a slight look of disappointment in his eyes. "All the munitions, commissary stores, hardware, and regimental clothing that General Gaines ordered has arrived and been loaded onto the two vessels at the end of the pier. We'll be ready to sail as soon as the *Phoebe Ann* arrives and you shift what you've got in your boats into her hold."

Muhlenberg's brow furled. He remembered the last thing he'd seen as they pulled away from Blakeley that morning. "The *Phoebe Ann* at Blakeley?"

Tankersley was embarrassed. "Aye, sir, that's the one. Sent her up there two weeks ago to let the fresh water kill the barnacles, and for some reason she hasn't come back yet. Sent word four days ago to the captain, but he hasn't written back. Probably caught that Alabama Fever and just left her there. Damn darkies what made up his crew probably run off to Florida when they saw there wasn't no one looking over them."

Muhlenberg sat upright in the chair and glowered down at the shipping agent. "Mr. Tankersley, your crew problems aren't my business. I need a ship. How do you propose to get one?"

"Well, Major, you're right, my troubles aren't your business, but they are your problem, if you know what I mean. Now, I found a new captain, but it'll take a few days to round up a crew. If I could use some of your soldiers to run up to Blakeley and bring the *Phoebe Ann* back, we can get on our way."

Muhlenberg shook his head. He didn't have a problem with sending some men to get the ship; they would just be sitting around anyway. He was more concerned with all the other problems brought on by the delay. "And what am I to do with my people and all the cargo on those boats while we wait?"

Tankersley squirmed. "Well, there is the fort, and I've got plenty of warehouse space here."

"Mr. Tankersley, you were instructed to have the ships ready to sail on the twentieth. I shall not be authorizing payment for the days that we have to sit here because the *Phoebe Ann* isn't ready."

"I fully understand, Major, and I'll not be charging the army for the warehouse space either."

Muhlenberg looked Tankersley coldly in the eye and said, "I should hope not. How many of my men will you need?"

"I suppose eight would be enough. If they've got any sailing experience, that would be a help."

Muhlenberg huffed, stood up, and turned for the door. There wasn't much else he could do. If Tankersley had been a soldier under his command, he'd have had him whipped. In the end, he needed the man's ships, so he was forced to cooperate. "I'll have the sergeant pick a crew."

Private Jesse Greenlee wasn't very impressed by the captain Mr. Tankersley had found for *Phoebe Ann*. Greenlee had grown up around the docks of Mystic, Connecticut, and had served two years on a whaler before entering the army. He knew a true captain when he saw one, and James Shirley fell far short of the criteria. "I've been coasting this shore for twenty years," was Shirley's favorite saying, and that was one of the things that worried Greenlee. The man had no knowledge of the river or how to navigate the many meanders they would face.

With a good breeze behind him, Shirley ordered full sail, and *Phoebe Ann* began to move swiftly down the river. As far as Private Greenlee was concerned, it was a little too swift. When an approaching vessel was spotted coming around a bend in the river, Shirley ordered the boat to the left of the channel instead of holding to the right, as he should have. The master of the other vessel, confused by the maneuver, quickly dropped his sail and threw out an anchor. Shirley, even more confused, ordered *Phoebe Ann's* sail dropped. Now out of control, the ship was carried by the current onto a sandbar. It wasn't a hard grounding, but with the wind and the current to their backs, they were not about to get free.

For four days *Phoebe Ann* didn't move, until the wind shifted from the south, blowing more water in from the bay. With help from several other boats and the high tide, the ship broke free of the bar and made its way downriver. An hour later they were sailing across Mobile Bay in an intermittent rainstorm, pushed along by a strong southerly wind.

Once again, the soldiers worked well into the night, loading their equipment and belongings onto *Phoebe Ann*. It was slow work, often halted by an occasional thunderstorm. Muhlenberg, already behind schedule, was determined to leave Mobile at first light. Tankersley wasn't so sure it was going to happen. "The barometer's fallin' fast, Major. We may be in for a big blow hereabouts."

By the time morning arrived, even the major had to agree that leaving the dock was not advisable. The wind had reached gale force, and the rain was strong and constant. For many of the soldiers, accommodations became a problem. The majority of them had been camped out in their tents in the parade ground of old Fort Charlotte. As the wind and rain increased, most of the soldiers were forced inside crowded storerooms or unused offices. Most of the officers took rooms at one of the town's hotels. Joining them were Jack, Annie, Elizabeth and Nellie. Jack had deemed it a worthy use of a portion of the sutlery's profits.

The storm raged for two days. On the third day, when Major Muhlenberg and Mr. Tankersley went down to the docks, they found a near-disaster. Several boats had sustained damage and one, a small bay fisherman, had hit *Phoebe Ann's* stern and sunk. Until repairs were made and the sunken boat removed, Muhlenberg and his vessels were going nowhere.

The work took two exasperating days. Muhlenberg was constantly pacing, beating a path between the dock and Tankersley's office. His orders had specifically said to be at Fort Scott no later than November tenth. The earliest he could expect to get underway was the sixth. With a favorable breeze (something that was certainly not guaranteed), it would take three days to reach Apalachicola Bay. If the wind held fair and was from the proper direction, they might be able to ascend the Apalachicola in two days, thereby arriving on the tenth. Muhlenberg wrung his hands. He knew timing was an essential factor in military success. People lived and died depending on who was in the right place at the right time or the other way around. There was the distinct possibility that if the ships didn't arrive at Fort Scott on the tenth or very soon thereafter, something very unfortunate was going to happen. If everything went unexpectedly right and absolutely nothing went wrong, he just might make it by the deadline.

20 Nov. '17
Ft. Scott, Flint River, Georgia

To:
Maj. Gen. Andrew Jackson
Nashville, Tenn.

General,

In compliance with your orders, I have transferred my Head Quarters to Fort Scott on the Flint River in preparation for the defense of the frontier against aggressions by the various Indian tribes south of the border. I regret to inform you, however, that opportunities for offensive operations are very limited for the time being. The first and foremost reason for this situation is the utter lack of supplies at this post. Major Muhlenberg was to have arrived at this place from Mobile with three shiploads of rations, ammunition, clothing, and other military stores by no later than ten days passed. Much was my mortification to find upon my arrival today that no word has been received of his whereabouts. His orders were to leave Fort Montgomery nearly three weeks ago on a voyage that should have taken but a week. Even allowing for the vagaries of wind and other causes unpredictable, I cannot imagine what has delayed the major. My worst fears are that his vessels have been waylaid by the many pirates and privateers that now frequent the Gulf of Mexico or that he has been attacked by hostiles while ascending the Apalachicola. I shall dispatch a boat downriver in the morning to hopefully ascertain his location and to assist, if possible, his ascent of the river.

Without Muhlenberg's supplies, the force at this post is unable to venture very far afield. Major Wooster had already placed the men on half rations, and what is on hand is nearly exhausted. There is perhaps a week's worth of flour available, the small amount of bacon is mostly rancid, and there is no coffee. The men exist primarily on the meat of a few beeves appropriated, most unwillingly, from the few settlers in the area, venison purchased from friendly Creeks, and fish caught in the river. Of greater concern, however, is the lack of ammunition. There are barely enough rounds on hand to fill the men's cartridge boxes. Without ammunition we can do little more than defend the area around this post.

In addition to the difficulties of supply, I have received orders from the War Dept. that forbid our crossing the line into Florida. Being thus circumscribed, there is little we can do to punish the marauders, as they will quickly flee to the safety of Spanish territory after committing their depredations.

In spite of these concerns, we shall not be inactive. I have been informed that Major Wooster is, at this moment, meeting with Neamathla, headman of the Mikasuki village of Fowltown, some few miles upstream from this place on the eastern side of the river. The major has gone to receive the Indian's reply to our demands for the murderers of the Garrett family. Should they not agree to turn the miscreants over to us, I feel it well within my authority to bring Neamathla and other such chiefs into custody as hostages until the murderers are apprehended or surrendered. Indeed, considering the limited means and authority I have, the only action I can take to punish the Indians dwelling south of the line is to harass their cousins who live north of it.

I will, as often as practical from this remote place, keep you informed of our situation and apprise you immediately when I learn the fate of Major Muhlenberg's convoy.

Please extend my best wishes to Mrs. Jackson,

Your Most Obedient Servant
E. P. Gaines
Bvt. Maj. Gen., U. States Army

Neamathla, headman of Fowltown, sat cross-legged upon the low platform of his village's council house and stared at the white officer who sat across from him. The officer looked as if he had not yet attained his thirtieth summer, yet seemed very much at ease for a man who was in such a dangerous position. The chief knew the soldiers at the fort were few in number and were without large stores of ammunition and food. If Neamathla cared to, he could wipe the fort and its soldiers off the face of the earth in a day. For the moment, there was simply no reason to do it. War with the whites might very well come, but today was not the day to start it.

Major William Wooster stared at the chief who sat before him. Neamathla was somewhere near his fortieth birthday, sported a thin mustache, and had a look of supreme confidence. That confidence, however, was based on false assumptions. Yes, Wooster's men at Fort Scott were vulnerable, but only until the arrival of Muhlenberg's convoy. With those ships would be an additional hundred soldiers and enough supplies to render the fort secure. Neamathla was also unaware that General Gaines was expected to arrive soon with several more companies of soldiers. The Indians may have been contemplating an attack, but today was not the day they would do it.

Wooster leaned forward slightly, determined to make his intentions understood. His gaze remained on Neamathla, but his words were directed at an Indian with surprisingly light hair who served as the chief's interpreter. "Weeks have passed since the talk of General Gaines was sent to the Mikasuki towns. Your chiefs have had time to consider it and provide an answer. What do they say? Will they surrender these murderers, or will they face the wrath of the long knives?"

Neamathla listened to the interpretation, though he already knew what the question was. There was really no other reason for the white man to be at Fowltown. Taking a deep breath, Neamathla prepared to deliver the response from the chiefs of the Mikasuki towns located south of the Florida border. Because Fowltown was located north of the line, the whites often came to him with their complaints and demands. He had occasionally thought of moving his people south so he would no longer have to deal with the whites, but could not abide the thought of being driven from his land by nothing more than white harassment.

Neamathla looked at the interpreter and said, "Tell the white man this": He then shifted his gaze to Wooster. "We do not have the men he seeks. They are from the Alachua Seminoles, who live to the south. They are our cousins, not our brothers. What they do is their own business and if the whites wish to speak to them of this matter, they should go to the Alachua chiefs. Yet we desire peace and wish no misunderstanding with our white neighbors, so we have spoken to Bolek and the other Alachua chiefs, and they have told us this: The white woman and her two children were slain as satisfaction for three of our young men who were slain when the whites stole their cattle. We found, in possession of the white woman, a cook pot that had been the property of one of the young men, and thus believed her husband to be one of the murderers. Thus spoke the Alachua chiefs, but there is more they wish to say:

"The white man always complains of murders and thefts by the Indian, but never says anything about murders and thefts done by the white man. The killings you talk of were done in just retribution for murders done by white men. Just this past summer two of our warriors were killed while riding from St. Augustine to the Alachua towns, and their horses stolen. In the winter before that, an old Mikasuki woman was slain when she refused to surrender her basket of corn to a white thief. You ask us to turn over our people—who have done nothing more than take just satisfaction for the deaths of Indians—to face the justice of the white man. Will you turn the murderers of our people over to us so that they may see the justice of the red man? By our count, we have yet to take satisfaction for the murder of three Indians. Do we not have the right?" Neamathla paused, letting the interpreter catch up. "So say the Alachua chiefs."

Wooster did not respond, and Neamathla didn't expect him to. In reality, the officer was nothing more than a messenger. Having spoken the official responses from the Mikasuki and Alachua chiefs, Neamathla decided to make his own feelings clear. He had been disturbed by reports of soldiers from Fort Scott crossing the river to cut trees on the southeast bank. As far as Neamathla was concerned, they were trespassing. For many years, the Flint River had served as one of the dividing lines between Mikasuki land and that of the Lower Creeks. The Creeks may have allowed the whites to build their fort on Creek land, but Neamathla had certainly not given the soldiers permission to enter Mikasuki land. "I have heard that your soldiers have cut timber from the south side of the river. These are our hunting grounds, and they are not allowed to do this. There are good trees on the Creek side of the river. Use those, if they will let you have them. I have been told that the Creeks gave to you much of their land after the defeat of the Red Sticks. If this is true, it does not concern us. This side of the river is Mikasuki land. It was not for the Creeks to give away. I have been told that there is a line in the earth south of here that divides the American whites from the land claimed by the Spanish whites. I have never seen this line and do not believe it exists. No white man, Spanish, American, or the English before them, marked such a line in the earth. Since the time of my grandfather's father these lands have belonged to the Mikasuki. You Americans have been here for no more time than it takes a child to grow to a man. You cannot call this land yours." Neamathla rose to his feet. The discussion was over.

Wooster also rose to his feet and extended his hand to the Mikasuki chief. The Indian's words had been firm, but not threatening. Wooster doubted General Gaines would see it that way.

Elizabeth watched as Major Muhlenberg paced *Phoebe Ann's* deck. For the past two weeks the man had been a smoldering powder keg, and everyone was waiting for the explosion. They had left Mobile on November 6 after the wreckage from the storm had been cleared away. At first the major had been optimistic. The wind was strong and from the northeast, precisely what he needed if they were to make Fort Scott by the deadline. Once clear of Mobile Bay and out in the Gulf, however, the waves increased in size and the vessels began to strain. After about an hour, signal flags were hoisted on *General Gates,* notifying the major that a crack had developed in the small ship's only mast. *Phoebe Ann* came alongside and the officers shouted back and forth, assessing the situation and discussing what could be done. Finally it was decided that a jury-rigged brace could be fastened around the break, but the sail would need to be lowered while the repairs were underway, costing them much-needed time. Muhlenberg fumed, but there was little he could do about it. It was either that, or send the boat back to Mobile for repairs.

The repairs took several hours, and in the late afternoon the little three-ship fleet once again set sail for the Apalachicola. An hour later, people near the aft end of *Phoebe Ann* heard a loud snap, and the vessel began a wide, uncontrolled turn. The crew immediately dropped the sails while Captain Shirley peered over the stern rail. What he saw wasn't good. The rudder stock had broken, and the rudder had come partially off its hinges. It had probably been damaged when the fishing boat slammed into it during the storm, but no sign of trouble had been evident until a greater strain was put on the rudder. More hours were spent making temporary repairs while *General Gates* and *Perry* stood by. Sunset came and passed, and the work continued. Sometime around midnight the vessels attempted to get underway, but the rudder proved nearly useless. Muhlenberg reluctantly ordered the anchors dropped until sunup.

In the morning, Muhlenberg and Captain Shirley inspected the rudder. Both agreed the one they had tried to fashion was never going to work properly. Muhlenberg ranted and swore, but in the end he was forced to order the ships back to Mobile. The repairs took five days to complete, requiring *Phoebe Ann* to be completely unloaded and carefully beached at high tide so she would be partially out of the water when the tide went out. For the entire time the work was being done, Muhlenberg paced nearby, either on the dock or along the shoreline, swearing and badgering the workers, trying to make them work faster. By the time the repairs were complete and the fleet once again set sail, they were already two days past the November 10 deadline.

The major's demeanor did not improve once the ships were at sea. The wind had fallen to nothing more than a faint breeze directly out of the southeast, the precise direction they wanted to go. Forward progress was measured in nautical miles per day instead of per hour. On the third day out a ship was sighted slowly closing in from the east, a two-masted brig carrying at least a dozen cannon. As it came near it hoisted the flag of the Venezuelan revolutionaries. It was no doubt a privateer, nothing more than an officially sanctioned pirate. The only cannon Muhlenberg had were two army six-pounders that had been removed from their gun carriages.

For several hours the privateer chased the three smaller vessels, but the faint wind prevented it from accomplishing the task with any speed. As the largest and slowest of the three American vessels, *Phoebe Ann* appeared its most likely target. As it drew within range, the pirate fired a warning shot, a signal for *Phoebe Ann* to drop its sails and surrender. Muhlenberg swore and ordered Shirley to maintain his course. He then ordered the women and children below decks and instructed the soldiers to load their weapons and take cover behind the ship's bulwarks. If they were to be boarded, he meant to put up a fight.

Jack Dill looked at the distant pirate ship and pondered the situation. Stepping over to Muhlenberg, he said, "If I may be so bold, sir . . ."

The major snapped, "What?"

"It's a pirate ship, sir, not a warship. They'll not try to sink us. There's little booty to be had from a sunken ship."

"And what of it, Sergeant? That certainly won't stop them from boarding us."

"Yes, sir, but a strong show of force might make them change their minds. Have the men stand tall at the gunnels, their muskets at the ready. Have the women and older children get weapons from below and do the same. If the other boats follow our lead and draw close, the pirates may decide we aren't worth the cost."

"And what if they decide to open fire on us?"

"We're in a pickle either way, sir. The way I see it, it's not like war, where everyone's out to kill the other fellow. For them it's business. They want their plunder at the lowest cost possible. If half their crew is going to get killed trying to board us, they may decide whatever we've got on board here just isn't worth the expense."

Muhlenberg looked at the privateer. Dill was right. "It's worth a try, Sergeant. Tell the women and older children to grab a musket. Those that know how to use them are free to do so, if it comes to that." He then turned to the soldiers sitting on deck. "On your feet, damn it! Show the bastards what they're up against! Captain Shirley! Signal the other vessels. Tell them to draw close, but do your best to maintain a distance from that pirate."

Within minutes, the women and older children were on deck, armed with muskets, bayonets, and any other weapons they could find. Elizabeth smiled at Dill. "Should Johnny see me now!" She then looked at the slowly approaching pirate ship. If it did come to a boarding, she would not flee below deck. Although she had never fired a musket, she had seen it done enough to know the procedure. She could also use the bayonet, if need be. She looked at the line of soldiers and women at the rail. They were standing perfectly still, a well-disciplined rank ready for battle. But battle wasn't what they wanted. They wanted to frighten the pirates off. She took a deep breath then shouted "One, two, three: Huzzah!" Muhlenberg was about to tell her to be quiet when Dill and a few of the other soldiers followed her lead. Within moments everyone was following suit, in perfect unison. Soldiers on *General Gates* and *Perry* took the cue and were soon doing the same. Then Muhlenberg did something no one expected. "Captain Shirley, signal the other vessels to follow our lead. Alter course to intercept that damned pirate. If we're going to bluff, let's make it a good one. I don't have time to waste waiting for them to make up their minds whether or not they're going to attack us."

For several long minutes the pirates held their course, inching closer in the light breeze. Then ever so slowly, they turned away. Elizabeth set her musket down and turned to Nellie, giving the woman a big hug. Captain Vashon would have been proud.

Free of the pirate threat, the little fleet sailed on toward the Apalachicola, making time as best the scant breeze would allow. Muhlenberg's mood brightened, but only temporarily. The successful repulsion of a pirate boarding party would have provided some psychological cover when he finally reached Fort Scott. He would be a hero, and Gaines would have no choice but to excuse the tardiness. Now, though the threat of pirates had been removed, Muhlenberg was back to his original predicament: He was inexcusably late.

As each hour passed, the major became more irritable. He should have been grateful for Dill and Elizabeth's help in driving off the pirates, but instead, their quick thinking embarrassed him. Even more annoying were the children. Crying babies and toddlers underfoot brought forth a tirade that made even the sailors blush. At those times when the wind completely died, he could do little more than pace the deck, swearing under his breath. The ship soon became divided, with Muhlenberg and the crew occupying the aft deck, the soldiers keeping to the fore deck, and the women and children staying below, no matter how nice the weather or how filthy the quarters.

On the morning of the eighteenth, the fleet finally dropped anchor outside Apalachicola Bay. Reaching the bay had been a goal, but for the moment, it was just out of reach. The storm that had struck Mobile earlier in the month had shifted the sands, and no one could find a break in the bar. A launch was dispatched to explore the bar and by late afternoon the crew had found an opening, but there was a problem. It would be barely more than six feet deep at high tide. *Perry*, the smallest vessel, could make it through, but loaded as she was, *Phoebe Ann* drew seven feet of water. The deeper water of the bay was only yards away, but Muhlenberg's ship couldn't reach it.

Muhlenberg and the captains got together to discuss their options. In truth, there was but one thing to do: Offload all *Phoebe Ann's* passengers and cargo so she rode high enough in the water to make it over the bar. *Perry*, drawing the least amount of water, would ferry the cargo across the bar to the *Gates*, which would become dangerously overloaded until *Phoebe Ann* was in the bay and could once again assume her burden.

The work commenced before dawn, with everyone working as hard and fast as they could. Their efforts were limited, however, by the speed at which *Perry* could cross the bar and offload its cargo to *General Gates*. Despite the hard work, *Phoebe Ann* was still sitting too low when the tide began to go out. Having missed the morning's opportunity, work continued at a slower pace, with additional supplies and personnel being transferred in the launches when the tide was out. By that evening, *Phoebe Ann* was riding high in the water and was manned by no one but Captain Shirley, a few black sailors, and Private Greenlee. Everyone on the two smaller ships watched intently and held their breath as *Phoebe Ann* approached the bar. No one spoke a word as she slowly slipped over the shallowest spot, and a collective cheer arose as she entered deeper water. Even the irritable Muhlenberg let out a shout. He ordered an extra gill of rum for everyone, and then reminded them all that everything needed to be transferred back to *Phoebe Ann*.

General Edmund Pendleton Gaines drummed his fingers on the table and looked at the officers gathered around him. He was a man of middle years, weathered and thin, with a full head of graying hair. He had arrived at Fort Scott that morning and found nothing as it should have been. No food, few weapons, not enough soldiers, and the Indians as insolent as ever. He wanted to blame someone, but the best he could do was say, "Where the hell is Muhlenberg?" He had no way of knowing *Phoebe Ann* had crossed the bar the evening before. He looked at Major Wooster. "We need to send a boat downriver to ascertain his whereabouts and help get those boats up here."

Wooster turned to Captain Vashon, who in turn looked at Lieutenant Scott. "Lieutenant, select forty men from between our company and Captain Allison's and prepare to leave at first light in boat number two. Take no more than two days' rations. Muhlenberg should have plenty."

Allison quipped, "If they haven't eaten it all."

Wooster shook his head. "What if he isn't there, and they need to come back? They need to take a week's worth, but the bare minimum. We haven't any to spare." Both Vashon and Scott nodded. They all assumed Muhlenberg had been nothing more than delayed. No one wanted to believe that out of three ships, not one had been able to reach the Apalachicola.

Gaines nodded and looked to Scott. "Take five days' rations. You'll have to stretch it to seven."

The morning of the twenty-first dawned cloudy and with little breeze. Lieutenant Scott and forty soldiers walked down to the landing and stepped aboard a crudely built flatboat. It was a simple vessel, rectangular in shape, about thirty feet long and half that in width. The bow was slightly undercut and rounded, but was certainly not designed to cut gracefully through the water. The deck was flush with the sides of the boat, which gave Scott and his crew some cause for concern. They would be totally exposed and if attacked, there were no bulwarks to take cover behind. The only cover on deck was a small deckhouse, eight feet long by five feet wide, but only four feet high, which served as the entrance to the hold below. For propulsion there were two large oars on each side, and for steering there was a rudder on a long pole mounted at the stern. In truth, the oars were more for steering than propulsion. The current would move them downriver, not the men's exertions.

From atop the bluff, John Stuart watched the men load their weapons and supplies into the hold. He turned and approached Captain Vashon. "Sir, I should be on that boat. Half of those men are from our company."

"And the other half are here, Sergeant." Vashon smiled slightly. "We both want to be on that boat, son. Fear not, Elizabeth will be here soon. You know as well as I do that your health is not fully restored. How much food have you been able to hold down?"

Stuart sighed. Sooner or later everyone in the army would have to deal with a bout of dysentery, and the past week had been Stuart's turn. "Not much, sir. Still, I feel well enough."

"I'm sure you do, Sergeant. Be that as it may, both I and Major Wooster feel you are needed here. When Lieutenant Scott catches up with Major Muhlenberg, he'll have Jack to assist him. He doesn't need you both." Vashon didn't mention the other reason he hadn't sent Stuart with Scott. While Scott had come to accept that Johnny and Elizabeth were married, he hadn't accepted the fact that Elizabeth had chosen a common sergeant from the Louisiana frontier over a refined officer from Virginia. Without Vashon to keep an eye on things, trouble might arise between the two men. Keeping Stuart at Fort Scott was the best way to avoid that.

As Vashon and Stuart watched the boat push off from the dock, the captain said, "Godspeed, gentlemen. Bring our beloved swiftly to the safety of our camp."

Stuart nodded and added, "Amen to that, sir."

The pair was soon joined by General Gaines and Major Wooster. After Scott's boat had cleared the first bend in the river, Gaines turned to Wooster and announced, "We'll have to deal with this Neamathla fellow. I'll not have a damned Indian telling me where I can or cannot cut timber."

Wooster was hesitant. "It was not a threat, sir. He was simply making his position known."

"He can prate about and beat his chest all he cares to. The United States will not be dictated to by savages."

"Sir, I see little need to provoke them. We don't need their timber. There's plenty on this side of the river."

"It is *our* timber, Major, and I'll not have some damned redskin disputing that fact. It's a bad precedent and can only lead to further insolence."

Wooster saw there was no use to argue. Gaines had decided to take issue with Neamathla, and there would be no reconsideration of the matter. It was, as it had always been and would always be, the same story: The settlers and speculators wanted the land, and with the army behind them, they would eventually get it. The Indians, no matter how long they had been on the land, had no real say in the matter.

Gaines stiffened slightly and made his pronouncement. "Major, take two hundred men, go to Fowltown, and escort this Neamathla fellow here to Fort Scott. He needs to be shown the authority of the United States Army."

Wooster's eyes narrowed. He knew trouble was coming and wanted it perfectly clear what his orders were. "And if he refuses, sir?"

"Then compel him by force, major."

"And if we are fired upon, sir?"

"Then run them out of town and don't give them anything to return to."

On that same grey morning the boats of Major Muhlenberg's convoy raised anchor and approached the mouth of the Apalachicola River. The breeze was light, but enough to make a decent headway. In a way, the light breeze was a blessing: They needed to move carefully to avoid the shallow oyster beds that dotted the bay.

It took over an hour to cross the wide waters of the bay and draw near to the mouth of the river. There was a swift current coming downstream; the summer rains that had inundated Alabama and Georgia had ceased only weeks ago, and the land was still draining. The boats formed into a single line with *Perry* in front. As the vessel with the shallowest draft, she would have to find the safest path upriver. A few of the men had been this route before, during the attack on the Negro Fort the previous year. They knew that even *Phoebe Ann* should have no trouble.

As the boats worked their way upstream, a sailor at the bow of *Phoebe Ann* worked a lead line, shouting out the depths as they inched along. As long as he kept yelling "mark twain!" they were safe. It was a fairly wide river, about two hundred yards across, though it would certainly narrow as they ascended. For the most part, it was a reasonably straight river. Over the eons the strong, immense flow from Georgia had found little resistance from the soft limestone and sand that formed the Gulf coast. If the wind cooperated, within two or three days they would be at Fort Scott.

Their ascent of the river had not gone unnoticed. Within minutes of entering the river, one of the lookouts on *Perry* caught sight of a canoe paddling northward. Several hours later, someone else thought he saw an Indian peering out from behind a cane break. After that, everyone saw Indians everywhere, though few of the sightings could be confirmed.

Hostile natives weren't the only consideration on Muhlenberg's mind. First of all, there was the matter of food. Even though they had taken on considerable stores destined for Fort Scott, the delays had forced him to use many of those supplies to feed the people on board the ships. He could have purchased more provisions before departing, but the extra costs associated with the delays would have forced him to exceed the allocated funds for the trip. If someone higher up the chain of command didn't approve the expenditures, they might well come out of his own pocket. Considering that General Gaines was sure to be displeased with his late arrival, Muhlenberg had decided not to spend any more money than he absolutely had to. If they were hindered any more, the barrels and crates would be empty by the time they reached their intended destination.

There was also the problem of the sick. Muhlenberg had started the journey accompanied by those who had been deemed too ill to make the march. Some of those men had recovered, others had not. More than a few had taken sick while on the voyage. By his best guess, there were about twenty men and women who ought to be under a surgeon's care. Considering the poor food, close quarters, and dismal sanitation aboard the vessels, the number would only get higher. Worst of all, there was absolutely nothing he could do about any of it. He couldn't control the depth of the water, couldn't make the wind blow, couldn't stop the Indians from watching, couldn't tell the men to quit eating, and couldn't stop the spread of disease. The only thing he could do was curse his situation and soldier on.

It was late afternoon and they had gone barely ten miles when they came to a snag. A tall magnolia had fallen into the river at one of the narrower points, and quite a bit of debris had built up behind it. Although the river wasn't completely blocked, none of the ships could get past the obstruction. The three ships pulled close together, dropped anchors, and the various officers conferred as to the best way to remove the obstacle. Saws and axes were broken out and two launches were lowered into the water. Before the boats could reach the snag, however, several shots rang out from shore. One of the soldiers cried out and fell to the floor of the boat. On all the ships, everyone took cover. Soldiers rested their muskets on the gunwales and watched the shoreline, looking for any sign of Indians. Reluctantly, Muhlenberg ordered the boats to take cover behind the ships and await further orders.

There seemed but one course of action. Chances were the Indians who had fired on the boats were scouts and few in number. Muhlenberg ordered *Phoebe Ann's* two boats lowered and every healthy soldier assembled. If they could chase the Indians off, the men from the other boats could work at clearing the obstacle. They would have to work fast. Darkness was approaching, and it was a good bet that a large force of Indians would be gathered by morning.

As soldiers on *Perry* and *General Gates* provided cover, Dill and his men boarded the boats and rowed toward the bank. A few shots were fired from shore, and one man was wounded, but otherwise they landed unopposed. Dill formed the men into a line, ordered them to fix bayonets, and began to fan out around the base of the fallen magnolia. Out in the water, the men from the other boats began to work on the snag. It was a massive tree, and much of it was under water, which made cutting difficult. The crew continued their work after sunset, even after it had become too dark to see very well. Finally, late in the evening, they felt a shift in the snag. It appeared to have broken loose.

Unfortunately, the snag wasn't going anywhere. The tree was too big, the river too narrow, and the ships were in the way. Muhlenberg realized that if he were going to proceed upriver, he'd first have to go back downriver to a point where the snag could float by them. With great reluctance, he gave the order that at first light the ships would weigh anchor and drift back down to a point a mile or two below, where the river was much wider.

It was just as well that they did. In the early morning twilight, as *Phoebe Ann's* anchor broke the surface of the water, shots rang out from the shoreline. It soon became apparent that this time it wasn't just a few scouts. Judging from the war whoops and the number of guns firing, there were at least a hundred warriors hidden in the forest. *Perry,* being closest to the shore and the smallest vessel, received most of the hostiles' fire, and a few of her crew were wounded. In the end, it was simply too dangerous for the crew to stand up and man the anchor windlass. They cut the anchor line, set sail, and followed the other ships downriver. Muhlenberg sighed. Unless there was a very strong wind, it was going to be difficult to get past that narrow spot in the river without heavy loss of life. The only safe place for the moment would be where the river widened. Until the wind picked up, the Indians left, or reinforcements arrived, the relief convoy was stuck.

Lieutenant Richard W. Scott took one last look at Fort Scott as it fell from view, hidden by the trees as the boat rounded a bend in the river. *Someday I'll be able to tell everyone that Fort Scott was named in my honor,* he thought. Visions passed through the lieutenant's mind of the thriving community that would grow up around the fort site, a town no doubt called Fort Scott, or maybe Scottsville. The history books would say the city, for surely it would eventually be a true city, had been founded by General Richard W. Scott, hero of the War of 1812, and conqueror of Florida and

Havana during the Spanish-American War of the 1830s. All of that was in the future, of course, because at the moment, everyone knew the fort had been named in honor of General Winfield Scott.

The late November air was crisp, the Flint River was flowing nicely, and the flatboat was making good progress. Scott, as commanding officer, stood at the back of the deckhouse, issuing orders to the steersman and the four soldiers who manned the sweeps on either side of the boat. Not that the orders were needed. Steering the vessel to keep it in the center of the river was an instinctive process that required little coaching. By the time Scott issued his commands, the actions had already been executed.

The river was wide at this point, with several streams, large and small, emptying into it. Just ahead, about seven miles, was the biggest juncture of all, the confluence with the Chattahoochee. Somewhere, perhaps three or four miles to Scott's left, was the imaginary line that separated the United States from Spanish Florida. Once Scott and his crew passed through the confluence of the Flint and Chattahoochee, they would cross that line. They would be on the Apalachicola River, and they would be in foreign territory. Scott wasn't sure of the propriety of the situation. Did United States troops have authority to enter Spanish lands? Scott had seen Gaines's orders prohibiting him from entering Florida to chastise the Seminoles. Evidently it was permissible to cross the line in support of a supply mission. Not that it really mattered. There was nothing the Spaniards could do about it anyway. There was a garrison at Pensacola and a few troops at Fort St. Marks, but rumor had it they were ill-equipped, poorly paid, and disinclined to do anything without direct orders from the Captain-General in Havana, who usually waited on instructions from Madrid. In all probability, by the time the Spanish authorities discovered there were American vessels on the Apalachicola, there would no longer be American vessels on the Apalachicola.

The pace of the current quickened as Scott's boat came to the confluence and entered Florida waters. The flow from two large river systems was being forced into one channel, and their energies combined. About a mile below the juncture they came to a bend in the river, and the strong current pushed them toward the eastern embankment. Scott called out to Reason Crump, who was manning the rudder, "Hard to starboard, Private!"

Crump responded, "That she is, sir, but she's goin' where she wants to!"

Scott looked about in a slight panic. "Oarsmen! Polemen! Keep her off the rocks!" There was no direction on how to accomplish the feat, only an order to do it, and, in fact, no real sign of rocks. Several of the soldiers picked up stout poles and prepared to push the boat off the bank, but beyond that, there was little they could do. The boat was now moving more sideways than forward. Corporal Edwards, a man who had grown up on the Tennessee River, instinctively reached for a grappling hook and threw it over the side. As the hook dug into the bottom, he wrapped the line around a wooden cleat and eased the boat to a halt.

Scott spun around, an angry look on his face. "Who ordered that hook thrown out?"

The corporal shrugged slightly. "You said to keep her off the rocks, sir, and that's how you do it."

Scott couldn't really argue with the logic. "Very well, bring in the hook, and let's be on our way. Next time, await my order."

Edwards answered, "Yes, sir," and turned and winked at Crump. He then took the line, walked to the stern of the boat, and called out to a pair of soldiers standing on the deck. "You two, take hold of the line and start pulling." The men pulled against the current until the boat was over the hook and the line went slack. Edwards then brought the hook to the surface, and the boat resumed its course. He stepped over to Crump and put a hand on the big man's shoulder. "Damn good thing there weren't no Injuns hidin' in them bushes."

The boat continued down river. Near sunset, Scott spied a large house situated on a low bluff over the river. It was, he supposed, a good place to stop for the night. The boat was eased up to a wide dock and tied off. The lieutenant walked up the sloping path toward the house, where two men stood on the veranda, waiting to greet him. Over their heads hung a simple sign that read, "Forbes & Co." Scott had heard of the trading post, but had imagined a much smaller facility. This was a handsome, two-story building, with glass windows and a balcony on the second floor. It was, he had to admit, larger than his own home in Virginia.

As he walked up the steps of the house, the two men stepped forward. The older one extended his hand, and then spoke in a thick Scottish brogue. "Good evening, good sir, I be William Hambly, and this is my assistant, Edmund Doyle. Welcome to Spanish Bluff." After Scott introduced himself, Hambly quipped, "A Scot! Well, that certainly makes you welcome. What can we be doing for you?"

Scott wasn't sure. "We were, in truth, looking for no more than a convenient place to tie the boat up for the night. With your permission, of course." He then noticed a pair of Indians sitting against the wall at the far end of the veranda. In a lowered voice he asked, "Are they friendly?"

Doyle chuckled. "Friendly? Not so I'd imagine. Still, unless you Yanks have given them some new reason to be unhappy, I'd not say they were hostile. All the same, you wouldn't want to get too comfortable, if you know what I mean. Best keep your lads on the boat tonight, post a couple of sentries on the dock, and be ready to cast off in a hurry, if needs be."

Hambly was more reassuring. "They're not looking for war, lad, so unless you give them some cause, they'll not bother you. Make yourself comfortable, and if your men have any coin on 'em, we'd be glad to let them have a look through our emporium." Scott gave him an apprehensive look, and the man smiled. "We promise not to sell them more than their normal ration of whiskey. We'd also be honored if you would sup with us tonight. It isn't often we get officers of the American government visiting here."

Scott replied, "You have not yet dined?"

Doyle shook his head and smiled. "We were awaiting your arrival."

It was a pleasant meal, better than Scott would have expected on the frontier. As the leading merchants in Florida, Forbes & Co. were able to bring a little bit of Britain to the wilderness. The china and silverware were of the highest quality, and the furnishings were as fine as could be seen in any average British home. Even the two handsome Indian women who waited upon them were dressed in the latest European fashions. Scott assumed the women were Hambly and Doyle's "wives," but no introduction was made, and the lieutenant didn't ask.

As he gazed about, Scott was amazed at the variety of goods in the store. There were numerous bolts of cloth of every fabric and color imaginable, along with beads and ornamental trinkets of every description. There were practical items such as cook pots and utensils, and frivolous items such as toys and amulets. Most disturbing to Scott were the numerous weapons. The rifles were of the highest quality, and a wide variety of knives and tomahawks covered the shelves. The store was, in effect, the Seminole and Creek arsenal.

Scott mentioned, "The Seminoles appear to be well armed, by the looks of this store."

Doyle smiled. "They are, my friend, hunters by trade. A good rifle is as valuable to the hunter as a good hammer is to the carpenter." He laughed. "We carry those also, along with the nails."

Scott was curious. "You are British, yet you reside and conduct your business in a Spanish colony. Where do your allegiances lie?"

Hambly was quick to answer. "Our allegiance, Lieutenant, lies to this store and our employers. As long as the Spaniards hold Florida, we'll work with the Spanish authorities. Should your nation someday acquire the colony—as we hear you are attempting to do through negotiations with His Most Catholic Majesty—we will strive to work with the American government. We ask for nothing more than the opportunity to conduct our business. We care little for the business of empires."

Scott knew there was much more to it than that. "And the Indians?"

Doyle felt the need to deliver a polite message. "They are our customers, Lieutenant. Without them, this whole enterprise ceases to exist. We cannot cheat them, we never lie to them, and we must always keep their best interests in mind. Between the Spanish crown, you Americans, other British merchants who would like to steal our business, the Indians, and the need to make a profit, we find ourselves with a five-armed balance that is forever in need of adjustment. Our greatest fear is that someone will tip the balance farther than we can compensate for."

After the meal Scott returned to the boat. He had trouble sleeping that night, despite the merchants' assurances that the Indians would not attack. At first light, he bid his hosts good-bye and ordered the boat back into the flow of the river.

The morning was, thankfully, uneventful. About noontime they passed the remnants of the Negro Fort, where a group of runaways and Indians shouted insults at them and fired several shots, more for the purpose of making a statement than to do them any harm.

An hour or so later they passed a narrow spot in the river where a snag had obviously been cut loose. Most everyone on Scott's boat agreed it must have been done by Muhlenberg's vessels, but if so, where were they? If they had gotten that far, why hadn't they gone farther? It made no sense. They all began to worry that something had happened to the convoy and that it had been forced to return to Mobile. If so, that meant a long, difficult return trip to Fort Scott, fighting the current every inch of the way. If for some reason the Seminoles wanted to start a war, Scott and his soldiers would be their first victims.

As Major Wooster led the four companies of soldiers through the woods on the southeast side of the Flint River, he had plenty of time to reflect upon his mission. At Fort Erie, during the war with England, Gaines had ordered him to undertake what both of them knew could very well be a suicide mission. By the end of the day, the majority of the men in the company were dead and most of the others, Wooster included, were seriously wounded. Yet no one had thought twice about the propriety of the order. Now, faced with a much less dangerous command, Wooster had to admit he had serious doubts about what he was being asked to do. It was one thing to put the lives of your men on the line when a war was raging; quite another to ask them to actually begin a war.

Wooster had seen little value in arguing the point. Gaines wanted to start something, but he wanted it to appear as if the Indians had commenced the hostilities. If Neamathla and his warriors put up any resistance, which they most certainly would, Gaines could use it as an excuse to attack Fowltown. Yet as onerous as the orders were, what bothered Wooster most was the timing. Without the supplies on Muhlenberg's boats, the army was in no position to start a war. Worse than that, it would give the Indians every reason they needed to attack any vessel that attempted to ascend the Apalachicola. Muhlenberg's larger vessels might not be in any great danger, but a small boat like Scott's would be a sitting duck.

Wooster didn't know why Gaines was in such a hurry to start a war, but he had a good idea. The most likely cause was pressure from Andrew Jackson. If Old Hickory had decided the Mikasukis, Seminoles, and refugee Creeks in Florida needed to be punished, then he would want it done without delay. Most of all, Jackson wouldn't want to give the officials in Washington time to interfere. Jackson was the type who would shoot first and defend his actions later. Wooster didn't like the entire situation, but he also knew there was little he could do about it. Even if he refused to carry out the order, Gaines would just find another officer to lead the mission. He knew it was a poor excuse for ignoring one's conscience, but there was a certain lovely lady in New Orleans that he intended to marry, and this was not the time to throw away his military career.

Wooster turned to Tom Perryman, the half-blood Creek Indian who was serving as their guide. "How far?"

Perryman rubbed his chin. "Another mile, maybe."

"Think we've been spotted?"

The guide broke into a big grin. "Oh. I'm sure they saw us cross the river at Fort Scott. You know they've been keeping an eye on us ever since we built the place."

Wooster nodded. He'd assumed as much. He called out to Captains Vashon and Allison, who quickly came to his side. "Vashon, keep your company near the front of the column. Allison, keep the other three companies about a quarter mile behind us. The Indians are no doubt aware of our approach, but may not know our strength. Better to let them think we're only about fifty men, instead of two hundred. Keep your march as quiet as you can, but if you hear gunfire, fix bayonets, yell at the top of your lungs, and run like hell to our aid." He gave both men a hard look. "Never hesitate in the face of the enemy."

The column marched on until the village came into view. Wooster called a halt and surveyed the situation. Fowltown was built on a sloping hillside, about half a mile from the river, high and far enough away from the water to be safe during a flood. Between the soldiers and the village was open grassland, presumably where the Indians grazed their cattle. It was a presumption because none of the animals were in sight, a sure sign that Neamathla's people knew he was coming. It was also obvious that the village was deserted. Behind and to the right of the village was a pine forest. To the left, in low ground near the river, was a thick hardwood hammock. If the warriors were gathering against the white soldiers, then that was where they would be.

Wooster turned to Stuart. "The white flag, Sergeant." Stuart unfurled the flag and moved to the major's side. Wooster stepped into the clearing, the sergeant by his side, the rest of the company following closely behind. They marched across the field and into the village. No one came out to greet them; no one fired a shot or tried to stop them. When he reached the central fire, the major stopped, and then ordered Vashon to have his men fan out and search the cabins. Not surprisingly, they found no one at home.

From the largest of the huts, a soldier came out carrying a tattered red coat and a rolled piece of parchment. Wooster took the items and smiled. The coat was similar to what would be worn by a British officer, though in its present condition no Englishman of rank would dare be seen wearing it. The parchment, partially torn, proved even more interesting. It was a certificate declaring that Neamathla was a captain in His Majesty's Militia, and a loyal friend to the crown. Wooster chuckled. The chief probably had no idea what the certificate said, and most likely kept the coat because it proved useful on cold winter nights. Wooster knew that people would read what they wanted to into the articles, no matter how they were obtained. If the certificate had been one of the numerous peace medals the United States handed out, the bearer would have been considered a friend to the Americans, even if he had been wearing it while fighting against the government. If the coat had been an American officer's coat, people would have assumed it had come from a butchered soldier, never stopping to consider that the Indian might have found it in a pile of castoffs. Wooster also knew that Gaines would be thrilled to get his hands on the articles and would make the most of them in dispatches to Washington and the press.

Vashon strolled up and asked, "Shall we burn the village, sir?"

Wooster thought for a moment. Perhaps there was still time to avert a war. "No, I feel little justification. They have not opposed us in any way. We do, however, need to send them a message. Have the men go through every hut and put anything of value into a pile in the center of the village." He then looked down at the smoldering fire. It was laid out in a symmetrical fashion, with four logs pointing to the cardinal directions. He sensed a significance in the pattern and thought it might be spiritually important. "Sergeant Stuart, start a new fire, then douse this one." He knew he was sending a message, but wasn't sure what it was.

Neamathla watched from the cover of the woods as the soldiers went from cabin to cabin in his village, removing everything that could be found and throwing it into a pile in the middle of the compound. The next thing he saw puzzled him. The soldiers built a new fire near the pile, and then deliberately put out the sacred central fire. If they were intending to burn things, why didn't they simply use the fire that was already burning? Then he understood. The white man in charge, the one he had spoken with the day before, knew the significance of the central fire. By putting it out, the white officer was telling the people of Fowltown that their village had no life in it. The white man wanted them to be gone.

He watched as the soldiers sorted through the pile of goods they had taken from the huts. Some items were thrown onto a new pile, and others were thrown into the fire. Weapons, ornamental objects, and ceremonial items all went up in flames. Metal objects and foodstuffs were set aside. He assumed the soldiers would take those things with them. They were little better than common thieves.

A warrior came to his side. It was the same fair-haired man who had done the interpreting when Neamathla and the major had met the previous day. Neamathla turned only slightly, keeping his eye on the activities in his village. "Yellow Tom wishes to speak?"

"Our warriors grow angry and wonder why we do not fire on the soldiers."

"The white man wants war, so that he can destroy all our villages, not only this one. I shall not give him that satisfaction."

Yellow Tom nodded. "Will they burn our homes?"

Neamathla shook his head. "I do not think so; we have given them no cause. If they intended to burn the houses, why remove everything from them?"

The pair watched as the soldiers began to pick up the items that had not been thrown into the fire and distribute them. The white men were preparing to leave. Neamathla bit his lip. It was a sad day, but he had prevented a war from starting, thereby saving many other villages. He only hoped the people of those villages would appreciate the sacrifice.

As he rose from his concealment and began to turn away, he heard a shot ring out, followed by a loud war whoop. Suddenly the forest erupted with gunfire. He looked angrily about, wondering who had defied his orders and fired on the whites. Then he realized it didn't matter anymore. The war he had sought to avoid had just begun.

Wooster spun around as he heard gunfire coming from the woods. He quickly ordered everyone to take cover behind the buildings and return fire. He saw one soldier who appeared to be dead and several who were wounded. He then heard yelling from behind, and turned to see Captain Allison run into the open field with his men close behind. As soon as there were sufficient men on the field, Allison ordered them to form ranks and fire a volley toward the woods. Wooster, running as fast as the leg that had been injured in 1814 would allow, charged onto the field, his sword held high. When he caught Allison's attention he began to swing the blade in a circle that pointed to the sky, then stopped and pointed it at the woods. Allison got the message, and told the bugler to sound the charge. Screaming their own war cry, the soldiers ran toward the trees, bayonets facing the enemy.

The major waited until Allison's men had gained the hammock, and then ordered the bugler to recall them. They had run the Indians off, which was all they needed to do. As the troops gathered in the field, Vashon approached Wooster and asked, "Do you still want to leave the village intact, sir?"

In truth he did, but he knew the option was no longer available. He had hoped to avoid a war, and assumed Neamathla wanted the same. In the end, a hot-headed warrior had defeated both men's best intentions. He spit on the ground in disgust, slid his sword into its scabbard, and said, "Put it to the torch, Captain."

6

22 Nov. '17
Ft. Scott, Flint River, Georgia

To:
Hon. Geo. Graham, Sec. of War, Acting
Washington City

Sir,

It is my duty to inform you that events on the border with Florida have taken an ominous turn. Yesterday, near noontime, a column of U. States forces under the command of Maj. William Wooster, 4th Infantry, was fired upon by Seminole and Mikasuki warriors outside the village of Fowltown, located several miles up-river from this post, within U. States territory. Maj. Wooster had been dispatched to Fowltown for the purpose of escorting the headman, Neamathla, to this post for a conference.

The Major had found Fowltown deserted and, while inspecting the village, was fired upon by a large force concealed within the adjacent woods. Fire was immediately returned, and a vigorous bayonet charge served to dislodge the enemy from his fastness. The savages forthwith fled to the safety of nearby swamps and canoes that had been positioned in the river. Casualties consist of one private slain and five wounded. It is believed perhaps a dozen of the savages were killed, though no bodies were found, it being the habit of the Indian to remove his fallen comrades from the field.

Obviously, this thoroughly unprovoked attack signals a significant change in the attitude of the Florida Indians and their allies. It is worth noting that found among Neamathla's possessions were a fine British officer's uniform and a Captain's Commission in King George's Army. Maj. Wooster, being under orders to drive the red men from their village if hostilities were commenced, razed Fowltown upon his departure. The village being situated on land ceded by the Creeks, I saw no legal impediment to the expulsion of such a hostile band. This being some of the finest land in Georgia, we can only hope that it may soon be brought to market and properly settled.

I await further orders, but must inform you that my means are at present very limited. The supply vessels dispatched from Mobile under Major Muhlenberg have yet to arrive, and our provisions and ammunition stores are inadequate for the purpose of any offensive action. Lt. Scott, 4th Infantry, was dispatched down the Apalachicola yesterday morning to ascertain the cause of the delay and assist if necessary.

I am, respectfully,
Your Most Obedient Servant,
Edmund P. Gaines,
Maj. Gen. U. States Army

P.S. Rumor here has it that Mr. Calhoun of S. Carolina is soon to become Sec. of War. If so, extend to him our congratulations, and assure him of our full support and cooperation.

EPG

Soon after the battle was over, Neamathla hunted down the warrior who had fired the first shot. The young man was trembling as the chief approached. Neamathla shouted, "I said not to fire on the whites! Can you not hear?" Before the warrior could answer, the chief pulled out his knife, cut off one of the offender's ears, and threw it at the man's face. "Now you have reason for not hearing the words of your elders!"

Neamathla's anger lessened the farther south he and his people marched. It was a comparatively easy trek, primarily because his people were unencumbered by a large number of personal possessions. Believing that if he gave the whites no provocation they would not destroy the village, he had told the villagers to take only what was necessary when they went to hide in the woods. The actions of one rash warrior had ruined everything.

As they walked somberly along, the chief was approached by Lah-nee-tay Fixico, the young kinsman better known as Yellow Tom. Though barely past his twentieth year, the man had already made a name for himself as a fierce fighter. Tall, lean, and strong, the most notable thing about him was the light color of his hair. Though not truly "yellow," as some white people's hair was, it was the lightest brown imaginable. Coming alongside, the young man asked, "What now, uncle?" From someone else, the question might have sounded like an insult or a challenge. After all, the welfare of the villagers was Neamathla's responsibility, and they were now homeless and destitute. From Yellow Tom, however, the question was like that of a student. He wanted to learn from the experience, and Neamathla was the best teacher he knew.

The chief gave a simple answer, though he knew the truth was much more complicated. "We will go live among our brothers near Miccosukee Lake. When the war is past, we will build a new village farther south, away from the whites."

"There will be a war?"

"Did you not see the gunfire this morning? Did you not see our homes go up in flames? The whites have the war they wanted, the only question is when it will end and how far they will go into our homeland. Only the Breath Giver knows these things."

"Will we have satisfaction for the loss of our village?"

"We may, but do not be foolish enough to think it will end the matter. The white men do not see justice when a red man takes satisfaction for wrongs that are done; they only see another excuse to make war upon us. Beware of satisfaction, for in dealing with the white man, such a thing can never be."

A rush of excitement ran through the crew of Lieutenant Scott's boat when Reason Crump shouted, "A mast! There! Above the trees; around the next bend in the river!"

Corporal Edwards smiled. "Thank the Lord. I was afraid we were going to have to pull this damn boat all the way back upriver."

The soldiers manning the oars on either side of the boat began to pull a bit harder, and before long the ships of Muhlenberg's fleet came into view. A cheer arose from the crews of all the vessels when they saw the flatboat come around the bend. It came alongside *Phoebe Ann*, was tied off, and a rope ladder extended over the side of the larger vessel so Scott and his men could come aboard.

Scott was the first to board. He immediately approached Muhlenberg, gave a crisp salute, and said, "General Gaines sends his respects, sir, and inquires into the reason for your delay in reaching Fort Scott. The supplies you bring are much looked for."

Muhlenberg nodded. "I'll wager they are. By God, Lieutenant, I think we've had every hindrance imaginable. We just crossed the bar two days ago. We ran into a snag not too far upstream that had to be cut away, and by the time we cut it loose, the damn redskins had gathered on the shore and were starting to pick us off. We fell back here to let the snag float by and were waiting for a good wind to fill our sails and get us past the narrows where the Indians are gathered. You weren't fired upon?"

Scott shook his head. "No, sir, just some harassing fire at the old Negro Fort site. We did see where you had cut loose the snag, but saw no Indians."

"Is the river clear the whole way to Fort Scott? I'd hate to get three-quarters of the way up and realize we can't get through."

"You should have no problem, sir. I've brought forty men with me, to use as you see fit."

Muhlenberg looked at the men coming aboard from the flatboat. He wasn't sure if they were a welcome sight or not. His own provisions were getting low, and he certainly didn't need forty more mouths to feed. "Well, the sun will be down in less than two hours, so there isn't much any of us can do today. Join me and the other officers for supper in about an hour, and we'll decide our next course of action. Your men can stay aboard and socialize for the evening, but they'll probably have to go back on board the flatboat for the night. As you can see, we're rather full-up here, and the other ships aren't much better."

Scott rendered another crisp salute, said, "Very well, sir, I'll see to my men, then join you for the evening meal," and turned away.

Muhlenberg stepped over to the railing and surveyed his little fleet. If the Indians weren't gathered at the narrows, there really wasn't any reason to delay the trip upriver. Even a light wind would be good enough. If the breeze died completely, he could put the launches over the side and use them to tow the ships. It would be difficult, but with the additional forty men, it was now an option. The biggest problem was what to do with forty more men. There was precious little room left on the ships, and no good place to put them. He'd have been happier if Gaines had sent only twenty.

There was also the problem of the sick and wounded. Some of them were in need of medical attention that only the surgeon at Fort Scott could supply. Others carried infectious diseases and needed to be kept away from the rest of the men as much as possible, which was impracticable on the small, crowded vessels. He would also like to be rid of the annoying women and children. He looked down at Scott's flatboat. Perhaps there was a way to solve some of these problems.

As the crewmen from Scott's boat came aboard *Phoebe Ann*, the happy sounds of old friends coming together could be heard throughout the vessel. Near the bow of the boat, however, a tense conversation was taking place between Sergeant Dill, Private Driver, and Annie. Dill had been dreading this day ever since Annie had crept into his tent soon after the majority of the company had left Fort Montgomery, headed for Fort Scott. True, there had been no legal marriage between Driver and Annie, and everyone knew that the woman would eventually move on to someone else, but that didn't prevent Dill from feeling as if he'd somehow stolen Annie from the man.

Driver, for his part, had some cause to feel betrayed. He had known Annie had her eyes on Dill before the troops had left Fort Montgomery, and wasn't the least bit surprised to find them together. Yet unlike most of Annie's other liaisons, she had not formally left her lover before taking up with another. It seemed a serious breach of etiquette, and Driver felt he was owed some sort of explanation. He looked first at Annie. "If you were planning on taking up with the sergeant, you should have told me, Annie. I wouldn't have stopped you, not that I could have." He then turned to Dill. "And I thought you a more honorable man, Sergeant."

Dill winced slightly. He *did* feel guilty, just not guilty enough to beg forgiveness or to offer Annie back to the man. She was his now, and as long as she was content to remain with him, he would not give her up. The best he could do was apologize and hope the private accepted it. "My regrets and apologies, Driver, I should have been stronger." He then looked at Annie. "It was more of a temptation than I was prepared for."

For a moment, the two men stared at each other. Dill, as well as anyone, knew the potential for violence between soldiers. As one of the company sergeants, it was often his responsibility to settle disputes between his men, and the worst ones were often over a woman. It was the sort of situation that could easily lead to a knife in the back. Had they been officers, the matter might have ended in a duel. Would Driver recognize the inevitable and accept the apology, or would his pride force him to take an unreasonable stand? Dill wasn't sure, and his body tensed, ready to take defensive action. Driver, his fingers nervously drumming on the ship's railing, contemplated his reaction.

Annie already knew the outcome. She could recognize a violent, possessive soldier, and had made it a point never to take up with that sort. It had happened once, when she was much younger, and she'd vowed never to let it happen again. She knew precisely what to say to get her former lover to back down. "Now Jonathan, you know it was pretty much over between us. I'm sorry; I just didn't expect you to get sent off so soon, and didn't want to make a scene before you left." She took his hand and said, "You know I gave more than I got, and didn't take nothin' I didn't come with. I made no promises I didn't keep, and didn't ask more of you than you had to give. Them was sunny days, Jonathan. Don't complain about the rain." With her other hand she reached out to Dill. "Now Sergeant Jack here feels sorry for what happened, but didn't mean you no harm, no more than you meant harm to the fellow I was with before." She gripped both hands tightly and raised them up a bit. "And I sure ain't nothin' worth fightin' for."

For some reason Dill wasn't so sure, but said nothing. Driver, never one to court a conflict, was happy to let the matter rest. Still, he cared enough about Annie to offer some advice. "You know you can't keep doing this forever, Annie. Someday someone's going to want you bad enough not to let you go, no matter how many times you tell 'em it ain't going to last. Ain't no one as free as they think they is."

After the officers had finished their sparse afternoon meal, Muhlenberg took Scott to the side for a private conversation. He knew Scott wouldn't be happy with the order he was about to receive, but the major's mind was made up. "Lieutenant, I want you to take your boat back to Fort Scott."

"Sir?" was about all the lieutenant could think to say.

"I don't like it, Mr. Scott, but I don't see much choice. General Gaines needs to know we're coming, but unless we get a good strong wind, we just aren't going to make much headway up this river. Plus, I have sick and wounded who need to see the surgeon. Pick twenty men to handle the warp lines, and take as many of the sick and wounded as you can." Before Scott could protest, Muhlenberg added yet another burden. "I also want you to take some of the women and children."

Scott stood tall, every inch the Virginia aristocrat. "At that, sir, I must protest. I cannot, on my honor, allow women and children to be put in such danger. If there is an attack by hostiles, we shall all be in fear of our lives. Even sick men can handle a musket. Women and children would only add to our peril."

"Lieutenant, some of these women are as sick as the men. One is having a difficult pregnancy. They all need to see a doctor."

"If there are women in need of medical attention, Major, I cannot refuse. Children are another matter. A small, crowded flatboat is no place for children, sir."

"The army is no place for children, Lieutenant, but we have them none the less."

"Sir, I cannot be more adamant in my protestations. Ailing women if we must, but no children."

Although the stern look on his face didn't change, Muhlenberg had to admit inwardly to a feeling of satisfaction. One sign of a great leader was the ability to make men willingly follow orders they would normally want to refuse. He could tell Scott didn't like the whole idea of taking the boat back upriver. Giving in on the children would prevent the lieutenant from raising any other protest. "Very well, no children." It was, in fact, an easy concession. All the children were on the *Perry*, out of sight and generally out of earshot.

Scott, unaware he had been taken in, was also pleased with himself. He had stood up to a superior officer on the highest moral grounds and had prevailed. He snapped a salute and stood at attention. "If the major has no further orders, I shall select my crew."

Muhlenberg smiled. His father, hero of the Revolution, would be proud. Yet Muhlenberg also realized the potential pitfall. If anything happened to that boat full of soldiers and women, he would be held responsible.

Yellow Tom was nearly the last of the Fowltown refugees to reach Kinnachee's Town, the main Mikasuki village near Miccosukee Lake. It was a typical Indian town for that part of the world, no different from the usual Creek or Seminole town. The cabins of the town's leaders surrounded a central square, and in the center of the square was the sacred fire. Cabins and lodges were scattered about, some close to the square, some almost out of sight, near sources of water or cultivated fields. Unseen were the numerous satellite villages that dotted the surrounding countryside. Although physically separate, they were politically associated with the central town and considered Kinnachee their headman. In times of danger or for a major social gathering, the central town was where the people from the outlying villages would gather. After the attack on Fowltown, it had become a very crowded place.

Neamathla had dispatched Tom to make sure no stragglers had been left behind or no hot-headed warrior had gone off to take revenge on his own. By the time he reached the safety of the Mikasuki villages, a large number of warriors from other parts of Florida had begun to gather. It surprised him how fast word had gotten out of the American's attack, and how quickly the other tribes had responded. Searching out Neamathla, he found the chief sleeping beneath a large oak tree by the side of one of the lakes. The older man awoke as the young warrior approached, then shifted his position so that he was leaning against the tree. Looking up at the overhanging branches, he smiled. "My new lodge."

Tom nodded. "Then I must find my own tree, for if this is suitable lodging for Neamathla, it is more than enough for me."

Neamathla laughed. "Tomorrow we build a hunting lodge. Trees are not good for keeping the morning dew from my head. Did all my people arrive safely?"

"All that I could find. It was hard on the old men and women, but the young ones stood by them and helped them walk. They have suffered much."

"As will we all, should the white man come this way."

Tom wondered what had transpired since the arrival of the refugees. "Has the council met?"

Neamathla seemed unsure of the answer. "We have met, but little was decided that was not already known. The mood of the chiefs is like the stampede of cattle. It thunders forward, and little can stop it. The only ones who speak caution are Tukose and Abraham, who have been sent from the Alachua and Suwannee towns by Bolek. They live far from the border with the whites and do not wish to give the Americans cause to travel south and destroy their homes."

"I see Micco Phillip is here from the St. Johns towns. His voice is strong and people will listen to him. What says he?"

"Phillip is a young chief and has not yet learned the hardest lessons, as has an older man like Bolek. There is fire in Phillip's words, and only blood will cool them."

"And Abee-Aka?"

Neamathla nodded. Abee-Aka was the most highly respected medicine man in the tribe. His opinion would carry great weight.

"He says little, nor does he have to. He spends all his time making war medicine. It is like a whisper that all can hear."

That left but one major group, and there could be little doubt as to their wishes. "What of the Creeks?"

Neamathla shook his head sadly and told Tom what both men already knew. "They speak of nothing but revenge. Homathlemico rants all day and curses through the night, as do all his warriors. The fools believe what the Englishmen tell them, that they will bring guns and powder, and that the lands lost to the Americans will be returned. Only Hillishadjo remains quiet. He knows the Great King in London cares little for our people, that he only uses us when it suits him. But he says nothing, for he was the one who led his people into war against the Americans, and cannot now admit his error."

Both men sat in silence for a moment, until Tom asked the next obvious question. "So what has been decided?"

"Our warriors are to gather at the border, where the rivers meet. There are boats waiting at the lower end of the Apalachicola, bringing soldiers and supplies to the fort on the Flint. If we can, we will stop them from reaching the fort. If the whites are without those supplies, they cannot attack us."

Tom knew better. "That will not stop them for long."

Neamathla had to agree. "It will only gain us some time, so that we can better prepare our defense. With luck, we can turn the boats back, for they will be surprised to see us in such force on the river. The soldiers on those boats do not know their friends at the fort have started a war."

Lieutenant Scott looked over the boat as it worked its way up the Apalachicola River. At first, the journey had been difficult and tension-filled. Soon after they had left the convoy, the river split as it went around a large island in midstream. One side of the channel was too narrow to allow anything but a small launch or canoe to pass. The main channel wasn't as bad, but still worrisome. The current was swifter, the shore closer, and at the end of it stood the remains of the Negro Fort. If they were going to be attacked, that would be the most likely place.

Everyone peered at the destroyed fort as they slowly passed. For those who were inclined to believe in ghosts, this was certainly the haunt of a large number of tortured souls. The destruction wrought by the massive explosion was still visible, and no one had trouble imagining the suffering of the inhabitants. Muhlenberg had sent two launches with musket men to escort them past the fort, but after that, Scott and his crew would be on their own. Once they were past the old fort site, the launches fell back, and a sense of vulnerability fell over the crew and passengers.

Although a few of the men had wondered why there were no Indians at the Negro Fort site, Scott saw little reason to ponder the matter. There was nothing of particular value at the site, other than its being a good vantage point. There might well have been an unseen warrior at the place who would report their presence, but what of it? He had more or less assumed they were being watched, and there was little he could do about the situation anyway.

Progress was slow, at best. The boat was slightly rounded at the front and the bow curved under, which resulted in it pushing the water aside more than plowing squarely into it. Still, with no keel and a wide beam, the vessel was certainly not made for speedy travel against the current. The two large oars on either side of the craft provided just enough forward motion to balance the flow of the river, but not enough to make much progress toward their destination. To do that, Scott was forced to use the laborious warping process. One of the soldiers would stand at the bow of the boat and throw a heavy iron grappling hook as far forward as he could. When he felt the hook grab hold of the bottom, he would hand the line off to four other men, who would then haul in the line as swiftly as they could. Once a rhythm was established, a good forward motion could easily be maintained. The hard part was keeping the crews from tiring.

To accomplish that, Scott had divided his twenty men into four groups. One group manned the oars and the tiller, two manned the port and starboard warp lines, and another one rested. The sick men and the women, unable to do much else, kept a lookout for any hostile activity. Scott felt confident that if he could keep up the pace, they would reach Fort Scott in three or four days.

Selecting the twenty men who made up the crew had been an easy task. It had required nothing more than going up to Sergeant Dill and saying, "Sergeant, I need you and Corporal Edwards to select the eighteen strongest men of our crew. We're taking the boat back to Fort Scott. We'll also be taking twenty-five sick and wounded, so provision the vessel accordingly." With that, the lieutenant had left to find out who the sick and wounded were.

Some of the men Dill and Edwards had chosen had been obvious. The first to come to mind was Reason Crump. His wife Nellie was among the sick, and Crump was one of the strongest men in the company. Darbey and Henderson were both tall and well built. Driver and Gravit were good, steady men, as were Asbury and Fail. Greenlee was an accomplished seaman, and that could certainly prove useful. Then there was McIntosh. He was a massive Scot, supposedly related to the half-blood Creek chief William McIntosh, and was always a good man to have around in case there was a fight.

Besides the twenty healthy soldiers and twenty-five sick and wounded, there were two other people on the boat whom Scott would rather not have had on board. The first was Elizabeth Stuart. Scott was still unhappy about her rejection of his romantic attentions, but more than that, he feared taking the daughter of his commanding officer into a dangerous situation. There was really no cause for her to be on the boat. She certainly wasn't ill, and there was no special reason why she had to get to Fort Scott any quicker than anyone else. She had, however, been adamant. If Jack Dill and Nellie Crump were on the boat, Elizabeth was going to be there with them. Along with Elizabeth and Dill had come Annie. There seemed no reasonable way to separate the trio. One would not go without the other two. Scott had thought of dismissing Dill, or even bringing him up on charges, but he feared how Captain Vashon would react. Vashon had put Elizabeth in Dill's care, and the sergeant would not relinquish the duty. In the end, Scott had acquiesced, giving in to the argument that Elizabeth and Annie were needed as nurses for the sick and wounded.

The first day of the trip had been uneventful, even pleasant. The weather was sunny but cool, and there was a light breeze to their backs. Scott only hoped Muhlenberg was able to take advantage of the wind and start upriver. The sick were crowded at the center of the vessel, either in or around the deckhouse, and were as comfortable as they were likely to get. If nothing else, Scott could enjoy looking at Elizabeth Stuart. Why such a beautiful girl had chosen such an unworthy man was beyond him. As far as Scott was concerned, Captain Vashon was a fool for letting it happen. A man like himself had so much more to offer. Perhaps, in some unimaginable way, he could make an impression upon her, make her forsake her husband and come to him instead. Just one night would be enough to prove he was the better man. Unfortunately, with Jack Dill and Reason Crump aboard the crowded vessel, there was nothing much he could do at the moment. Things might change, however, when they reached Fort Scott. It was definitely something to think about.

The second day of the trip was looking as if it would be about the same, though one of the fevered men had taken a serious turn for the worse overnight. Scott was impressed by the way Elizabeth and Annie cared for the sick and wounded. One of the soldiers had been shot in the chest, and the two women saw to it that his bandages were cleansed and changed often. Nellie Crump was plagued by constant vomiting and diarrhea. The once-plump woman had lost a considerable amount of weight, and no one seemed to be pulling on the warp lines harder than her husband.

At around noon on the third day, the Forbes & Co. store came into view. Scott intended to stop there for an hour or so, perhaps to have a good meal and give the men a rest. As the boat approached the dock, Hambly, the proprietor, came down to meet them, a worried look on his face. Scott stepped off the boat and greeted the trader warmly. Hambly was less cordial. The pair stepped away from the boat, where the storekeeper delivered his message in hushed tones. "I don't think it would be wise for you to stay around here, Lieutenant. I'm sure we're being watched by the unfriendlies. Something has got them mightily upset. Most of them have left the area, and I've heard rumors that they're gathering at the line where the rivers come together, hoping to stop your convoy. The longer you wait here, the greater danger you'll be in. If I were you, I'd just cast off and head back on down to the Gulf and meet up with that convoy of yours. I don't think the river's a safe place to be anymore."

The news placed Scott in a quandary. Could he even think of turning around? How would it reflect upon his reputation if he retreated from nothing more than a rumor? Would he be any safer going south than going north? The Indians may be gathering at the confluence of the rivers, but they may also be at the narrows near the Negro Fort. He also had to consider the invalids. Would some of them die without the surgeon's care? He had been given a task, a direct order from a superior officer. How could he explain to his fellow officers, his family, or his friends why he had not completed his assigned mission? A true soldier would not retreat, and neither would he. He had but one question for Hambly: "Can you procure me a runner to take a message to Fort Scott?"

The trader nodded. "I can, though I cannot guarantee that he'll get there. The path is treacherous at the moment."

Scott understood. He turned and shouted to Dill, "Sergeant, bring me a paper and pencil. Also bring me my leather bag." He looked back at Hambly. "How much do you think it will cost?"

"I doubt that he'll take less than three dollars. Too much chance of him getting his head skinned if he gets caught."

Dill arrived with the paper and pencil and the leather bag. Scott stepped over to a wooden handrail, set the paper down, and began to write. It was a short note, addressed to General Gaines at Fort Scott. When finished he folded the paper and handed it to the trader, along with a letter from Muhlenberg to the general. He realized the runner may not make it to the fort. He also realized the runner's chances might be better than his own.

Yellow Tom could smell the camp long before he came upon it. First there was the aroma of roasting venison and the occasional whiff of gunpowder, both of which were soon replaced by the less pleasant odors of several hundred warriors occupying a relatively small patch of ground. As he entered the center of the camp, some of those present cast a suspicious look in his direction. His light hair and other European features made those who were unfamiliar with him wary. It was only after several old friends greeted him warmly that the looks disappeared and those who were concerned turned their attention to more pressing matters.

One of the first to greet him was Peter McQueen, another half-blood, but a man who looked much more Indian than white. McQueen was a Red Stick leader from Alabama, one of those who had been driven south by Andrew Jackson in 1814. A strong leader and fierce warrior, he had a large following and was one of the men most feared by the Americans. As he grasped Tom's hand, he asked, "Does our friend Neamathla follow close behind you?"

Tom shook his head. "Our people are much in need of care, especially the old and the very young. He will not leave them until all are safe and cared for."

McQueen understood the situation all too well. When his own people had sought refuge in Florida they had arrived totally destitute, weary from a hurried march, and with many of their warriors slain. They had survived with the aid of their Seminole and Mikasuki cousins and had set up new camps far from the border. Although they had recovered physically, the scars of the defeat would never heal. Many of the women were without husbands, and some of the warriors were still without the confidence necessary to take on the Americans in a new war. McQueen hoped that coming events would restore some of that confidence. "It is a pity, but such is the duty of a chief to his people. With the help of the Breath Giver you shall return to Neamathla with news that will make his people smile. Our scouts tell us that there is a single small boat coming up the river, full of white soldiers. They will be near this place tomorrow."

Tom was intrigued. "How many soldiers?

"Less than fifty. Many look sickly, and they are tended by some women. They will be no match for us."

Tom looked around the camp. Everywhere he looked he saw men preparing for battle. "How many warriors have arrived here?"

McQueen smiled. "I have lost count, but there will be at least ten warriors for every soldier on the boat. My greatest fear is that there may be fighting over the trophies."

Tom looked out over the Apalachicola River. He was standing perhaps a mile from where the river split, the point that was supposed to somehow separate the American land from Spanish Florida. To his north, less than ten miles away, was Fort Scott, the place he assumed the soldiers were going. Even after the destruction of his village, he felt a slight touch of pity for those soldiers. They would never live to see Fort Scott.

It was dark, cold, and all too quiet. The thin crescent moon had set hours ago, and the sun would not rise for a few more. It was the last day of November, 1817, and Jack Dill had serious doubts that he would live to see December. As he leaned on the tiller, he looked out over the anchored flatboat, straining to see the front of it. Most of the crew and nearly all of the sick and wounded were sleeping. The routine of the day and the throwing of the warp lines had ceased. It was just too difficult and dangerous to be pitching a heavy grappling hook in the dark. Besides, the men needed to sleep. As a very necessary precaution, one of the four squads stood by the oars, while another stood lookout.

As Dill adjusted the rudder to keep the boat centered in the current, Annie came and stood close beside him. He put one arm around her and held her tight, trying to fight off the chilly air. Just having her there made him feel safer.

Annie looked up at him, though in the darkness she could barely see his face. Speaking in a low voice, she asked, "Why doesn't the lieutenant go back, Jack? I just know there's a bunch of Indians just waiting for us out there."

Dill knew it too. It had been too quiet. On the way down the river, whenever an Indian scout had seen them, he would let out with a war whoop or fire his rifle into the air. No such bravado greeted them on their return trip. For whatever reason—and none of the reasons he could imagine seemed friendly—the mood of the natives had become much more serious. There had been much speculation as to what Hambly had told Lieutenant Scott when they had stopped at the store, but no one assumed it was good news, and Scott wasn't talking about it. The boat had immediately left the store, and the lieutenant seemed more determined than ever to forge ahead. Still, for the sake of Annie, Dill tried to sound confident. "Don't fret, sweets, by this time tomorrow we'll be sitting at Fort Scott, laughing over a glass of whiskey and a hot meal."

Annie fell silent and snuggled tighter to Dill. She realized just how wonderful that felt, having someone to hold on to. For the most part, all her past liaisons had been for the sex. As long as the man excited her when the sun went down, she was happy. When that excitement died or he was no longer around, she went looking for someone else. She knew it was shameful and that people looked down at her, but it satisfied a strong need in her. Yet ever since they had stepped on board *Phoebe Ann*, the sex had stopped. There had simply been no private time or place. What amazed her most was that for once in her life, she really didn't miss the lovemaking. Just being close to Dill had been enough, especially now, when she felt the most vulnerable. She turned a bit, and looked straight in his eyes. "Jack, when we get to Fort Scott, will you marry me?" He didn't say anything, and she wasn't sure how he was reacting. It was just too dark to make out his features with any certainty. "I mean for real. With a preacher or a judge, or something. I don't want nobody else, ever again. I just want to be with you."

Dill wasn't sure what to say. He'd never really thought much about marriage to anyone, certainly not to someone who'd had so many lovers. It was something he assumed would happen after he left the army, after he had settled in some town and was the owner of a prosperous business. When he reached that point in his life, he might well have his choice of eligible young women from fine families. Marriage at this point in time was more suitable for a couple like Johnny and Elizabeth. They were both passionate people, and the need for each other was so strong. For him, passion was something that started when the clothes came off, and passed within the hour.

Yet the past few weeks had brought a change in him. Like Annie, he was happy just to have someone to hold on to. True, her past was questionable and people might talk, and yes, she was certainly not a refined lady, but she was honest, strong, and adaptable. If she put her mind to it, she could be a fine wife.

Besides, this was the frontier. A person's past and the lack of eastern manners counted for much less out here. He looked down at her and smiled. "I think I would like that." Then he leaned over and kissed her.

Homathlemico was excited. The day for revenge had finally arrived. A runner had brought news that the boat full of soldiers would soon be in sight, and the chief had given orders for his warriors to take their places and remain concealed behind the trees, the brush, and the tall grass by the river. The sun was high, and he didn't want anyone to be seen. He wanted the surprise to be complete.

Not that the lives of the few soldiers on the boat would be sufficient to give total satisfaction for all that he and his people had lost and suffered through, but it would be a start. Life for the Upper Creeks had started to turn bad soon after the visit of Tecumseh and his brother, the Shawnee Prophet. The Prophet's visions and Tecumseh's orations had inspired them all, including Hillishadjo, who also began to preach defiance against the encroaching white men and their insidious ways. To Homathlemico and the others who followed the Prophets, the thought of driving the white man out of Creek land had been intoxicating.

Equally exciting had been the thought of returning to the ways of their ancestors. The temptations associated with living like the white man were destroying the Indian way of life. The native traditions, the strength of the clans, and the ways of the spirit world were all fading. Tecumseh and the Prophets had preached a return to those traditions as the only way to be truly free of the white man. The only way to defeat the Americans was for all Indians to come together and rejoice in those things that made them Indian. Homathlemico had tasted the hope, and it was sweet.

And then it had all turned sour. The Americans made war on the British, and the Great King in London sent his soldiers among the Creeks, making promises of support if the natives would aid in the fight against the Americans. Then the war ended, and the Great King in London called his soldiers home. The Red Sticks were abandoned.

Not only had the wars been hard on his people, it had been personally devastating for Homathlemico. His two wives and all his children had been lost along the way. He had no idea if they had been killed, taken prisoner, or were living among some other tribe. Had his children starved to death? Had his women been violated by the soldiers? He didn't know. They were simply gone, and his sadness was exceeded only by his anger. For Homathlemico, the need for revenge was greater than any need for caution. He had been personally shamed by the war. He, as much as anyone, had led his people to a humiliating defeat. He needed something to revive the spirit of his people, something to make up for all the pain and disappointment. He needed revenge.

Homathlemico knew the attack on the boat would bring more soldiers into Creek land, and that the dreaded settlers would soon follow. He knew that Andrew Jackson would once again come in search of his people, bent on annihilating them. Jackson might even enter Florida and destroy what little his people had left. None of those facts meant anything to Homathlemico. All he wanted was to kill as many whites as he possibly could.

Elizabeth was enjoying the midday warmth as the boat made its slow progress north along the Apalachicola. It had been a cold night, and she missed having Johnny beside her. Nor did it help when she saw how close Jack and Annie held each other. *One more day*, she thought. *One more day and we'll be at Fort Scott, and I'll be spending the night with Johnny*. Lieutenant Scott had told her there was one more big bend in the river before they reached the point where the Apalachicola split into the Chattahoochee and Flint Rivers and entered United States territory. From there, it was about seven or eight miles up the Flint to Fort Scott.

Dealing with Lieutenant Scott had been awkward, but not troublesome. She knew she had wounded his pride by rejecting his advances and marrying Johnny, and she also knew that pride was everything to a man like Scott. The lieutenant had spoken to her often on the trip upriver, partly because he wouldn't lower himself to hold a casual conversation with any of the enlisted men, and partly because he was still trying to impress her. For Elizabeth, it meant treading a fine line. Scott was one of her father's fellow officers so she had to be cordial, but she couldn't be too friendly for fear he would attach more meaning to a smile than she intended to convey. For the most part she stayed close to Jack and Annie or Nellie Crump, and she never spent the first moment alone with the lieutenant. *Yes, just one more day.*

She stood at the back door of the deckhouse and looked down into the boat, where Nellie Crump lay on a blanket set atop a bale of uniforms, curled up in sleep. Whatever intestinal problem Nellie had been suffering from had largely passed. Still, she was unbelievably weak. The vomiting and diarrhea had taken more out of her than her constitution had been prepared to give. With any luck, sometime that evening they would reach their destination, and Nellie would be resting comfortably at Fort Scott under a surgeon's care.

Elizabeth shifted her gaze forward, past the low roof of the deckhouse, surveying the activity on deck. Standing at the front was Lieutenant Scott, his form erect, trying to look the part of the leader. On either side of him stood Reason Crump and Corporal Edwards, alternately throwing their grappling hooks into the water ahead of the vessel. Behind them were the soldiers who would haul in the warp lines, while two men stood on each side manning the oars. Just behind her, Jack was again at the tiller, with

Annie sitting off to his side. The four oarsmen did their best to aid the men on the warp lines, but progress was agonizingly slow.

Sitting atop the deckhouse were five men who were resting, but also performing the task of lookouts. Two on each side were scanning the shoreline for any sign of hostiles, while another kept an eye astern. Scott was determined not to be surprised. Scattered across the deck were some of the invalids, who also were keeping an eye out for trouble, while the remainder of the sick and wounded were below, some too weak to come out in the fresh air. Both the invalids on deck and the men on watch kept loaded muskets by their sides.

As the boat entered the bend in the river, Elizabeth heard Jack tell the oarsmen on the port side to slack off some so the boat would turn more toward the center of the stream. Just as Jack was beginning to adjust the tiller to accomplish the same task, Lieutenant Scott turned and commanded him to, "Keep her in the middle of the river, Sergeant." The current, coming from the left, was pushing them toward the eastern bank, and no one wanted to get too close to the wooded shore. There was no telling what might be lurking there.

At the bow of the boat, Edwards motioned for Crump to throw the hook more toward the opposite shore, hoping to draw the boat away from the eastern side. The effort helped, but only so much. The flatboat, rectangular and bulky, tended to go where the current pushed it, not where the crew wanted it to go. As the boat began to drift toward the shallows, Scott became more animated, directing Edwards to throw his hook off the side to keep the boat from drifting any closer to land. He shouted at the oarsmen and then at Dill, in effect telling them to do what they were already doing.

Suddenly and without warning, there was one loud crack, followed by hundreds of rifles firing from the woods and undergrowth along the east side of the river. In one quick instant, Elizabeth saw Lieutenant Scott crumple to the deck and Reason

Crump fall over the side of the vessel. She heard screams and shouts from all over the boat, then a command from Jack telling her to get below. Before she could move she heard Jack cry out, and turned around to see him holding a bleeding right arm. Annie, who had been sitting on the deck and was partially shielded from the Indians' fire, leapt up to help him. "Get down!" he yelled, but it was too late. A rifle ball smashed into her skull, and she fell lifeless at his feet. "No!" he screamed and fell to his knees. That probably saved his life, for both he and Elizabeth were now sheltered by the deckhouse.

With no one at the tiller and the oarsmen dead, wounded, or firing a musket, the boat began to drift closer to the shore. Edwards, wounded in the shoulder, threw his hook off the side in a vain attempt to keep the boat from drifting any further, but he couldn't hold it. Elizabeth took a quick look around. Besides her, perhaps only a half dozen of the nearly thirty people who had been on deck had not been killed or wounded. Some of the more exposed of the wounded attempted to crawl along the deck to take shelter behind the deckhouse, but most never made it. There were simply too many Indians firing from the shoreline.

As the boat drifted inevitably towards the river bank, the Indians ceased firing and began to gather in the shallow water. Shouting and yelling, they jostled and pushed each other, each vying to be among the first to board the vessel and exact their bloody revenge upon the living and the dead. Elizabeth cautiously raised her head above the roof of the deckhouse to have a look. Lying before her was Private Asbury, desperately gasping for breath, blood running from his mouth. She stared at him, her eyes wide open, her whole body shaking. He returned her gaze, his eyes pleading for her to do something, but then his eyes glazed over and the life left him.

Private Darbey, who had given her and Johnny his cabin when they were first married, lay atop the deckhouse, desperately clutching his thigh, watching the blood squirt from between his fingers. His life was draining away, and he was powerless to stop it. By the side of the house Elizabeth could see the lifeless form of Private Fail, the man whose wife had an inordinate love of pretty things and who was still on board one of Major Muhlenberg's vessels. Also dead were Privates Gravit and Greenlee, who had been manning the oars on the side of the vessel nearest the Indians. The warriors had obviously targeted the men who might be able to guide the boat to safety.

Elizabeth suddenly thought of Nellie Crump. She and most of the other invalids were down below, not fully aware of what was happening, and no doubt frightened beyond belief. She started to rise, to go to Nellie, but a firm hand drew her back down. Sergeant Sissom, one of the invalids who had been on deck, shook his head. "Don't go down there. It'll be a death trap." He tried to push her to the side of the boat. "Jump over the side. Swim to the other shore."

"I can't swim!" She looked at the water. Four men had already gone over the side. Three were making their way away from the doomed craft, but the fourth was struggling to stay afloat. She looked back at Sissom. "Why don't you swim off?"

He smiled weakly. "I can't swim, either." He then looked down at his bloody left leg. "Anyway, the leg's shattered. I can't even stand up."

She turned to Dill, who was trying to load one of the muskets. "Jack, you need to swim away from here."

He shook his head. "I'm not leaving Annie. I'll not let them take her hair. Go with the others. I'll be fine."

Elizabeth looked toward the shore. The closest Indians were only ten or fifteen feet from the boat. Edwards was still struggling to stop the boat with his warp line, but it was a losing effort. In a minute or two, the warriors would be boarding the vessel. If the only thing holding Jack back was her and Annie, she'd have to remove that encumbrance. Lifting Annie's limp corpse, she started to drag it toward the side of the boat. Dill, with his unbroken arm, helped her, and they slid Annie over the side as carefully as they could. Hopefully the same current that was carrying them to the Indians would carry Annie's body safely away from the scalping knives. She then turned to Dill and asked, "Can you help me swim?"

Before they could jump into the water, they heard a scream from the cabin. It was Nellie, calling for her husband Reason. Elizabeth looked at Dill. "I can't leave her." They both knew the futility of it, but they would have to try and bring her from the cabin and put her in the water. There wasn't enough time, but they had no choice.

As they stepped toward the cabin door, they were pushed aside by McIntosh, the gigantic, wild-eyed Scot, who was exiting the cabin. In his arms was a small swivel cannon they had been carrying to Fort Scott. "This'll sweep the deck clear!" He turned toward the bow of the boat. The first warriors were taking hold of the vessel and starting to climb aboard. McIntosh cradled the cannon in his arms and pointed it toward the Indians. "C'mon, you red bastards! Have a taste of this!"

About a dozen warriors were either on the front deck on climbing aboard. McIntosh turned to Private Gray, who was standing by his side. "Let 'em have it, lad!" Gray touched a smoldering stick to the touchhole, and the cannon roared. A handful of warriors fell to the deck or plunged into the river.

It was a valiant gesture on the part of McIntosh, but it was the last thing he did. The force of the discharge was so great that it forced the cannon into his chest, sending him reeling backwards. He stumbled into Dill, and both men fell over the side. Dill quickly came up for air, but the Scot never did.

It only took the warriors a moment to recover from the discharge of McIntosh's cannon. As they began to climb aboard, only three uninjured soldiers were left to defend the boat, Privates Mullis, James, and Gray. Mullis and James, near the front of the vessel, charged at the warriors with their bayonets. Close hand-to-hand fighting ensued, but the men were in danger of being overwhelmed. James suddenly yelled out as a tomahawk cut into his hands, forcing him to drop his gun. Mullis quickly came to his aid, swinging his musket like a club. James, knowing all was lost, dove into the water. Mullis, raging like a madman, continued to swing his weapon, forcing the warriors back. Then, from the shore, a rifle rang out, and the soldier fell to the deck.

At the back of the boat, Private Gray took hold of Elizabeth's arm and yelled, "Into the water! It's our only hope!" Just then, Nellie cried out again. Elizabeth tore her arm free, pushed Gray away from her, and lunged toward the cabin. As the soldier fell into the water, she ran down the steps and into the cabin. She tried to lift Nellie, but even with the loss of weight, the woman was still too heavy for a slim girl of seventeen to lift. Nellie tried to get up, but couldn't raise herself off the bales of uniforms she had been lying on. There was simply no strength left.

From outside the cabin Elizabeth could hear the war whoops of the Indians and the screams of the soldiers who were being slaughtered. Then suddenly the light coming in the door of the cabin was no longer there. She turned to see a warrior standing at the door, a wild grin on his face and a bloody tomahawk in his hand. Her eye caught sight of a musket lying nearby with its bayonet fixed. She quickly grabbed the weapon, pointed it at the man, and pulled the trigger. Nothing happened. The warrior laughed, then took a step down into the cabin. Suddenly his foot slipped on the blood-drenched step, pitching him forward. He looked for something to break his fall, but the only thing in front of him was the frightened white woman holding the bayonet-tipped musket.

Elizabeth's eyes widened as the bayonet plunged into her attacker's chest. The warrior's momentum carried him towards her, and they both fell to the floor. Pushing the lifeless form aside, Elizabeth ran up the steps and out onto the deck. There was no time to do anything for Nellie. More than anything, she needed to get off the boat, find Jack, and somehow get back to Johnny. She didn't care if she couldn't swim. She needed to get into the water. It was her last chance to escape alive. She bounded toward the back of the boat, only a few feet away. Out in the river she saw Jack, being helped along by Private Gray. She didn't know how, but she was going to reach them.

One foot was already in the air when she felt the grip of a strong hand on her arm. The hand pulled, stopping her forward motion. Elizabeth was swung around and back onto the deck. She looked up, fully expecting to see a dark, angry face and a tomahawk coming toward her head. Instead, she gazed into bright blue eyes, an expressionless face, and the lightest hair she had ever seen on an Indian.

29 Nov.
Forbes' Store
Spanish Bluff

General:

Enclosed you will receive Major Muhlenberg's communication, which I am forwarding to you by express from this place. Mr. Hambly informs me that the Indians are assembling at the junction of the river, where they intend to make a stand against those vessels coming up the river. Should this be the case, I am not able to make a stand against them. My command does not exceed forty men, and one half sick, and without arms. I leave this place immediately.

Your Obedient Servant,
R. W. Scott, Lieut. 4th Infantry,
Commanding Detachment

Note: The bearer of this is entitled to three dollars on delivering this letter.

News of the arrival of an Indian runner had brought the officers of Fort Scott into the west blockhouse, where General

Gaines had set up headquarters. By the time they were all gathered, the general had read the letter and passed it on to Major Wooster. Gaines looked at the Indian, who was obviously waiting on something, and stepped over to a chest in the corner of the room. He opened it, shuffled through the contents until he located a small leather pouch, then poured the contents of the pouch into his hand and picked out three silver coins. *Three dollars!* he thought. *That's half a month's pay for a private!* Gaines handed the coins to the runner, who muttered something, and then left Fort Scott as unceremoniously as he'd arrived.

Gaines turned to Wooster and said, "Make out a voucher stating that I had to pay some damn Indian three dollars for a stroll through the woods, and have every senior officer at the post witness it." Long experience had taught him that getting money back from the War Department required determination and more than a few sheets of paper. He then motioned toward the letter from Lieutenant Scott. "What do you think, Major?"

Wooster shook his head, and then handed the letter to Captain Vashon. "Should have been here by now, sir, or getting very close. Two days is sufficient from Spanish Bluff. Depends on what time of day he wrote this letter." He thought for a moment then added, "Then again, sir, the letter says, 'I leave this place immediately.' It doesn't say which direction he's going. He may have decided it was too dangerous and returned to Major Muhlenberg."

Gaines nodded. Wooster might be right, but who could know? At the moment, it was academic. The afternoon was swiftly fading and if a rescue party was going to be formed, things would have to move quickly. The general turned to Lieutenant Clinch. "Lieutenant, I want you to take twenty men and find out what happened to Scott. For all we know, he might be a mile down river or all the way back at the Gulf with Muhlenberg." He then looked to Vashon. "Captain, have your men plank up the sides of one of the boats. That should give adequate protection if they run into hostile fire along the river." Vashon departed and Gaines turned back to Clinch. "Take three days' rations. We can spare no more, and that should be enough to get you to Muhlenberg, if that's where Scott is. If you do go all the way to wherever Muhlenberg is, tell him there can be no further delay. If the damn redskins have taken to the warpath, I'll need those supplies he's carrying more than ever. Stay with him, help him however you can, but do not attempt to return on your own."

Clinch saluted, said, "Yes, sir," and left to gather his men.

Gaines looked at Wooster. "We'd better see to the defenses of this post, Major. Finish the breastwork between the buildings, send a detachment to the spring to fill the water barrels, and post a double watch tonight. If they're going to attack someone, this is the most likely place." He shook his head. "I hope Scott had the presence of mind to turn around and go back to the safety of Muhlenberg's convoy instead of trying to force a passage past half the damn Indians in Florida."

Wooster didn't answer. He knew how proud a man Scott was. He also knew that pride could easily get a man killed.

The Indians had left no one alive on Lieutenant Scott's boat, but not everyone had been slain. At least twelve men had jumped into the water, but some had been unable to swim, while others were too badly injured to go very far. Of the six who made it to safety, three were injured, only two still had shoes, and only one had a coat. The only tool or weapon they had was a jackknife that one of them had been carrying in his pocket. Beyond that, they were defenseless and vulnerable.

The first men to reach the opposite shore had waited anxiously for the others, urging them on as they swam, watching helplessly as Seminole warriors fired at them from the east bank. After helping their comrades ashore, the survivors hurried west, trying to put as much distance as possible between themselves and the site of the massacre. They had no idea if they were being pursued, but had to assume they were. Progress in the march was agonizingly slow. One man had a broken arm, while another had a badly wounded leg. They hadn't spoken much, not wanting to make any noise that might alert an unseen Indian scout. Now, several hours later and with the sun nearing the horizon, they rested. They spoke quietly, assessing their situation and making what plans they could.

The first priority was the care of the wounded. Three of the men—Privates Gray, Wheadon, and Gorman—were uninjured, and each selected one of the others to care for. Gray looked at Sergeant Dill's upper right arm. He saw a bullet hole and touched the area lightly. Dill winced in pain. Gray nodded. "My guess is the ball hit the bone and broke it. Probably still in there. I don't think the bone's completely broken, though. More likely just a crack in it." He took the jackknife and cut off the blood-soaked sleeve. Looking around, he found a stout twig, broke it to the proper length, and bound it next to the arm with strips of cloth from the sleeve. "I suppose that will help until we get you to the surgeon at Fort Scott."

Next to them, Gorman was examining Private Thompson's lower left leg. A Seminole bullet had cut a long, wide gash through the calf muscle. It wasn't a deep wound and no bone had been hit, but it was bleeding and Thompson could barely walk on it. Gorman carefully removed Thompson's coat. "I know you'll probably wish you had this when it gets cold tonight, but I think it will serve you better as a bandage." Getting the knife from Gray, he cut one of the sleeves off and slid it over the wounded leg. It was a tight fit, and Thompson had to stifle his cries of pain as the bandage was slid up, but it appeared the best way of stopping the flow of blood. Gorman cut a strip of cloth from the back of the coat and used it to tie off the ends of the bandage, securing it in place. Standing up, he handed the knife and the remnants of the coat to Wheadon, who was tending to the wounded hands of Private

James. Gorman then went in search of a branch that he could somehow fashion into a crutch for Thompson.

Wheadon looked at James's hands and shook his head. "How on earth did he get both hands at once?"

James shrugged and smiled weakly. "Lucky, I guess." The tip of his left thumb was gone, along with the first two fingers on the right hand. Cutting strips of cloth from the coat, Wheadon bound the hands as best he could. It wasn't pretty, but there was little else he could do.

As the only noncommissioned officer, Dill knew it was his responsibility to take command, yet all he could think of were Annie and Elizabeth. Wheadon and Gorman, the first ones to reach the safety of the opposite shore, had watched the conclusion of the battle and confirmed that Elizabeth had been taken prisoner and appeared to be unharmed. No one cared to mention the fact that she might not stay that way for long.

Gray knew Dill needed to focus on the present situation. He gently asked, "What's next, Jack?" Dill just shook his head. The only thing he could focus on was the image of Annie's bloody face and her body floating down the river. Then he imagined Elizabeth being carried off. Worst of all, he could see John Stuart's face. How could he tell his best friend that his young wife had been taken prisoner by the Indians? He would also have to break the news to Captain Vashon. He wasn't sure he could do it.

Gray kept up the gentle pressure. "We need to get to Fort Scott, Jack. We need to report to the general. We need to tell Johnny and Captain Vashon that Elizabeth is still alive."

Dill closed his eyes and shook his head, as if that would somehow drive the painful images from his mind. Concentrating, he tried to imagine the path ahead. "We need to get north of the junction of the rivers. It can't be far. We were only a mile or so below it when we were attacked. At some point we'll have to cross the Chattahoochee, and that will put us in Georgia. From there, we move east until we come to the Flint, and then follow that until we reach Fort Scott. Depending on how hard it is to cross the Chattahoochee and any other streams we come across, it shouldn't take us more than two days."

Gray added, "I figure we ran west, maybe northwest, from the river, maybe two or three miles. If we head northeast, we'll hit the Chattahoochee somewhere north of where the Flint comes in."

Wheadon pointed out, "Don't expect we'll find much to eat along the way."

Thompson quipped, "I sure as hell ain't goin' to light no fire and do any cookin'."

James laughed. "And Fort Scott was on half-rations when we left. Probably won't have anything to feed us when we get there." They all chuckled, momentarily forgetting the catastrophe they had all survived. It would be difficult, but they would make it.

Dill used his good arm to raise himself up and prop his back against a tree. "We'll rest here for the night. Gray and I will take the first watch, Wheadon and James the second, Thompson and Gorman the last."

Wheadon handed the jackknife to Gray. "Don't shoot until you see the whites of their eyes."

As the other four men lay down, Dill and Gray turned their backs to each other, watching in opposite directions. Dill sighed and stared out into the twilight. Once again, the image of Annie's bloody face came to mind. Could he ever forget it?

It was well after dark by the time Lieutenant Clinch's boat reached the confluence of the rivers and entered Spanish territory. About a mile farther down, they came to a gentle bend in the river and were forced to adjust their course to stay in the center of the channel. The moon was setting and the clouds obscured the stars, removing what little light there was. Although they were keeping a sharp lookout, they saw no sign of an attack, nor did they see the flatboat that had been hauled up one of the small streams that fed into the river. They also missed seeing the young woman's body that had become entangled in the growth along the riverbank.

As they passed Spanish Bluff early in the morning, the soldiers were greeted by catcalls and a few shots from some Indians standing on the dock. That in itself was worrisome. Forbes's store was obviously not the welcoming place it had been for Scott just three days earlier. Could something have happened to Hambly and Doyle? Clinch had no idea, and he was certainly not going to go back to the store and ask any questions. At the same time, the lieutenant felt a slight sense of relief. If Scott was nowhere between the fort and the store, then he must have turned back. As far as he could tell, the people on Scott's boat were safe with Muhlenberg's convoy and had not fallen prey to an Indian attack.

The three-day march to the villages at Miccosukee Lake was exhausting, but for the most part Elizabeth had been able to keep up with her captors. Thankfully, the pace was unhurried. Two wounded warriors, carried on litters, served to regulate the rate of travel. Surprisingly, there seemed no sense of urgency to reach the villages. The warriors were euphoric after their triumph and had no concern about being pursued. Elizabeth was well aware of what might happen if she was unable to keep up the pace. Jenny Holley, one of the invalid women, had also been taken prisoner, but it soon became apparent she could not endure the march. Although Elizabeth did not see what happened to the woman, the distinct crack of a rifle told her all she needed to know.

The march had commenced about an hour after the attack was over, early in the afternoon. For the first hour or two of the trek, Elizabeth was too frightened and stunned to think of anything else but the horrible sights she had seen. The initial volley from the concealed warriors had killed or wounded over half of the exposed people on the boat. Another volley took out many of those who had not been hit the first time. Then, when the boat reached shallow water, the Indians rushed aboard, tomahawks and war clubs at the ready. For the most part, the soldiers were able to put up nothing more that a feeble defense. Only McIntosh and his little cannon had been able to slow the attackers down, and only for a few seconds.

The most horrible sight had been when the warriors entered the deckhouse. Enraged that Elizabeth had killed one of their brethren, they showed no mercy to the invalids and women they found huddled against the bulwarks. Only Jenny, who was no older than Elizabeth and six months pregnant, had been spared, but not for long. Most painful to Elizabeth's ears were the screams of her dear friend Nellie Crump. It was a terrifying sound that would remain with her for the rest of her life.

After all the whites had been slain, the Indians began to ransack the vessel, intent on finding anything of value. They had hoped to find gunpowder and lead, but in this they were disappointed. Being in a hurry to depart and knowing they would be pulling the boat against the current, Scott had ordered only lightweight and easy-to-handle items packed on board. For the most part the contents of the boat's hold consisted of uniforms and some of the passengers' personal belongings. As far as the Indians were concerned, it was all worthless. Unhappy with their loot, the warriors pulled the boat down to a small tributary nearby, and pushed it a short way up the stream. Most of the corpses were still on board.

The Indians kept up a steady pace, rarely taking time to rest or eat, and not stopping until twilight was near ending. On those occasions when the war party did take time to rest, Elizabeth's light-haired captor would toss her a piece of dried meat, along with a leather bag filled with water. Never did he say a word to her, nor did he touch her, except to prod her on when her pace slowed or jerk her to her feet when she stumbled. And while the grasp of his hand was certainly not gentle, it was never harsh. He showed absolutely no emotion toward her, friendly or hostile.

Almost everything her captor did during the march forced Elizabeth to re-evaluate her situation. His reactions to the attention paid to her hair by his companions proved the most interesting and troubling. She had always been proud of the long, bright red tresses, but soon realized they were turning into a curse. Not an hour went by without some passing warrior pointing to or touching her hair and making some comment she couldn't understand. Her captor's responses left her bewildered. If the passing warrior made a comment but didn't touch the hair, her captor would usually make some remark that caused both men to laugh. If someone touched her hair, there would be a warning of some sort, but that, too, usually ended up with both men smiling.

On one occasion, however, the touch almost led to violence. An especially malicious-looking warrior grabbed her hair and twisted it tightly. Crying out in pain and anger, she lashed out and slapped the man. Stunned, the warrior drew his knife and held it menacingly in front of her face. Just as quickly, her captor drew his own knife and touched the point to the other man's throat. He said a few slow, obviously threatening words to the offender, who, after a few moments, let go of her hair and lowered his knife. The two men stared at each other, each one looking for some weakness in the other. Before it could come to blows, however, one of the chiefs walked up and shouted at both men, who then backed off a step and slowly sheathed their knives. The warrior who had grabbed Elizabeth's hair muttered what she took to be an insult at her captor, then turned and walked away. She looked at her captor. He was smiling slightly, a satisfied look on his face.

What Elizabeth couldn't decipher, through all these incidents concerning her hair, was whether her captor was protecting her personally, or just a future trophy. It was no use asking; she couldn't speak the Seminole tongue. The warriors seemed obsessed with taking scalps, and hers would obviously be a coveted prize. Would he kill her just to obtain a trophy he could brag about? Was that all she was worth?

Other conversations her captor had with fellow warriors were just as perplexing. Most were completely unintelligible to her and what she could make out from gestures and expressions only increased the confusion. The most troubling exchanges often began with a lewd gesture by a warrior, which usually elicited some humorous response from her captor. And although he made no advances toward her while on the trail, she could never be sure how she would be used once they reached their destination. The thought made her shudder. Her body belonged to Johnny. Would she be able to protect it?

Jack Dill and his five companions reached the Chattahoochee River midmorning on the day after the attack. Seeing the river and being able to cross it, however, were two different things. Uncountable eons of flow had cut steep bluffs in the river bank, and it was going to prove difficult for the three wounded men to make it down to the water's edge. They assumed there would be Indian paths that led down to the river, but they had no idea where they were, and were hesitant to follow well-used paths for fear of running into hostiles. There was also the problem of finding a suitable place to exit the river on the other side. Just because there was a path to the river on one side, it didn't necessarily mean there was a corresponding path on the opposite shore.

Then, of course, there was the problem of actually crossing the river. Although they all could swim, three were suffering from injuries that would make swimming difficult, and all were exhausted and hungry. The current, though not especially strong, was still swift enough to be an obstacle of its own. It was also the first day of December, the water was cold, and building a fire was out of the question. What they needed were a guide and a boat, but neither were likely to be found.

After working their way along the heavily wooded bluff for almost an hour, they located a gully that appeared to lead down to the river. Looking over to the far shore, they spotted a valley in the opposite bluff that seemed to be a natural landing. Unfortunately, it was a little north of where they were standing, and the current would be carrying them south. Still, it was the most promising site they had seen, so they decided to give it a try.

On their trek from the site of the attack, the six men had found little that was edible, and only one item that they felt might be useful. Earlier that morning they had found the scavenged remains of a doe that appeared to have been killed some weeks previous. Why the hunter had left the skin after removing it was a mystery, but they were thankful he had. After scraping it clean with the knife, Gray bundled it up and threw it over his shoulder. He wasn't quite sure what he intended to do with it, but a large piece of deer hide could always prove useful, especially if they were going to have to cross a river.

It was a difficult descent into the gully. The trees were small and tangled, and it was hard to find a path through them. Although not too steep, the slope was sharp enough to make them worry about slipping. This was an especial concern for the wounded men, so their uninjured fellows kept close by their side, ready to lend a steadying hand if needed. Both Dill and Thompson stumbled a few times, but both managed to stifle any shouts of pain. Still wary of being discovered by an Indian scouting party, the soldiers worked their way down in silence, except for the occasional whispered profanity.

When they at last reached the river's edge, Gray unbundled the deerskin and tossed it on the ground. "Time to get as naked as the day your Momma dropped you, lads. The last thing we need on the other side of the river is wet clothing."

Dill sat down on the riverbank and hung his head. "Boys, I need to rest." His arm was throbbing, his stomach was empty, and his mind was still filled with visions of Annie, Elizabeth, Johnny, and Captain Vashon. He knew that as sergeant he should be more commanding, but he just didn't have it in him at the moment. Gray had sensed as much and had taken over as the group's leader. Dill was both grateful and relieved.

Gray nodded. "Aye, we all do. But not too long. Fort Scott's not getting any closer." As the men took their seats on the moss-covered ground, each one retreated into his own thoughts of the massacre and of the path ahead. James began to remove the blood-soaked bandages from his hands. Examining the ragged stumps that had once been fingers, he wondered how he would make a living after he left the army. Thompson stared at a thin stream of blood running down his leg. The bleeding had stopped overnight, but even with the aid of the crude crutch Gorman had fashioned, the task of climbing down the hill had reopened the wound. Getting in the water would only make things worse. Still, there was little choice.

Gorman began to feel a sense of guilt for having survived the attack. Why had he been spared while all the others had been taken? What had any of them, even the survivors, done to deserve this? Should he have fought on, or had he been too quick to jump into the water and swim to safety? He thought of his slain friends and of the women who had been killed and mutilated. Could he have done anything to prevent it?

Wheadon picked up a stick and began to absent-mindedly probe the mud at the edge of the small creek he was sitting next to. They had all taken a drink, but none of them had enjoyed any substantial amount of food for the past day and a half. As he turned the mud over, his eye caught sight of a shiny brown shell, about an inch and a half long. Picking it up, he smiled. "Mussels. Toss me that knife, Gray." Prying the shell open, he cut the meat out and swallowed it. He smiled broadly. "Dinner is served, lads."

He probed the mud with his hands and soon found another. Opening it up, he handed it to James. The others took the cue and also began to dig. When one of the creatures was found, it was handed to Wheadon, who opened it and passed it on to whomever was next in line. By the time the mussels became scarce, each man had consumed about a dozen. It wasn't much, but it was better than being hungry.

Gray began to cut some small saplings and lengths of vine with the knife. After fashioning a crude boat-shaped frame and wrapping the skin around it, he told the others to roll up their uniforms and toss them inside. Naked and shivering, the six men ventured toward the water's edge, looked up and down the river to make sure there were no Indian canoes coming, and then waded in. It was shockingly cold, and they all halted momentarily before plunging in. Dill went first, with Gray alongside him. Gorman helped Thompson into the water, keeping close to him, always keeping an eye on the wounded leg. James pushed off next, his swimming little hampered by the loss of his fingers. Wheadon came last, pushing the small deerskin boat before him, making sure no water got in.

It was not an especially wide river, no more than a quarter mile across, but their general fatigue and the strength of the current made the swim difficult. They tried to swim against the current so they would come ashore closer to the landing, but it proved impossible. When they finally reached the east side, they rested in the cover of some large trees, and then began to swim along the bank, working their way toward the landing. At last, after having spent a good half hour in the water, they were able to crawl onto dry land.

Although fully exposed for any passing Indian to see, the exhausted men sat on the dirt, letting the noonday sun dry their skin and warm their bodies. After dressing and resting for about half an hour, they resumed their march, heading almost due east. After traveling no more than a mile, they came upon another river, nearly as wide as the Chattahoochee. Gray smiled. "It's the Flint, and right where we want it to be. It'll run north for a bit, and then start to turn east. The fort's only six or seven miles away, boys."

The warriors who had attacked Lieutenant Scott's boat arrived at the Mikasuki villages on the morning of the second day after the battle. The villagers, alerted by runners, were gathered outside the central town, anxious to welcome their victorious kinsmen. When the two groups came into sight of each other, joyous shouts and yells came from both sides. As Elizabeth and her light-haired captor broke into the open, the crowd, mostly curious women and children, began to gather around them. Some of them tried to reach out and touch her hair, others poked sticks at her. Most of them were laughing and jeering. Yet if any approached too close or looked as if they might do her real harm, Elizabeth's captor shouted a warning and shook his gun at them. He was still protecting her, but to what end, she did not know.

When the excitement and novelty wore down a bit, the man who had taken Elizabeth prisoner called out to a pair of older women. When they came close, he spoke to them in a stern and commanding voice, and pointed to one of the cabins. He then looked at Elizabeth. "You will go to the lodge of the unclean women."

Elizabeth was stunned. He spoke English! She had so many questions to ask, she didn't know where to start. She started to stammer something, but the warrior shouted, "Silence! Do not speak!" Never one to let someone tell her what to do, she started to speak again. This time his look turned exceedingly angry, and he raised his hand as if to strike her. "Silence! I will tell you when to speak!"

She cowered slightly and looked away. Satisfied that he'd gotten his message across, he told her, "These women will take you to the lodge of the unclean women, those with their moon-bleed." He saw a quizzical look on her face. "You are white. You are unclean." The angry look left his face. "You will be safe there."

The two women grabbed her by the arms and led her toward the cabin. As they approached the dwelling, one of them called out to the occupants, and a young woman came to the door. The older one spoke to the young one in a commanding tone, no doubt relaying orders from the yellow-haired warrior. The young one nodded and stepped aside as the older women nudged Elizabeth toward the door.

There were about twenty women of childbearing age within the building, a few with suckling children at their breasts. They momentarily looked up, and some gave her a contemptuous look, while others muttered something she couldn't understand. Within a minute, all went back to their domestic chores. The young woman who had brought her in pointed to a vacant corner of the cabin and motioned for her to sit. Elizabeth asked, "Does anyone speak English?" but no one answered. Realizing there was nothing else to do, she went to the corner and took a seat on the dirt floor. The young woman soon approached carrying a bowl and a wooden spoon. Elizabeth took them and stared at the contents of the bowl. It appeared to be a watery gruel with bits of meat and vegetables mixed in. It didn't smell bad, so she took a small mouthful. It was a bit distasteful but not revolting, so she leaned back and began to eat.

Outside the cabin, toward the center of the town, Elizabeth's captor was approached by Neamathla. "Lah-nee-tay, I am glad to see you have returned unharmed." He glanced toward the cabin where Elizabeth was. "You have taken a fine captive. What shall you do with her? Take her to wife? Sell her to the Creeks? Ransom her to the whites?"

Yellow Tom shrugged. "The choice may not be mine, Uncle." He motioned toward one of the cabins at the other end of the compound. There, the warrior who had threatened Elizabeth the previous day was talking to a wailing woman. "My captive slew

Soo-lee Tustennuggee, and now Efa-Hadjo will claim her as satisfaction for the death of his brother. He has spoken to Homathlemico, who will no doubt call a council to decide which of us has claim to her."

Neamathla was surprised. "The little white woman slew Soo-lee Tustennuggee?"

Tom smiled. "She is stronger than she looks. There is a brave spirit in this one."

The six survivors continued on their way to Fort Scott. They were traversing relatively level pine woods, and had it been a normal march across such open terrain, they'd have covered the distance in two or three hours. As it was, their progress was much slower. Thompson's leg was not doing well, which limited the pace of everyone else. Gorman had found a strong hickory sapling that had split into two branches, and managed to make it into a usable crutch. The "Y" at the top was a bit narrow, but he had wrapped it in leather from the deerskin and covered it with some of the cloth from the cut-up coat, making it tolerable for Thompson to put his weight on. The one thing the crutch couldn't relieve was the fatigue. For every half hour spent walking, the group spent a quarter hour resting.

Thompson wasn't the only one who needed to rest occasionally. Although the two pairs of shoes were shared as much as possible, that still meant four men were walking barefoot. There was also the problem of food. Other than the occasional berry bush or nut they found, there simply wasn't anything to eat. Every now and then they ventured down to the water's edge to get a drink, but when they probed for mussels, they came up empty handed. They stumbled across a dead raccoon, but the maggots were already feasting on it, and they had no intention of attempting to make a fire anyway. Several deer were spotted, but all the men could do was stare at them and dream of roast venison.

The group also felt it was safer to avoid open areas, so they skirted clearings, not wanting to be caught in the open should a hostile warrior appear. Of course chances were just as good a warrior this close to Fort Scott would be friendly, but there was no way to find out without exposing themselves. There was also the knowledge that Indian loyalties could quickly change. Yesterday's ally could be today's sworn enemy. All in all, it was best to avoid contact with anyone but a white man.

Late in the day they came to a wide stream. It was only about two hundred feet across, but looked too deep to wade. They knew Fort Scott was no more than a mile or two away, but for the moment, the stream seemed an insurmountable obstacle. They would have to swim it, and with the sun getting low, they might not dry out until after dark. They had all suffered from the cold on the previous night and didn't want to make this night any worse than it promised to be. On the night before, they had slept in a deciduous forest and had covered themselves with the abundant autumn leaves as a sort of blanket. Tonight there would be nothing but pine needles to sleep on. They all agreed that the remaining hour or so of daylight should be spent building some sort of shelter to protect them from the morning frost. By huddling close together under adequate cover, they could survive the night and hopefully reach Fort Scott in the morning.

Elizabeth remained in the lodge, surrounded by other women, but very much alone. It was a simple dirt-floored log cabin, not that much different from what a white settler might build. The primary difference was in the roof. White men tended to cut wooden shingles, while the Indians preferred thatching with palmetto fronds. There was also no solid door on the Indian cabin, just a low entrance that forced a person to bend over as she came in. Considering that none of the other women in the lodge paid her more than minimal attention, Elizabeth decided the isolation was intentional. Several times she had seen one of the other women gazing at her intently, when they thought she wouldn't notice. She knew that many of them despised her, yet she felt in no real danger. Obviously, her captor had given strict orders concerning her treatment.

It wasn't until late the second day that anyone came to see Elizabeth. She recognized the voice of her light-haired captor calling from outside the cabin, though she had no idea what he was saying. The young woman who had attended her the day before motioned for her to go outside. Elizabeth rose and stepped out into the sunlight.

Her captor pointed to an open patch of ground off to the side of the lodge. "Come, sit here. We shall talk."

As they both took a seat on the dirt she tried to be friendly and gave him what she considered a compliment, saying, "You speak good English."

He laughed and responded in a voice that sounded as if it had come straight from the Highlands. "Aye, lass, as true as any Scotsman you're likely to meet." The voice changed slightly, and out came, "Or perhaps you'd like a wee bit o' the Irish." He then tilted his head back and spoke in the condescending tone of an aristocrat. "Or, if your ladyship would prefer, I am quite eloquent in the King's English." The accent and expression then shifted to something more common. "Or blimey, Miss, maybe something from down 'ere at the east end of old London Town." His expression then changed to one of slight distaste. "Hell, Missy, I can even talk like one o' them damn Georgia boys."

She laughed, something she'd had no reason to do for the past four days. Yet he wasn't finished. "Yo también hablo un poco español." He then recited a few sentences in one of the Seminole dialects. Although she couldn't understand a word of it, she knew from the expression on his face and the gestures he made that this was his native tongue and the one he was most proud of.

She was amazed at his command of language and asked, "Who are you? Do you have a name?"

His facial expression reverted to the one of indifference she'd gotten accustomed to while marching from the site of the attack, and his voice changed to an odd mixture of British and Indian influences. "No, Miss, we Indians are not intelligent enough to give our people names."

She realized how stupid and insulting the question sounded and apologized. "I'm sorry. Will you please tell me your name, sir?"

He smiled again. "Which one would you like? Let's see, there's the one my people gave me as a child, Lah-nee-tay Sakah Sischeh." Knowing she neither understood what it meant nor could easily remember it, he took a finger and flipped a lock of his hair. "Yellow Hair." She nodded, and he went on. "Then there is the name my father gave me, Thomas Campbell, though I much rather prefer Tommy. Next there is the name my people gave me when I became a man, Lah-nee-tay Fixico, which means Fearless Yellow Warrior." He leaned forward and lowered his voice, as if passing along a secret. "They don't know that 'yellow' is the white man's word for a coward." He sat upright again and told her, "You can call me what the British soldiers do: Yellow Tom."

She smiled at him. For the first time in days, she began to feel relatively safe. Surely someone as friendly as Yellow Tom would not let her come to harm. "Very well, Mr. Yellow Tom, you may call me Elizabeth."

His face turned serious. "No. That is a white name. You are with the Seminole now, and shall have a Seminole name." He looked at her for a moment, trying to think of a suitable name. A satisfied look came across his face as he announced, "Kitisci Bess. Red Bess. Like the old queen they speak of in England, Elizabeth. Good Queen Bess!" Although she was not willing to part with her true name, she had come to realize that Yellow Tom did not like being challenged. For her own safety, she decided it was best to accept his edicts.

Feeling more relaxed and hoping he would be forthright with his answers, she asked, "What is to become of me?"

The indifference returned to his face. "I cannot say. Another warrior has laid claim to you, and a council will decide which of us shall have you."

She was stunned. "What? How can that be? You're the one who captured me. No one else laid a hand on me!"

He shook his head. "The warrior you killed, Soo-lee Tustennuggee; his family lays claim to you as satisfaction for his death."

"But it was an accident! Anyway, he was going to kill me."

Tom shrugged. "A white woman's death is of no consequence to us. A warrior's is."

"You can't let this happen!"

"If the council rules it so, I cannot stop it. The warrior who took hold of your hair and drew his knife when we were on the trail is Efa-Hadjo, the brother of Soo-lee Tustennuggee. He is a warrior who is greatly feared and has many followers among the Red Sticks." There was no sign of remorse in his voice, no indication that he would dispute the decision of the council.

Her heart sank. "What will become of me if the council rules in his favor?"

Yellow Tom looked her straight in the eye and did not withhold the truth. "He has already said that he will have your scalp and build a fire around you, and the louder you cry in pain, the harder he will laugh at you." He watched the color drain from her face. "And he will do it."

Jack Dill and the other survivors climbed out of their crude shelter early in the morning, stripped off their clothes, and easily crossed the stream that had seemed such an obstacle the day before. They moved on at a slow, steady pace, knowing that unless some strange tragedy befell them, they would reach Fort Scott sometime that day. Most of all, they wanted to take it easy on Thompson. He had weakened considerably since the march began, and could put no weight on his injured leg. He needed to see the surgeon as soon as possible, but he didn't need to be pushed to the point of collapse.

It was near noontime when they heard shouts and the crashing of timber. From long experience, all of them knew it was the sound of an army logging party. They all moved forward with purpose in their strides, even Thompson, who winced with every step, but would not slow down. They heard another tree fall, and clearly heard the voices of some of the soldiers, but could not yet see them. During the momentary silence that occurred after the tree fell, Dill and his men began to call out, and Gray and Wheadon broke into a run.

Gray reached the clearing first, but froze when he saw several muskets pointed at him. Then he smiled and began to laugh uncontrollably. The soldiers slowly lowered their weapons, and one of them rushed forward. It was John Stuart.

When Gray saw Stuart's face, he stopped laughing and took a deep breath. Before he could speak, Wheadon came into view. Falling to his knees, Wheadon clasped his hands and looked toward Heaven. "Thank thee, Lord, for delivering us from evil, amen."

Stuart looked at the two men, not knowing what to think. What were they doing here? Where did they come from? What had happened to them? Before he could ask, he saw Dill and the others come into view. Thompson, realizing the journey was over, stumbled a few steps and then collapsed. Stuart quickly turned to one of the soldiers standing by. "Run back to the fort and sound the alarm. Bring a litter for Thompson. Go!"

Stuart was bewildered as he approached his closest friend. The last he knew, Dill and Elizabeth were both on one of Muhlenberg's boats. For Dill to be wandering wounded through the Georgia woods could only mean there had been some sort of attack. He also knew that his friend would not have left Elizabeth unless he absolutely had to. A sickening realization began to sweep over him. The look on Dill's face only seemed to confirm it. Stuart stopped moving and started to gasp for air. Dill quickly stepped forward and put a hand on Stuart's shoulder. "She's alive, Johnny, she's alive."

Stuart closed his eyes and breathed easy. "Thank God, Jack. I saw your face and just knew . . ."

Dill could not look his friend in the eye. "She's been taken by the Indians, Johnny. She's a captive."

Yellow Tom had told Elizabeth very little after he'd announced that a council would be deciding her fate. He'd told her the council would meet at noon on the following day, and that while all the elders would be part of the council, only three chiefs would actually vote, but that in reality, only one would make the final decision. When she asked why, he explained that one of the three chiefs was his uncle Neamathla, who would surely support him, while another was the Red Stick leader Homathlemico, who would just as surely stand behind Efa-Hadjo. The deciding vote would fall to Kinnachee, headman of the villages there at Miccosukee Lake. As to how Kinnachee would vote, Tom had no idea. True, he was a Mikasuki and therefore a kinsman to Neamathla, Tom, and all the displaced Fowltown Indians, but he was also intent on cementing the relationship with the Red Sticks, whose alliance he would need if they were to fight the Americans. If nothing else, Kinnachee prided himself on being hard to predict. He felt an immense advantage in doing the unexpected.

When Elizabeth pressed for more details, Yellow Tom rose to his feet and said, "I have nothing more to say. All your questions will be answered after the council has ruled and your fate is known. Go back into the lodge. You will be sent for when all is ready." She tried to read some insight into her situation from his face, but could sense nothing. Indifference and nonchalance seemed to be the emotions he preferred to display, and she began to feel as if it were just that, a display.

For the moment, there was little for her to do but think. She had been given a pair of moccasins to sew, and she performed the task as instructed, though with little care as to how they turned out. She realized they were probably intended for her own feet, but also knew there was only a 50:50 chance she would survive to wear them. Her feelings moved between despair, frustration, and anger. Despair overcame her when she thought about what would happen if the council ruled in favor of Efa-Hadjo. She had seen his face and the anger in his eyes. His only thought was to kill her in as painful and prolonged a manner as he could. Frustration swept over her when she realized her fate was totally out of her hands. There was little or no chance of escape, even at night, as the women had positioned themselves between her and the door, and one of them always kept watch. Frustration would soon give way to anger, of a kind she had never felt before. These people had killed Annie, Nellie, and other of her friends in a most horrible manner. Sooner or later, given the opportunity, she would take satisfaction of her own.

Interspersed with the concerns of her captivity and possible fate were thoughts of Johnny and her father. Did they even know she was alive and a captive? Would they try to rescue or ransom her? Would they come too late to save her? Beyond thinking, there was little else for her to do, and there was simply nothing good to think about. Even if Yellow Tom won out over Efa-Hadjo, there was little to look forward to. She would, in essence, be his slave, and he could do with her as he pleased. As to what that meant, she could only speculate. For the moment, she was simply biding time, and it gnawed at her to know there might be precious little of it left to her.

Late the following morning she heard a voice call out from outside the lodge. The young woman motioned for her to get up and leave. Standing outside was a warrior she was unfamiliar with. He put his hand around her arm and led her toward the village's central fire. On one side of the smoldering fire, seated on a low platform, were three middle-aged men, dressed in their finest regalia. Opposite them were Yellow Tom and Efa-Hadjo, with several feet of open space between them. Her escort led Elizabeth to the open space and motioned for her to sit down. After doing so, she looked at Yellow Tom. He did not look back, and seemed, as ever, quite detached from the proceedings. She then looked at Efa-Hadjo. He gave her a threatening scowl, and then laughed menacingly. Surmising that nothing she might do would have any bearing on her fate, she spit in Efa-Hadjo's direction. He instantly turned angry and reached for his knife, but a quick shout from both Kinnachee and Neamathla stayed his hand. Elizabeth had decided that if Efa-Hadjo wanted satisfaction, she would give him as little as possible. She then looked at Yellow Tom. Although he was still not looking at her, she could detect a slight smile on his face.

Kinnachee's voice boomed, and everyone turned their attention to the three men on the dais. The chief first addressed the crowd, presumably telling them what the gathering was about, and then spoke to Efa-Hadjo, who stood up and began to address the chiefs, the elders, and the assembled townspeople. To Elizabeth it seemed a very long speech, if all he was asking for was possession of her based on his need for satisfaction after the killing of his brother. What worried her most were the shouts of agreement and encouragement from the crowd. She turned to Tom and whispered, "What's he saying?"

He leaned over and told her, "In order for him to show that his claim to you is greater than mine, he must prove how great the loss of his brother was. He is telling everyone about how great a man Buzzard Warrior was, how many enemies he slew, how many scalps he collected, and how fine a hunter he was. The last point is significant, because he has to show that his brother's death will cause great hardship for his family."

"Why do they call him Buzzard Warrior?"

"Whenever he would kill an enemy, he would take a bite out of the man's flesh, chew it up until the blood ran from his lips, then spit it out. He thought it would intimidate his fellow warriors and make them fear him, but I laughed at him and told him it was all for show. He didn't like me after that." She began to realize that the argument might have less to do with her and more to do with an animosity between Tom and Efa-Hadjo.

At length, Efa-Hadjo finished his oration and took his seat. Elizabeth expected Tom to present his case next, but before he could, a voice called out from the back of the crowd. They all turned to see a young man wearing a British officer's uniform. He stepped forward and addressed the chiefs. They nodded in agreement to whatever he was proposing, and then Kinnachee spoke directly to Tom. The light-haired warrior rose up and stepped aside, and the British officer took his place next to Elizabeth. He leaned over and whispered, "My name is Robert Ambrister, formerly of His Majesty's Royal Marines. I have prevailed upon the chiefs to let me interpret while Yellow Tom speaks, and to protect you from our belligerent friend here."

A glimmer of hope ran through Elizabeth's mind. "You have influence with these people? Can you help me?"

He shook his head. "Sorry, Miss. I never take sides in Indian disputes. It's the fastest way I can think of to lose what little trust they have in me."

She was wondering why a British officer was even in Florida, but before she could ask, Tom began to speak. Ambrister listened, and then leaned over toward Elizabeth. "My Seminole is not that good, but I can give you the gist of what he's on about. First off, he's telling them it's long been the tradition of his people that a captive's fate is in the hands of the captor, and that Efa-Hadjo is insulting them and wasting their time. Good point, but if that argument held any weight, we wouldn't be sitting here, would we? Ah, now he's getting down to the finer points, disputing how great a warrior old Buzzard Breath really was."

"Did he really call him that?"

"Not exactly, but just as insulting." He laughed, finding Tom's sarcasm amusing. "He says Buzzard Breath claimed a lot of kills but had few scalps to prove it. Most of them were supposedly taken in battles with the Americans where the Red Sticks lost, so maybe he didn't have a chance to lift the scalps. Now he wonders if maybe the Buzzard dropped them while running from the battlefield. Then he asks just how many losing battles a warrior has to be in before they call him 'great.'" They watched as Tom pointed at Elizabeth. "Oh! Now he wants to know just how great a warrior the Buzzard was if a little thing like you could so easily do him in. Well, if there wasn't bad blood between Yellow Tom and Efa-Hadjo before, there certainly will be now." Elizabeth looked at the crowd and began to feel more assured. Many of those who had been shouting their support for Efa-Hadjo were now supporting Tom. For them, the argument over whether she should live or die was nothing more than an amusement.

Ambrister listened intently as Tom continued. "Now he's bringing Buzzard Breath's abilities as a hunter into question. He wonders why, if he was such a good hunter, was his debt so high with the traders? He asks why, if he was such a great provider, are his squaw and little one always so hungry? Then he wants to know what kind of father and husband leaves his old squaw and little ones in Alabama to be captured or killed by the Americans."

Elizabeth cast a glance at Efa-Hadjo. The man was seething. The Englishman went on, obviously enjoying Tom's speech. "Now he's making the logical arguments. He says that on the one hand, Efa-Hadjo and Buzzard Breath's new squaw wants you to replace the person they've lost, but if Efa-Hadjo puts you to death like he's promised to, what possible benefit can that be to their clan? Then he says that once you are dead, you'll have no value. You cannot be sold to another tribe, you cannot be ransomed, and you cannot bear him many warriors to make his people proud."

The last line made Elizabeth's jaw drop. "I shall do no such thing! I'm a married woman."

Ambrister chuckled. "Well, that will be between you and him, Miss. Right now I'd worry more about staying alive than anything else you might be concerned with. Ah, I see he's starting to wind down. Well, if this were a proper English court of law, I'd say he's won his case. Unfortunately for you, Miss, this isn't a proper English court of law. Those chiefs are going to do what they want, no matter what anybody says." He rose to his feet as Tom approached. "Well, good luck, Miss. I truly hope to see you in the morning."

As Tom sat down next to her, she looked at him in a different light. What were his intentions for her if the chiefs ruled in his favor? Would he really sell her to another tribe like a common slave? Did he actually intend to take her as his wife? Up until his speech, she had looked upon him as a savior of sorts. Was he nothing more than a slaver and a rapist?

A number of lesser chiefs and elders stood up and addressed the council, as did the Buzzard Warrior's widow. The council listened respectfully, nodded their heads, but made no sign of real commitment. When all were done speaking, the chiefs began their deliberations. She could see that Neamathla and Homathlemico were doing their best to convince Kinnachee to go one way or the other. At times he seemed to agree with one or dispute the other, but never gave an indication that he was being swayed completely to one side. Elizabeth was nearly at the point of screaming at him to make up his mind. It was, after all, her life they were arguing about. Didn't she have the right to say something about it? Then she felt Tom put his hand on her leg. She looked over at him. He shook his head slightly. Speaking out would offend the chiefs and probably force Kinnachee to decide against her.

Then Ambrister approached the platform. He spoke respectfully, in a low tone that no one else could hear, making gestures that seemed to indicate he was offering an option they may not have considered. The three men listened, nodding slightly. Homathlemico seemed to make an objection, but the Englishman gently countered it. Ambrister then stepped away. Kinnachee closed his eyes for a moment, deep in thought. Then all indecision seemed to leave him. He quickly consulted with Neamathla and Homathlemico, who nodded in agreement.

Kinnachee came to his feet to announce the decision. Tom interpreted. "Brothers and sisters! We have come to one mind in this matter. The arguments of Lah-nee-tay Fixico and Efa-Hadjo are both good and with much merit. We have listened to those who have spoken in favor of one or the other, and none could convince our hearts that one course of action was more just than the other. Our minds could not come to an agreement, and we knew not how to resolve the issue. Then our friend from across the sea offered us a path that appears just and proper. Let the woman decide her own fate."

Even Tom looked surprised at the announcement. Ambrister approached Elizabeth and said in a low voice, "I have given you an opportunity, Miss, not a guarantee. The choice is obvious, but remember, all choices have consequences." He then turned and motioned toward Kinnachee. The chief was speaking, and Elizabeth soon realized he was addressing her. Ambrister interpreted. "He says you must choose. Will you go with Yellow Tom or with Efa-Hadjo? The choice is yours."

Elizabeth looked at Efa-Hadjo, who was busily conferring with Homathlemico and the Buzzard Warrior's widow. Then she looked at Tom, who seemed almost unconcerned. Ambrister had said the choice was obvious, but there would be consequences. She took a quick look at Ambrister's face and knew it was useless to ask what those consequences might be. Kinnachee barked a command, which she understood to be a demand for her answer.

Keeping her eyes on Kinnachee, she turned slightly toward the Englishman. "Tell the chief I shall go with Yellow Tom."

Almost immediately there was a shout from Efa-Hadjo, who stepped forward, pulling Buzzard Warrior's widow by the wrist. Addressing Kinnachee, he pointed first to Elizabeth then to the widow. Kinnachee nodded his assent. Once again, Ambrister interpreted. "The widow claims she has received no satisfaction for the death of Buzzard Breath and demands the right to challenge your life against hers."

Elizabeth looked at Tom. "What does he mean?"

"A fight to the death."

Elizabeth was stunned. "Women do not fight to the death!"

Tom corrected her, saying, "White women do not fight to the death. You are among the Seminole now. If you wish to survive, you must live by our rules. Refuse the challenge, and you will be put to death."

Elizabeth looked at the widow. She was at least ten years older, twenty pounds heavier, and fifty times more dangerous looking than Elizabeth. Ambrister leaned towards her and said, "An opportunity, Miss, not a guarantee. It was the best I could do for you."

There was really no choice. Certain death in some horrible fashion, or possible death while fighting for her life. "Tell the chief I accept the challenge."

As soon as Ambrister said the words, the villagers started to form a large circle in front of the platform where Kinnachee and Neamathla sat. Efa-Hadjo tossed his knife and tomahawk toward the center of the circle, and Tom began to do the same. Elizabeth stopped him, saying, "The club, not the tomahawk." Tom usually carried a stout wooden war club, nearly two feet long, with a thick shaft and a massive round head. It seemed more intimidating than the tomahawk, and she desperately needed something to make her look more imposing to her opponent. She also felt she could use it more effectively than the tomahawk. One of the favorite games for the boys in Baton Rouge had been a stick and ball game called Skinny. It involved a lot of running and jostling, which Elizabeth had no use for, but it also required a ball to be hit with a stick. Her brother Robert loved the running, pushing, and shoving, but with his deformed left arm, he could not use the bat to hit the ball. Somehow he had talked the other boys into allowing Elizabeth to take his place when it came to the hitting. She had actually gotten quite good at it. She even enjoyed the household chore of beating the rugs. The war club was something she could handle.

She turned to Ambrister and asked, "Are there any rules?"

He shook his head. "Only one: Kill your opponent." He then added, "This is no time to be a lady."

Tom offered another bit of advice. "She is angry. You need to be smart."

The fight almost ended before it had a chance to really begin. As Elizabeth bent over to pick up Tom's knife, her opponent lunged, her knife held high, ready to plunge into the white woman's back. Forgetting about the knife on the ground, Elizabeth quickly spun around, swinging the club as hard as she could. More by luck than design, the head of the club smashed into the widow's left hand, sending the tomahawk flying. Elizabeth realized she was now at an advantage and may have even broken some bones in the other woman's hand. She remembered how her father had always taught his troops to fix bayonets and charge when confronted by Indians. Taking the initiative, she slowly approached her adversary, swinging the club with both hands, forcing her opponent to retreat.

The widow knew that as long as she remained out of range of the club she was safe. She also knew she could not kill the white woman unless she got close enough to use the knife. Exactly how to use the knife was another problem. All she had ever used one for was to skin game, prepare food, or for other domestic chores.

She had never used one to kill anyone or to defend herself from harm.

Elizabeth kept up the pressure, but could not get close enough to strike the woman. She was also aware that while the club might cause pain or break a few bones, the only way it was likely to kill the woman was with a firm blow to the head. That wasn't going to be easy.

The widow was getting angry. She wanted to kill the white woman, but could not get within striking distance. Yet she knew enough to be patient. The frail white woman was working much harder than she. Swinging the club took effort; dodging it was easy. Sooner or later her opponent would tire. Then she would attack and bury the blade deep within the breast of the woman who had slain her husband. She would be satisfied.

Elizabeth was swinging the club less now, opting to hold it aloft in a threatening position while taking deep breaths. The Indian woman occasionally slashed the air with her knife, but always a club's length away. This could go on forever, if they both continued with the same tactics.

The widow was watching, waiting for Elizabeth to tire. Then she saw what she was looking for. The white woman stepped back a bit, took a deep breath, and lowered the club slightly. It was time. Screaming at the top of her lungs, she lunged.

Elizabeth swung the club with all her might. The Indian woman had taken the bait. Elizabeth felt the club head smash into the woman's ribs and thought she heard them crack. The widow fell to her knees. Elizabeth swung again, this time straight into her enemy's chest. The widow dropped her knife and fell on to her back, gasping for breath. Elizabeth quickly dropped to her knees and picked up her adversary's knife. She remembered Ambrister telling her it was, "No time to be a lady." She remembered Tom's advice to, "Live by our rules." She plunged the knife into the other woman's chest.

She heard shouts from the spectators. Looking around, she tried to understand what they were saying. The words were unintelligible, but the gestures were clear. They wanted her to take the other woman's scalp. Getting to her feet, she turned to Yellow Tom and handed him the knife. "White women do not take trophies."

8

2 Dec. '17
Ft. Scott, Flint River, Georgia

To:
Hon. Geo. Graham, Sec. of War, Acting
Washington City

Sir:

It is my painful duty to report an affair of a more serious and decisive nature than has heretofore occurred, and which leaves no doubt of the necessity for the immediate application of military force and active measures on our part. A large party of Seminole Indians, on the 30th ultimo, formed an ambuscade upon the Apalachicola River, a mile below the junction of the Flint and Chattahoochee, and attacked one of our boats ascending the river. The unprovoked attack killed, wounded, or took the greater part of the detachment, consisting of forty men, commanded by Lieutenant R. W. Scott of the 4th Infantry. There were also on board, killed or taken, seven women, the wives of soldiers. Six men of the detachment escaped, and after much hardship, have returned here to Ft. Scott. Three of them were wounded.

The supply convoy commanded by Major Muhlenberg has been detained near the mouth of the Apalachicola due to hostile fire and a lack of wind. I shall immediately strengthen Major Muhlenberg with another boat secured against the enemy's fire. He will, therefore, move up with safety, keeping near the middle of the river. I shall, moreover, take up position with my principal force at the junction of the rivers, near the line, and shall attack any force that may attempt to intercept our vessels as they ascend.

I feel persuaded that the order of the President prohibiting an attack upon the Indians below the Florida line has reference only to the past, and not to the present or future outrages, such as the one just now perpetrated. Our nation is now placed strictly within the pale of natural law, where self defence is sanctioned by the privilege of self preservation. Of the force engaged, the survivors differ in opinion, but all agree that the number was very considerable, extending about one hundred and fifty yards along the shore, on the edge of a swamp or thick woods.

I am assured by the friendly chiefs that the hostile warriors of every town upon the Chattahoochee prepared canoes and pushed off down the river to join the Seminoles as soon as the account of my movement from the Alabama reached them. The Indians now remaining upon the Chattahoochee, I have reason to believe, are well disposed. Several friendly chiefs have offered me their services, with their warriors, to go against the Seminoles. I have promised to give them notice of the time that may be fixed for my departure, and then to accept their services.

I am, respectfully,
Your Most Obedient Servant,
Edmund P. Gaines,
Maj. Gen. U. States Army

Lingering grey clouds hung over Washington, D.C., left over from a storm that had passed through the day before, dumping at least an inch of rain onto the dirt streets of the capital. The trees, having lost their leaves for the winter, braced their skeletal limbs against a cold northwest wind, while the city's residents turned up their collars and pulled tight their hats.

Inside the presidential mansion, the mood was no better than the weather, despite the fact that Christmas was but a few days away. President James Monroe and his most important cabinet members had come together to discuss a letter that had just arrived from General Gaines. They were gathered in one of the smaller rooms of the mansion, the Green Drawing Room. Monroe had chosen the room because its small size made it easier for the fireplace to heat. Besides, it was one of the few places in the mansion where workmen weren't present. The building had been burnt by the British during the War of 1812, and there had been a concerted effort to repair it before Monroe's inauguration in March, 1817. The promise had been kept, but the final details seemed to drag on forever. Monroe would be happy if he never smelled paint again.

The president considered the three other men seated around the low, marble-topped table. Would they offer suggestions that were in the nation's best interest, or would they be thinking of their own political futures? They were, after all, ambitious politicians who were close to the highest office in the land, and it was always a hazy line between patriotism and self-interest.

The man most likely to have the nation's interests in mind was the Secretary of State, John Quincy Adams. The man from Massachusetts certainly had hopes of someday occupying Monroe's position, and was, at present, the president's most likely successor. A strange pattern had developed, one that Monroe had benefited from, so he certainly couldn't speak against it. It had become customary for a president's Secretary of State to rise to the presidency after his predecessor's retirement. Madison had done it after Jefferson, and Monroe had done it after Madison. Then again, as far as Adams was concerned, the office was due him simply because he was the son of John Adams. Monroe thought little of that notion, but at the same time, he did have to admit that Adams was probably the most qualified. No one could argue against the man's intelligence, patriotism, or dedication to duty. As a diplomat, he was second to none. Unfortunately, as a human being, he was close to insufferable.

If anyone was a threat to Adam's ascendancy, it was the Secretary of the Treasury, William H. Crawford. The man was without a doubt a great public servant, having served in the Senate, as Minister to France, and as Secretary of War before assuming the position at Treasury under President Madison. Be that as it may, Monroe knew an ambitious man when he saw one. The Georgian was robust, confident, quick minded, and knew the workings of power politics. He had taken the position of Secretary of the Treasury because he understood that power and money were forever intertwined. Congress could appropriate all the funds it wanted to, but only Crawford could write the check.

Monroe was unsure of his new Secretary of War, John C. Calhoun. The South Carolinian was certainly a young man of towering ambition, but he was also fiercely nationalistic. He had not been the president's first choice for the position, but everyone else Monroe approached had turned it down. No one wanted to take on a Congress that was determined to cut the military to the bare bones. Calhoun, on the other hand, was looking forward to the challenge, and had come up with some very good proposals to actually strengthen the army. Not that Congress would go along with any of them, but to an extent, even a lost battle with the legislature would enhance Calhoun's reputation. But those battles were in the future. Right now, there was an Indian war to fight.

And not just any Indian war. If it had been an Indian nation within the territorial limits of the United States, there would have been no great problem. The Seminoles, however, resided in Spanish Florida, and that meant invading foreign territory. True, Spain and the United States were on reasonably good terms, but the situation would still have to be handled carefully. In truth, he was more worried about the British. During the War of 1812 they had supplied and encouraged the Seminoles and Creeks to make war against the United States. Rumors had it that British agents were still operating in Florida, still causing trouble. The last thing Monroe wanted was another conflict with England.

Monroe began the discussion with the War Department. "Well, Mr. Calhoun, two weeks on the job and you've got a war on your hands. Is the army up to it?" It was meant as a joke; everyone knew the army was never ready for war.

The only one who didn't smile at the remark was Calhoun, who responded in the characteristic tone of a southern aristocrat. "No, sir, it is not, but I can assure you, we shall prevail. General Gaines has insufficient troop strength, inadequate provisions, and a woeful lack of munitions, but all these matters shall be addressed forthwith."

Adams, never one to let a sarcastic comment slip by, quipped, "They don't even have General Gaines."

Crawford looked confused. Although as much a southerner as Calhoun, Crawford had little of the aristocratic bearing cultivated by the older families of the south. His roots were in the frontier, and he spoke in a more common manner. "What's that supposed to mean?"

Adams explained that Gaines had been ordered to the east coast of Georgia to dislodge a band of pirates that had taken over Amelia Island, just across the border in Florida. Due to the fact that even an express rider took three weeks to make the trip between the Georgia wilderness and Washington, there was simply no way to recall the general, who would have received the order soon after the destruction of Lieutenant Scott's command. The pirates, who fancied themselves privateers sailing under the flag of some new South American republic, were disrupting trade in the Gulf Stream and smuggling everything they could get their hands on into the United States, including slaves. It was an indication of how weak the Spanish Governor at St. Augustine was if he couldn't even drive a handful of pirates out of one of his own towns. Adams smiled, enjoying what he assumed would be the general's frustration. "Gaines will be fuming all the way to St. Marys, just in time to receive orders telling him to proceed posthaste back to Fort Scott. That should put him in a fighting mood."

Monroe asked, "Who else did Gaines notify about this massacre?"

Calhoun answered, "General Jackson, of course, and Governor Rabun of Georgia. I also assume he told David Mitchell, the Creek Indian Agent."

Monroe nodded. He could envision the news spreading like wildfire throughout the nation. At every town the express riders stopped in, tongues would immediately start flapping. Newspapers would print any rumor they heard, passing it off as fact. Each story would be slightly exaggerated and embellished until it reached New England, where the papers would report that several hundred people had been killed on Scott's boat, a thousand Indian canoes were ascending the Flint and Chattahoochee, and that all of western Georgia was laid waste. The only good thing about all the overblown rumors and the resulting cries for revenge was that Congress would once again be in love with the army. Perhaps with a little skill and luck, Mr. Calhoun might actually get some of his reforms approved.

The president asked the next obvious question. "So what is our course of action, gentlemen?"

Calhoun offered that, "We have no choice, sir, but to enter Florida and severely chastise the Seminoles. That will, of course, mean raising a sufficient army."

Crawford, the Georgian, proudly noted that, "The Georgia Militia will certainly do their duty."

Adams remarked, "I'm sure they shall." There was a distinct tone of sarcasm in the remark, but Crawford let it pass. Adams held nearly everything in disdain—with the exception of John and Abigail Adams—so there was no need to take the comment personally. The Secretary of State then went on to add, "I shall have to inform the Spanish Embassy, which means I will no doubt have to sit through a long lecture on the rights of sovereign nations. Then I shall receive a formal list of restrictions upon our movements and whatever other such diplomatic niceties Señor Onis and his compadres can devise, which we will, of course, ignore." He shook his head in a slight sign of frustration. "I do so wish they would name their price and let us get on with the negotiations for the place. Perhaps these troubles will hasten His Most Highly Exalted Imbecilic Impotent Catholic Majesty's government toward a decision."

Crawford broached the most delicate subject. "I'll suppose we'll have to put damned Old Hickory in charge."

It was Calhoun's turn to feel as if he'd missed something. "General Gaines can certainly handle the situation."

Adams laughed. "Young man, do you honestly think Jackson's going to give up the chance to invade Florida and slaughter a bunch of Seminoles? He's been dreaming of it since 1814. Unless you're prepared to remove him as commander of the Southern District, I don't think you can stop him."

Monroe expressed his hope that, "Perhaps he will be indisposed."

Adams doubted it would make a difference. "If both he and his beloved Rachel were on their deathbeds he'd go. It's a fight he's been spoiling for, and he won't pass up the opportunity if it's there."

Crawford noted that, "We'll have to issue orders telling him not to bother the Spanish in any way. He dislikes the Spaniards almost as much as he hates the English."

Calhoun pointed out that, "He'll be operating under the same orders as General Gaines, which specifically prohibits molesting the Spanish without first consulting with our office."

Adams smiled. Calhoun may have been extremely intelligent, but he didn't understand Old Hickory. "Jackson has two boxes by his desk. One is labeled 'Orders that suit me,' and the second is for orders that do not. Most of us call that second box a trash basket. He'll be the first man to shout, 'I take full responsibility,' and the first man to shoot anyone who tells him he's responsible for the problems he's created."

Monroe couldn't disagree, but the best he could do was tell Calhoun, "Make sure you send him copies of Gaines's orders." He then asked, "How many men can we raise?"

Calhoun began to think. "We can bring perhaps five hundred regulars to Fort Scott, mostly from the Fourth and Seventh Infantries. If we do put Jackson in charge, he'll no doubt raise a thousand Tennessee Volunteers. We can supplement the force with the Georgia Militia, perhaps a thousand men."

Crawford shook his head. He knew the situation in his home state. "You may get a thousand men, but only about half of them will go to Florida. The other half will cry that they need to stay near home to protect their families, all while collecting their militia pay. If you want fighting men, call out the Lower Creeks. There's bad blood between them and the Seminoles, not to mention the Red Sticks. I can guarantee you a thousand, maybe fifteen hundred warriors."

Calhoun did the math. "That means 3,000 to 3,500 men. I should think that would be more than sufficient, gentlemen. I doubt the savages can count more than 2,000 warriors."

Adams sneered slightly. "Counting is the easy part, Mr. Secretary. Now you have to get all of them to the war front, feed them, clothe them, and somehow get them the munitions they'll need. Then you'll have to convince Congress to pay for it all."

Monroe and the others nodded. The war may have started, but it would be months before the army was able to make any sort of effective response. In the meantime, the Seminoles were free to do as they pleased.

If she had been given the time, Elizabeth would have burst into tears or vomited when she gazed down upon the woman she had just slain. The look of mortal fear was still on the widow's face, and blood was still oozing from the knife wound in her chest. Yet before Elizabeth could truly grasp what had just happened, women and girls rushed around her, grabbed her by the arms, and began to lead her toward the nearby lake. At first she felt fear, thinking they meant to accomplish what the widow couldn't, but then she heard laughing and saw smiles. She was being cheered. The women also began to tear at the tattered remains of her blood-stained dress. By the time they reached the water, she was naked.

Laughing and shouting, the women led her into the cold water of the lake. She began to wonder what would happen next. Would they simply leave her there, forcing her to exit the water totally exposed? The idea mortified her. No one but Johnny should ever see her naked. To her surprise, the women began to scrub her with coarse cloths, paying particular attention to any small cuts they saw. They were in no way trying to be gentle, and while the cleansing may have been painful at times, the frigid water also made it invigorating.

The women then began to lead her out of the water. At first she resisted, not wanting anyone to see her nudity. Then she felt someone wrap a blanket around her. She shivered from the cold, wet cloth, but at least she was no longer exposed for all to see. Then a second and third blanket covered her, and she began to feel warmer. Somehow, she managed to slide the first blanket off, and the relatively dry wool of the second blanket felt wonderful.

The women led her to a cabin and escorted her in. They pulled the blankets away, and she once again stood naked before them. Then one of the women handed her a skirt. It was a simple design of printed cotton, the cloth no doubt imported from England, received in trade for Florida deerskins. It was not as colorful as those worn by the women around her, and she assumed it was someone's castoff. There were no undergarments or pantaloons, and she felt horribly underdressed, but it seemed to be the fashion of the natives, and there was little she could do about it. Another woman then placed a large circle of cloth with a hole in the center over her head. It fell comfortably around her shoulders and hung down to her waist. Again, there were no undergarments, and she realized she was going to have to be careful not to expose her breasts whenever she bent over or raised her arms.

The women then motioned for her to take a seat on the ground. She did, and one of the women drew a knife and began to cut the laces of her soaked and tattered shoes. Elizabeth thought of trying to show the woman how to undo the laces, but a few swift strokes of the blade made the lesson unnecessary. The shoes came off, and the pair of moccasins she'd made went on. They felt surprisingly soft and comfortable. Elizabeth smiled at the women and nodded her approval. She may have been a prisoner, but for the moment, she felt completely welcome.

A familiar voice called from outside the cabin. "Red Bess! When you are ready, come forth. We have much to speak of."

Elizabeth rose, adjusted her dress, and ran her fingers through her hair in a vain attempt to make it presentable. Stepping out of the building, she saw Tom, Mr. Ambrister, and a middle-aged Indian woman. Tom motioned them all toward a small clearing, where they all took a seat on the grass. Elizabeth was careful how she moved, well aware of her exposed condition under the dress. Ambrister chuckled at the awkward motions, to which Elizabeth curtly responded, "I do not wish to encourage any notions of impropriety."

The Englishman laughed. "Miss, there isn't a red-blooded redskin in this village that hasn't already had the notion. But fear not. Old Tommy here shall keep the howling wolves at bay."

Tom nodded. "You are now a member of our clan, and shall be shown the same respect as any woman of my family." He nodded toward the woman by his side. Her features were weathered by the hard years of living life in the wild, but Elizabeth could see that she had once been a lovely woman. The curl of her dark brown hair and softer facial features showed her to be of mixed parentage. The most noticeable thing about her, however, were the innumerable strings of beads around her neck.

Elizabeth had noticed it to be a fashion among the Seminole women, but this lady appeared to have taken the fashion to excess. Still, Elizabeth had to admit they were eye-catching accessories, with different patterns and colors that seemed to dance when she moved. "This is Conowaw, the Bead Woman, my mother. Obey her in all things, and there shall be no cause to punish you or treat you unkindly."

Elizabeth smiled at the woman, but the return gaze was little more than an acknowledgement of the white woman's presence. Elizabeth asked Tom, "Does she speak English?"

"A little. You shall help each other learn the other's tongue." He then turned to Conowaw and said a few words in his native language. The woman nodded, rose, and went to the lodge. Tom again turned his attention to his captive. "You are my prisoner, and your fate has been given to me, as much as the God Spirit will permit it. The cleansing in the lake has washed the whiteness out of you, and your having slain both Soo-lee Tustennuggee and his widow has proven your worth. You are now a Seminole and shall live like one. You will work with the other women, and you shall eat like the other women. When they toil hard, so will you. When they are hungry, you shall also be hungry. When they laugh and feast, you will laugh and feast along with them. Do not try to once again be a white woman, for that will only bring us displeasure and bring punishment upon you. You are among us now, and must forget your old life."

Elizabeth was stunned. In a few short sentences, Tom had erased all her previous life and taken away all the things she held dear, including her husband, her father, and her nation. Angered at the thought, she shouted, "I shall not!"

Tom's gaze turned cold. Ambrister chuckled. "Honestly, Tom, did you really think it would be that easy? She's a white woman; a Yank no less. You can't tell them anything." He then gave Elizabeth a serious look. "Miss, you're in Rome. Do as the Romans do. Displease this man, and he can do whatever he cares to with you." He then made sure she understood the gravity of the situation by emphasizing the most important word he'd just said. "What-ever." He then laughed. "Oh, bloody hell, there's a war coming. We might all be dead in six months. Neither one of you should be too worried about what the far-off future holds. For you, Miss, the best thing to do is to consider yourself a lucky young lady and not do anything stupid that would cause this fine savage gentleman to want to be rid of you, one way or another."

Elizabeth stifled her pride. Ambrister was correct. Right now, the most important thing for her to do was to stay safe. General Gaines would soon be raising an army to avenge the loss of Lieutenant Scott and the others on the boat. As part of that army, both Johnny and her father would not rest until she was rescued. As long as she stayed safe, there was always the chance of rescue or even escape. For the moment, the safest place she could envision was to remain under the care of Yellow Tom. She lowered her gaze to the ground. "I shall bring you no displeasure."

Tom's easy smile returned. "Good. Now go to my mother. She shall put you to work and see to your needs."

Elizabeth may have been willing to swallow her pride a bit, but she wasn't going to be ignored. "You said you would answer all my questions after my fate was decided."

Tom sighed. Ambrister told him, "You might as well get it over with, Tommy."

The Indian reluctantly agreed. "Very well, Red Bess, what have you to ask?"

He was expecting questions about his heritage, his proficiency in English, or what he intended to do with her, but her first question was, "Why did you save me?"

He really hadn't thought about it. When he had taken part in the attack on the boat, he was as willing to slaughter whites as any other warrior. What had prevented him from killing this particular woman? He looked at her closely for a moment, and then a warm smile of remembrance came to his lips. "You reminded me of Miss Alice."

Even Ambrister, who knew something of his friend's background, was surprised. "Alice?"

Tom was enjoying the memory. "The loveliest, most caring woman I shall ever know. The hair, the face. You could well have been her sister." He saw the curiosity on both his companions' faces. "My governess," he explained, but it was obvious that a more detailed account was necessary. "My father was a merchant in Charleston before the American rebels took power. When the war started he remained loyal to the king and fled with his family to St. Augustine. After the war ended, he stayed on in Florida, working at the Panton and Leslie store on the St. Johns. He was sent as factor to one of the Mikasuki villages, and there he took my mother to wife, and I was born soon after.

"When I was about four years of age, my father went to England to conduct some business and thought it would be good to take me with him. 'To learn some proper manners,' he would say. It was only supposed to be for about a year. While there, he hired Miss Alice as my governess. Sadly, before the year was out, my father took ill. For two years he suffered, never gaining enough strength to hazard the long voyage back to Florida. After much pain, the God Spirit took him. His last request of my uncle in London was for me to be returned to my people here in Florida. My father was a wise man, for he knew I did not like life in England. I longed for the forest, for the warmth of my homeland, for the love of my mother and my people. He knew I would never make a good Englishman. So I returned to this place and have never thought to leave it again."

Tom's personal history lesson served to answer most of Elizabeth's questions about the man, so she turned her attention to Ambrister. "And what is an English officer doing in Florida? The war is over."

The Englishman laughed, but there was an obvious note of indignation in his reply. "And what are all these American ships doing on the Apalachicola? As for myself, I haven't been in His Majesty's Service since the war ended, and therefore I have just as much right to be here as anyone. As for my business, it is my own, and no concern of anyone but those I deal with."

Elizabeth was slightly annoyed by Ambrister's tone. "So why do you continue to wear the uniform?"

"Quite honestly, Miss, it is the best coat I own, and winter is fast approaching. Also, it affords me some prestige and authority amongst the savages. Even Tommy is impressed." Tom laughed at the thought, and Ambrister continued in a more serious manner. "You Americans seem to think you own this place, and that everyone else has to have your permission to set foot in Florida. Who gave you consent to destroy the Negro Fort and kill all those hundreds of people? The last time I looked, the Spanish flag flew over St. Augustine and Pensacola."

"Those Negroes were our runaways. We had every right to bring them back."

"Did you? Seems to me that once they crossed into Florida, they were free." He then drove home the point. "You belong to Yellow Tom now. If you run off and find your way back to Georgia, will you still be his?"

"I will never be anyone's slave!"

Ambrister laughed heartily, but his response sent a chill down Elizabeth's spine. "Foolish woman! What do you think you are now? What do you think you agreed to when you chose to go with Tom instead of Efa-Hadjo? Tom owns you, Miss, as much as any white master owns any black slave."

Major Wooster was becoming concerned. Instead of the force at Fort Scott getting larger, it kept getting smaller. About a week after the massacre of Lieutenant Scott and his men, General Gaines had received orders to lead an attack against Amelia Island, far to the east. With him had gone his staff and a company of soldiers. Gaines had fumed about the order for a full day before leaving, complaining about being sent off to chase pirates while there was a war going on. "Let the damn navy deal with the pirates. That's their job, isn't it?" In the end, Wooster had convinced the general that the army could walk to and from Amelia Island twice before more men and supplies arrived at Fort Scott, so there was really no reason to disregard the order. Besides, clearing the pirates out of Amelia would remove one more source of weapons for the Seminoles.

As if the departure of Gaines and his compatriots wasn't bad enough, the general had dispatched yet another thirty men down the Apalachicola to help Major Muhlenberg get his ships upriver. No one could be sure what Muhlenberg's problem was, but sending more men always seemed a good solution to any problem. This time the general had sent the men in two keelboats, which were well protected from enemy fire and powered by ten oarsmen. Because the keelboats could move against the current much better than the flatboats that had gone before, Gaines had also ordered one of the boats to come back with word of what the holdup was.

In the meantime, Wooster had been left in charge of Fort Scott with barely one hundred men to defend it, and a good number of them were on the sick list. In a way, that was good, because there simply wasn't enough food to keep everyone fed. The flour was almost gone, the salt had just run out, and no one had tasted coffee in weeks, a situation that was especially annoying to Wooster, who normally would have gone through four cups in a day. Meat was being rationed, and no one had any idea when more would arrive. As it was, they were living on what fish they could catch in the river, along with the occasional deer or beef—probably stolen from some white settler or Florida Indian—that the friendly Creeks brought in.

Even if Muhlenberg arrived that day, his cargo would do little to ease the food shortage. Wooster had to assume whatever foodstuffs those ships carried were nearly gone. Indeed, there was always the possibility they had been forced to return to Mobile to resupply. Still, there were other things on those vessels that Wooster needed. Foremost, of course, was ammunition for the soldiers' muskets. If the Indians attacked, he might be reduced to throwing clods of red Georgia clay at the warriors. He also needed nails and other hardware to complete construction of the fort's defenses, and the surgeon was in desperate need of medications and other hospital supplies. As for the soldiers, they needed uniforms and shoes, and certainly some soap. Unfortunately, from what the survivors of the massacre had told him, most of the uniforms had been lost with Scott's boat. That was a real problem, because winter was setting in, and the men's clothing was in tatters. Most of all, Wooster just wanted to see Muhlenberg's ships safely at the dock and the men they carried standing at their posts. And perhaps they could deliver just a little bit of coffee.

In another part of Fort Scott, Captain Vashon, Sergeant Stuart, and Sergeant Dill were gathered for their daily prayer meeting. That wasn't what they called it, and no one got down on their knees, clasped their hands together, and called out to the Lord, but the conversation shared over a glass of whiskey always revolved around prayers for Elizabeth's safety and quick return.

At least some of the doubt as to her condition had been removed by the arrival of Creek spies who had traveled to the Mikasuki villages and asked discreet questions. The reports had been conflicting, but all indicated that her life had been spared, and she was living under the protection of a half-blood warrior who seemed to go by several names, all of which had something to do with "yellow."

Each man was handling the news in his own way, according to his own concerns regarding Elizabeth. Dill was the most relieved, having felt guilty for somehow letting her get captured in the first place. Even though both Stuart and Vashon held him blameless and even praised him for keeping her alive during the attack, he could not shake the feeling of responsibility. He also couldn't get Annie out of his mind. Six months earlier, if anyone had mentioned her, he might have referred to her as a "strumpet" or something worse. Close familiarity had changed all that. He had been only a few days away from willingly, even happily, calling her "wife." Now she was gone, having died in his arms, and tossed over the side of the boat like so much rotted meat. He was having a hard time coping with the loss and feared what would happen if something horrid befell Elizabeth. For the most part, he said little about the incident, and everyone was polite enough not to ask. He went about his duties as best he could, though with little enthusiasm, and except for his time with Stuart and Vashon, he avoided company. He was pleased that the broken arm was healing satisfactorily, but feared the scars to his spirit might never fade.

Captain Vashon was turning to the solace he best understood, the bottle of whiskey. Food might be scarce at Fort Scott, but cheap liquor could always be had. For whatever reasons, the Indians might prevent traders from entering their territory, but the whiskey sellers were always welcome and tended to move about more freely than most other whites. For Vashon, it was the easiest way to escape the fears of what might happen to his beloved daughter. As with most fathers, she would always be a little girl, no matter how grown-up and independent she may have gotten. In his mind, she was totally defenseless, in great danger, and there seemed nothing he could do to help her. When news had first arrived of her whereabouts, Vashon had offered to lead a rescue mission, but both General Gaines and Major Wooster had immediately turned down the request. Their reasoning was sound—too few men and little ammunition—and he couldn't say they were unsympathetic, but the inability to do anything for his daughter was eating at him. His stomach was always in some sort of pain, and he often woke up at night needing to vomit. He knew the whiskey was killing him, but he didn't really care. All he wanted to do was live long enough to see Elizabeth's face again.

For John Stuart, the news that his wife was alive and unharmed was a welcome relief, but the fact that she was living under the protection of a half-blood warrior was bothersome. The more questions he asked, the more concerned he became. Yellow Hair or Yellow Tom—he wasn't sure which—was often described in glowing terms by the Creeks who knew him. One had even said, "She is lucky to be the squaw of such a fine warrior." Doubts about Elizabeth's fidelity began to creep into his mind once again. After he and the rest of the company had left Fort Montgomery, Stuart had been concerned that Elizabeth might take up with Dill. Seeing how Jack mourned the loss of Annie had erased all such notions from his mind, but now Elizabeth was living with another man, one who, by all accounts, was much less a savage than his fellow warriors. Stuart knew how passionate a woman Elizabeth could be. Would she turn to her protector for comfort or physical satisfaction? Even if her will was strong, would she be able to protect herself from unwanted advances or outright force? Images worked through Stuart's mind, all of them lurid. Scenarios played out in his imagination, and none of them concluded with a chaste Elizabeth.

After an hour's commiseration, the three men raised their near-empty glasses for a final toast. Vashon wiped a small tear from his eye, took a breath, and said, "May God watch over and protect our dear Elizabeth." The other two added their "amen," and the trio drained their glasses. For them, and all the sympathetic soldiers at Fort Scott, it was going to be a long wait before they could take the care of Elizabeth out of God's hands.

Don Francisco Caso y Luengo knew full well why he had been given command of one of the loneliest outposts in Spain's crumbling Atlantic empire. An inappropriate drunken remark to the Captain-General's daughter while at a reception in Havana had brought him almost instant banishment to the small fort at St. Marks on Florida's Gulf Coast. If Florida was the forgotten corner of the empire, St. Marks was the forgotten corner of Florida. Perhaps once every three or four months a boat would arrive with dispatches from Havana or St. Augustine, the capital of East Florida. Pensacola, the capital of West Florida, was much closer, but the governor there could not be bothered with anything happening east of the Apalachicola River, the dividing line between the two colonies.

If it weren't for the stagnation of his career, the isolation wouldn't have been that bad. True, the seventy-man garrison hadn't been paid in six months, but the money was on the books, and sooner or later the paymaster would come from Havana and matters would be set straight. In the meantime, there really wasn't anything to spend the money on. Yes, there was Arbuthnot's store a mile or so up the Wakulla River, but the Bahamian was more than happy to extend the garrison credit, so the shortage of gold and silver was no real problem. The lack of communications from Havana and St. Augustine could be viewed two ways: On the one hand, Luengo didn't have to deal with the countless royal proclamations, edicts, regulations, or directives that arrived in every mail—and which he was totally incapable of doing anything about—while on the other hand, he truly missed the letters from his family in Valencia. Meanwhile, the weather was generally pleasant, the soldiers were not unmanageable, and he had a lovely Indian mistress to help relieve the boredom.

The presence of Arbuthnot's store was also a mixed blessing. In the first place, it was totally illegal. Forbes & Co. was the only trader licensed by His Most Catholic Majesty, and Arbuthnot's entire venture could be viewed as nothing more than smuggling. Whatever the legal situation, Luengo was powerless to close the store down. Arbuthnot had the good will and support of the native population, and the Spanish officer was in no position to make those natives angry. Besides, when provisions ran low or there was some other necessity that Havana would not supply, Arbuthnot was generous enough to meet the garrison's needs. In exchange for those favors and the occasional keg of rum, the merchant had earned an unauthorized license to operate in Florida. It may not have been completely proper, but with all the corruption Luengo had seen in Havana and elsewhere in the empire, his own minor transgressions seemed almost saintly.

Militarily, the need for a fort at St. Marks was a bit of a mystery to Luengo. Being five miles upriver, there was nothing he could do to prevent pirates or some enemy's vessels from moving along the coast or making landfall nearby. With only seventy men at his disposal, there was also nothing he could do to protect or control the hundreds of Indian warriors and their families who made up the population of his jurisdiction. The only other purpose for the fort's existence was to collect duties on any goods imported into the region, but he had already given up on that. Like most Spanish officers, Luengo was just doing his duty, passing time while the empire slowly disintegrated. Still, the duty was not unbearable, and so long as nobody attacked the fort, he had little reason to complain.

Up until this day, Luengo had never seen any reason why anyone would want to attack his isolated little fort. Now, as he looked at the men gathered in his quarters, he sensed a change in the status quo. Seated at the table were two powerful Red Stick chiefs, Homathlemico and Hillishadjo, the Prophet. They looked awkward, not being accustomed to sitting in chairs. Across from them were Hambly and Doyle, the proprietors of the Forbes & Co. store on the Apalachicola, who had been forcibly brought to St. Marks as prisoners of the Indians. At the far end of the table was

Alexander Arbuthnot. The news these men brought was troubling. Several weeks earlier, the American army had attacked a Mikasuki village in southern Georgia. A week later, the Mikasukis, Seminoles, and Red Sticks had retaliated by attacking an American boat on the Apalachicola, killing about forty people, mostly soldiers, and taking one woman prisoner. No one doubted that United States forces would soon be entering Florida to take revenge. Luengo had to assume that somewhere in the not-too-distant future, his quiet little post would get caught up in the conflict.

The Spanish commandant felt sickeningly powerless. A quarter of his force was unfit for duty, and he barely had enough gunpowder to conduct the weekly cannon and musket drill. The only thing he could do at the moment was defuse the situation in front of him. The two chiefs were intent on executing Hambly and Doyle, something neither Luengo nor Arbuthnot wanted to have happen. Hillishadjo, who spoke English tolerably well, pointed his finger at the two merchants and made his accusations. "They have been friendly to the Americans and have been spying against us. We have seen the American boats stop at their store, and we know they have sent runners to the American forts. For this they must die!"

Both Hambly and Doyle looked haggard. It was obvious that they had been roughly handled since being taken prisoner several weeks earlier. Both men hoped Luengo might be able to save them, but they weren't sure he had sufficient sway with the Indians. As for Arbuthnot, they weren't sure he even wanted them saved. Doyle turned a pleading eye toward the Spanish officer. "Don Francisco, you know we cannot be inhospitable to the Americans if they stop at our store. It would not be honorable, nor would it be wise. While we have always been loyal to the Spanish crown, you know as well as we that your country and the United States are engaged in negotiations for Florida. When Spain leaves, we will have to deal with the Americans, whether we like them or not. We cannot afford to alienate them. Please do not mistake our courtesy for support." Doyle knew he and Hambly had been treading a fine line when dealing with the Americans, and that they'd been more than courteous. They had sold supplies to Fort Scott and had passed on information about the Indians to the American authorities. It made good business sense, but it was also dangerous.

Hambly looked to Arbuthnot. "My friend, don't let this business rivalry turn to murder. It will do you no good. Already it costs you, for these people have looted our store, and every item they have stolen is one they will not buy from you. Please don't think that by eliminating us you will profit from this war."

Arbuthnot could not have agreed more, but he was not inclined to tell his rivals as much. Indeed, he would not even tell them that he had already saved their lives by advising the Indians to bring their prisoners to St. Marks and let the Spanish authorities decide their fate. It was an odd position to be in. For years, nothing would have pleased him more than to have Forbes's store disappear. It was, after all, his primary competition. But to have the store burned and looted, and for the proprietors to be savagely murdered would do him little good. Such an act would almost certainly force the Spanish authorities to take some sort of action. Right now, he was more or less free to conduct his business as he saw fit. He didn't want to risk that. He was seventy years old, and all he really wanted was to enjoy his remaining days as he had for the past several years, sailing his boat and trading with his Seminole friends. This war between the Indians and the Americans threatened to end all that.

Arbuthnot also agreed with Hambly's comment about not being likely to profit from the war. True, he might sell the Indians plenty of guns, powder, and lead in the near future, but much of it would be on credit, and if the natives lost the war, as was almost certain, there was little chance he would see the debt paid. Wars were generally thought to be good for business, but in this case, he could see no profit in it, only danger. He turned to the two chiefs, directing his words to Hillishadjo. "My friend, these are serious charges you make against these men, and if so proven, they must be punished. But you know these men trade here at the pleasure of the Great King of Spain, and that to harm them may make him angry. For all these years he has been satisfied to let the Seminole live free, without disturbance or restriction. It would not be wise to give him cause to change his feelings toward his red children. You must let the Great King of Spain and those who serve him decide this matter." He then cast his eye toward Luengo, hoping the officer would take the cue.

Luengo was more than happy to go along, if only because Arbuthnot's warning also applied to him. Nearly every set of dispatches he received from Havana contained copies of letters from the American government complaining about Spain not fulfilling its part of the Treaty of 1795 that required the colonial authorities to control the Indians living along the border. The fact that the Americans were not keeping their end of the bargain by controlling the whites who lived in Georgia would make little difference if the authorities in Madrid or Havana needed a scapegoat for the troubles in Florida. Nor would it matter if Luengo pointed out the fact that seventy men was a ridiculously small number to control thousands of well-armed natives. "Mi amigos, the words of Arbuthnot are true. His Most Catholic Majesty of Spain does not cast an angry eye toward his Seminole children because they have given him no cause to. His fury and his might are thrown against those who have brought him displeasure, and he has sent many soldiers to smash them and destroy their villages. Do not give him cause to do the same to you. You must leave these prisoners here with us. We will send word to our chiefs in the great city of Havana, and they will look into these matters. If they find these two guilty of the charges you make, it shall go hard on them. This is the advice I give you."

Hillishadjo interpreted the two speeches for Homathlemico, who responded with a few words of his own. Hillishadjo turned back to Luengo. "My brother and I must talk." With that, the two chiefs rose and left the room. The four white men looked at each other, but no one said a word. All of them could sense that while the Prophet was willing to accede to the proposal, Homathlemico had reservations. Homathlemico had often complained about Forbes cheating him, not understanding that a licensed trader was bound by the higher costs associated with duties, taxes, and payoffs to corrupt officials. Everyone knew that part of the reason the two merchants had been taken prisoner was nothing more than simple revenge for imagined wrongs.

After several minutes, the two chiefs re-entered the room and took their seats. Hillishadjo announced their decision. "We shall do as you ask and leave them with you. But we will not wait forever for the Great King of Spain to make his decision. We will leave this place and return to our villages and prepare for the war with the Americans. When we return after defeating the Americans, if your Great King has not yet spoken his mind, then we will take our prisoners back and deal with them as we see fit. Of this we have no more to say." Luengo nodded and smiled. Once again, another disaster had been postponed, hopefully to be avoided completely as events changed peoples' priorities and other catastrophes took precedence. That was, after all, what life at a remote outpost was all about.

Major Muhlenberg stalked the deck of *Phoebe Ann*, trying to imagine some way he could salvage his military career. General Gaines had ordered him to arrive at Fort Scott no later than November 10. Unless something in the present situation changed soon, he would be lucky to make it by January 10. What possible excuse could he give for being two months late?

He could no longer blame the weather. Certainly, sometime within an eight-week period the weather had to have been good. He could not bemoan the lack of manpower. Gaines had seriously depleted the command at Fort Scott in order to send him enough personnel to pull the boats upriver if it needed to be done. He couldn't blame the lack of provisions. Granted, there wasn't much, but no one was starving yet.

So how could Muhlenberg explain the holdup? First off, it was the weather, at least in part. It hadn't rained or stormed in weeks, meaning there was little breeze to fill the sails and not enough water flowing in the river. When the ships had arrived at the mouth of the Apalachicola, the water level had been sufficient to get them over the shallowest part of the river. That was no longer possible. Another reason for the delay did have something to do with manpower. Indian manpower. Hundreds had gathered near the old Negro Fort, where the river was narrowest, and were doing their best to prevent the boats from ascending. In that, they were successful. The one time Muhlenberg had attempted to force his way through, the warriors had held their ground, killing two soldiers on one of the towboats and wounding several others.

In all these situations, there was little Muhlenberg could do. He couldn't put more water in the river, he couldn't blow wind into the sails, and he couldn't protect his men from the Seminole bullets. The only thing he could do was sit and wait, and try to think of some way to convince General Gaines that a simple supply mission hadn't been an utter failure.

Elizabeth couldn't sleep. The look of fear and pain on the widow's face and the words "thou shall not kill" kept running through her mind. She had, indeed, killed someone, and in a very violent, brutal manner. It wasn't like when she'd killed Buzzard Warrior on the boat. There had been no choice—not even a chance to think about making a choice—in that situation. Killing his widow had been different. The blows with the war club had incapacitated the woman, and Elizabeth had been in no immediate danger. She could have spared her opponent's life and walked away the victor. Instead, she had taken up the knife and willingly pushed it into the woman's heart. Was she little more than a cold-blooded murderer? Was she damned for eternity?

Ambrister, the young Englishman, had assured her she was not. He was quick to point out that had the situation been reversed, the widow would have had no second thoughts on the matter. He also pointed out that once the widow had regained her capacity to fight, the contest would have continued. Yellow Tom had seen no moral dilemma. He had simply reminded Elizabeth, "It was a fight to the death."

All that may have been true, but she also knew that initially she had reveled in the victory. There had been an overwhelming feeling of relief, power, and perhaps even joy. It hadn't lasted long, but it was real, passing only when she gazed down at the lifeless form of her adversary. The thought frightened her. She was a white woman, a Christian, a person who had been brought up to be a lady. Was it all a lie? Was she as savage as her captors?

9

6th January 1818
Headquarters
Southern Division of the Army
Nashville, Tenn.

To:
His Ex'cy James Monroe
Pres't of the U. States
Washington City

Confidential

Sir,

I respectfully acknowledge receipt of the order to take command of United States forces along the border with Spanish Florida for the purpose of severely chastising the savages who have so lately brought such wanton destruction to our frontiers. I also acknowledge receipt of the enclosures, containing copies of the orders issued to General Gaines.

Will you permit me to suggest the catastrophe which might ensue by strict compliance with the last clause of your order, the one that denies the commander the right of pursuing the Indians should they take refuge under the Spanish flag? Suppose that the savages are beaten and seek protection at St. Augustine or Pensacola? We must then halt our pursuit, as ordered, to communicate with the government in Washington City. While waiting some weeks for the necessary reply, the militia grows restless and returns to their homes, leaving the army much reduced in size and vulnerable to attack by the Indians, now aided by the Spanish or British Partizans. Permit me to remark that the arms of the United States must be carried to any point within the limits of Florida where an enemy is permitted and protected, or disgrace results.

Your orders to General Gaines to seize Amelia Island are, I conceive, very proper. The Government should not, however, allow an opportunity to pass that would afford much greater security to our frontier. This order ought to be expanded to include the seizure of all Florida, including St. Augustine and Pensacola. This can be done without implicating the Government. Let it be communicated to me through any confidential channel (perhaps Congressman Mr. J. Rhea) that the possession of the Floridas would be desirable to the United States, and in sixty days it will be accomplished.

I am, with the utmost respect,
Yr. Mo. Obt. Svt.
Andrew Jackson
Major General, U. States Army
Commdg. Southern Division

Secretary of the Treasury Crawford shook his head, leaned across his desk, and handed the letter back to the Secretary of War. "What did the president say?"

Secretary Calhoun shrugged. "He never opened it. His servant reports that the president is ill, and that he simply passed it on to my office to deal with."

"Can't say I blame him. Letters from Jackson tend to make me ill, too. So how are you going to respond?"

"What the general is proposing is highly improper, and he shall be informed that no action is to be taken against any Spanish installation. To do otherwise would be an act of war against Spain, something only Congress has the power to authorize."

Crawford looked dismissive of the idea. "If I were you, John, I would take that letter, hide it away in your desk where no one can find it, and never mention it to the president or anyone else."

"How can you advise such a thing? The subject has been broached, and I cannot in good conscience ignore it."

"Then you answer it at your own and the president's peril. Think on it, John: What answer can you give Jackson that will not come back to haunt us, as surely as the Ghost of Banquo came back to haunt Macbeth?" Calhoun's brow furled as Crawford continued. "If you tell Jackson not to molest the Spaniards and something goes wrong, you and the president will be the scapegoats. I can hear it now: 'I asked for permission, but they denied me the power I needed to protect the frontier.'"

Calhoun had to admit Crawford had a point. Crawford then looked at the other option. "Suppose you give Jackson permission to attack the Spaniards. My God! You've usurped the powers of Congress! Do you know how far your head will roll? And don't think just because you've slipped word to him through Mr. Rhea that everything will remain confidential. Congress will certainly launch an investigation into who authorized Jackson to make war on Spain, and the general will have no choice but to produce the letter you sent him through Mr. Rhea."

Crawford then summed up his argument. "Right now, anything Jackson does beyond the orders issued to him or Gaines is his responsibility. Answer that letter, John, and it's yours. Only you and I are aware of this proposal Jackson has made, and the president, in all honesty, will be able to claim complete ignorance when all this blows up. For rest assured, sir, Jackson will do as he pleases, no matter what the order. The man is as dangerous to America as Napoleon was to France. Let him take Florida. Only good can come of it. Either by conquest or negotiations we wind up in possession of Florida, and with any luck at all, Jackson ends up with a sullied reputation, and his star begins to fall."

As General Gaines sat wet and shivering on the bank of the Flint River, he realized he had been pushing things a little too hard. He had always been impatient, and once again his restlessness was costing people their lives. First there had been the trouble with Fowltown and the subsequent massacre of Lieutenant Scott and his crew. Had he been in too much of a hurry to confront the Indians? If he had only waited until Scott had returned from his mission to Muhlenberg, no one would have gotten killed. Now, if he'd only waited until sunup, four more lives could have been spared.

It had been a difficult two months for the general. First there had been the unwelcome order to take possession of Amelia Island, two hundred miles away. The trip to Amelia had been an exhausting affair. It had taken about two weeks of marching and boating to get there, a few days to run the pirates off and take possession of the island, then two more weeks to get back to Fort Scott. While at Amelia, he had received news that Andrew Jackson had been given command of the campaign against the Seminoles. At first Gaines had felt insulted. Wasn't he good enough to lead a campaign against the Florida Indians? He certainly had the experience and was outranked by only two or three men in the entire army. On the other hand, Gaines knew Florida and the Seminoles were an obsession of Jackson's, and the old man would never be happy until both the Spaniards and the Indians were driven into the sea. In the end, Gaines had to admit that it was better to let Jackson run the show.

Gaines had hoped to find time to rest when he returned to Fort Scott, but relaxation wasn't in his nature. Perhaps it was the old injuries, or perhaps it was old age coming on, but whenever he attempted to get comfortable, something would hurt. It might be his back, his shoulders, his knees, or some other joint, but the only time he seemed to be pain-free was when he was in motion and didn't have to think about it. All that movement, of course, wore him out, but no sooner was he in a comfortable position then something would ache, and he'd be on his feet again. The upshot was that after two days at Fort Scott, he was ready to go again.

Finally, on the third day after Gaines's arrival, Muhlenberg's little fleet had sailed into view. After carefully assessing the supply situation at Fort Scott, the general had once again packed his bags. This time he had gone to Hartford, Georgia, the site of the Creek Indian Agency and the mustering point for the Georgia Militia. While there, Gaines had been able to meet with General Glasscock of the Georgia Militia and General McIntosh of the Creek Volunteers, who were already gathering and demanding to be mustered in immediately. The orders, however, had been to organize and prepare, not gather and muster, and until the War Department issued further orders, Congress would not authorize the funds. Using militia and volunteers was the government's way to fight a war on the cheap, but it always ended up costing more when the final tally was made.

Gaines had also made contact with supply contractors while in Hartford, but the results had been mixed. No one could supply all he needed, and delivery times were questionable. Prices were high, but no worse than he had expected so far into the interior with a war imminent. All in all, it had been a bothersome trip, but that was life in the military: Months of boredom, moments of excitement, and years of frustration.

Having finished his business in Hartford, Gaines began the return trip down the Flint to Fort Scott. The first day of the trip had gone well, and Gaines and his five-soldier escort had made good progress. It was warm for a January and the river was flowing smoothly, making for a pleasant trip. It had been the sort of day that made the general glad to be stationed on the frontier. Other officers might wish for a posting in Washington or at one of the massive stone fortresses guarding a place like New York or Boston, but Gaines was happiest at a simple wooden fort near the edge of the wilderness. As far as he was concerned, it was America at its best.

And then he got impatient. With a bright moon overhead and Fort Scott only twenty miles away, Gaines elected to rise early and take to the river an hour or two before sunrise. One of the men suggested that it might be better to wait until daylight, but Gaines was adamant: He was ready to get on with the trip. At first the water had been serene, and the boat moved with only a little direction from the oarsmen. Then they heard the rush of water ahead of them. Viewed in the bright moonlight, the approaching set of rapids appeared manageable, so they steered the vessel toward the widest opening in the rocks and braced themselves for the slight drop. Suddenly an unseen rock caught the vessel in just the wrong place, and it spun quickly around and capsized, sending all six men into the frigid water. Gaines struggled against the current, coming to rest against a large rock in the middle of the river. He called out to the other men, but only one answered.

He started to shiver. January was no time to be swimming in the Flint River, no matter how pleasant the day might have been. He could barely make out some trees on the shoreline, perhaps fifty feet away. The lone soldier who had answered his call seemed to be in that direction. Taking a deep breath, he pushed off from the rock and into the current. Following the voice, he swam against the current toward the eastern bank. After an exhausting struggle, he was able to grab hold of a tree limb and rest momentarily. The soldier called out from a small clearing just ahead, and once again Gaines pushed himself out into the current. After swimming several yards he caught hold of the soldier's outstretched hand and was pulled onto dry land.

So there he sat, cursing his own impatience. In the predawn light, they scanned the river and called out to the other men, but saw or heard no one. After the sun rose, the pair began to walk south, in the direction of Fort Scott. A mile or so down the river they saw the first body. Not far beyond, they found another. Soon after that they saw the overturned hull of the boat, a hole punched in the side. All their clothing, supplies, and weapons were gone. If a hostile Indian happened upon them, they were as good as dead. Moving as quietly as they could and seeking whatever cover was available, the two men marched silently on. If only he could learn to be patient.

Many miles to the south, Hillishadjo gazed at the pitiful white man who lay curled up, naked, and tied to a tree. He watched as the young soldier looked desperately around, fearful for his life. The man had been captured by a Red Stick scouting party while fishing just out of sight of Fort Scott. The warriors had bound and gagged the man, placed him in their canoe, and taken him south to their camp on the Apalachicola River. Along the way they had beaten the man, poked him with their knives to the point of drawing blood, and continually made threats against his life. In truth, the soldier had been in no real danger of being killed until they arrived at the camp, where the execution could be properly carried out in a process that would consume many painful and torturous hours.

Hillishadjo hated all white men, but for some reason he began to take pity on this one. Perhaps it was the soldier's frailty or his youth. Perhaps it was because he understood the white man's language and the pleas the captive was making. Perhaps he was just tired of the killing. Yet whatever the reason or his sympathies, there was little he could do for the soldier. By custom, the warrior who captured someone had the privilege of deciding a prisoner's fate, and this warrior was demanding revenge for a sister he had lost to the whites.

Hillishadjo began to wish the soldier had never been captured. Spies among the Lower Creeks had informed him that a large American army was gathering, and he didn't need to provide the Americans with yet another reason to slaughter more

Indians. In years past, he had preached fervently for war with the whites. Now he knew the futility of it. He also knew he could expect no help from the British, despite all their promises. Like all white men, they were liars. Killing this captive might provide some temporary satisfaction for his people, but in the end it would only bring more suffering. His people had suffered enough.

The warriors began to taunt the captive, brandishing their knives in front of his face or making small incisions into his skin. The soldier screamed and cried out, which only served to encourage his tormentors' cruelty. One of them approached and poked the muzzle of his rifle into the captive's side. The white man's eyes widened as the warrior's finger went to the trigger. Suddenly the gun fired, the captive screamed, and the warrior burst out in a malicious laugh. There had been no ball in the rifle and little powder, but the small explosion had left a burnt, bleeding hole in the man's flesh. As the execution went on, there would be many more.

The shouts and war-whoops attracted the attention of Hillishadjo's fifteen-year-old daughter, Milly, who was frolicking down by the river. Leaving her friends, she approached the gathered warriors and worked her way to the center of the crowd. She gazed down at the condemned soldier with an ambivalent eye. If this was an example of a white soldier, her people would have little to fear.

As the torture continued, Hillishadjo called out to Milly, took her aside, and spoke a few words to her. She seemed confused at first, not understanding why her father was asking her to do what he proposed. He explained again, and she nodded her acquiescence. Milly then approached the vengeful warrior and asked that the soldier's life be spared. At first the warrior scoffed at the idea, but as Milly continued to beg for mercy, the warrior's attitude softened. At last he relented. Taking his war club in hand, he beat the prisoner one more time on the back, hard enough to cause pain and bruising, but not with enough force to break any bones. Hillishadjo smiled. The pleadings of a pretty face were often more powerful than anything he carried in his medicine bundle.

Hillishadjo wasn't sure what he would do next. He could not risk taking the man back to Fort Scott in his present condition. The soldier needed time to heal. In the meantime, the village was not a safe place for him. The effect of Milly's smile might soon wear off. After a few minutes thought, he decided to take the soldier to the Spanish fort at St. Marks and ransom him, maybe for a keg of rum. That would make the warriors happy and perhaps show the Americans that the Indians wanted peace. Still, he had to wonder: How would the white men treat him if the situation were reversed?

Alexander Arbuthnot sensed something wasn't right. As he checked the inventory at his store on the Suwannee River, things weren't adding up. The rum tasted slightly off, the gunpowder was just a little low in the barrels, and the bolts of cloth seemed a bit smaller than they ought to be. It looked as if everything had been skimmed. It would be a hard thing to prove. Had they been short when he bought them, or had someone been stealing from him when he was gone? If it had been just one type of item he might have thought it happened before he bought the supplies, but for the pilferage to be so widespread indicated theft by his employee.

In a way, he was not surprised. Peter Cook, the young clerk he had left in charge of the store, did not have the best reputation. He had been fired by a store owner in Nassau for theft, but the evidence was so thin and the boy seemed so honest in his protestations of innocence that Arbuthnot had considered him worth the risk. He was now beginning to regret the decision. Arbuthnot's opinion of the youth had also been swayed by Cook's own words. The clerk was forever scheming, trying to gain some advantage over his customers, the competition, or the Americans. The old trader was convinced it was Cook who had put the Red Sticks up to taking Hambly and Doyle prisoner and looting their store. The boy had even gone off with the Seminoles to participate in a raid against the American fort in Georgia, something Arbuthnot had warned him not to do. For that reason alone, the merchant felt he had just cause to dismiss Cook. The suspected thievery just added to the bad feeling he had about the youth.

Unfortunately, dismissing Cook would not be as easy as simply telling him to walk out the door. Like it or not, he'd have to take the boy back to the Bahamas. If he were to abandon the young man here in Florida, Cook's family would certainly raise a fuss. Besides, for the moment, he needed the man's services. There was a war coming, and if things went badly, he would have to pack up his merchandise and go back to Nassau. All in all, it was not the time to have an employee he couldn't trust.

Elizabeth was surprised at how quickly she settled into life among the Indians. The daily routine at the Seminole village was not that different from what she had known at Fort Montgomery. Food preparation, mending or making garments, watching over someone's child, or simply tending a garden were universal tasks requiring minimal instruction. The language barrier could sometimes present a problem, but for the most part she followed the example of her companions and was able to complete her assigned tasks with little difficulty.

As might be expected, there were some tasks she enjoyed and others she loathed. She detested leather work but enjoyed cooking, especially when there was something new to learn or create. Laundry was much easier to do. Indians appreciated clean clothing as much as anyone, but their garments were much simpler and fewer in number. The one task she seemed to enjoy the most was grinding corn. She wasn't sure why. Instead of using a heavy millwheel or cumbersome grindstone, the Seminoles used the stump of a tree with a bowl hollowed out in the top as a mortar, and a length of small diameter log as a pestle. She and another woman would stand in front of the stump, put corn in the bowl, and then drop the pestle log onto the corn, thereby smashing it. She and her companion would alternate strokes, soon falling into a rhythm. Sometimes they would chant, at other times they would gossip. It was a simple task, but the log felt good in her hands, and she soon developed the habit of occasionally skipping a stroke and tapping the stump with the log, all without breaking the rhythm. It was almost like a little dance.

Elizabeth quickly learned that the other women, especially Yellow Tom's mother Conowaw, were strict taskmasters. If she was slow to respond, lax in her work habits, or did not do the assigned job properly, she would be verbally abused and occasionally struck with a branch. At first she thought it was because of her status as a captive, but then she noticed that the other young women were treated in a similar manner. It was simply the Indian way, and as the weeks passed, she learned to accept it.

During the initial days of her captivity, her worst fear had been that Tom would take her as a wife and then expect her to act as one in every manner. She had no idea what she would do in such a situation. Could she allow anyone other than Johnny to know her in that way? What if she became pregnant with Tom's child? On the other hand, could she risk angering Tom? It had been made very clear to her that he could do with her as he pleased, and all of the alternatives were frightening.

Fortunately, she found he was rarely at the village, and so the subject didn't come up for quite awhile. There was always some hunting, scouting, trading, or war party that kept the warriors busy and on the trail. Still, she knew the matter was only postponed, not forgotten. There was always the fear he might return from an expedition and demand the physical comfort only a woman could give him. Worst of all, she had to admit she also longed for the same sort of comfort. She loved Johnny and had no intention of giving herself willingly to another man, but if rescue didn't come soon, she wasn't sure what would happen.

As it was, the subject didn't arise until mid-January, after she'd been a captive for over six weeks. Tom returned from a hunt and came upon her alone in the lodge he shared with his mother and a few other kinfolk. Taking a seat across the ground from her, he nonchalantly announced, "Conowaw says you work hard and would make a good wife, Red Bess."

Elisabeth stopped her sewing and looked at the ground between them. "I already have a husband."

"So you have said. But he is not here and can do you no good."

She would not be tempted, no matter how handsome he was or how considerate he'd been. "Be that as it may, Yellow Tom, I have sworn an oath and given my vow. I shall not dishonor the man I love."

He nodded thoughtfully, but otherwise showed little expression. "Well spoken, and I shall not force from you that which you would not give freely. But who can say what the coming months may bring? The Americans raise their army and will soon be upon us. Perhaps they will rescue you, as I am sure you hope for. Or perhaps we shall drive them back to Georgia with the loss of many scalps. Perhaps this man you love will be slain in the war, or perhaps it will be me. When this war is over, you may be with him, you may be with me, or you may be with someone else. Then you may see things differently. For now we will wait for the God Spirit to do his work."

Up until this moment, she had avoided letting herself get too friendly with Tom. The chance of commencing a romance was simply too great, and she needed to maintain some emotional distance. Now that she knew his intentions, she felt less constrained. He was an oddity among the Indians, and she wanted to get to know him better. "Why do you call him the God Spirit?"

Tom smiled as a fond memory came to mind. "Miss Alice was a God-fearing woman, and every Sunday when I was in London, she would take me to the church. Some of what I leaned there I have brought home with me, though most of what they taught me I left behind, as it was worthless."

Elizabeth was a bit surprised. "You heard the word of God and rejected it?"

"It may be fine for the white man in his great cities, but here it's of little use. Here we have Hesaketa-Mese, the Breath Giver. Can there truly be one Great Spirit for the white man and a different one for the red man? I can't believe it. I can only believe that we really don't know. Therefore I have taken what is good from the white man's God and from my people's Spirits and have chosen to call him the God Spirit."

She laughed. "You make it sound so simple."

He shrugged. "It is."

Something else came to Elizabeth's mind. "Can you read and write?"

He winked, seeming to tease her with the answer. "Perhaps I can read better than you. Miss Alice was a good teacher." Then a more thoughtful look came across his face. "Writing is another matter. I was taught, but have lost the skill. Paper and ink are not something we have in our village, and there is no one to read what I write." Then his face lit up. "But I have a book!" He got up and walked over to a small chest in the corner of the lodge, opened it, and brought forth two small books. "It was a gift from my father, who said it was the greatest book ever written. It is all I have left from my village, the one your soldiers burned."

He handed her the book and sat down. She opened the cover and found the title page. Then she laughed. She had been expecting it to be a copy of the Bible. Instead she saw *An Inquiry into the Nature and Causes of the Wealth of Nations, Vol. I.* Below the title was the name *Adam Smith.*

Tom explained. "My father knew that even though I was returning to my people, I would still have to deal with the white man. He told me that if I really wanted to understand both the English and the Americans, I should study this book. He also told me that just like the Christian holy book, there is much truth in these words, but that evil men will always find a way to turn those good words to their own dark purposes. My father was a wise man."

Elizabeth had to agree. She was also beginning to understand Tom. He had somehow managed to find his place in this world and seemed genuinely happy with it. And that surprised her. It was something she couldn't understand. "With your light hair, your softer features, and your excellent command of our language, you could easily pass for an Englishman or an American. Why do you remain an Indian?"

The smile left Tom's face and was replaced by a look of annoyance, bordering on anger. "Is it so much better to be an American or an Englishman? Is it so bad to be an Indian? Is an Indian less a man than a white?" His resentment was growing, and he pointed out the door at three boys who were playing together. "Does my light hair make me less an Indian? Look at those three boys. The tallest one is the son of Micco Phillip, and a pure Indian. The black one, John, is the son of a slave woman who fled her cruel master. The shorter one is a Creek, the son of Powell, a white man. All have different blood, but all are Seminole." He looked hard at Elizabeth and knew she still didn't understand. "These are my people! We choose to be Seminole! We do not want to be like the white man!"

Tom took a breath then continued his tirade. "Is the white man really so grand? I have seen the great city of London and all the princes in their fine coaches and handsome clothes. I have seen the servants who bow down to them as if they were the God Spirit.

I have also seen them drunk and chasing after whores. I have smelled their foul air and stepped in their filthy streets. I have seen these princes feast so much that they become sick, while all the other white people of London are starving. I have seen the plantations of Georgia, where the white man whips his black slaves because he is too lazy to do the work himself. I have seen your white soldiers cry as they are slain and plead to keep their scalps. What in all this makes the white man better than the Indian? Do our children starve while our chiefs grow fat? Do we foul our land and water so much that it makes us sick to live here? Do our warriors die less bravely than the white soldiers?" He then gave Elizabeth a cold, penetrating stare. "Do we continually whip our captives and rape the women we have taken prisoner?"

Elizabeth was shaking. No one had ever given her such a scolding. Wiping away a tear, she said, "I'm sorry. I did not mean to insult you."

Tom shook his head and stood up. She was so beautiful, so delicate, yet so strong. He wanted her to understand that he was no better or worse than any other man. He lowered his voice and began to turn away. "Yes, I could pass for a white man, but I could never *be* a white man."

Like most of his fellow Americans, Andrew Jackson feared a large, standing army. As a boy, he had lived through the Revolution and had suffered at the hands of the British army, losing his entire family during the war. He still bore scars from the time an English officer had slashed him with a sword when he'd refused to shine the officer's boots. Large armies were the tools of tyrants, and they were also expensive to maintain. If there wasn't a war, why spend money on the military? Unfortunately, the answer to that question cropped up every time a conflict broke out. Saving money has its cost, and right now Andrew Jackson was paying the price. A war had started in November, and it would probably be sometime in March before he would be able to fire the first shot against the enemy. In the meantime, while troops were mustered, supplied, trained, and moved, the Seminoles were free to carry on the war.

Jackson had received the War Department's orders at his home in Nashville in late December. That very day he had sent word out across the state, calling for volunteers to fight in Florida. Such was the reputation of the Hero of New Orleans that he could expect a thousand men to answer the call. But word moved slowly through the thinly populated frontier, and it had taken nearly a month to gather and provision the initial companies. Others would follow in the weeks to come, but at the lightning pace Jackson waged war, they might arrive too late. Impatient to be on his way, Jackson and a few companies of volunteers left Nashville a week after New Years.

It was not going to be an easy march. January and February were not the best months to be traveling through the American wilderness. Cold weather, ice, and snow would be the least of his impediments along the way. There would be rivers and streams to cross, small mountains to skirt, and forests to cut through. Roads were almost nonexistent, and what few there were tended to be nothing more than dirt paths. Getting men and wagons over the hills and through the valleys was going to be hard work, and the men would be grumbling the entire way. Some would come to regret having volunteered, and a few would decide they could un-volunteer if they cared to. Jackson had dealt with that sort before. To his mind, they were nothing but deserters and would be shot. If an old man in ill health like himself could make the march, anyone could.

The first week of the journey had been relatively easy. Although his ultimate destination was southeast from Nashville, the best way to get there was to go southwest, down the Natchez Trace into the northwest corner of Alabama. Months earlier, in late fall, the Trace had been a relatively busy pathway, loaded with

Kentucky and Tennessee boatmen who had unloaded their cargoes on the lower Mississippi and were making the month-long trek back to their homes via the Trace. By January the road was more or less deserted, and many of the inns and ferries were shut down. No one expected to see hundreds of men treading the path in the middle of winter.

Now, as he stood at Colbert's Ferry on the Tennessee River, Jackson had come to his first major obstacle. Parts of the river were frozen, but the ice was nowhere near thick enough to cross over. At the ferry crossing, only one boat was still in the water, the others having been hauled up on land for the winter or trapped in the frozen waters of the little bays that made up the ferry landings on either side of the river. The one usable boat was a small barge, barely big enough for a two-horse wagon, and would require many trips to shuttle the men and supplies across. The crossing itself would also be difficult. The temperature was below freezing and would be colder out on the river. The current was moving swiftly, and large chunks of ice would collide with the boat as it crossed. Jackson ordered a pair of rowboats put back in the water, and along with the barge, the volunteers began to work their way across the river, pushing large blocks of ice aside as their frozen hands worked the oars and ropes. The crossing took all day.

The army resumed its march on the following morning. From this point on, the path would become more tenuous. Turning east, they would leave the Natchez Trace and head for central Alabama. From there, they would cross central Georgia until they reached the Flint River, then follow it down to Fort Scott. It was not the most direct route, but one of the few available. The roads that did exist were minimal, many of them having been cut four years earlier, when Jackson had marched against the Red Sticks during the Creek Civil War. Four years of neglect and natural regrowth would make those roads difficult to pass. If the snow fell heavily, it might make them impossible to find. If such was the case, they would just have to cut new ones.

As Andrew Jackson rode away from Colbert's Ferry, he knew getting to Florida was simply a matter of putting one foot in front of the other. Yes, there would be pain and hardship along the way and some of the men might succumb to disease as they traveled, but that was life. You didn't worry about those things; you just faced them as they came and pushed on through. The war was many thousands of footsteps and many weeks away, but eventually he and his army would get there, and when he did, the Seminoles, the Spaniards, and any Englishmen he encountered along the way were going to pay dearly for making him leave Nashville in the middle of winter.

10

March 2, 1818
Fort Scott, Georgia

To:
Mr. Robert Vashon
St. Louis, Missouri Terr.

Dear Robert,

For once I am able to report something other than "Elizabeth is still a captive and there is nothing we can do about it." An express rider arrived this morning with news that Gen'l Jackson and much of the Tennessee Volunteer Army will be upon us in a few days. Then, perhaps, we shall be able to leave the horrid confines of this God-forsaken fort, take the war to the bloody savages, and thereby rescue our beloved wife and sister. I cannot describe the impatience and anxiety I feel, waiting for the march to begin. Pity the Seminole who puts himself within range of my bayonet, for he shall see no pity from me. I could feel remorse for the Redcoats we killed at New Orleans, for they were fellow soldiers, doing their duty while serving their country. These are naught but blood-lusting savages, and for me, the matter is personal. And woe be it to the warrior who holds my Elizabeth captive, if I find he has laid but one hurtful hand upon her. The very thought of another man, let alone some damn heathen Seminole, being with my wife torments me beyond all reason.

Calculations are that our army will number some 3,500 men, when one considers the regulars, Tennessee Volunteers, Georgia Militia, and Creek mercenaries. Let us see how brave these Seminoles are when faced with a real army, not a defenseless boat full of invalids and women. With any luck, what few we leave alive will be forced into the sea and left to drown. Such an easy death would be too good for them.

Where we shall encamp all these men and how we shall feed them is a question I cannot imagine an answer to. We have barely a week or two's provisions on hand to sustain the 500 regulars presently bivouacked outside the fort. When Gen'l Jackson arrives that will quickly disappear. Word has it that there are ships waiting with supplies at the mouth of the Apalachicola, but considering it took Maj'r Muhlenberg two months to make the passage up-river, I can't see where that does us any good. Ah, but that's the concern of generals, not sergeants.

My greatest concern at the moment is your father. Since Elizabeth was taken captive, his drinking has become more serious. As always, he is the dedicated soldier, but his demeanor has become more sullen, and he neglects both his health and appearance. This change has not escaped the notice of Gen'l Gaines, who has mentioned it to Maj'r Wooster. We can be thankful the major holds your father in high regard, for he has gone out of his way to shield him from any embarrassments. I can only pray that he does not fall foul of Old Hickory. Perhaps his mood will lighten when we begin the march, and he feels we are drawing closer to finding Elizabeth. In the meantime I will do what I can, but the powers of a sergeant are extremely limited.

I shall close for now, as an express rider soon leaves for Hartford. As always, Jack sends his most kind regards to both you and Anna Lynn, as do I. Knowing it will take weeks for this to reach you, I can only hope that by the time you read these words, Elizabeth will once again be safely within our company.

Yours, with greatest affection,
Johnny

The sound of shouting woke John Stuart from a deep sleep. Recognizing the voice and knowing it could only mean trouble, he threw off his bedroll and sprang from his tent. Running across the parade ground, he swiftly climbed a ladder and stepped out onto the wooden platform outside one of the Fort Scott's watchtowers. There he found his father-in-law, Captain Vashon, leaning drunkenly against the picket wall. Standing before him was a mortified soldier, shaking and standing at attention.

Upon seeing Stuart, Vashon bellowed, "Sergeant! Confine this man for sleeping while on watch! Give him a hundred lashes! Hell, put his worthless ass before a firing squad! I'll not have such dereliction of duty from any man in my company. I'd rather have him shot."

Stuart looked at the soldier. He wasn't even in Vashon's company. While saying, "Yes, sir," to Vashon, Stuart turned to the soldier and made a gesture of reassurance. "I'll bring it to the major's attention."

From behind him he heard Major Wooster's voice as the officer ascended the ladder. "Bring what to my attention, Sergeant?"

Stuart had no choice but to answer the question. "The captain found this man sleeping on watch, sir."

Wooster stepped onto the platform and looked at the wide-eyed young man. "Were you sleeping, soldier?"

The soldier, fearing he was close to being sent to the firing squad, hurriedly answered, "Yes, sir, but I wasn't on watch, sir. I go on duty at midnight, sir. It was a nice night, so I thought I'd sleep out here until I was called for, sir."

From across the compound, they heard the angry voice of General Gaines call out. "What the hell is going on over there? A horde of attacking savages would make less noise!"

Wooster sighed and turned to answer the general, shouting, "False alarm, sir. Nothing to be worried about. Everything is in order."

No one, not even Gaines, was fooled. "Like hell it is, Major. See me in the morning."

Wooster looked at Vashon, who was leaning against the picket wall, barely able to stand. Shaking his head, he turned to Stuart. "How the hell did he even get up the ladder?"

Stuart shrugged. "This is how I found him, sir."

"Well, see if you and Private Sleeper here can get him safely down the ladder and back into his quarters." He looked at the soldier Vashon had accused of sleeping on watch. "Don't worry, son. He won't remember a thing in the morning." The major then took Stuart aside. "You and Lieutenant Clinch are going to have to watch over him. General Gaines understands the situation, but his understanding will only go so far. He'll tolerate this behavior here at the fort, but neither he nor Old Hickory will put up with it when we get into enemy territory. I'll take him aside in the morning and talk to him, but I can't watch over him every night, and I can only make so many excuses to the general."

Stuart nodded. "I know, sir, and I thank you, sir."

Wooster put a hand on Stuart's shoulder. "He's a good officer, Sergeant, and we'll need him in the weeks ahead. The last thing I want to tell your wife when we find her is that her father has been court-martialed."

General Jackson and the first part of his army arrived at Fort Scott on March 9, 1818, and on the following morning he called a council of war. The various commanders leading the invasion force gathered in the small two-story building used as the officer's quarters, anxious to hear what the general's plans would be. The senior-most officers were on the lower floor, sitting on chairs and chests, while the junior officers watched from the bunkroom on the second floor or just outside the doorway.

Major Wooster sat on the stairway, as if he were trying to decide if he were a senior or a junior officer. Up until mid-January he had been the Commanding Officer at the post, but with the arrival of Major Muhlenberg, that had changed. Muhlenberg was a real major, not a brevet like Wooster, and therefore entitled to command, along with the extra pay and privileges that accompanied the position. Now, with the coming of Jackson's army, there were a host of generals, colonels, and lieutenant colonels around to outrank them both. For Wooster, that was fine. He was young, which gave him plenty of time for advancement. There was also a war on the way, which would hopefully provide an opportunity to enhance his reputation. For the moment, he was content to sit on the step and watch the higher-ups make their plans and give their orders.

Among those present was General Glasscock of the Georgia Militia. Glasscock had been appointed to his position by Governor Rabun, more on the strength of his political and family connections, rather than any military experience. Still, he was acknowledged to be an effective leader, and no one doubted his commitment to the cause. For the Georgians, whose own homes were in danger of attack, driving the Seminoles away from the borderlands was a matter of survival. Whether or not they were a welcome part of the force was another matter. Jackson had experienced run-ins with both Secretary Crawford and Governor Rabun, which led to a disdain for anything Georgian. Looking to General Glasscock, Jackson commented, "The muster reports for your regiments are appalling, General. Where are all the patriotic hearts of Georgia?"

Glasscock was quick to respond. "Where was our government when all those patriotic hearts answered the call, General? My men turned out with enthusiasm when called, but for two months we sat in our camps, shivering from the cold, with neither orders nor provisions from Washington, which has yet seen fit to pay them for their time of duty. If you wish a respectable army, sir, you should treat it with proper respect."

In another place or time, Jackson would not have stood for such an insolent response, no matter how justified it was. He knew Glasscock was right, and that the Georgians had been poorly treated. At the same time, he didn't really care. The war was now, not two months ago, and he expected everyone to dance to his tune without complaint or question. Yet now was not the time to argue, especially since many of his own Tennessee troops were still weeks away. Besides, he was suffering from a terrible cold and needed to save his strength for the real enemy. He decided to end the conversation with a simple, uncontestable statement, saying, "I expect your rolls to be filled within two weeks, General."

Glasscock had made his point and saw little advantage in prolonging the conversation. Congress had just gone into session for the year, and the Georgia delegation would see that the payments were made. "So it shall be, sir."

On paper, Jackson had a huge army, but in truth, little of it was at Fort Scott, and none of it was ready to launch any sort of invasion. Over a third of that force would be composed of Indian allies. Once again, as had happened when Colonel Clinch had attacked the Negro Fort, the Lower Creeks were anxious to go to war against their Seminole and Upper Creek cousins. Also as before, William McIntosh, the half-blood Creek leader, was in charge of the forces and assumed the title of general. Unlike the Upper Creeks and Seminoles, most of the Lower Creeks had decided the future, good or bad, lay with the white man, and they were attempting to accommodate the new ways as best they could. It wasn't easy. Whites had no use for them and were continually trying to steal everything they had. Even Jackson had betrayed them, taking much of their land after the Creek Civil War. Yet they also knew there was no turning back. To have not taken up arms against the Florida Indians would have cast them as enemies to the Americans, a distinction they neither wanted nor needed. Besides, the government would pay them well, and much of the money would go into McIntosh's own pocket.

Unsure of the willingness of the Lower Creeks to fight, Jackson directed his next question to McIntosh. "How many of your Creek warriors can we depend upon, General?"

McIntosh knew that Jackson meant, "How many men can you raise?" but the Indian leader chose to respond in a manner that better suited his mood. "You can depend upon every warrior who answers my call, General Jackson. A Creek never turns his back on a friend."

Jackson understood the double meaning of McIntosh's words, but again decided against any sort of confrontation. If the Lower Creeks were going to be troublesome, he would deal with them later. "How many, General, and where are they?"

"Many hundreds. They are gathering at their villages and at Fort Hawkins. They will take up the path when I send word and will gather where I direct them." Both men understood that the Indians would cooperate with the army, but it would be on their own terms. For Jackson, that wasn't a real problem. He understood the Indian character and could mold it to his needs.

He next asked, "How stand the regulars?"

Both Muhlenberg and Wooster came to their feet. Muhlenberg, as senior officer, spoke first. "The Seventh Infantry stands ready, sir, awaiting only provisions, ammunition, and your orders."

Wooster had little to add. "As does the Fourth Infantry, sir."

And that was the real problem. Andrew Jackson was, as ever, impatient to get on with the fighting. He wanted to commence the war immediately, and he wanted to destroy anything in his path. It was hard to know who he considered the greatest enemy: the Indians, the English, the runaway slaves, or the Spaniards. For the moment, however, most of his wrath was reserved for whoever was in command of the supply ships that had been dispatched from New Orleans. He turned to General Gaines. "Where the hell are those supplies, General?"

Gaines didn't take Jackson's attitude personally. The only time he had ever seen the man truly happy was when he was resting at his home in Nashville with Rachel by his side. And even that was temporary. If anything wasn't running smoothly at the plantation, Jackson's temper would flare. Gaines knew the man was in constant pain from the many wounds he'd received in his lifetime. He also noticed the handkerchief Jackson used to cover his mouth when he coughed was blood stained, a reminder of the pistol ball still lodged in his lung following a duel. Sometimes it seemed as if anger was the only thing that kept Andrew Jackson alive. He couldn't die yet; there was someone else to punish. To the question of where the supplies were, Gaines answered, "I have no idea, sir. I've dispatched runners to ascertain that information, but none have yet to return. We can only assume they are at Apalachicola Bay or making their way upstream."

Jackson couldn't understand the problem. "He's got a pair of gunboats for escorts, damn it!" At least it gave him an opportunity to vent his anger on someone who wasn't there. "Just blast the damn redskins aside and load the supplies on smaller boats! Worthless damn naval officers. You can't win a war by sitting at anchor."

The meeting went on for another hour or so, as maps were looked at and assignments given. All of it, however, depended upon the arrival of the much-needed supplies. Fort Scott was nearly out of food, and though ammunition supplies were adequate for their immediate needs, there was certainly not enough for a major campaign. Everyone began to wonder when Old Hickory's patience would run out.

Near the end of the meeting, Jackson asked, "Any news on where they're holding that woman they took prisoner from Scott's boat? I assume she's a happy little squaw by now."

Only Jackson's aides, as ignorant as he was as to who the prisoner was, laughed at the joke. Captain Vashon quietly turned and walked out the door. Jackson looked around, his normally chilly stare a few degrees colder. Casting his eyes toward the departing Vashon, he turned to Gaines. "I smelled whiskey on that man's breath, General."

Wooster stepped forward. He didn't care if it was Andrew Jackson; the matter needed to be set straight. "If I may, sir?"

Jackson quickly turned his head in the major's direction. "What!"

"That female prisoner, sir, is Captain Vashon's daughter."

Even Jackson knew he had stepped over a line. Still, it was beyond the ability of Andrew Jackson to make an apology. The best he could do was say, "Thank you, Major. Inform Captain Vashon that rescuing his daughter shall be my highest priority."

Farther south, other men were also making plans. At Fort St. Marks, in the quarters of Commandant Luengo, three worried men sat around the table and discussed the latest news. In front of them was a bowl of paella, or at least the closest thing Luengo could make to what he lovingly remembered from his childhood in Spain. There was rice, some beans he had gotten from the Indians, and a few pieces of meat he couldn't identify. A few peppers added some flavor, but it was nothing like what he'd had at home. It was like duty at St. Marks: It wasn't very bad, it just wasn't very good.

Robert Ambrister, the young English adventurer, relayed the latest intelligence from scouts near Fort Scott. "General Jackson has arrived with several hundred men from Tennessee, the Georgia State Militia is gathering, and McIntosh has called out his warriors."

Luengo looked concerned. "And how long do you think, Señor, before the invasion begins?"

Ambrister shook his head. "Not soon. His soldiers are still gathering, and he cannot move until the supply boats reach him. I don't see him crossing the line for several more weeks."

Alexander Arbuthnot, the old Scottish merchant, had already made his decision. "I think it would be wise for us to be as far from Florida as possible when he pays a visit."

Luengo nodded. "I agree, amigos. It is said that Jackson hates the British more than anything. It would be dangerous if he found you here."

Arbuthnot looked to Ambrister. "It's best we packed up our things and made our way back to Nassau, laddie." He motioned out toward the bay, where his schooner lay at anchor. "Why don't you get on board the *Chance* and go with my son down to the Suwannee. You can help Cook get things ready—if the rascal hasn't stolen it all—and you can also warn Bowlegs and his people as to what's coming. I'll stay here and pack up the merchandise at the store upriver. When you get everything on board at the Suwannee, come back and we'll load up what's here, and then set sail for home."

Ambrister was a little concerned. "Shouldn't we pack up here first, then head south?"

"I don't think so, lad. Jackson will probably head for the Lake Miccosukee towns first, then for Alachua and the Suwannee. If he stops here at all, I imagine it won't be until after he's done with the Indians."

Luengo tended to agree. "Even should Jackson come here before you return, Señor Arbuthnot is my guest and is under the protection of the flag of Spain. It is a sacred protection the Americans dare not violate."

News of Jackson's arrival at Fort Scott had also reached the Seminole towns surrounding Lake Miccosukee, where warriors were gathering and making preparations for war. Tomahawks and knives were sharpened, and powder and lead were passed out. The chiefs met in council, trying to decide on the best course of action. There seemed but two choices: abandon the villages or stand and fight. Moderate chiefs, such as Neamathla and Micco Phillip, favored abandoning the villages. The more militant, such as Kinnachee and Homathlemico, were determined to fight it out. After much acrimonious debate, no consensus was reached, so it was decided the warriors would remain at the villages and prepare for battle while the women and children fled south.

Yellow Tom was pleased with the plan, as it was precisely what he'd recommended to Neamathla, but was frustrated by how the council had arrived at the decision. As much as he loved the Indian way of life, every now and then he saw certain disadvantages to the way his people did things. This uncertainty over the best way to defend their homeland was a prime example. Major decisions were usually made in council, and when the council couldn't come to an agreement, events were simply allowed to take their course. In this situation, they were letting the white men decide the when and where of battle, which could prove disastrous. Neither the Americans nor the British would allow such a thing. There was always someone in charge, someone that had ultimate authority. True, that person might be totally incompetent and make a horrendous decision, but in times of crisis, indecision could be fatal. A bickering council was the last thing they needed.

As far as Tom was concerned, abandoning the villages but fighting for them was the best thing they could do. If the reports were true, the size of the American army made it unstoppable. In light of that, it was best to remove the women, children, elders, livestock, and valuables out of harm's way. Yet it would have been foolish to simply let the enemy advance without opposition. Left unchecked, it was difficult to tell where they would stop. Would it be the Suwannee, or would they push on to the St. Johns, Ocklawaha, or the Withlacoochee Rivers? Would they even go as far as the Okeechobee? The more obstacles the Indians threw in the Americans' path, the sooner they would decide they had gone far enough.

The plan may have been good, but the differences within the council meant that the implementation was spotty. Kinnachee, determined to save his town, issued instructions for his people to flee, but did little to actually encourage it. As a result, women were unsure whether or not to leave their husbands, and not enough attention was paid to removing the livestock and food stores to safe places. If the Americans weren't stopped, the people of the Miccosukee towns would lose nearly everything they had.

At the moment, however, Tom had other things on his mind. Of primary concern was the safety of his captive. He had promised Elizabeth no harm would come to her, but he wasn't sure he could keep that pledge once the fighting started. He might be killed or captured or somehow prevented from protecting her. And now, more than ever, she needed protection. Many of the Red Sticks had gathered at the villages, and among them was his old enemy Efa-Hadjo. More than once the Red Stick leader had made a threat against Elizabeth's life, and Tom had no illusions that he was simply bluffing.

Tom knew that Elizabeth's flaming red hair was a trophy any warrior would covet. Efa-Hadjo had also mentioned that it would look especially nice hanging next to Tom's light brown locks. Tom began to feel he had more to fear from the Red Sticks than the white men. Several scenarios crossed his mind, and he began to wonder what he would do if any of them came to pass. If it came to a point where he could no longer protect Elizabeth from Efa-Hadjo or his warriors, would he break away from his people and take her to the whites? Worse yet, if it came to a personal confrontation between him and Efa-Hadjo, could he take the life of a fellow Indian to save the life of a white woman? On the other hand, what if his people were defeated and the whites appeared as if they might rescue her? Could he simply let her go, or should he try to flee with her, abandoning his place among the warriors? Any of those acts would make him a traitor to his people, and he recoiled from the thought. Yet he had to admit that for her, he might well do it.

It had taken about six hours for Andrew Jackson's patience to run out after the meeting with his officers on the morning of March 10. Shortly before sunset he called the officers back together and announced they would be heading south first thing in the morning. If the supply vessels couldn't reach the army, the army would go to the supply vessels. It was as simple as that. A few people raised questions about whether there was enough food, ammunition, wagons, and pack animals, but the general quickly dismissed those concerns. Others wondered whether it might not be better to wait for the remaining troops to arrive or for the friendly Creeks to gather, but Jackson insisted the laggards would quickly catch up. There was a war to be fought, and he was ready to fight it.

The news brought about an instant change in Captain Vashon. Returning to his tent, he corked the bottle of whiskey and said, "None of that tonight. I've got work to do." He then went in search of Sergeants Stuart and Dill. He found them by the river, sitting on the dock, looking longingly toward Florida. "On your feet, lads! We head south in the morning! Assemble the company and get them ready to march. Let's go find my little girl!"

The bugler sounded reveille about an hour before dawn. Sleepy soldiers struck their tents, rolled up their bedrolls, gathered their few possessions, and checked their weapons. The one thing they didn't do was partake of a large breakfast. There was precious little to eat, and even the coffee was watered down. Pieces of salted pork and meager rations of hard bread were distributed among the men, who placed the items in their haversacks, knowing it would have to sustain them until they reached the supply vessels. Of course no one could be sure the supply vessels were actually there.

As each company finished their preparations and mustered for duty, they were marched down to the dock and were ferried across the river. It was a time-consuming business, especially when dealing with the horses and wagons. The regulars, better organized and disciplined than the militia and volunteers, were the first units to disembark and begin their march down the south bank of the Flint. It took several hours to get everyone across, and by the time the march was fully underway, the column of soldiers stretched for nearly two miles.

Jackson, mounted at the head of the column, kept sending word toward the rear, demanding that the units at the back quicken their pace and close ranks with the companies in the lead. It was a futile demand, because Jackson kept pushing the men at the front of the column to forge ahead, to make as many miles as possible before sunset. He was driven now, anxious to reach the supply ships and prepare for the fight. Yet it was important to keep the army as tight as possible. Stragglers were vulnerable, and he was not yet ready to engage the enemy.

What had been a narrow trail was fast becoming a road, as the pioneers cleared trees and brush to allow the wagons and cannon to pass through the woods. After a few miles' march, the army turned south and entered Spanish territory, though no one could say precisely when they crossed the unmarked line. By mid-afternoon they reached an east-west trail that looked more heavily traveled. Knowing it would take them to the Apalachicola, they followed it west, hoping to make the river by nightfall.

They had gone barely a mile down the path when one of the Creek scouts approached Jackson and handed him an army canteen. The general looked at it and then passed it to the other officers. At first none of them said anything, simply sighing or nodding, acknowledging what they all knew: It had belonged to one of Scott's soldiers. Jackson finally broke the silence, saying,

"This unnamed soldier shall be avenged." He then ordered the column to resume its march at an even quicker pace.

About an hour before sunset, one of the scouts again approached Jackson, this time reporting bones had been found, probably one of the victims of the massacre. Jackson turned to Wooster. "Have one of the survivors see it they can identify the remains, Major."

Wooster turned his horse and rode back to Vashon's company. Stopping next to Vashon, he said, "Captain, the scouts have located some skeletal remains. I'd like Sergeant Dill to go forward and see if he can determine if it's the body of one of Scott's detachment." Vashon helped Dill climb onto the back of his mount, and the three men trotted off toward the front of the line.

What they found was a widely scattered pile of bones, obviously human, but spread out and jumbled from the actions of wolves and other scavengers. Vashon closed his eyes and turned away. Might it be Elizabeth? Dill walked among the bones for a few minutes, shaking his head. Then he stopped, bent over, and picked up a tattered piece of cloth. Turning to the officers who were watching from their horses, he said, "It's Jenny Holly, sirs. Gorman said he thought he'd seen her taken prisoner." He picked up a stick and began to probe through the leaf litter. After a few moments he bent over and picked up a small piece of bone. In his hand was a miniature human jawbone. "She was near due with child, sirs."

Vashon relaxed and let out a deep breath. Wiping a tear from his eye, he turned to Wooster. "Perhaps 'tis better her husband died in the massacre than to have seen this, sir."

Wooster nodded and looked down at Dill. "When the company arrives, Sergeant, have them scour the area for any other remains or artifacts. We shall afford this young lady a proper burial, with full military honors. She suffered as much as, if not more than, her companions on that boat, and in as much as we cannot bury them, her grave shall represent them all."

Jack Dill awoke the next morning and walked down to the river. *This is where they waited for us,* he thought. *Did he yell out a victory cry when he killed Annie? Did he even know he'd done it?* He took a seat on the ground, lowered his head, and began to cry. He heard footsteps coming from behind, but paid them no mind. He knew who it was.

John Stuart sat down next to his friend and put an arm around his shoulder. "We'll get even, Jack. I promise it. We'll slaughter every damn one of them."

Dill kept staring at the sand in front of his feet. "We slaughter them; they slaughter us. I don't care anymore, Johnny. I just miss Annie."

"I know. I feel it, too. All I can think about is Elizabeth, and wonder what it will be like when we find her. Will she be the same? Will she still love me? It eats at me, Jack, but at least I have hope. I stand a chance of getting her back. Nothing will bring Annie back."

"I didn't want much, Johnny. Just a nice home, a good business, and someone like Annie by my side. And now they've taken it."

"Blood-thirsty redskins. Kill every damn one of 'em, for all I care."

In a way, Dill admired his friend's simple way of thinking: The Indians had attacked the boat, and they should be punished. Yet when Dill attempted to place blame, he always found a deeper layer of responsibility. There seemed no end to it, and no one who could be called guilt-free. "It's not just them, Johnny, it's everybody. It's the squatters, it's the land grabbers, it's the politicians in Washington, the bloody Brits, and the damn Spaniards. Everybody wants an empire, be it big or small, and Annie was just another victim of all that greed. Worse than that, we're part of it. The settlers take the Indians' land, the Indian fights back, and in comes the army to kill off the Indians. And when we get out of the army, we'll be land-hungry settlers, just like the rest. I wonder how many Annies I'll kill before it's over." Dill gave a shake of his body as if trying to throw off a chill that had settled over him. Rising to his feet, he said, "I'm thinking too much, Johnny, and the army doesn't pay me to think. Let's get back and join the march, so we can get this damned war over with. I won't be happy until Elizabeth's home safe with you and the captain. I don't want you to have to feel what I do."

It was late on the second day of the march when they saw the first supply vessel. It was one of the smaller boats and was well ahead of the others, but it was laden with cases of hardtack and barrels of bacon, and the boat's crew were welcomed as saviors. The army made camp, and everyone ate his fill. Andrew Jackson's determined scowl was replaced by a triumphant smile. His one great doubt about the mission had been removed. With a well-fed and properly equipped army, there was nothing standing between him, the enemy, and the conquest of Florida.

The news that the American army was headed down the Apalachicola and not straight for the towns at Lake Miccosukee caught the Indians by surprise. Everyone had expected Jackson to wait for his supplies to arrive, after which he would strike at the heart of the Seminole nation. Huddled around a warm campfire, Yellow Tom and Neamathla discussed the situation. Neamathla noted, "Jackson is impatient. He cannot wait to kill the red man."

Tom nodded in agreement. "His army will be well fed, and their cartridge boxes will be full. There will be little that can stand in their way. Why have the towns not been abandoned and the people moved south?"

"Kinnachee and the Red Sticks still think they can fight off the Americans. They have listened too eagerly to the Englishmen and believe their promises of aid. Homathlemico leaves in the morning to join Hillishadjo, then both will go to St. Marks, where they believe the English ships will come. I fear the war will be over and our people scattered like the wind-borne leaves of autumn before any English ship comes to our aid."

"A man often sees with his heart, not his eyes."

Neamathla gave his young friend a knowing smile. "And the white woman you hold captive: Do you see her with your heart or your eyes?"

Tom laughed. "Both. My heart wishes to take her as my wife, but my eyes tell me that her love belongs to her white husband. But I shall be patient. Time and the Breath Giver shall sort such matters as best they see fit. For now, I will keep her safe."

Jackson's army reached the remains of the Negro Fort on the fifth day of the march. The other supply vessels had been contacted and told to rendezvous at the site. It was here that Jackson intended to build his base of operations for the Florida campaign. He instructed his aide, Lieutenant James Gadsden, to erect a new, smaller fort within the confines of the old fort, and then honored the young man by naming the post Fort Gadsden. Loyalty was something Old Hickory appreciated and cultivated. He knew the concerns of the politicians and diplomats in Washington, and how they fretted over offending Spain or England. Jackson didn't care about such things. Whoever stood in the way of the growing American nation, be they foreign or domestic, would be swept aside, and he would have no qualms about doing it. To accomplish his objectives, rules would have to be bent, perhaps broken. When it came time to explain his actions, Jackson would need loyal men like Gadsden to back him up.

Lieutenant Isaac McKeever, United States Navy, was not a devious man by nature. What he was about to do was certainly dishonorable, but he found justification in the fact that he was dealing with what he felt were murderous savages who had little regard for personal honor. Jackson had asked him to find out if the Seminoles and their allies were expecting any aid from the British. Before leaving New Orleans, McKeever had come up with an easy way to accomplish the task. Now, as the anchor of the U.S.S. *Thomas Shields* went down outside St. Marks, a British Union Jack was unfurled off the taffrail. What better way to lure the Indians out to the ship than to present them with the long-awaited British supply ship?

It was easy enough to make the ship look English. *Shields* wasn't a big man o' war, just an eight-gun topsail ketch used to patrol the Caribbean in search of privateers and pirates that might be raiding American shipping. It was the sort of vessel either England or Spain might employ, and didn't appear all that different from a merchant vessel.

It was also a relatively easy task to impersonate a British officer. Wounded and captured during the War of 1812, McKeever had spent three months as a prisoner of war and had learned the mannerisms of an English naval officer. The accent may not have fooled a Londoner, but it was certainly good enough to hoodwink an Indian. What he wasn't sure of was whether or not it would fool a Spaniard.

The first test came that afternoon, when a launch rowed out from the fort carrying a young Spanish lieutenant. Luckily, the officer spoke little English, so McKeever made use of a black crewmember from the islands as an interpreter. The Spaniard welcomed McKeever to St. Marks and asked his business. The American officer told him he was bringing supplies to the Indians, after which the Spaniard politely informed him that no British ships were allowed in Florida waters without written permission from the Captain-General in Havana. McKeever just as courteously told the lieutenant a British frigate was on the way from Havana with precisely those papers. Both men knew the truth. The Spanish lieutenant may not have known McKeever was American, but he knew there was no ship coming from Havana, and McKeever knew there was nothing the Spaniards could do to make him leave. It was all a formality.

After the Spaniard departed, McKeever leaned against the ship's railing and wondered if he'd passed the test. For all he knew, the Spanish lieutenant would go back to the fort and tell everyone to stay away from the American ship flying the British flag. Only time would tell.

A few days passed, and McKeever began to fear he'd been found out. Then a lookout reported a canoe approaching. The American officers once again donned their British uniforms and patiently awaited the arrival of their guests. As the canoes pulled alongside *Shields*, McKeever could tell he was about to greet two important chiefs. He wasn't sure who they were, but the finery of their clothing and the ornamentation they wore indicated they were not common Indians.

The first man to come aboard was a younger chief, strong and fierce. The next man to step on deck was older and more thoughtful looking. McKeever stepped forward and offered the older man his hand. "Welcome aboard, my friends. I bring you greetings from His Majesty's Navy. I am Captain McKeever, and who might I have the privilege of welcoming?" He had no idea if either one spoke English, but he used his best British accent anyway.

The older man took McKeever's hand and shook it warmly. "I am Hillishadjo, and my friend here, who does not speak your tongue, is Homathlemico. Long have we waited to see the flag of the Great King in London. Do you bring us aid for out fight against the Americans?"

McKeever could not believe his luck. He had hoped to capture a few warriors for the purpose of extracting information. He had not dreamt of capturing two of the Red Stick Creek's most important leaders. Jackson would be ecstatic.

McKeever was anxious to spring his trap, but wanted to get as much information from the pair as possible before letting them know they had made a fatal mistake by venturing out to greet him. "I bring you presents and implements of war. We have muskets, lead, and powder for our friends, and scorn for our enemies. How many warriors await our help?"

Hillishadjo smiled. "Many hundreds. With the help of our English friends, we can drive the Americans from our homelands."

McKeever had hoped for a more specific number, but doubted the old man really knew. "Are there any of our English brothers nearby that we might talk to? We should like to know where best to unload our presents."

Something struck Hillishadjo as odd. He'd noticed that none of the crew were speaking or moving about, and had spent enough time on ships to know that sailors were a talkative, active lot. He began to feel uneasy and tried to think of a gracious way to exit. "Our friend Arbuthnot stays with the Commandant of St. Marks, and the young Ambrister should return in not too many days. We will go back to the fort and tell Arbuthnot that you wish words with him."

McKeever wasn't sure what had spooked the old chief, but he had no intention of letting either of them off the ship. "Wait. We have presents for you." He turned to a young officer standing nearby. "Mr. Bainbridge: The rifles, please." A few of the sailors leaning against the railing moved to block the Indians' path to the ladder and their canoe. Two others threw off the tarpaulin covering a hatch, revealing a pair of muskets. They quickly picked up the weapons and pointed them at the Indians, while out of another hatch poured a squad of Marines, their muskets fitted with bayonets.

Homathlemico immediately lunged for the railing, hoping to jump over the side and swim to safety. A burly sailor stepped in front of him, club in hand, and swung it into the chief's stomach. Homathlemico doubled over in pain. Two other sailors pushed him to the deck and quickly removed his tomahawk and scalping knife. Hillishadjo didn't move or struggle as a sailor took hold of him. His own desperate longing for the oft-promised English aid had led him into a trap.

McKeever smiled. "Mr. Bainbridge: Run up a proper flag. I'll no longer stand under that damned Union Jack." He then turned to one of the Marines. "Sergeant, take our guests below, and show them the comfort of our brig."

It took ten days for Fort Gadsden to be erected and for all the supplies to be off-loaded from the ships and into the storehouses. It had also taken nearly a week for the remaining troops to arrive and the friendly Creeks to show up. General Jackson had rushed things as much as he could, but he also wanted the men to rest and to get everything in order. On March 26, Jackson gave the order to move out. The timing seemed right. The men were well rested, their stomachs were full, and they were anxious to go to war. That was good, because once they resumed the march, the army wouldn't stop until the Seminoles were destroyed.

Elizabeth could hear the young warrior and his woman making love at the other end of the lodge. It had started out with muted giggles from the woman, followed by heavy breathing accompanied by an occasional grunt from the warrior. Neither one seemed to be in a hurry, and they certainly weren't trying to conceal their pleasures. They were simply doing what came naturally, something Elizabeth sorely missed.

She could also see, by the moonlight that filtered into the lodge through the cracks in the walls, the handsome form of Yellow Tom, asleep, and not more than four feet away from her. It was a temptation she was finding harder and harder to resist. She still loved Johnny and her mind recoiled at the thought of being unfaithful, but at the same time, his memory was starting to fade. She knew this, and tried to think of him, of his face, his touch, his kiss, and his body, but somehow Tom's image kept intruding into the mental picture. It wouldn't have been such a problem if Tom had been in any way repugnant, but he was quite the opposite. Not only was he physically attractive, he was also protective, considerate, and certainly not the savage she had feared. Indeed, with the exception of a few belligerent warriors such as Tom's enemy Efa-Hadjo, she was hard pressed to find anyone in the tribe she considered truly savage. True, their customs were different and often violent, but there seemed to be far fewer people she could define as "evil."

One of the things that bothered her most was that she'd never attempted to escape. In the early days of her presence among the Indians, she had been too well guarded to even consider the idea. As she became more accepted by the tribe and settled into a routine, there were occasional opportunities to flee, but she always shied away from taking advantage of the situation. She wasn't quite sure why. Part of it had to do with the knowledge that sooner or later the army would come to punish the Seminoles and would rescue her in the process. There was also, she had to admit, this growing attraction to Yellow Tom. Beyond that, there was the fear of what would happen to her if she were unsuccessful in her bid for freedom. At present, she was reasonably well treated. That might change if she betrayed the trust these people had shown her.

And that, more than anything, was what prevented her from attempting an escape. In exchange for treating her with a modest amount of respect, her Indian captors had relied on her not to abuse that trust. In a sense, she was cooperating with the very people who had brutally slain all those people on Lieutenant Scott's boat, including Annie and Nellie. And while she could never forgive them for what had happened, she also understood that equally cruel depredations had been carried out upon the Indians by the whites. No one was to blame for the bloodshed, but everyone was responsible. When she thought back on all the times she'd spoken callously about the Indians or had reveled in their defeat or destruction, she began to understand that she was as much a part of the animosity as any gun-toting backwoodsman. Like everyone else, she had accepted them as inferior savages. If she had been wrong about that, what else was she wrong about?

It took six days for the army to march from Fort Gadsden to the Seminole towns around Lake Miccosukee. Indian runners had given the towns a few days' advance warning of the army's approach, allowing the remaining women and children a chance to gather their belongings, leave their homes, and move into the dense forest. No one had any intention of totally abandoning the area. Some chiefs confidently predicted that the Americans would come, there would be a battle, and the invaders would be driven off. The more realistic leaders entertained no such fantasy. The villages would be destroyed, the remaining cattle stolen, and the crops consumed. Yet no matter what happened, the Mikasuki people would remain, eventually to return and rebuild. The Americans were like fires, floods, or fierce winds: The damage would be real, but not everlasting. As long as Spain owned Florida, it could be no other way.

In the meantime, Andrew Jackson was faced with a tactical problem. Lake Miccosukee was a fairly large body of water surrounded by a number of small villages and towns and a few smaller lakes, some with their own villages. While Kinnachee's town was the largest, destroying only one settlement would have a negligible effect on the Indians. If the Seminoles were to be driven from the borderlands, everything would have to be destroyed. To do that, Jackson would have to spread his army out, sending detachments to locate the many scattered villages. He could have gone about the attack in a slow, methodical manner, but that wasn't the way he did things. He would press the attack with all the speed and fury his army could deliver, destroy everything in his path, then move on to the next objective. It wasn't a very elegant way to fight a war, but when you had overwhelming force, it was certainly effective.

To accomplish his mission, Jackson approached the area from the west, and then had his forces fan out, each division heading off in a slightly different easterly direction. The orders were simple: If they saw enemy warriors, kill them. If they saw women and children, take them prisoner. If they found a village, burn it. If they found cattle and horses, round them up. If they found food, take what they could carry and destroy the rest. By the end of the day, nothing of value was to be left for those who had escaped.

Major Wooster, in charge of three companies of the Fourth Infantry, attempted to do his fighting a bit more scientifically. He instructed his men to move as quietly as possible, with an advance guard and flankers, and with everyone always on the lookout for an ambush. Vashon and Stuart were placed near the forefront, in hopes they would recognize Elizabeth before any harm came to her. In truth, Wooster doubted she would be in the area. He assumed the Indians had received several days' notice of the army's approach and had subsequently removed the non-combatants to safe locations. Still, it did give the father and husband an opportunity to feel as if they were doing all they could to rescue the young woman. Wooster would have wanted the same privilege, had it been someone he loved in a similar situation.

For Captain Vashon, the anxiety was becoming almost unbearable. His primary mission was not to kill the enemy, but to rescue his daughter. Happily for the cause of the army, one objective seemed to mesh with the other. The sooner the Seminoles were crushed, the sooner they would be forced to return his daughter. He was not, for some reason, especially concerned for her safety. Spies had informed him that she was being well treated by her captors, and he knew she was more valuable as a hostage or bargaining piece than as a dead woman. His greatest fear was that she might get injured in a crossfire.

John Stuart's priorities were a bit different. Although he was determined to rescue his wife, he was even more firm in his resolution to wipe out those who had taken her from him. Stuart was also bothered by a feeling that he'd lost control of Elizabeth. The one thing that made his life special had been taken from him, and he didn't like the feeling. He began to feel like some miser, more intent on hoarding his money than enjoying it. She was *his* woman, and only *he* would have her. Now she was *theirs*, or, more specifically, some Indian's named Yellow Tom. He had no idea in what manner the savages were using her, but he could only assume the worst, and for the past four months, it had been nearly all he could think about. To him, she had been perfection, and now that perfection had been sullied.

Also at the forefront of Wooster's column was Jack Dill. Like Stuart and Vashon, he was intent on rescuing Elizabeth. Although he had no familial attachment to her, he did consider her one of his closest friends, perhaps more so after the loss of Annie. He felt it had been his responsibility to protect them both while on the voyage from Fort Montgomery to Fort Scott. In that, he had failed miserably. Rescuing Elizabeth and asking her forgiveness was now an obsession. He only wished there was some way to ask Annie's forgiveness.

As he watched from his concealment, Yellow Tom could see a line of soldiers approaching through the pine forest, heading directly for the hardwood hammock where he and his fellow warriors were concealed. He also noticed fixed bayonets on their muskets, which meant they intended to charge into battle, not form a line and shoot volleys at the Indians hidden in the dense foliage. He knew his own warriors were no match for the white men, being predominantly untried young men that Neamathla had assigned him to lead. Still, if the Americans could be delayed, it would help ensure the women and children of his clan could make good their escape. There was a certain young woman among them he did not want falling into enemy hands.

The men of the Fourth Infantry were about a mile from the first villages when Major Wooster called a halt. They were marching through a relatively open pine forest, and up ahead was the edge of a thick grove of low oaks interspersed with palmetto bushes. It was the perfect place for someone to stage an ambush. Stopping just out of rifle range, Wooster let his men catch up, and then met with his two senior officers. Pointing toward the oaks, he said, "We have to assume that is where they'll make their first stand. Allison, deploy your men to the left, Vashon, you take the right. We'll advance cautiously in line, taking cover behind the trees whenever possible. When they open fire, sound the charge and run at them in an orderly manner. Once we've gained the hammock, halt the advance, take cover, and regroup. When all is in order, we'll press on and take the town." He looked at Vashon. "We do this in an orderly fashion. No heroics from you or your men. I want you alive when we find your daughter."

The soldiers fanned out and began to approach the woods. When they were about fifty yards from the first oaks a shot rang out, followed by a hundred more and the sound of innumerable war whoops. As Vashon raised his sword to lead the charge, he felt a musket ball tug at the edge of his coat as it passed through. To his right, he heard a soldier cry out, then fall to the ground. As the bugler sounded the charge, the rest of the soldiers pointed their bayonets at the enemy and began to advance at an easy run, shouting at the top of their lungs.

Off to Vashon's right, Sergeant Dill felt a pull on his chin strap as a ball hit his tall, cylindrical hat. He took no time to reflect on how close it had come to killing him. The shot had missed, and that was that. The only thing he had to concern himself with was reaching the hammock with as many of his men as possible. He looked down the line of soldiers, shouting at those who advanced too eagerly, while checking for those who might be lagging behind. He could tell a few had been wounded, but otherwise the company was holding together as well as might be expected.

Sergeant Stuart was one of the first men to reach the woods. Anxious to spill Indian blood, he'd moved a bit faster than the other men, and had purposely headed for the closest puffs of smoke. Seeing the back of a retreating warrior, he leveled his musket and fired. "Have that, you red-skinned bastard!" he shouted as the man fell to the earth. As he began to reload, another warrior sprang up from a nearby tree and charged at him with a tomahawk held high. Turning quickly toward the threat, Stuart lowered the musket and drove the bayonet into the man's stomach. With fiery eyes and teeth clenched, he pierced the warrior's abdomen again and again. As the man fell to the ground, Stuart kicked him onto his back and drove the bayonet into the warrior's heart.

Back at the center of the company, Captain Vashon was swinging his sword in the air, leading his men in the charge. Suddenly he felt a pain in his side, and put his hand over the spot. Looking down, he saw blood, but stopped his advance only momentarily. No matter how serious the wound, he would not stop until he'd reached his objective. A few yards later, he passed the first oak tree. He advanced another twenty yards and began to call out for the men to halt and regroup. Leaning against a tree, he called out for Lieutenant Clinch, his second-in-command. The other officer ran up, and then turned white as he saw the blood on Vashon's coat. The wounded man slowly lowered himself to the ground, resting his back against the tree. He looked up at Clinch and said, "The company is yours, Clinch. Do your best to find my daughter." Closing his eyes, Vashon slumped to the earth.

Yellow Tom was breathing hard. The soldiers had been impossible to stop, and his warriors had been forced to fall back. Still, it had not been an all-out rout. They were retreating slowly, keeping up a steady fire, making the whites advance with caution. It would be that way all day.

John Stuart watched with some relief as the wounded were carried from the field. Captain Vashon's wound, though serious, had been declared non-mortal by the surgeon. As he returned to his company, a firm resolve came over him, a determination to find Elizabeth as quickly as possible and reunite her with her father. He knew there was little he could do in a practical sense, other than push his men forward, hoping they could somehow break through the defenses and catch the women and children before they made their escape.

When the order to advance was given, Stuart and his men were at the forefront, pushing toward the villages as fast as Clinch would allow. With Captain Vashon out of action, the company was down to one officer, effectively leaving Stuart, as the senior sergeant, second-in-command. After some confusion as to where the allied Creeks were, Stuart pressed on, cursing the time that had been lost. Brandishing his musket high above his head, he shouted encouragement to the men, telling them when to keep together and when to spread out, when to take cover and when to advance.

The fighting continued for several hours, the army advancing against an enemy that was almost unseen. The combat was fiercest around the villages, but the Indians never showed themselves in any concentration, and always from some sort of concealment. It was obvious they were not trying to repulse the Americans, only slow them down, and the very thought of being delayed only made Stuart push all the harder. Finally, as the sun inched its way toward the western horizon, word came down that General Jackson had called a halt. There would be no further pursuit of the enemy that day. The villages were to be secured; the troops were to gather and regroup. Stuart was angry, not yet willing to give up the chase. Dill calmed him down, assuring him the women and children were long gone, and warning him not to take foolish chances. Stuart was breathing hard, exhausted from the pursuit. Dill was right. Elizabeth was already in danger of losing her father. If he wasn't careful, she might be rescued, only to find out she was a widow and an orphan.

6th April 1818
Before Ft. St. Marks
E. Florida

To:
The Honorable John C. Calhoun
Secretary of War
Washington City

Sir,

It is with exceeding pleasure that I have the honor to inform you of the rapid advance of our forces and the complete chastisement of the barbarous savages populating the border lands with Georgia. After having erected the depot on the Apalachicola, the army was provisioned, supplied with the necessities of war, and otherwise prepared for the ensuing campaign. Departing Fort Gadsden on the 26th ultimo, we marched at a brisk pace to the northeast, arriving at the Mikasuki towns on the morning of the 1st instant. The enemy, no doubt having been forewarned by British agents of our approach, had abandoned their villages and fled to the safety of the inhospitable swamps. A spirited, though disorganized, resistance was encountered, but after some initial confusion as to location of the allied

Creek forces, we were able to enter the towns largely unopposed.

I can report with some confidence that the savages will not soon be returning to their homes, nor shall they be of a mind to commit further depredations upon our frontier. In total, in all the villages the army visited, several hundred cabins were put to the torch, and many acres of cultivated land stripped of any crops. Although the Seminoles no doubt drove many of their cattle into hiding, several hundred head were captured, and those that were not needed to supply meat to our troops were sent north with several companies of Georgia Militia, and the proceeds of the sale will serve as prize money for the volunteers and militia.

As if any further justification for our actions were needed, I find it painfully necessary to report that in the center of the principal village, no doubt the home of the chief Ken-Hadgee, a red pole was discovered, festooned with the scalps of over fifty hapless victims of the Indians' cruelty and barbarity. Several of the scalps were identified as belonging to members of Lt. Scott's party, including those of several females. Also discovered was evidence of a British presence in the village, no doubt those scoundrels Arbuthnot and Ambrister, who have neglected no opportunity to delude the savages with promises of military aid and the return of lands lost during the late war. Should these miscreants have the misfortune to fall within my grasp, it shall go hard on them.

I have now encamped the army approximately one mile away from the Spanish post of Fort St. Marks, having received intelligence of the Seminoles and their allies being supplied and aided by the commandant of this post. I shall endeavor to communicate with the commanding officer in the morning to ascertain the veracity of these reports. Spain is bound by treaty to prevent depredations upon United States soil, and I shall not countenance a Spanish officer violating those obligations.

Casualties during the storming of the Mikasuki villages were light, with fewer than half a dozen men lost and no more than twenty wounded. Among those wounded is Captain Vashon of the Fourth Infantry, who has suffered a ball to the chest, but hope is entertained for his eventual recovery. It was Vashon's daughter who was taken prisoner from Lt. Scott's boat, and it is my fervent wish to have her reunited with her father as soon as possible.

In part because of Captain Vashon's delicate condition, I will leave the Fourth Infantry here at St. Marks while the army presses south toward the Suwannee. Besides the large Seminole village at Old Town, it is believed several hundred escaped slaves reside nearby. If I proceed with haste, we may be successful in capturing these fugitives and thereafter return them to their rightful owners.

I am, with the utmost respect,
Yr. Mo. Obt. Svt.
Andrew Jackson
Major General, U. States Army
Commanding, Forces of the Southern Division

Hillishadjo was resigned to his fate. He stepped proudly from the cell located in the filthy bowels of the small warship anchored off St. Marks and offered no resistance to the sailors leading him away. Homathlemico, on the other hand, was not done fighting. The chief struggled with the sailors dragging him from the cell, but the heavy iron manacles that bound his wrists and ankles severely limited his motion and rendered him practically powerless to resist.

The two prisoners were brought on deck and pushed toward the railing. Looking over the side, Hillishadjo could see two boats with about half a dozen well-armed sailors in each. He wasn't sure what that meant. Was he being sent to the Spanish commandant at St. Marks? It didn't seem likely. Don Francisco might well have agreed to ransom him from the Americans, but what did the Spaniard have that the Americans would take in trade? The more likely reason for his being taken ashore was that the American army had arrived, and he was being turned over to General Jackson or one of his officers. Whatever happened next was likely to be unpleasant.

Hillishadjo watched as Homathlemico continued to struggle with his captors. Pushed to the railing, the man refused to climb down the ladder and into the waiting boat. Tiring of the struggle, one of the sailors wrapped a rope several times around the chief's arms and chest, making it nearly impossible for him to move. The sailor then took a rope hanging from the mast and attached it to the bindings. Bundled and restrained, Homathlemico was hoisted over the side and lowered into the boat. Laughing lustily, the sailors kicked the chief into position at the center of the boat and began to row ashore. The other boat approached the ladder, and Hillishadjo stepped to the railing, climbed down the ladder, and took a seat near the back of the boat. There was, quite simply, no fight left in him.

It took about half an hour for the boats to reach the shoreline, then another half hour to ascend the St. Marks River to where it split into its two main branches. Strategically positioned at the center of that split was the small Spanish fort. The boats took the right fork, and as they glided past the fort Hillishadjo could see Spanish soldiers on the parapet, a bewildered, concerned look on their faces.

It was near noon when the boats finally came ashore, about a mile above the fort. Hillishadjo waded onto the landing as confidently as he could, his gait restricted by the manacles that bound his ankles. Homathlemico, still bundled in ropes, struggled defiantly and shouted curses at his captors. Three sailors lifted him from the bottom of the vessel, carried him ashore, and dumped him unceremoniously on the ground.

A group of about thirty American soldiers were awaiting the Indians' arrival. At the center of that group stood a tall, older man with a full head of graying hair. No one had to tell Hillishadjo that this was Andrew Jackson.

Jackson looked at the two Red Stick leaders with a cold, satisfied look in his eye, and then turned to one of the other officers. "Very well, Major Wooster. You may string them up."

Hillishadjo noticed that even the other Americans were surprised at the abruptness of the order. The one named Wooster had a puzzled look on his face. "Sir?"

Jackson looked slightly annoyed. "I said hang them, Major. Do you have a problem with hanging murderous savages?"

"No, sir, but should they not be questioned first, or perhaps given some sort of trial and allowed to defend themselves?"

The general shook his head. "A waste of time and words, Major. Show them to the nearest suitable tree and be done with them." With that, Jackson turned and walked away.

Wooster took a deep breath and then turned to one of the soldiers. "Sergeant Stuart, we have our orders. Shall we proceed?" Hillishadjo watched as a sailor walked down to the boats and returned with a length of rope. An officer motioned toward a large, wide-spread oak tree. Homathlemico was hoisted to his feet, and the group started to march toward the tree.

So this is where I end my days, Hillishadjo thought. *It is time.* He looked around. *It is a pleasant place.* They stopped under the tree, and the rope was thrown over a stout limb. Homathlemico was pushed forward toward the waiting noose. The struggle had finally gone out of the chief, but not the defiance. As the noose was placed over his head, he spat in the face of the man named Stuart.

Stuart's fist lashed out, hitting Homathlemico square in the jaw and drawing blood. "Have a quick trip to Hell, you son-of-a-bitch!" the soldier shouted.

The major calmly said, "That is enough, Sergeant," then nodded to the men who were holding the rope.

Hillishadjo called out in his native tongue, "Fear not my friend, we shall soon be with our ancestors."

Homathlemico could not respond. As his body was jerked from the ground, the noose tightened around his neck, cutting off his breath. He struggled against the pain, jerking his body from side to side in a futile attempt to ease the agony. Hillishadjo watched as a minute or two passed, until the motion stopped and his friend hung limply at the end of the rope.

Homathlemico's body was lowered to the ground, and Hillishadjo was led forward. As the noose was placed around his neck, the major stepped up and asked, "Do you have any last words?"

Hillishadjo thought for a moment, and then said, "My daughter saved the life of one of your soldiers. For this I have no regret. I die an honorable man."

Stuart stepped in front of the condemned man. Hillishadjo could see pure hatred in the white man's eyes. The sergeant's voice seethed as he asked, "Where is my wife, damn you? The one you took from the boat on the river."

Hillishadjo understood the man's rage. It was really no different from what many of his people had felt after being defeated by Jackson several years earlier. "You have cause for your anger, and I forgive you. The last I saw her, she was at Lake Miccosukee, but that is many weeks ago, and she may no longer be there." He thought to offer to find the woman and return her to her husband in exchange for his life, but knew the offer would be denied. Jackson would rather risk the life of a white woman than spare the life of a red man.

The major put a hand on the sergeant's shoulder and gently pulled him back. He then nodded to the soldiers who held the rope. Hillishadjo felt an excruciating pain in his neck and a torturous pressure in his lungs. His legs involuntarily thrashed, and his vision began to fade. The last thing he perceived was the face of his daughter, and it gladdened his heart.

Yellow Tom was worried. For some reason, his clanswomen, Elizabeth among them, had gone south to the camp of the Red Stick leader Peter McQueen, instead of east to the Mikasuki towns along the St. Johns River, as had been intended. The fighting at the villages had lasted a few days, with the Seminoles always forced to fall back and eventually watch their homes go up in flames. With outlying villages spread out over a large area, the exodus had been anything but organized. In reality, it was no surprise that some groups had taken a path they had not planned to. Some had even wandered into the hands of the whites. His concern grew as he hurried his mount south, trying to close the distance between himself and McQueen's camp. Would his mother, Elizabeth, or any of his people be safe if Efa-Hadjo and his band arrived at the camp first?

Don Francisco Caso y Luengo felt trapped. Two hours earlier he had been informed that boats from the American ship anchored in the harbor had brought Hillishadjo and Homathlemico ashore and turned them over to the American army. Not long after, the boats returned to the Gulf, and one of the sailors had shouted at the sentries, making a gesture indicating someone had been hung. They also indicated that the Spaniards might be next. Now, barely an hour later, American soldiers were at the gate, awaiting Luengo's response to a letter from Andrew Jackson.

Unable to read English with any fluency, the Spanish officer handed the letter to his friend Alexander Arbuthnot. The old Scotsman read the letter and shook his head. "The arrogance of the man! He demands the surrender of this fort, as if a state of war existed between the United States and Spain. All very politely said, of course, but that's the tally of it."

Luengo was shocked. "Has the man no respect for the law of nations? On what grounds can he possibly demand the surrender of this fortress?"

"Believe it or not, he says it's for your own protection. He states he has reliable intelligence that a large force of Seminoles and Red Sticks intend to overrun your fort, and to prevent this, he must occupy the fortress with American troops."

"That is preposterous. The Indians flee south to avoid the Americans. They would certainly not seek refuge here."

Arbuthnot nodded in agreement, but understood the reality. "Since when does a thief need an honest excuse?" He looked hard at Luengo. "How will you respond?"

"If he fears this fortress being taken by the Indians, I will tell Jackson his troops are welcome to encamp nearby, but honor and duty will not allow me to surrender my post without permission from my superiors in Havana. I will even offer him the use of our infirmary for the care of his wounded, should he need it. Surely a soldier must understand the responsibilities of command."

Arbuthnot was doubtful. "Any man who would make such a demand in the first place cares little for the niceties of honor and duty, except when they can be used to his advantage."

Luengo looked at his Scottish friend. "I begin to fear for your safety, mi amigo. A man who would violate a sacred treaty between friendly nations would not think twice to violate the protection I have offered you under the flag of my country. It would have been better had you gone to the Suwannee with Ambrister and your son."

"Do you plan to defend the fort?"

"I must defend the honor of our flag. Yet what can seventy men do against the thousands that are gathering outside our walls? There is not enough powder in the magazine to fire the cannon ten times." Luengo also questioned the loyalty of his troops, but said nothing. Perhaps if Havana paid them regularly, they might have been more dependable. "Should I be forced to surrender, I will say you are my father. They would have little cause to question it."

Arbuthnot gazed toward the Gulf of Mexico and saw the masts of the American warship. There was nowhere for him to go. As long as that ship remained anchored at the mouth of the river, there was no way for his own vessel to approach and rescue him. With the American army beginning to encamp all around them, there was no chance of escape overland. Like Luengo, he was trapped.

For the first time in months, Elizabeth felt she was in danger. From the moment she and the other clanswomen had walked into McQueen's camp, she had sensed the eyes upon her and had seen the cold stares. These were Red Sticks, Upper Creeks who had been driven from their homes in Alabama after suffering a bloody defeat at the hands of Andrew Jackson. Their animosity toward the white man ran deep.

The Red Sticks had welcomed them, but certainly not with open arms. Food was scarce, and little of it was doled out to the newcomers. Shelter was minimal, and Elizabeth and the other women had been forced to construct their own crude lean-tos. Although the Mikasukis and Upper Creeks shared a common enemy, they had never been extremely friendly. She felt isolated, and that made her extremely nervous. Beyond that, she was bothered by the knowledge that her presence was putting the lives of her friends in danger.

The strange fact that she suddenly felt like an outsider was an irony that did not escape her. In truth, she had been an outsider for the past five months. Why should she feel any different now? The realization soon came to her that it was because she had been accepted by Tom's extended family, especially his mother. Unfortunately, being accepted by Conowaw was not the same as being accepted by the tribe. At best, she was tolerated. By some, she was despised. Her situation was no different from that of a free black in the white society she had been taken from. No matter how much a person tried to fit in, there would always be those individuals who would not give him or her a chance. At the Mikasuki villages, those who continued to hate her just because she was white had been in the minority. In this village, they were the vast majority.

The whole matter of being accepted by her captors was beginning to weigh heavily on Elizabeth's mind. Why should she want to fit in? These weren't her people. She might make a few friends, but the large part of the Indian population would never truly welcome her. They would accept mixed bloods, like Yellow Tom, because they were born into the tribe, but a pureblood white American would always be seen as an outsider. As far as she could tell, there was nothing she could do about it. And did it really matter? After all, Andrew Jackson, Johnny, and her father were coming to rescue her. All she had to do was stay safe, and before long, her time among the Indians would be nothing but a memory.

Her thoughts were interrupted by the sound of a woman's scream. Rising quickly, she ran in the direction of the sound, stopping only to grab a corn-grinding log that happened to be nearby. Like all Indian women she carried a knife, but it was a small, utilitarian instrument and not much of a weapon. The stout log, on the other hand, felt comfortable in her hands, almost like a war club.

Breaking into a clearing, she saw Tom's mother kneeling, with Efa-Hadjo standing behind her. The warrior had Conowaw's hair gripped tightly in one hand, while the knife in his other hand was pressed firmly on her forehead. He smiled menacingly as he saw Elizabeth approaching, and called out, "Yours, white woman, or hers."

A small crowd had gathered around Efa-Hadjo and Conowaw, and as Elizabeth came near, the circle parted to let her through. Efa-Hadjo laughed. What did he have to fear from the little white woman?

Elizabeth never broke her stride. In one fluid motion, she elevated the club she was carrying and swung it as hard as she could. Efa-Hadjo raised his arm to protect himself, but the momentum was too great, and the club struck him a glancing blow on the side of the head. Dazed, he dropped his knife and loosened his grip on Conowaw's hair. Breaking free, the Indian woman rolled swiftly away, leaving Efa-Hadjo exposed. With a quick change of direction, Elizabeth swung the stick up, squarely between her adversary's legs. Efa-Hadjo fell to his knees in agony, his eyes wide with surprise. Once again she swung her club, this time bringing it crashing down onto his skull with all the force she had within her. As the warrior collapsed dead at her feet, she glowered at a stunned group of men she knew to be his followers. "*Never* threaten a friend of Red Bess."

Commandant Luengo hoped he had averted a disaster. General Jackson had accepted his offer of allowing the Americans to post a protective guard outside Fort St. Marks in exchange for the use of the fort's infirmary. Perhaps by permitting Jackson free access to the fort, the American general would see no need to take it, and Luengo could avoid the shame of having to surrender his post. Still, with three companies of United States Regulars encamped just on the other side of the small moat, the Spanish commander had a right to feel nervous.

From the small window in his quarters, Luengo watched as a group of litter bearers approached the fort. When those that had been felled by disease were added to the casualties from the battle at Lake Miccosukee, there were almost as many American sick and wounded in the fort as there were Spanish soldiers. He had visited one of the wounded, a captain by the name of Vashon, who had once been a militia officer when Baton Rouge had still been under Spanish authority, less than ten years earlier. Although the two had never met, they had known some of the same Spanish officials and held similar opinions of them all. It had been a pleasant conversation, and Luengo truly hoped the man would recover, if only to see the daughter that had been captured by the Seminoles.

Luengo turned from the window and took a seat at the large table that filled much of the room. At the other end of the table was Alexander Arbuthnot. The old Scottish trader had been hiding out in Luengo's quarters ever since the Americans had arrived. He looked over to his host and asked, "Well, laddie, do you think they know I'm here?"

The Spaniard shrugged. "They have not asked, which does surprise me much."

"Do you think Hambly or Doyle told them?"

Luengo shook his head. "They know you saved their lives when Hillishadjo and his friend were here. They swore they would not reveal your presence, and I believe them. What I fear more is what Hillishadjo may have inadvertently said while he was being held on that ship, or what one of my disloyal soldiers might have revealed. I only hope you can remain hidden until the Americans leave."

The words were barely out of his mouth when he heard a commotion from below. Moving to the window, he saw American troops running across the bridge that spanned the moat. Grabbing a sword off the wall, he ran out onto the balcony and looked down at the parade ground. Standing there were the American soldiers and about half of his own men. The Americans had their muskets raised; his soldiers had their hands raised.

Luengo ran down the stairs and up to the American officer. "Who are you, and what is the meaning of this? This is an act of war!"

The officer bowed slightly and politely delivered his message. "Lieutenant Clinch, Fourth United States Infantry at your service, sir. General Jackson sends his regrets, but he does not have the luxury of spending time negotiating the finer points of Spanish honor. This post has been found to be offering aid to the enemy, in violation of the treaty between our two nations, and must therefore be surrendered until such time as His Most Catholic Majesty can properly control the inhabitants of his colony. Your personal property will be respected, the fort's supplies will be inventoried and a receipt given, and you and your men will be transported to the nearest Spanish installation. Do you accept these terms, sir?"

The Spanish officer was stunned. His career, already in jeopardy, was now at an end. He unbuckled his sword and threw it on the ground. "Are these the sons of the illustrious and honored General Washington? How quickly they become corrupted! The shame shall rest on your honor, not mine!"

Clinch smiled. "One more thing, Don Francisco. Please inform Mr. Arbuthnot that he is no longer your guest, but ours."

Andrew Jackson smiled broadly as he watched the Stars and Stripes being raised over Fort St. Marks. If the politicians at Washington played their cards right, it would fly there forever more. He turned to the officers gathered around him, speaking first to General Gaines. "General, I want the army ready to move south in the morning." He next turned to McIntosh, the Lower Creek leader. "General, can your warriors head out this afternoon to scout the road ahead of us to the Suwannee?"

The half-blood Indian nodded. "They have already found the path, my friend, and are several miles to our east. Friends have told us that McQueen and his Red Sticks have a camp not far from here, on Econfina Creek."

"Thank you, General." Jackson next turned to Major Wooster. "Major, the Fourth carried the brunt of the battle at Lake Miccosukee and deserves a respite. I'm going to leave you in command here at St. Marks. If nothing else, it will afford the wounded a chance to recover in a proper infirmary, even if it is a Spanish one. I fear Captain Vashon's injury is more serious than first we thought. Tell him to take heart. I shall have his daughter back to him within the week."

Yellow Tom sensed trouble the moment he rode into Peter McQueen's camp. People were milling about, packing belongings and breaking camp. Tying his horse to a tree, he approached the first warrior he saw. "What news is there? Why do you break camp?"

The warrior looked distracted. "The Americans have taken the Spanish fort at St. Marks. We fear they will be upon us in a day or two."

Tom now understood what was happening. If the reports were true, he needed to get Elizabeth away from there quickly. "Where are the Mikasukis who have come here? I look for Conowaw, the bead woman."

The warrior pointed south. "Not far down that path."

"Has Efa-Hadjo arrived yet?"

The man smiled oddly. "Come and gone, in the worst way."

Tom broke into a run. He may have been too late. Efa-Hadjo would have wasted no time taking his revenge upon Elizabeth.

As he stepped into a clearing, Tom came upon a sight he did not expect to see. His villagers and clanswomen were preparing to leave like everyone else, but the person in charge was not one of the elders, but Elizabeth. She stood in the center of the group, pointing this way and that, telling people to hurry, what they could and could not take, and offering reassurance to those who were frightened. What had happened?

Peter McQueen walked up and put a hand on his shoulder. "Your white woman may be the best warrior you have." All Tom could do was look puzzled. McQueen continued. "Efa-Hadjo threatened your mother, so the little white woman beat him to death with a corn-grinding stick." He then broke into a deep laugh. "I don't know if I would keep her or send her back to the whites." Still laughing, he walked away, leaving Tom bewildered.

Elizabeth, hearing the laughter, turned and saw Tom. Dropping a basket she was holding, she ran up to him, threw her arms around him, and began to cry. Then she slowly pushed away, ever so slightly. The army was only a day or two away. Johnny was close; she could feel it. Yet she also felt something else. She felt safe. Conowaw and the other women had stood by her. Tom had come to protect her, even if he had come too late. He had been worried about her as a person, not as a captive. What on earth could she do that would not betray either him or Johnny?

Tom looked into Elizabeth's tear-filled eyes. Then he kissed her. She didn't move, but just looked into his eyes. They both knew what it meant, and they both knew what would happen that night. She could deny it no longer.

Suddenly there was the sound of gunfire in the distance. A boy came running down the path yelling "Lower Creeks! McIntosh is here!"

He turned to Elizabeth, and then pointed to a heavily wooded area by the stream. "Take the women and hide in that hammock. Don't come out until you hear me call." He looked deep into her eyes and squeezed her hand. "Do what you must. I will understand." He then gave her a quick kiss and ran off down the path.

Elizabeth began to gather the women and children and urge them into the hammock. Some of the younger ones were in a panic, looking around for some prized possession or a missing sibling. Elizabeth grabbed them by the arm and pushed them on their way, assuring them their brother or sister was already in the hammock or that their prized possession wasn't worth their life. When all were accounted for, she ran deep into the woods and threw herself to the ground behind a thick stand of bushes.

For the better part of an hour she lay there, hearing the sound of gunfire come ever closer to her position. Then it stopped, and she could hear the voices of warriors calling out to each other. She knew from their words they were Lower Creeks. Her heart raced. If the Creeks were that close, Johnny and her father could not be far behind. All she had to do was call out, and she would be rescued. Then she thought of the other women. If she revealed her position, the others would surely be taken prisoner. They would be separated from their loved ones just as surely as she had been.

Her thoughts turned to Tom. If she allowed herself to be rescued, she would be reunited with Johnny. If she remained concealed, she would be with Tom. There was no escaping it. The choice was hers, and she had to make it. She closed her eyes and tried to sort it out. She didn't belong in Tom's world, but had been fully accepted into it. She belonged in Johnny's world, but after seeing the cruelty and injustice the whites were inflicting on the Indians, she wasn't sure she wanted to be in it anymore. She cried softly and let her mind wander between the images of the two men's faces. Which one? She closed her eyes, took a deep breath, and made her choice.

Suddenly a shot rang out, and she heard a bullet hit a nearby tree. One of the women had been spotted. The Creeks, thinking there were warriors hidden in the hammock, began to open fire. The other women kept low, trying to remain concealed. Elizabeth knew they would never surrender and risk losing their husbands and brothers. She also knew the Lower Creek warriors would continue to fire until they realized it was the women they were shooting at. Picking up a palmetto frond, she began to shout "White woman, I'm a white woman!" and waved the frond above her head. One shot rang out and perforated the frond, but then someone shouted and the firing ceased. Rising to her feet, she ran out to greet the warriors. She had to somehow convince them that she was the only person hiding in those woods.

One of the warriors approached her. He didn't look like an Indian, and his voice proved her right. He took her hand and said, "It's all right, Mrs. Stuart, you're safe now. My name's Tom Woodward, and I'm a friend of General McIntosh. I'll see that you are safely returned to your husband and father. They've been anxious for you."

She gripped his hand tightly and began to lead him away from the hammock. "Oh, please! Take me away from here! Take me back to Johnny!" She pointed down the path that led back to the center of the camp. "The warriors went down that path. When they fled, I saw my chance to escape and hid out in those woods. Oh, please! Take me to my father!"

The deception seemed to be working. The warriors began to turn toward the path, intent on following their enemy. Then one of the hidden women stood up, followed by another. Soon they all were on their feet, walking out of the hammock. Elizabeth looked at them in disbelief. She caught sight of Conowaw and saw a look of scorn in the woman's eyes. Her heart sank. They thought Elizabeth had revealed their location. They didn't understand what she was trying to do. They thought she had betrayed them. She lowered her head and fought back a tear. The trust had been broken and could never be mended.

Jackson's army moved swiftly south, reaching the scene of the battle the next day. The general greeted Elizabeth warmly, asked her if she'd been mistreated in any way, and attempted to glean as much intelligence from her as he could. For the most part, he was disappointed in what she told him. On the whole, she had been treated well, almost like a member of the tribe. As for any military intelligence, there was little she could tell him that he didn't already know or was the least bit useful. She knew the remaining warriors were headed south, but had no good idea as to their strength.

The information she got from Jackson, however, was of extreme importance. For the first time she learned her father had been wounded at Lake Miccosukee. Even though the general assured her the wound was not life-threatening, she insisted on being taken immediately to St. Marks to be with him. Jackson graciously consented, and after conferring with General McIntosh, a party of Lower Creek warriors commanded by Tom Woodward was detailed to escort her to the captured fort. For Elizabeth, the war was over.

As far as Andrew Jackson was concerned, the war was far from over. No sooner had he finished the interview with Elizabeth than the order was given to continue the march south, toward the

Seminole villages on the Suwannee River. There was reported to be a large settlement of runaway slaves in the area, and he wanted to get his hands on them.

The Suwannee River flowed lazily toward the Gulf of Mexico through the flat, lush Florida landscape. Breaking the calm movement of the water were three boats, all heavily laden with trade goods and making their way toward the mouth of the river. The two smaller vessels were Indian dugout canoes, while the largest was the battered launch from Alexander Arbuthnot's schooner *Chance*. As the launch steered to avoid a small group of manatees, Jonathan Arbuthnot took the time to poke at one of the large, lumbering creatures with an oar. It would have been easy to kill the beast, he thought, but what would he do with it? It was too heavy to drag ashore, especially along the thickly wooded banks of the Suwannee. The thick hide made the creature difficult to skin, and the meat was reported to be fatty and distasteful. All in all, more trouble than it was worth.

He was beginning to think the same of Florida. His father seemed to love the place and its inhabitants, but Jonathan could not see the attraction. The business was good, but was it worth all the dangers and complications? Between the Spaniards demanding payoffs, the pirates to be avoided, and the gifts to be distributed to the Indians, the cost of simply setting up shop was almost too high to justify the expense. The Indians, though usually friendly, could not be entirely trusted. If prices were too high or changes in leadership brought new alliances, their mood could change in an instant. Whenever he came to Florida, the younger Arbuthnot always felt as if he had to watch his back. Now, with news of the approaching Americans, he saw even less reason to like the place.

In the closest canoe was Robert Ambrister, who wasn't quite sure what he was doing in Florida. He had been hired to go to

Florida, maintain friendly communications with the Seminoles, and keep an eye out for any opportunity to make a profit. Maintaining friendships with the Indians had proved the easiest part of the job. All you had to do was shower the chiefs with cheap presents and tell them what they wanted to hear. He made it a point not to tell them outright lies, but he was certainly not above bending the truth, almost to the breaking point.

Finding business opportunities was the difficult part. He had originally been told he was laying the groundwork for an effort to displace Forbes and Co. as the principal merchants in the area, but as the months passed, he wasn't so sure. Forbes still had the Spanish monopoly, and there was a limited market for small traders like Arbuthnot. Ambrister began to suspect Governor Cameron and Captain Woodbine, the people who had hired him, had designs on Florida itself. The Spanish were losing control of the colony, and someone was going to step in and take their place. Revolutionaries from Mexico and South America had shown some interest, but they were more akin to pirates than anything else. In truth, there were only two powers that had any real interest in Florida: the United States and Great Britain. The Americans had been trying to negotiate a purchase for some time and now appeared to be attempting to take it by force. But the King of Spain had little use for the Americans, with all their talk of democracy and republics. If His Most Catholic Majesty truly wanted to be rid of the place, he'd much prefer to hand it over to his fellow monarch, George III of England, even if the man was a Protestant.

In the other canoe was eighteen-year-old Peter Cook, the clerk who worked for Arbuthnot. Unlike Jonathan Arbuthnot, Cook liked Florida. Compared to the small, somewhat barren islands of his native Bahamas, Florida seemed a lush and boundless place. Unlike Ambrister, Cook knew exactly why he was here. He needed the work. Not that Arbuthnot was paying him all that well, but there was always the opportunity to make a few shillings on the side, as long as the old man didn't notice when things were missing. Unfortunately, Arbuthnot had noticed things weren't right, and had threatened to turn him in to the magistrates when they returned to Nassau. Not that the old trader could prove anything. Cook was careful to pilfer only those things that were not easily counted or that could in some way be diluted. He'd gotten away with it with his first employer and would probably do so again. After all, it was his word against Arbuthnot's, with no tangible evidence to back up the charges.

He would need the money if his master plan was going to work. Courting Liz Carney was going to take some cash, but not more than he could reasonably expect to raise. After all, Liz wasn't royalty, she was just the daughter of Nassau shipwright Ted Carney. True, Liz was no great beauty, but that wasn't the attraction. She was an only daughter, and old Ted probably had a considerable sum of money stashed away somewhere. At least that's what Cook surmised. Carney's shipyard was a busy place, but the old shipwright lived a very frugal existence. The profits had to be somewhere, and Cook intended to get his hands on them by the easiest means available. Getting a wife was just a means to an end.

As the three boats came to the mouth of the river, they could see *Chance* anchored just outside the sandbar. It would be another hour before they reached the schooner, making their way through the winding passages of the small delta and around the shallowest parts of the bar. It would take several more hours to unload the cargo and stow it away. When that was finished, Cook and Ambrister would take the canoes and bring down the final load of merchandise from the store. They had to hurry, because for all they knew, the Americans were only a day or two away.

Yellow Tom sat on the south bank of the Suwannee River and watched as the Americans set up their tents and built their campfires amid the cabins and huts of the abandoned Seminole villages. It had been a desperate fight, but the native forces had simply been overwhelmed. They had also been surprised. Scouts had warned them of the enemy's approach, but the news had come too late, and the Americans had come too fast. There had barely been enough time to get the women, children, and elders safely across the river before the first attackers arrived. The black Seminoles had fought with the most ferocity. They had a special hatred for the whites, especially the Georgia Militia, and were determined to kill as many as possible. They were also determined not to be taken alive.

Tom lowered his head and closed his eyes. Was there anything left for him? His village was gone, and his people were scattered. He had no idea where he would go. Neamathla spoke of returning to the Apalachicola after the Americans went back to Georgia. Others spoke of joining the bands living in the Alachua Prairie or along the St. Johns. Many had decided to go farther south, to a place known as the Cove of the Withlacoochee, an area of lakes and islands where the whites would never find them. Most of the blacks talked about a settlement called Angola, south of Tampa Bay. None of these options sounded especially inviting or foreboding to Tom. They would simply be a place to lie down at night, a place to take his meals. None of them could be home, because the things that symbolized home had all been taken from him. The cabin he had constructed with his own hands at Fowltown had been reduced to ashes. His few possessions had been destroyed or lost along the way, including his copy of *The Wealth of Nations*, his only memento of his father. He had no idea where his mother was and could only assume she was a prisoner of the whites. Most painful of all was the knowledge that he'd lost Elizabeth. Perhaps the dreams he'd had were all hopeless fantasies, but they had given him joy. Now they brought nothing but sadness.

Robert Ambrister and Peter Cook hauled their canoes onto the embankment and started down the path toward the village. It was late at night, but the bright moonlight and their familiarity with the wide path made it an easy trek. There was one last load of trade goods to take out to *Chance*, and then they would raise anchor and work their way father down the coast, probably to Cedar Key. It had been a tough decision for Jonathan Arbuthnot to make. They had left his father at St. Marks with the intention of returning for him after the store at the Suwannee was emptied. Unfortunately, the Americans had moved swifter than any of them could have predicted, and the whereabouts of the elder Arbuthnot was unknown. Perhaps he had fled to one of the Indian camps, or perhaps he had been captured. Maybe he was still hiding out at St. Marks. Until they found out something definite or until the Americans left, it would be foolish to sail in that direction. Reports had it there was a heavily armed American warship anchored off the coast of St. Marks, and none of them wanted to risk running into that.

Despite the tension of the situation, the pair were laughing heartily, having just shared a bawdy story about a certain tavern maid in Nassau. Catching sight of a campfire near the edge of the woods, they turned toward it, hoping there would be some Indians sitting around who might give them some food. Breaking into the clearing, they sauntered up to the fire and called out to the half-dozen warriors seated around it. Suddenly Ambrister realized something wasn't right. Not far away were other fires, more than there should have been. He also noticed some military-style tents. A cold chill ran through his body as he realized these were not Seminole warriors but the American's Lower Creek allies. Before he could even think to run, the warriors were on their feet and coming towards him. Cook just stood by, totally unaware of what was happening. Ambrister raised his hands and shook his head. If only he hadn't been wearing his old Royal Marines uniform coat.

April 21, 1818
Fort St. Marks, Spanish E. Florida

To:
Mr. Robert Vashon
St. Louis
Missouri Territory

My Dearest Robert,

Oh, what a great joy it is to at last communicate with you and inform you that I have been rescued from my captivity among the Indians and reunited with Father and Johnny.

And yet, for all the happiness I should feel at this moment, a deep sadness hangs over my heart that destroys all the joyousness of this reunion. Alas, dear Robert, it is with exceeding dread that I must tell you that Father has died, succumbing to wounds received in battle with the Indians some four weeks past. As befits a man of such courage and honor, Father was struck down by a ball to the chest while leading a charge against the Indians at Lake Miccosukee. At first, I am told, the injury was not considered to be that serious, and hopes were entertained for a speedy recovery. As is often the case, however, infection soon set in, and Father's condition began a slow decline.

If I have any good news to report in this matter, it is that I was able to see and speak with Father before his passing. I was rescued from a camp of the Red Sticks a little over a week ago and immediately brought here to St. Marks, a Spanish fort that has been occupied by General Jackson's army. The general, with great concern for Father's health, had kindly left the Fourth as garrison of the post while the remainder of the army pursued the fleeing Seminoles. Upon my arrival at this place, I was, of course, greeted most warmly by Johnny and Jack. The immense joy of being enfolded once again in Johnny's arms cannot be adequately described. Yet I instantly sensed a reservation in the welcome, and when I asked how Father was, Johnny burst into tears and could not face me. It was Jack, always the stalwart one, who told me of Father's grave condition, much worse than I had been led to believe.

Amid tears and anxiety greater than any I felt while in captivity, I was led to the fort's infirmary, where Father lay, attended by the regimental surgeon. Oh, it was a sight that tore at my heart more than I can relate. His skin was most pale and his frame withered. Yet at the sight of me he rose in his bed, and the joy upon his face was greater than ever I have seen. We embraced for the longest time, our tears flowing and mixing as they fell, and not a word said between us. At that moment, though Jack had warned me there was little chance of Father's recovery, I truly felt that my mere presence would restore Father to health, but it was not to be. Johnny told me the only thing that seemed to keep Father alive was the hope of once again having me near.

For the next five days I did not leave Father's side, knowing my hours in his presence would be few. Oh, the tears I cried, but I regret not one, for my presence seemed to comfort him so. He spoke often of Mother and of you, of New Orleans and Baton Rouge, and of Uncle Paul and Aunt Mae. We laughed, and he held my hand so tightly that at times it fell asleep and began to tingle. Yet I would not suffer him to loosen his grip, for it is a feeling I will forever keep in my heart.

When I awoke yesterday morning I found I could not awaken him, and I immediately called for the surgeon. The doctor examined Father and found life still in him, but he could not be roused. Johnny and Jack soon joined me in my vigil, and at an hour before noon Father left this world, once again to be reunited with Mother, I am confident. He was quietly buried at the fort's cemetery with muted honors, there being but one musician at the post. Major Wooster assures me full honors will be paid upon the return of General Jackson and the entire army.

As for the details of my captivity, there is little I care to relate, other than that I am happy it is over and am once again safely in Johnny's care. Contrary to what rumors may be adrift, I was not mistreated in any significant manner, and the greatest scar my mind carries is the sight of so many of my dear friends meeting such a horrible fate. As to the miracle of my survival, it can be attributed to my capture by a half-breed warrior known as Yellow Tom, who then took it upon himself to be my protector. Having spent a portion of his youth in England, he was more a gentleman than a savage, and treated me with great kindness and respect. Indeed, once I was accepted by his family, they all showed me no animosity and became my friends. I know the Indians have committed murders upon the whites of Georgia and for this they must be punished, but equal wrongs have been committed upon them, and no white man has yet to feel the lash or swing by the noose for these crimes. And while I cannot forgive them for the deaths of my friends on Lt. Scott's boat, I do not see any justice in this war. I know not whom to blame for all this suffering and can only hope it soon will end.

With this, I must close. My heart is full and should I continue to write, my tears would stain the page, and I would be forced to commence the effort again, which I cannot do. Please give my love to Anna Lynn. I will send a similar letter to Uncle Paul and Aunt Mae, for I know they are equally anxious for the news I have. Johnny and Jack, of course, extend their respects and condolences. We all miss you very much.

Your loving sister,
Elizabeth

The column of soldiers marched solemnly past the newest grave in the Fort St. Marks cemetery, each regiment in its turn, as a small group of musicians made three unhurried circuits around the mound of earth that covered the remains of Capt. George Vashon. Off to the side were the Lower Creek volunteers, some of them slightly baffled by the simple pageantry. Standing by the graveside was Elizabeth, still wearing her Indian dress, with Johnny by her side. It had been a week since her father had died, and she still felt slightly numb. She went through the motions of a daily routine, but there had been little for her to do. Everyone had been waiting for the return of General Jackson and his army. Now that the army had returned and the funeral rites had taken place, the rest of her life could commence.

But what was that to be? The talk between her and Johnny, and within the garrison at St Marks in general, had been that when Jackson returned, the war would be over. The Seminoles had been thoroughly punished, driven well south of the border, and would no longer pose a threat to the frontier. Other than holding St. Marks until the Spanish could adequately police the area, there seemed nothing else for the army to do. That being the case, the regiment would be assigned to some permanent post, and a sense of normalcy could return to their lives.

The big question was where that permanent posting would be. Speculation was rampant, with each individual hoping for some favorite place. Major Wooster wanted Baton Rouge, primarily because the woman he hoped to marry resided in New Orleans. Jack wanted Fort Gaines, believing its location on the Chattahoochee would make it a transportation hub for the rapidly growing portions of western Georgia. Lieutenant Clinch, now in command of Jack and Johnny's company, had fallen in love with the Gulf coast and hoped to remain as garrison commander of St. Marks until it was returned to the Spanish, if that ever happened.

As far as Elizabeth was concerned, her desired posting was Fort Montgomery. It was where she and Johnny had made their first home, if only for two weeks, and a point in her life she desperately wanted to return to. She knew it was impractical and impossible, but thought if she could somehow return to that place, she might be able to convince herself the past seven months had never actually happened and was nothing more than a bad dream. In the end, however, it didn't really matter where they went. What she wanted more than anything was a home.

As for Johnny, all he wanted was his wife back. True, she was there next to him, but her mind was somewhere else. At first, it had not bothered him. He fully understood that her devotion would and should be directed toward her dying father. Then, of course, there was the grief to deal with after his passing. But it had now been two weeks since her return, and they had yet to make love. It certainly wasn't for lack of opportunity. In consideration of what Elizabeth had been through, Major Wooster had assigned them a private room within the fort. Every night Johnny had held her close, often while she cried herself to sleep, but never once had she let the emotion overtake them. Considering how passionate she had been when first they were married, it was both surprising and troubling.

He was also bothered by her lack of willingness to talk about her captivity. He knew better than to ask about the massacre itself. The very mention of it made her shudder and turn away. During the initial interview with General Jackson she had given details about the deaths of certain individuals on the boat, but after that, she refused to mention it again. The only exception was to console a few soldiers who'd lost their wives or close friends on the boat. It was an obligation she felt she couldn't ignore, and the shared tears helped ease her own pain.

Johnny was quite perplexed by her response to rumors from Lower Creek spies that she'd killed two great warriors during her captivity. Her first reaction was one of shame or regret. When pressed for details, however, she seemed annoyed and would curtly reply, "It is not something a lady speaks of." As far as Elizabeth was concerned, the morbidly curious—including her own husband—could remain curious.

What bothered Johnny most, however, were the rumors about Yellow Tom. When he asked Elizabeth about him, she simply said that as the warrior who had captured her, her fate had been in his hands, and he had given her to the women of his clan to use as they saw fit. Johnny didn't ask if she and Tom had been lovers, but rather if anyone had abused her or treated her "inappropriately." She assured him that other than being treated very roughly immediately after her capture, no one had laid a hand on her, and, for the most part, she was treated just like any other woman of the tribe. She described her work as often being difficult and occasionally demeaning, but that no one had ever harmed her. When asked if Yellow Tom was handsome, she had smiled and replied, "For a half-breed," then added "but not near as handsome as my husband." All in all, Elizabeth's answers appeared truthful, but he didn't find them very satisfying. While they did not increase his anxiety about what had gone on during her captivity, they did absolutely nothing to ease it.

An hour after the funeral ceremonies for Captain Vashon were complete, Andrew Jackson called his senior officers together in what had once been Commandant Luengo's private quarters. Most of them assumed it was a meeting to discuss the termination of the war and the disposition of troops in the aftermath of the conflict, and at first it seemed that way. The first person Jackson addressed was the Lower Creek leader. "General McIntosh, as always, your warriors have proven their worthiness in battle, and the nation thanks you for their service. As soon as you are ready, you may proceed to Fort Scott, where your men will be mustered out and paid off." Jackson then turned to General Glasscock of the Georgia Militia. "General, we also thank the State of Georgia for its support, and you are to proceed at your earliest convenience to Hartford, where your men will be mustered out of United States service. To assist in having the men paid off in a prompt manner, I have instructed Lieutenant Gadsden to draft a letter authorizing Governor Rabun to pay the men out of the state treasury with the understanding that there will be immediate reimbursement from the War Department."

Both officers thanked Jackson, and then stood by to hear the disposition of the other units. What they heard surprised everyone in the room. "Gentlemen, I have received reports of approximately four to five hundred hostiles being welcomed and supplied by the Spanish authorities in Pensacola. It shall therefore be necessary for us to carry out an expedition west of the Apalachicola to determine the veracity of these reports. Colonel Williams, the Tennessee Volunteers will depart tomorrow for Fort Gadsden, where they will resupply and prepare for the expedition. Colonel King and Major Wooster, your infantry regiments will proceed to Fort Gadsden the day after tomorrow. Colonel Lindsay, you will detach two companies of the artillery to garrison this post until orders are received from the War Department as to its disposal. The rest will accompany us to Fort Gadsden. Are there any questions?"

Every officer in the room had questions, especially about the report of a large number of hostiles at Pensacola, but every one of them knew you did not ask Andrew Jackson awkward questions. Jackson paused but a moment, then said, "Very well, on to the next order of business. We will convene, in the morning, a courts-martial for our British prisoners, Messrs. Arbuthnot and Ambrister. General Gaines will preside, and Lieutenant Gadsden has made up a list of officers who will serve on the panel. I mean to see these scoundrels punished for the outrages the Indians have committed under their tutelage. The English must learn that we will not tolerate their presence on land that rightfully belongs to the United States."

The silence was almost embarrassing. General Glasscock, a prominent Georgia lawyer in civilian life and the man least intimidated by Andrew Jackson, finally asked the question that was on everyone else's mind. "General, this seems highly irregular. Do we even have jurisdiction in this matter?"

Jackson gave the man a cold look and brushed aside his concerns. "They're prisoners of war, General, and they shall be fairly tried in accordance with the laws of war. This will not be a trumped-up tribunal."

Glasscock, not one to shy away from legal arguments, countered with, "They were not captured on the battlefield, sir, nor could they be considered part of the enemy forces. If there is any law forbidding them from being in Florida, sir, or circumscribing their actions, it is Spanish law."

Jackson was getting angry. "This is a war against savages, damn it, and the normal rules of war do not apply."

Glasscock didn't bother to point out the incongruity of Jackson's last two statements. How could they be fairly tried according to the laws of war if the normal rules of war were not going to be applied? Yet he knew when an argument was lost and when further contentiousness could only lead to trouble. Andrew Jackson was his own authority and would set the rules as he saw fit. The Georgia lawyer had voiced his concerns, and if questioned later, he could defend his position. He also saw impending difficulties with Congress over Jackson's actions, and might well be called one day to testify against Old Hickory. In the meantime, he was on Jackson's turf and saw no advantage in further ruffling the old man's feathers. "My apologies, General. These are simply matters that needed to be discussed in order to avoid any future embarrassments."

Jackson huffed slightly and responded with, "No apologies necessary, General. You're just doing what a damned lawyer is supposed to do." They were odd words, coming from a former judge and United States Senator, but certainly not uncharacteristic of the man. Putting a tone of finality into this voice, Jackson then pronounced, "If there are no further questions, this meeting is adjourned. Those of you who are to serve on the courts-martial will be informed by Lieutenant Gadsden and will report to General Gaines." He then turned to Glasscock once again. "General, could I ask your indulgence to remain behind, along with Major Wooster and Lieutenant Clinch. Captain Allison, on your way out, could you have someone fetch Master Sergeant Stuart?"

Allison nodded, said, "Yes, sir," and left the room with the other officers.

Jackson began to explain the reason for having the three officers remain. "Clinch, with the death of Captain Vashon, command of Company G naturally passes to you, and I am therefore awarding you a brevet captaincy, which I am sure Congress will no doubt make permanent. Unfortunately, the murder of Lieutenant Scott leaves you without any junior officers, and it will be long after this campaign is concluded before the War Department sees fit to send you any replacements. Not that I expect any hostile action, but it would not be wise for the company to be without a second-in-command. In light of that, I am giving a battlefield promotion of Sergeant Stuart, making him an ensign until such time as a permanent replacement can be assigned. The lad's a good soldier and a natural leader. The men already follow him without question. Considering what his pretty young wife has been through, what with her captivity and the loss of her father, it seems the least we can do for her and the memory of Captain Vashon. Perhaps by giving this man a leg up, it will inspire him to greater things."

Wooster smiled. "I concur most heartily, sir. The man has promise and should be encouraged." The fact that the army no longer had the rank of ensign didn't really matter. It was an honorary thing, nothing more. Ensign had been the lowest rank among officers, and therefore put Stuart in his proper place in relation to the rest of the army.

Clinch was more noncommittal but saw little reason to raise any concerns. "He'll do a fine job, sir."

Jackson then turned to Glasscock. "General, the upcoming expedition to Pensacola may take some weeks and will entail a forced march through the wilderness, something I would not think to subject Captain Vashon's daughter to. Might I prevail upon you, as a gentleman of honor, to allow the lady to accompany you back to your home in Hartford and to keep her under your care until such time as her husband returns from this campaign? I plan on having his company stationed at Fort Gaines, so reuniting them should not prove difficult. Perhaps Mrs. Glasscock can assist Mrs. Stuart in her adjustment back to civilized life."

Glasscock gave a polite nod of his head. Jackson might be a bully, but he could also be a gentleman. "I would consider it an honor, sir. It is a most kind and generous suggestion on your part, and Mrs. Glasscock will be delighted to have a houseguest."

There was a knock at the door, and Jackson called out, "Enter."

"Sergeant Stuart reporting as ordered, General."

Jackson nodded and motioned for the young man to come forward. "We have some good news for you, Sergeant. Do come in."

It was near sunset when John Stuart approached Major Wooster as he walked along the parapet of Fort St. Marks. "Major Wooster, sir; may I have a word?"

"Of course, Ensign. What's on your mind?"

"A number of things, sir. First off, I understand you were the one who suggested the promotion to General Jackson. If so, then my wife and I owe you a great debt of gratitude."

"Other than the practical consideration of needing a junior officer, both the general and I thought it was especially cruel to part you from your wife after so long and anxious a separation. It seemed a fitting recompense, though Mrs. Stuart may not see it that way. Besides, your actions at Miccosukee did not go unnoticed. You are most deserving of the promotion, temporary and unpaid as it may be."

"Yes, sir, but am I fit to be an officer?"

Wooster smiled. "Stuart, you're a fine young man and will do a good job. The men already respect you and will follow your orders without question. Heaven knows, son, I served with—and under—far less intelligent and far more incompetent officers during the war with England. I think you'll rise to the occasion. If nothing else, Sergeant Dill and Captain Clinch will keep your feet on the ground."

The man who had been an orphan of modest means had other concerns. "But what of my breeding, sir?"

The comment forced Wooster to let out with a small laugh. "Come now, Mr. Stuart, this is the United States Army, not His Majesty's Redcoats, where being a member of the titled nobility is the only real qualification for office. You're well-read and a man of good moral standing and should rise on your merits, not your name. It's why we threw off the English yoke, remember?"

"Yes, sir. I just hope I do well."

Wooster put a hand on Stuart's shoulder. "Fear not, it will soon be nothing but a memory. There is nothing as ephemeral in this army as a temporarily brevetted non-commissioned officer."

"On that matter, sir, General Jackson said that when my enlistment is up, if I cared to apply for a real lieutenant's commission, he would give it his full support. Is that true? Could I actually hope to become an officer?"

"If General Jackson forgets his promise, I'll remind him, and I'll also remind General Gaines. There can be no guarantees, especially if Congress reduces the size of the army, but I'd hold onto your father-in-law's sword if I were you. You might have use of it someday." Wooster knew the talk wasn't over. "What else is troubling you?"

"I've heard talk that our occupying this post is an act of war against Spain, and that General Jackson is in violation of his orders. Isn't such talk insubordination?"

Wooster was happy to see the young man already thinking like an officer. "Of course it's an act of war, and this will be nothing compared to when we take Pensacola. But questioning your superior officer's judgment is not insubordination. Refusing to obey his orders is. A good officer will always question the propriety of his orders, and if he strongly disagrees, he should respectfully point that out to his superior. What the superior does with those concerns is up to him. If things go wrong, he'll have to answer for it later, either to God, the government, the people, or himself."

"But how can anyone question General Jackson? He's the greatest leader we've had since General Washington."

Wooster laughed. "Never declare someone's greatness until after he's been dead for twenty years." He then became more serious. "How many of us had the courage—or stupidity—to question his orders to his face? For that matter, how many of us wanted to question them? We all want Florida. The southern states can never be truly secure as long as some European power controls this peninsula. How many of us are willing to bend the rules to get it? Jackson certainly is. Yet as much as I respect the man, I also fear him. Given the right circumstances, he could easily become our Bonaparte, seizing power and setting himself up as dictator. What made General Washington great was that he walked away from power. Jackson hasn't faced that test yet."

Stuart was a little shocked. "Do you think it would ever come to that, sir?"

"I hope not. We are fortunate in that he worships the Union and the Constitution, although he'll be the first to disregard certain portions of it if he sees fit. But no, he would be loath to do anything to overthrow the government. We can only pray that circumstances never arise that force him to feel he's the only one who can save the nation."

Stuart turned and looked out over the marshes, toward the Gulf of Mexico. "There is one other thing, sir, if I may be so bold."

"Boldness is appreciated in a good officer. What is it?"

"Rumor has it that our prisoners are to be hanged, sir. This has caused some concern for my wife. It seems Mr. Ambrister interceded on her behalf when first she was taken prisoner and may well have helped save her life. She most respectfully asks that the court take this into consideration at the trial tomorrow. She understands that she is to depart with the Georgia Militia in the morning and will therefore not be here to testify in his behalf."

Wooster nodded. "Assure your wife that I will do what I can, Mr. Stuart, though I feel my voice may be in the minority." Wooster then reached into his pocket and pulled out a pair of cigars. "Come, enjoy one of the privileges of being an officer. I found these behind a rock in the wall of the Spanish lieutenant's quarters. He must have been storing them there to keep them cool. Probably the finest Havana has to offer."

The two men walked over to a sentry fire, lit the cigars and leaned against the parapet wall, enjoying the cool evening air, both thinking of the upcoming trial. Tomorrow was going to be a difficult day.

Elizabeth lay in bed, trying to convince herself there wasn't a problem, but was losing the argument. Ever since her return from captivity, she'd been afraid to make love to Johnny. Perhaps it was the fear of disappointment. So many nights during the past few months she'd wanted him, and she assumed the longing was just as strong for him. So much of their future depended on putting the past behind them and getting on with life. If the first night of passion did not go well, they might both have doubts about what the other felt.

But why should they? Did they love each other any less? Had something horrible happened to either one of them that would prevent them from making love as wonderfully as they had before they parted? She'd heard of women who had been raped by the Indians or forced to become a warrior's wife, and how they could no longer be intimate with their husbands after they were rescued. But that hadn't happened to her. She was physically no different than the day Johnny and his company had marched out of Fort Montgomery.

Yet there *was* something different, and she knew precisely what it was: Yellow Tom. She could not deny the attraction, and knew how close she had come to being unfaithful to her husband. She thought of Tom often and wondered what would have happened had she not been rescued. She'd heard of captives who had lived among the Indians for so long that they didn't want to be rescued. How close had she come to that point? Closer than she cared to admit.

Yet it was behind her now. Yes, she had been extremely drawn to Tom, but now that she was back with Johnny, Tom was just a pleasant memory. Had she been drawn to the Seminole warrior out of true affection or because she had needed his protection? She honestly didn't know. Was it simply a matter of wanting whoever was available? The longer she had stayed with Tom, the less she had thought of Johnny. She could only hope that the longer she stayed with Johnny, the less she would think of Tom.

She also knew her reticence to talk about Tom was beginning to raise suspicions in Johnny's mind. But what could she do? If she mentioned him in even the slightest complimentary way, Johnny might take it the wrong way and let his imagination get the better of him. She couldn't even talk about Conowaw for fear of Johnny's thinking she was more attached to her Indian family than she ought to have been. Elizabeth felt cornered. If she mentioned Tom, Johnny would get suspicious. If she didn't mention Tom, Johnny would wonder what she was hiding. Either way, she lost. She could only hope that by saying nothing, the matter would eventually fade away.

What they needed was one good night of joyous lovemaking to help erase the doubts. Perhaps this would be the night. Johnny was ecstatic about his promotion. He beamed as he strutted around the quarters, wearing her father's sword. Even Elizabeth was thrilled. The only disappointing news was her not being able to accompany him on the expedition to Pensacola. Once more, she was being taken away from the man she loved. When, she wondered, would they ever have a normal home life?

When morning came, the population of St. Marks decreased dramatically. The allied Creeks left sometime before dawn, while the Georgia Militia departed about an hour after sunrise. John and Elizabeth Stuart said their tearful good-byes, and he watched the departing wagon until she was out of sight. They had finally experienced a good night together. Seven months of fear were pushed aside by one happy hour under the sheets of a Spanish bed, and through tears and passion, they cleared away the doubts and were ready to face the future.

Facing a much more uncertain future were Alexander Arbuthnot and Robert Ambrister. The first trial, for Arbuthnot, commenced at nine o'clock and was held in Commandant Luengo's quarters. At one end of the table sat General Gaines, the presiding officer. Arrayed on either side of the long table were the eleven other judges, along with Lieutenant Gadsden, who was serving as clerk. Standing at the other end of the table was the old Scotsman, flanked by two soldiers.

Gadsden rose and read the charges. "The prisoner, Alexander Arbuthnot, a British subject and resident of Nassau, New Providence, in the Bahamian Islands, is hereby charged with inciting the Indians of Florida to make war upon the citizens and nation of the United States, for spying on behalf of said Indians, and for ordering the kidnap, torture, and execution of William Hambly and Edmund Doyle, merchants, residing upon the Apalachicola River in West Florida. How do you plead, sir?"

Arbuthnot was stunned. They were the most ridiculous charges he could imagine. Yes, he had stood up for the Seminoles, but he had always counseled them to avoid war. He had warned them that conflict with the United States would be a disaster, and recent events had proven him right. As for the charge of spying, he hadn't told the Indians anything that wasn't common knowledge or, at the most, a fair warning. And in regards to Hambly and

Doyle, he'd had nothing to do with their kidnapping, they had not been tortured, and were still very much alive. Hambly, in fact, was sitting in a far corner of the room, prepared to take the stand as a witness for the prosecution. Thoroughly insulted, Arbuthnot thundered, "Not guilty, as God is my witness!"

He soon realized as silly as the charges were, the Americans were taking them very seriously. Worst of all, they were using his own words against him. Found on board *Chance* were letters he intended to deliver or mail when he returned to the Bahamas, along with his letterbook, where he kept copies of all his correspondence. Captain Richard Call, the prosecutor and a close friend of Jackson, read excerpts from the letters, all of which pointed to a man who held the United States in contempt and warned British and Spanish officials of American designs on Florida. Arbuthnot couldn't believe his ears. "You call that spying? Since when is expressing one's opinions or passing along common news considered spying? Unless there be some secret information there that I should not be privy to, or some state of war existed between the United States and someone else when those letters were written, how can you in God's name call it spying?"

The point seemed to be well taken by the panel, so Captain Call went on to the matter of inciting the Indians to hostilities. Again, damning portions of the letters were recited to the judges, while none of the parts where Arbuthnot counseled peace were mentioned. Then the prosecution called its most damning witness, Arbuthnot's clerk, Peter Cook. The young man stood nervously before the panel, reciting his lines as he'd been instructed to, occasionally glancing at Call for a sign that he'd gotten it right. Cook had good cause to be nervous. One of the letters found on *Chance* had been from him to his sweetheart Liz Carney. In it, Cook told her how he had joined the Seminoles in an attack on Fort Scott, only days after the attack on Lieutenant Scott's boat. If the American army wanted to accuse anyone of aiding the

Seminoles in their war against the United States, Cook was the only one they had direct proof against.

Yet Jackson had seen little use in hanging a frightened youth of little import in the scheme of things. Jackson wanted Arbuthnot's skin, and he wanted just cause for carrying out the sentence of the court. It was easy enough to intimidate the boy, to put words in his mouth, to convince him Arbuthnot was the real threat to Cook's well-being, not an American firing squad.

So Peter Cook stood up and said what he had to. Why had he taken part in the attack on Fort Scott? "Mr. Arbuthnot said the experience would do me good, sir, if I didn't get meself killed." Had Arbuthnot supplied weapons to the Seminoles? "Yes, sir, the finest he could get." Had his employer encouraged the Indians to make war upon the Americans? "Very often, if it so please you, sir." Did Arbuthnot order the Indians to kidnap Hambly and Doyle? "That he did, sir. He often carried on about how he'd like to be rid of the pair. That way he could have the whole Florida trade to himself."

Arbuthnot tried to defend himself, but knew it was a wasted effort. If the Americans were willing to try a man on such worthless charges using such questionable evidence, the result was a foregone conclusion. "The lad's a liar and a thief! I specifically told him not to go on any war parties and leave my store unattended. As for selling guns to the Indians, that's what a merchant does, damn you! They're hunters. What in God's name am I supposed to sell them?" He looked at Hambly. "Never did I order anyone to harm Hambly or Doyle. And what concern is it of yours if I had? This is Spanish Florida, and neither of us are American citizens. Your laws don't apply here! Blessed hell, I even talked them out of killing him. Just ask him!"

Call then asked Hambly to approach the judges. "Did Mr. Arbuthnot tell the Indians to spare your life?"

Hambly wasn't about to lie, but he wasn't above bending the truth. The Americans were now the masters of Florida and would eventually gain title from Spain, either by cash or by conquest. If he wanted to stay in business, he would have to deal with the new landlords. "Not directly, sir, but he did advise Commandant Luengo to tell them not to harm Mr. Doyle and me until the Spanish Governor had ruled one way or the other. Of course we all knew we'd never hear from Havana before the Indians came back, so I don't know what he would have done then. I do know the Indians who came and took us from our store said that Mr. Arbuthnot had often told them he wanted to be rid of us."

General Gaines asked, "Mr. Arbuthnot, do you have any questions for Mr. Hambly?"

Arbuthnot had heard enough. "I'll not waste me breath on cutthroats and villains, nor give you the satisfaction of hearing me beg for me life. Officers and gentlemen? The whole lot of you are nothing but thieving liars and murderous scoundrels dressed in pretty uniforms. To hell with you all!"

Gaines nodded. "Very well." Addressing the guards who stood at the old Scot's side, Gaines said, "You may escort the prisoner out of the room while we deliberate."

Major Wooster, one of the judges, looked around the table and mentally counted votes. There were twelve officers on the panel, and eight were needed to reach a verdict. Five of them were Tennessee Volunteer officers, handpicked by General Jackson. General Gaines, though independent, was so similar in his thinking to Jackson that there could be little doubt of how he would decide. Colonel King of the Seventh Infantry idolized Jackson and would do the old man's bidding, no matter how distasteful. Then there was Major Muhlenberg, a man who would never rock the boat. That was all Jackson needed for his conviction. The rest of them were there simply to occupy the required number of chairs. Major Fanning might go either way, Colonel Lindsay always went counter to everyone else, and Captain Allison would vote his conscience. As for himself, Wooster would vote the evidence. Was he worried that General

Jackson would be angry with a vote to acquit? Not really. Old Hickory didn't want a unanimous verdict. He wanted to be able to say, "See, they made up their own minds."

The only real question to be decided was which charges to vote on. General Gaines immediately suggested the spying charges be dropped. Colonel Lindsay, always the contrarian, felt the spying charges were valid, but that the court had no jurisdiction when it came to the charge of ordering the kidnapping, torture, and execution of Hambly and Doyle, especially since the victims had suffered no real harm. Gaines, impatient to get on with it, said, "One or the other. I won't throw out both." A quick vote was held, and the majority sided with Gaines. Arbuthnot could die with the satisfaction of knowing he wasn't a spy.

Gaines then instructed Lieutenant Gadsden to hand out the ballots. As the slips of paper made their rounds, Gadsden issued the instructions. "If you would, sirs, kindly put a number 'one' near the top of the ballot and a number 'two' near the bottom. You will write 'convict' or 'acquit' next to the number when I finish reading the charge." After checking to see that everyone had completed the task, he read the charges. "Number one: On giving aid and comfort to the enemy, please vote." He waited while the pencils made their marks. He also noticed that no one was bothering to conceal their votes. "Number two: On ordering the kidnapping, torture, and execution of Messrs. Hambly and Doyle, please vote." No one bothered to ask if there might be some need to discuss the matter. Everyone's mind was made up.

The ballots were turned in, and the judges watched as Gadsden counted the votes. Wooster could take some satisfaction in the fact that his prediction had been correct. Eight voted to convict Arbuthnot on both charges, three wanted to acquit him. Fanning, the man who might have gone either way, split his vote.

Gaines then asked what sentence should be imposed. Once again, there was no need for discussion. They all knew what Andrew Jackson wanted.

Gaines nodded to one of the sentries. "Return the prisoner."

Arbuthnot was escorted back in and stood proudly in front of the panel. Gaines looked dispassionately at the condemned man. "Alexander Arbuthnot, hear the decision of this court. The charge of spying has been dropped. On the charge of giving aid and comfort to the enemy: guilty as charged. On the charges related to Messrs. Hambly and Doyle: guilty as charged. The court, therefore, sentences you to be hung by the neck until dead. The time of execution shall be at sundown tonight. Has the prisoner anything to say?"

Arbuthnot's gaze turned hateful. "May the murderous lot of you rot in hell."

As he was led from the courtroom, Arbuthnot passed Ambrister, who was being escorted from his cell to his own trial. The old Scot called out, "Make your peace with your Maker, lad. There's neither law nor justice to be found among the likes of these scoundrels."

The trial of Robert Ambrister began shortly after noon, after everyone had taken time for a quick midday meal. The prisoner was led into the courtroom and told to stand before the table where the judges sat. The charges against him were slightly different from those brought against Arbuthnot. There was no mention of spying, and he had never been implicated in anything to do with Hambly and Doyle, so those charges were never brought up. Instead of offering aid and comfort to the enemy, he was charged with aiding and abetting the enemy.

Ambrister wasn't sure what evidence the Americans had against him and didn't know that they actually needed any. Although he had come to Florida only with the intention of forwarding the vague interests of his friends back in Nassau, it was inevitable that some of his activities would result in trouble with the Americans. He could not win the friendship of the Indians without supplying them with weapons. He had never delivered any large number of guns, but his accusers would be more interested in quality rather than quantity. The Indians would not accept him as an Englishman of any influence unless he wore his old uniform and acted like a military man. That required training the Indians in the use of their weapons and in the tactics to be used against their enemies. And though he never encouraged the Seminoles to make war upon the Americans, everyone understood who the enemy was. Like it or not, he had to admit the charges against him were not entirely false, and if the court-martial had convicted Arbuthnot—whom he considered innocent of any wrongdoing—what chances did he have of faring any better?

Lieutenant Gadsden finished reading the charges, and then asked, "How does the accused plead?"

Ambrister realized the only hope he had lay in the one thing that had done the most to bring him to this point: his military uniform. The Americans might hate all Englishmen, but a soldier always respects another soldier, no matter what the color of his uniform. Standing at attention and putting on as martial a bearing as he could, the young man boldly proclaimed, "I plead no contest, sir, and, as an officer and a gentleman, throw myself upon the mercy of the court."

The judges were slightly stunned. It was the last thing they expected. They stared at each other in silence, wondering what came next. General Gaines finally gave the order, "You may escort the prisoner from the room while the panel discusses the matter of sentencing." He then turned to the two witnesses who had helped convict Arbuthnot. "Mr. Hambly and Mr. Cook, you are free to go."

After the room was clear of everyone but the twelve judges and the clerk, Gaines scanned the panel and asked, "Gentlemen? Any comments?"

One of the Tennessee Volunteer officers slapped his hand lightly on the table and said, "Well, that makes quick work of it. Let's hang the pompous little ass before he changes his mind."

Colonel Lindsay was quick to disagree. "I cannot be so callous toward a fellow officer, no matter what his nation. As a matter of honor, we should at least grant him the privilege of execution by firing squad, rather than by hanging."

The other officers, somewhat embarrassed by the coldhearted comment of the Tennessean, murmured their agreement. Gaines concurred, saying, "So be it. You may record the decision, Mr. Gadsden."

The officers sat quietly as Gadsden read the official order condemning Ambrister to execution by firing squad. Gaines nodded his approval, and then said, "Very well. . . ."

Wooster spoke up with a little hesitation. "Sir, if I may?"

"Yes, Major?"

"I do not feel comfortable with this."

Major Fanning, who had lost an arm during the war with England, shook his head. "Aye, me too."

Gaines looked at the two officers. "Go ahead, Wooster."

"I have it from Sergeant Stuart that Mr. Ambrister was instrumental in saving his wife's life after her capture by the Indians and had befriended her in that most anxious time of need. Surely that deserves some consideration."

Fanning waved the stump of his ruined arm and said, "I have little love for anything British, but I don't see much of King George in this young man. We all know he's not here at the behest of His Majesty's government. He's nothing more than a colonial trying to make his way and find a little adventure. He could be any one of us at that age."

Muhlenberg, the preacher's son, commented, "He did place himself in our mercy. It seems almost un-Christianlike to deny it."

Even the contrarian Colonel Lindsay tended to agree. "We wanted to make an example of the British, and we've done so with the old man. I see no value in taking the young man's life."

The murmurs of agreement convinced Gaines that the panel members were fairly uniform in their judgment. "Very well, but he cannot go unpunished. Any suggestions?"

Colonel King said, "Lashes."

Captain Allison offered, "Confinement at hard labor?"

Gaines nodded. "Very well, how about a hundred lashes and a year's confinement?"

Wooster suggested, "Perhaps fifty lashes, and a year at hard labor."

Fanning nodded. "That sounds reasonable."

No one offered any other suggestions, so Gaines said, "So be it. Mr. Gadsden, record that the court, upon mature reflection, has commuted the prisoner's sentence to fifty lashes upon his bare back and a year's confinement at hard labor."

Wooster and Fanning glanced at each other. Both had a look of relief in their eyes and were wondering if they had spared Ambrister out of compassion, or if they were attempting to ease their guilt over sentencing an unoffending old trader to the gallows. Maybe it was both.

Peter Cook was in a quandary. He had saved his life by cooperating with the Americans, but he could not go on as if nothing had happened. He was hundreds of miles from his home in the Bahamas and had no way to get back there. He certainly couldn't ask Arbuthnot's son for transportation back to the islands. In truth, he doubted if he could ever return there. Both the old Scot and Ambrister had many friends in and around Nassau, and all would be unforgiving when they heard Cook had testified against the old man. Even the Indians would have nothing to do with him once they found out. There was nowhere for him to go.

As he sat on the walls of Fort St. Marks, he watched the American soldiers going about their business. They seemed content, well fed, and reasonably well cared for. Most of all they seemed happy to belong to something. It was quite the opposite of what Cook was feeling. Coming to his feet, he began to walk along the parapet, moving in the direction of an American officer. It seemed strange, but he saw no other alternative. A few days ago he'd been talking about fighting the United States Army. Now he was going to ask if he could become part of it.

Andrew Jackson was in an especially bad mood. His stomach was hurting, his shoulder was aching, and he was anxious to get on with the war. There was a knock on the door, and Lieutenant Gadsden stepped in. "The results of the courts-martial, General."

Jackson looked at the death sentence that had been handed down for Alexander Arbuthnot. A satisfied look crossed his face, almost a smile. "Good."

Before handing the general the sentence for Ambrister, Gadsden said, "Mr. Arbuthnot's son has requested that he be allowed some time with his father before the execution, and that he be allowed to convey the remains back to their home in the Islands."

"The man's damn lucky we didn't string him up, too."

Gadsden nodded. "Yes, sir, but there was really no evidence against him, and one of the letters we found mentioned his disdain for the affairs here in Florida."

The general looked disgusted. "Very well, grant him his wish. Take them both out to that old tub of theirs, hang the old man from his own yardarm at sunset, and send them all on their way."

"Yes, sir." Gadsden then handed Jackson the paper with Ambrister's sentence.

The general's face began to turn red. "What the hell is this! I didn't give anyone permission to commute the sentence once it was handed down. The bastards have gone all womanish on us. You go back and tell Gaines that he will impose the original sentence, and that there will be no argument in this matter. I want that man dead."

Out in the harbor, Alexander Arbuthnot noticed that the clouds, thin and high in the sky, were beginning to redden. He had spent most of his seventy-odd years at sea and had always looked forward to a good sunset. It looked as if his last one would be glorious.

Back on shore, Robert Ambrister stood with his back to the wall of Fort St. Marks. He heard one of the senior officers addressing a man who appeared to be wearing an enlisted man's uniform but carried an officer's sword and had an officer's hat upon his head. The older officer said, "Ensign Stuart, if you intend to one day become a fully commissioned officer, you must learn that there are the occasional distasteful duties that must be performed. Carrying out an execution is perhaps the most dreadful. Are you up to it?"

The younger man looked nervous, but determined. "Yes, sir, Major Wooster."

Wooster nodded. "Very well, son, do your duty."

Ambrister watched Stuart approach. The look on his face was painful. In a wavering voice, Stuart asked, "Would you care for a blindfold, sir?"

Ambrister shook his head. "No, I want to see the muskets fire one last time."

Stuart leaned over and whispered. "My deepest regrets, sir. We all did what we could for you, but the general would not have it. I do thank you for the help you rendered my wife while she was in captivity."

Ambrister was slightly surprised. "Red Bess is your wife?"

Stuart was just as surprised. "Red Bess?"

Ambrister smiled slightly. "That's what Tommy called her." The condemned man might have lived to regret his words if, indeed, he had lived. He certainly had no intention of causing any trouble for Elizabeth and had no idea how her husband would receive those words. But living was not to be, and he watched as Stuart walked away and took his place near the end of the line of soldiers. He saw the men come to attention, saw Stuart raise his sword, order the men to ready their weapons, and then take aim. He never heard the word "Fire!"

29th April 1818
Fort St. Marks
E. Florida

To:
The Honorable John C. Calhoun
Secretary of War
Washington City

Sir,

It is with great pleasure that I have the honor to inform you of the progress of our campaign against the hostile savages residing in Florida. We arrived at this place on the 6th of April and found the post ill-garrisoned by the Spaniards and in immediate danger of being overrun by the enemy. Finding the post commander uncooperative, no doubt because of his collusion with the enemy, I deemed it necessary to occupy the fort in order to prevent its capture by hostile forces. Upon our securing the fortress, we were pleased to find in residence the notorious Arbuthnot, which provides ample proof of the Spaniard commandant's cooperation with the British instigators. The man was immediately confined to await trial.

By extreme good fortune, Lt. McKeever of the Navy was also able to take prisoner two of the most bloodthirsty Red Stick chiefs, the Prophet Hillis Hadjo and Homathlemico. Upon our arrival at this place, the murderous savages were brought ashore and summarily executed as an example to their fellows of the just retribution that will be meted out to those who see fit to make war upon the innocent women and children of our nation.

After two days' rest the army moved south, toward Bowlegs's town on the Suwannee, where it was reported that several hundred negroes had gathered with the Indians for mutual protection. On the 12th of this month, McIntosh's allied Creeks came upon a large encampment of McQueen's Red Sticks and a sharp action ensued. The enemy was routed with heavy losses, and many of their women and children taken prisoner. Also found among them was Mrs. Stuart, the female prisoner from Lt. Scott's boat. She was immediately returned to this place and re-united with her husband and Capt. Vashon, her father. Sadly, it is my painful duty to report the tragic death of Capt. Vashon from wounds received at Miccosukee, the only consolation being that his final days were spent in the company of his daughter.

The army continued its way south, arriving at the Suwannee on the 15th. When attacked, the Seminoles and their allies put up a spirited defense, but were soon driven to refuge on the opposite bank of the river, but not before having suffered heavy losses. I am happy to report that late that night we were able to capture another of the well-known English troublemakers, Ambrister. The following morning we were also able to take possession of Arbuthnot's schooner, upon which we found much damning evidence against both men.

Upon our return to this place some four days past, a courts-martial was convened for the purpose of punishing the British miscreants who had fallen into our hands. Under the weight of overwhelming evidence from their own hands and from reliable witnesses, both men were found guilty and forthwith executed.

Intelligence has arrived of a most alarming nature, informing me that the Spaniards at Pensacola are giving aid and comfort to upwards of 500 hostiles. Believing the reports to be true, I proceed at daybreak for the depot at Fort Gadsden, where the army will re-supply before taking up the march for Pensacola. Should the intelligence prove valid, I shall not hesitate to properly chastise the governor and thoroughly reduce his ability to offer succor to our inveterate enemy.

Having no further need of their services, I have dismissed McIntosh's Creeks and the Georgia Militia, and have dispatched them to Fort Scott and

Hartford, respectively, to be mustered out of service.
Trusting my actions have met with the President's utmost approbation,

I am, with respect,
Yr. Mo. Obt. Svt.
Andrew Jackson
Major General, U. States Army
Commanding, Forces of the Southern Division

President James Monroe closed his eyes and slowly shook his head. Up until this moment, it had been a fine spring day in Washington. The shade of the oak tree on the White House lawn and the warm, soft breeze had been delightful. Everything had been beautiful until his cabinet officers arrived with a letter from Andrew Jackson. "I should rather have loosed an elephant in a wine cellar than to have sent that man to Florida." Gazing off into the clouds, he handed the letter back to Secretary of the Treasury William Crawford.

Secretary of War Calhoun had already read the letter and was livid. "How dare he so brazenly exceed his orders! I specifically said to leave the Spaniards alone. We're at peace with them, damn him!"

Crawford chuckled and said, "Not anymore." In a way, he was perfectly happy with what Jackson had done. "The man's arrogance may yet be his undoing."

Secretary of State Adams knew the diplomatic fallout from Jackson's adventures would land squarely on his desk. "I can hear the British ambassador's carriage heading this way already, with Señor Onis plodding dutifully behind."

Monroe nodded in agreement. "I think we may safely assume the negotiations for the purchase of Florida will be suspended, perhaps permanently."

Calhoun was still fuming. "By what strange mutation of the laws of nations did he think he had the authority to try and execute two British subjects in Spanish territory? I should have his stars for this!"

Adams huffed. "He's more likely to have your balls, Mr. Calhoun. The Hero of New Orleans is the darling of the nation. You cross him at your own peril, sir."

Crawford was still smiling. "Speaker Clay will be pounding his pulpit over this one, leading his Congressional Choir in a rousing round of his favorite hymn, *Only Congress Has the Power* ..." Crawford pounded his fist into the palm of his other hand, doing his best to imitate Henry Clay. "Jackson the Usurper! Jackson the Caesar, the Cromwell, the Napoleon! King Andrew the First!"

Adams was unimpressed. He knew what the people would be saying. He drolly followed with, "Jackson the conqueror; Jackson the avenging angel who gave us Florida." The slightly aristocratic Adams loved the republic but had a disdain for the sort of active democracy Jackson represented. "The man can do no wrong, as far as the rabble are concerned. They'll cheer him to the gates of hell and then boast that his glow outshines the fires of damnation."

Crawford looked a little disappointed. "Oh, if only Congress had not adjourned for the summer. Now we'll have to wait until December for the fireworks to commence."

Adams told him, "Fear not, the newspapers will fan the flames until then."

Monroe was still shaking his head. "The British will raise the ghost of Lord Nelson and send him here with the entire Home Fleet. And we haven't even finished rebuilding from their last visit."

Adams huffed again. "Gentlemen, you do not see the great gift that has been placed before you because it comes in a rude wrapper. What ill can come of this, if we but play to our strengths and exploit the weaknesses of others?" The others looked at him with curious eyes, forcing him to explain. "Spain may shout and pound its puny fist, but what can it do? Their treasury is bankrupt, their navy is rotting at the wharves, and their army finds itself cornered in every corner of the southern continent. They are no threat to us. And while mad King George may rattle his sword and unfurl his many sails, he will not make war upon us. The editors at their writing tables and the Lords in their chambers may cry out and demand the protection of the crown, but the right honorable gentlemen of the Commons and the merchants in their counting houses would not dare take the nation to war again. They need our commerce much more than they need their pride."

He then went on to the matter of Florida. "Have we not all coveted Florida and felt it to be rightfully part of our wonderfully expanding empire? Let Señor Onis call off the negotiations! What good will it do him? The Spaniards will still be unable to adequately defend the place from the South American revolutionaries. It will still be a drain on what little treasury they have left. It will always be more trouble than it is worth. Now, at least, there can be no doubt in their minds that we will have the place, if not by negotiation and fair purchase, than by the sword of Andrew Jackson. Let His Most Catholic Majesty and all his Dons lick their wounded pride for six months or so. Soon enough, Señor Onis will be back at the table."

Adams then came to his conclusion. "And as for our headstrong Emperor Andrew, perhaps this will be his undoing, though I doubt it. If it is, then we have rid ourselves of a possible tyrant. If not, then we have gained a valuable piece of property and forever secured our southern border. Gentlemen, dark clouds often bring the life-giving rain. They do not always bring a raging flood."

The United States forces departed St. Marks on the last day of April, leaving the two companies of artillery to hold the post until either the Spaniards came to re-occupy it or Washington sent someone else to relieve them.

The advancing column of soldiers cut their way westward through the wilderness and reached Fort Gadsden two days later. There they rested, resupplied, and otherwise prepared for what they knew could be a journey of up to two hundred miles. Barges were built to ferry the soldiers, horses, cannon, and supply wagons upriver to a place where the guides said there was a trail that led to Pensacola. The army, over a thousand strong, would be on its own, without means of support, for any number of weeks. Everything they needed would have to go with them.

The guides were correct about where the trail began, but were unaware of the fact that it died out after passing through a pair of abandoned villages about twenty miles west of the Apalachicola. After consulting the few inaccurate maps in his possession, Jackson decided the army would hack and slog its way northwest until it found whatever remained of the old Spanish trail that had originally run between St. Augustine and Pensacola. Not that there would be much to find. The road, nothing more than a wide path through the woods when the Spaniards cut it over a hundred years earlier, had seen little use since then.

For two weeks they trudged on, never quite sure where they were or how far distant from their destination. For most of the way it was an easy walk, the land being flat, the forest relatively thin, and the ground firm enough to support the wagons. As usual, the river crossings slowed them the most. The rivers themselves were not especially wide or deep, but the swampy floodplains on either side were almost impenetrable. At one point it took nearly a day before they realized that they were walking parallel to a small meandering stream, rather than perpendicular. The heat of early summer, the occasional rainstorm, the heavy woolen uniforms, and the weighty packs upon their backs made everyone miserable. Yet to say they were totally lost would have been an overstatement. As long as they headed west, they would eventually run into the Escambia River, which flowed into Pensacola Bay. Exactly what they were going to do once they reached Pensacola was not entirely evident. There was the official story that up to five hundred hostile Indians were in the area, but few people took the report seriously. Even if there were that many, no one expected they would be standing around, waiting to do battle with the much larger American army. They would, as Indians always seemed to do, simply melt into the forest and disappear from the face of the earth.

The more persistent, and plausible, rumor was they were going to seize Pensacola itself. That had some of the men worried. They had been able to literally walk into the little, isolated fort at St. Marks. Pensacola would be another matter. Although the Spanish garrison might not be large, they had two forts to take refuge in, and Barrancas, the one defending the entrance to Pensacola Bay, was reputed to be one of the strongest on the Gulf coast. There was also the concern that attacking the capital of West Florida would start a war with Spain and her ally Great Britain. Many of the soldiers had fought in the last war with England, and although they were quick to brag of their exploits, none was in a hurry to repeat the experience.

On the other hand, most of the soldiers seemed quite excited by the proposition of kicking the Old World royalists out of Pensacola. All of them believed Florida should rightfully be part of the United States. Placing it under American control would eliminate any number of threats to the nation's security, be they from Indians, Europeans, or Latin American revolutionaries. Most of the men, however, were less than philosophical about their mission. For them, it was like a young buck challenging the head of the herd for supremacy. It made them feel strong; it made them feel superior.

If there was one thing driving the men on, it was the presence of Andrew Jackson. For the soldiers of the regular army, following the leader was simply something a soldier did. For the volunteers from Jackson's home state of Tennessee, it was like following in the path of a prophet. Everyone could see the general was in ill-health and suffering from a significant amount of pain. Yet he never slowed down, and he expected every man to keep up the pace. If Joshua could bring down Jericho with trumpets, Jackson might just be able to make the walls of Barrancas tremble and tumble into the Gulf with the thunder of his voice.

After so many months of fear, insecurity, and toil, Elizabeth Stuart was enjoying a life of ease and luxury. It almost made her feel guilty. Almost. She had ridden in a Georgia Militia wagon from St. Marks to Hartford, where the units disbanded and the men returned to their homes. She then went with General Glasscock to his plantation home a few miles outside of town. Although the general was a well-respected lawyer, he also participated in the lucrative cotton trade. For the most part, the management of the plantation was taken care of by the overseer and the work performed by slaves. It wasn't a large plantation, but judging by the fine furnishings and luxury goods of the plantation house, it and the law business were supporting the Glasscocks very nicely.

Mrs. Glasscock was an energetic, cheery lady of about thirty years who took it upon herself to see that Elizabeth was welcomed back into "civilized society" in the warmest manner possible. Upon seeing Elizabeth in the Indian dress, she immediately took the girl upstairs to her dressing room and found half a dozen dresses that would fit her with only the smallest of alterations. Elizabeth looked at the clothes and began to protest. "Mrs. Glasscock, I cannot take such fine clothing. Surely you must have some old castoffs." What she really meant was the thought of bloomers, petticoats, corsets, and other underclothing was not the least bit appealing after half a year in loose-fitting native dress.

"My dear girl, these *are* castoffs. I haven't fit into them in years." She then walked over to another wardrobe with shelves full of shoes. Sorting through them, she pulled out a pair and asked Elizabeth to try them on. "Oh dear, you *do* have petite feet!" Then she laughed. "Or are mine just large? Oh well, there's a cure for that." Turning to the young slave girl who was attending them, she said, "Maisy, go tell Caesar to take the carriage into town and fetch Mr. Durrance, the cobbler. We certainly can't have our guest walking about in those tattered old moccasins." As far as Elizabeth was concerned, the moccasins were the most comfortable things her feet had ever been in. Before Maisy could leave the room, however, Mrs. Glasscock called her back. "While you're downstairs, tell Cosimo to set a mess of water to boiling. This young lady needs a proper bath."

Mrs. Glasscock then took a close look at Elizabeth's hair. "Oh, my dear girl! It's so lovely and such a beautiful color, but such a frightful tangle! We'll have it done up properly in the morning, but for now, a good session with a brush and comb will do wonders. You have a seat here at the dressing table, and I'll see what I can do with it. I just love to brush my hair, and it's not near as beautiful as yours." Elizabeth didn't bother to tell the woman that she'd purposely let it get that way. Her hair had been a constant temptation to trophy-hungry warriors while she was a captive, and she hadn't wanted it to be any more of an attraction than it had to be.

It took the better part of an hour for the bath to be readied, and during that whole time, Mrs. Glasscock fussed over Elizabeth. The conversation was polite and buoyant, and she never questioned Elizabeth about her captivity. Instead, they talked about common things, like home and family, which caused Mrs. Glasscock to shed a tear when Elizabeth talked about her father's passing. "You poor child, what you've been through! You surely are as strong as the stories say." It was the first inkling Elizabeth had of a notoriety that extended beyond the confines of Florida, but she didn't bother to ask what those stories were. She was not yet ready to face the truth, much less whatever rumors were making their way around the countryside.

After doing what she could to untangle Elizabeth's hair, Mrs. Glasscock picked out a dress for her to wear, and then probed through a jewelry box until she found what she was looking for. "Here you are! You simply *must* wear this brooch, my dear. See how it sets off your lovely tresses?" Satisfied, she left her guest alone to soak in the hot water and wash six months of Florida off her body and out of her hair.

By the time she was called to dinner, Elizabeth felt like a completely different woman. The dress fit reasonably well, the shoes had been packed with enough cloth to ensure they wouldn't fall off, and Mrs. Glasscock had done a remarkable job with the hair. As she entered the dining room, General Glasscock rose from his chair and said, "Mrs. Stuart, you look truly beautiful." For the first time in a long time, she actually felt that way.

It was, beyond a doubt, the most wonderful meal she'd ever sat down to. She started with a small glass of Madiera followed by a thick vegetable soup. There were oysters, cornbread with apple butter, boiled potatoes covered with butter, ham, fried chicken, squash, succotash, and for dessert, the most wonderful sweet potato pie she had ever eaten. By the end of the meal, the loose-fitting dress was feeling a bit snug.

In the evening, the Glasscocks, their two children, and their guest sat in the parlor for awhile, sipping brandy and making polite conversation. They then returned to the dining room for a lively game of whist before retiring for the night. Elizabeth was thankful her mother had spent so many hours teaching her the finer points of being a proper lady. Such skills had been of absolutely no use among the Indians, of only minor value on the frontier, but in polite society, they were essential.

Having proven that an officer's daughter could play cards as well as any man, Elizabeth climbed the stairs and found her way to her room. She was exhausted. After changing into a simple cotton nightgown, she slipped between the sheets and luxuriated in the feel of a featherbed and a down pillow. She smiled. The only thing that would have made it a more perfect night was Johnny by her side.

It was a week into the trek to Pensacola, and Jack Dill was tired of walking. He was also a bit jealous of John Stuart. As an officer, even a temporary one, Stuart was privileged to ride a horse. By right of inheritance Stuart had acquired Captain Vashon's mount, and though he felt somewhat guilty watching his friends trudge along, he remained in the saddle. As it was, no one in the company was inclined to grumble about it, knowing they would have done the same in similar circumstances and that as soon as the war was over, Sergeant Stuart would once again be on his feet.

Though most of the men hadn't noticed much difference in Stuart, Dill did. The two men had worked closely together for over three years, and they had reached the point where one almost knew what the other was thinking. Yet for some reason, Dill was having a difficult time reading his friend's mood since they had left St. Marks. At times Stuart's frame of mind seemed low, as if there were some great weight on his mind. At other times he seemed almost elated, as if life could not be better. By nature, Dill liked the ship of life to run on an even keel. His friend's pitching and rolling bothered him.

Dill continued to observe Stuart, trying to figure out what the matter was. By the time they were nearing their destination, he began to notice a pattern. When Stuart was doing something related to his duties, he went about the task with vigor and enthusiasm. Take him away from those responsibilities, and he became sullen and withdrawn. On the evening after they had crossed the Escambia River, he decided to have a talk with his friend. In all likelihood they would be invading Pensacola in the next day or two, and he wanted to know the state of Stuart's mind. After camp was set up and the troops were settling in for the evening, Dill approached his friend and said, "Can we have a word, Johnny?"

Stuart looked slightly worried, knowing full well his friend never asked to "have a word" unless there was some problem that needed to be addressed. "Am I that bad an officer?"

Dill laughed. "No, quite the opposite. You seem to have a calling for it, and I've heard no unusual grumbling from the men. No, it's something else. I get the feeling something is bothering you, but just when I begin to think it's true, you seem the happiest man alive. Am I wrong?"

Stuart shook his head. "It's just the march, Jack. One minute I'm tired, hungry, and worrying about how I'll do once we get there, and the next I'm all caught up in the excitement of the campaign." He smiled broadly. "You know, Jack, I really love this. Being on the march, leading the men, thinking about the coming fight. I just can't get enough of it." He shook his head, as if he knew it was all a dream. "Look, I know I'm not a real officer and that soon enough I'll be back to being a sergeant, but things aren't going to be that way forever. When my enlistment's up I'm going to apply for a real commission, just like Jackson said I should. All that land out west is going to have to be explored and settled, and the army's going to be out in the middle of it all. That's where I want to be, Jack."

In a way it made sense, but Dill knew there was more to it. He was aware that Stuart liked the military life, and now that the man had gotten a taste of being an officer, the possibility of a career in the army seemed very inviting. There was, however, one thing his friend wasn't mentioning. "What about Elizabeth? Is that the kind of life she wants? We've both seen how hard it is on an officer's wife. Left alone with the children, always short of money, never having a permanent home. It may not be what she wants."

Stuart gave a disinterested shrug. "She's my wife. She'll go where I go."

The comment almost shocked Dill. It was as if Elizabeth didn't matter. Before the war, Johnny's first thoughts would have been of her. Now she seemed inconsequential. The finality of Stuart's statement also told Dill that his friend didn't want to go into the subject. Dill wanted to probe deeper, but thought it best to let the matter rest, at least for the time being. There was a battle coming up, and Stuart might feel different afterwards. He would certainly feel different after he returned to being a lowly sergeant. Patting his friend on the back, Dill called it a night, saying, "Guess we'd better find our tents. Big day tomorrow, if the general has anything to say about it. Glad I'm not a Spaniard." Smiling, he turned and walked away.

Stuart appreciated the fact that people were looking after him. Even Old Hickory seemed to care about his future. Reaching into his pocket, he pulled forth a handsome silver pocket watch. It had been Captain Vashon's, and Elizabeth had insisted Johnny keep it with him as a reminder of her father. Stuart missed the man, and hoped he could live up to the captain's expectations. He also knew he was fortunate to have a friend like Jack Dill. Few people would have cared to ask if there was some problem, and fewer still would have let the matter rest after receiving such an obviously evasive answer. Dill wasn't meddling or prying; he was just offering his support and giving his friend time to think.

And Stuart knew precisely what he had to think about: Elizabeth. Why was it bothering him so much that Elizabeth had gone by the name of Red Bess while she was a captive? Half of the name was obvious because of the distinctive color of her hair. The Indians would have focused on that above anything else. If it wasn't for the fact that it seemed to go hand in hand with the moniker of her captor, Yellow Tom, he might not have been concerned. In truth, it was the "Bess" part that gnawed at him. Bess was a familiar form of Elizabeth, something an Indian would not have known. Why had Yellow Tom given her the name? No matter what the exact circumstances, it had the sound of an affection and familiarity that went beyond the normal bounds between captor and captive. Stuart was also bothered by the fact that Elizabeth seemed to be holding something back. He could accept her being reluctant to talk about the massacre itself. It had to have been a horrible sight, and she would want to forget it. But what about those months in captivity? By all accounts, she had been well treated and accepted into the tribe. Why was she so reluctant to talk about it? What was she hiding?

The following morning, May 22, the army began its march down the west bank of the Escambia River, heading south toward Pensacola Bay. The closer they came to the bay, the more ill-defined the river became, gradually widening into an impenetrable swamp with no obvious center channel. About noon they reached the bay itself and could see hints of the town off in the distance. To call it a city would have been too imaginative. With a permanent population of less than five hundred people, including nearly two hundred from the Spanish garrison and administration, the entire settlement covered only a few square miles. If it weren't for the excellent harbor, Pensacola would have had no reason to exist.

About an hour after reaching the bay, someone noticed a pair of horsemen approaching. As they drew closer, it became obvious that one was a Spanish officer. Deciding it was a good time to stop for the midday meal, Jackson called a halt to the march and awaited the arrival of the two riders. Everyone assumed it was a messenger from the governor, bringing demands that the American army leave the area. No one expected Jackson to pay the least bit attention to the request.

As the Spanish officer and his companion drew close to the American force, Jackson and several of his officers walked out to meet him. The horsemen stopped in front of the Americans but did not dismount. The Spaniard turned and spoke to his companion, who was obviously an interpreter. The interpreter, who appeared to be an American, relayed the message. "We bring greetings from His Excellency Don José Masot, Governor of His Most Catholic Majesty's Province of West Florida, to General Jackson and his fellow officers. The governor wishes to know the purpose of your visit to our land."

Jackson looked at the officer but spoke to the interpreter. "We have received reliable reports of upwards of five hundred hostile savages in these parts who have wantonly made war upon the United States and have been supplied with arms and provisions by Governor Masot. We mean to put an end to it."

After hearing the accusations, the Spaniard responded through the interpreter, saying, "His Excellency wishes to inform you that all such reports are untrue. What few Indians reside near or in Pensacola are mostly women and the infirm, and receive only the charity of the Church. His Excellency points out that the idea that we might support so large a number of Indians is absurd. We have barely the means to support the population of the city and the garrison, and have nothing to spare. Those who have fostered such lies wish only to mar the peace which has heretofore existed between our two nations. Governor Masot insists that you depart His Majesty's lands and return to your own, and that you vacate the fort at St. Marks, the capture of which can only be viewed as a hostile act on the part of the American government."

Jackson huffed. No one, including the Spaniard, expected him to simply turn and walk away. This was nothing more than a formality that both sides had to go through. "Tell Governor Masot we shall determine the veracity of those reports for ourselves."

The Spaniard bowed his head politely and began to turn his mount. The interpreter already knew what to say. "We shall inform His Excellency of your intentions."

That afternoon, the army marched to within a mile of the city and made camp. Throughout the remainder of the day and into the evening, Jackson and his men made plans for the assault that would come the next day. No one was sure what to expect. Would the Spaniards offer any significant resistance? No one really expected it, but no one wanted to be unprepared. There were two places where the Spanish might mount their defense. One was at Fort San Miguel, located in the town center, and the other was at Fort Barrancas, which guarded the entrance to the harbor. If the Spaniards wanted to defend the city, Fort San Miguel was the obvious choice. Barrancas was several miles from town, and taking up position there meant abandoning the city to the Americans, which was what the defense was supposed to prevent. Intelligence, however, indicated that San Miguel was in poor condition and without sufficient cannon to mount a serious defense. Everyone hoped Masot would see the hopelessness of the situation and simply surrender without a fight.

Don José Masot was in a situation for which there could be no good outcome. As he paced about the courtyard of the Governor's Mansion, he tried to ignore the people who were standing by, awaiting his decision. There was a hostile army of over a thousand men approaching Pensacola, and he saw no way to stop it. Protestations of friendship and logical arguments had done no good and with only about two hundred men at his disposal, Masot was in no position to face the Americans in open battle. The best he could do was to somehow minimize the damage.

The mayor of the town broke the silence, asking, "When do you expect reinforcements from Havana?"

Masot almost laughed. "I don't. With revolutions in every outpost of the empire, no troops can be spared for such a worthless place as Pensacola. No, mi amigo, we are on our own."

The representative of the businessmen couldn't imagine why the American general wouldn't listen to reason. "Surely he must know our two nations are at peace."

Commandant Luengo, having been brought to Pensacola after Jackson had taken St. Marks, knew the futility of the statement. "The man ignores all laws of nations. If he wants this city, he will have it."

The businessman fretted, "He'll destroy every business in town! We'll have nothing!"

Masot shook his head. "I will abandon the city before I let that happen. Jackson doesn't want smoldering ruins, he wants a new state to add to their union. If the forces withdraw, he will destroy nothing."

Luengo, still smarting from the treachery at St. Marks, protested. "We cannot simply pull down the flag and surrender. I have been shamed once. I will not suffer such indignity again."

Masot nodded. "The honor of Spain must be upheld. We will withdraw to the Barrancas. With sufficient provisions, we can hold out there for weeks. I doubt that Jackson would attempt a frontal assault. Perhaps his supplies will run out, or his men will grow restless. It is our only hope."

Early the next morning, General Jackson marched his army into Pensacola without any opposition, issued a proclamation that the city was now under United States control, and that, as long as the population cooperated, they would be protected in their lives, property, and customs. He then appointed Colonel William King as military governor and set about instituting an administration. The fact that the Spanish flag was still flying over Fort Barrancas was an annoyance, but one that would be taken care of soon enough.

By midafternoon, Jackson was settled in at the Governor's Mansion and dealing with a steady stream of visitors and petitioners. Most were nervous local officials calling to make sure their families and property rights would be respected. Some were merchants hoping to make some sort of profit from the hungry and tired army. A few were Americans who had settled in Pensacola and wanted to somehow gain an advantage now that their countrymen had taken over. Jackson listened impatiently to them all, reassuring the worried, sending the merchants to the appropriate underling, and generally dismissing the obvious profiteers. Never one to waste time on administrative details, by the end of the day an annoyed Jackson was almost ready to give the city back to Masot.

The one visitor he spoke to the longest was an agent hired by his old friend John Coffee. The man had come to the city early in January and had proceeded to purchase desirable properties in and around Pensacola. Now he stood before Jackson, a map spread out on the table before them. Pointing to the map, the man said, "The properties with a 'J' over them have been purchased on your behalf, and the ones with a 'C' are for General Coffee. Most of them have already tripled in value, though I suspect those numbers will go down after things settle out. Still, once the colony officially becomes United States territory, they'll go back up, and in a few years will probably be worth five times what we paid for them."

Jackson nodded thoughtfully and told the agent, "After we run the Spaniards out of Barrancas, look at some parcels in that neck of the woods. Once we get Florida, the navy will be spending more time in the Gulf and the Caribbean, and there isn't a better spot for a Navy Yard than right here, and no better place to defend it than Fort Barrancas."

The army had been in Pensacola little more than an hour before Jackson dispatched Lieutenant Gadsden to Fort Barrancas with his demand that the Spaniards surrender. It was, considering the message, a rather polite letter. Jackson knew a siege would take days, or even weeks, and, as always, he was in a hurry to get things done. After beginning the letter in a very respectful and cordial tone, Jackson assured Masot that if he were to surrender without conflict, the people of the city would be secure in their customs, property, and religion. He also promised that Masot and his men would be given passage to Cuba, and shown all possible military courtesy. He then warned the governor that unless there was an immediate surrender, the American army would not be responsible for the resulting "effusion of blood."

The terms were as generous as Old Hickory would likely give, but Masot could not accept them. Honor dictated that he defend his post, at least for a reasonable amount of time, or until the position became untenable. Taking the moral high ground, Masot sat down to write a lengthy response, a copy of which would go into his official papers to prove he had done his duty to the best of his ability. First he denied and refuted Jackson's charge of his having aided the Indians who were making war upon the United States. True, he had given food and other supplies to the natives, but they were subjects of the Spanish crown, and as governor he had a responsibility to provide charity where needed. He pointed out that Florida was a Spanish colony, the assault on Pensacola could be viewed as nothing but an act of war, and force would be met with force. Next, to make his point, Masot quoted a speech President Monroe had made to Congress a few months earlier, pledging that Jackson's invasion of Florida was strictly for the purpose of chastising the Seminoles, and that the Spaniards would not be molested in any way.

Jackson had assumed Masot's reply would be much as it was. As a soldier, the governor had to do his duty, no matter how futile the cause. Accordingly, on the following day, Jackson and the bulk of his army approached Barrancas and set up their artillery. Once again Jackson called for the fort's surrender, and once again, Masot defiantly refused.

There was no option but to begin the siege. Jackson hoped that after the exchange of a few harmless rounds, Masot would declare he had done his duty and run up the white flag. Masot, with a career and reputation to protect, was not about to give in so easily. As the first of the cannonballs bounced harmlessly off the fortress walls, Masot smiled. The engineers had selected a good location and designed a solid structure. From where the American gunners were, their shots could only hit the outer walls and not come crashing into the fort's interior. As long as the food and water held out—and his soldiers didn't mutiny—he could stand his ground as long as he cared to.

Back at Hartford, Elizabeth was enjoying the simple loving atmosphere of the Glasscock home. As she watched Mrs. Glasscock go about her daily routine, Elizabeth saw a bit of herself and her own mother. The constant tidying up after the children, the checking of the food preparation, and the concern for everyone's comfort and health were common activities that seemed to hold so much importance. They were the sorts of things she had always enjoyed doing for her father and then for Johnny when they were at Fort Montgomery. They were the types of activities that she had seen Conowaw and Nellie Crump do with such care. She came to realize it didn't matter whether it was taking place in a stately plantation house or a humble Seminole lodge, it was the feeling of home that mattered. Keeping the home was as vital a task for Mrs. Glasscock and Conowaw as practicing law was for the general or hunting was for Yellow Tom. Everyone, male or female, was doing their part to help family and community survive. To Elizabeth, it seemed the most important thing in the world, the true purpose of a person's existence.

When Elizabeth had first arrived, Mrs. Glasscock was so excited about having her as a guest she immediately began to plan a gala reception in Elizabeth's honor. The general, proving himself a true southern gentleman, gently told his wife that it might not be such a good idea. Elizabeth probably wasn't ready to face a throng of people, and might not wish to answer all their probing questions. Her stay with the Glasscocks was meant to ease the transition back to a more normal life, and any undue attention might only make things more difficult.

The general was, of course, correct. Elizabeth looked healthy and had suffered no real physical abuse, yet her mind was certainly troubled. She'd had a few nightmares, but nothing recurring, and she had to admit that except for the first few days, her captivity had not been an exceedingly terrifying experience. Yet there were certain images that never left her mind. Foremost, of course, was the slaughter on the boat. Even after all these months, Annie's bloodstained face and Nellie's pleading eyes remained clear in her memory. She could recall every soldier's death and hear all their cries. She also remembered the forlorn looks of the Mikasukis after they'd been driven from their homes by Jackson's army, and the wailing of the women who had lost their warrior husbands. At times the thought of all that suffering overwhelmed her, and nothing could help her but a good, long cry.

At others times, however, anger overcame her and she needed to get it out. Yet there was no one to focus the anger on. She had experienced both sides of the conflict and had seen more than enough evil on both sides. She wanted to scream at someone, but there was no one to scream at. On several occasions she had gotten a horse from the stables and gone off by herself to some lonely place where she could shout obscenities as vile as any soldier could come up with. On one occasion she had found a stout stick and beat it against a tree until her strength gave out. It helped, but only for so long.

When another of those troubling days arrived, Elizabeth decided to take one of the horses and go off by herself. As she entered the stable she heard voices around the corner, in front of the stalls. She recognized one voice as the overseer's but couldn't place the other. When she heard the stranger ask, "How's your pretty little red-headed guest doing? I hear she's a regular vixen," she stopped in her tracks, just out of sight.

The overseer chuckled. "She is a right pretty one. Like to spend a little time on the haystack with that one."

The stranger warned, "Better be careful. I hear when that boat was attacked she picked up a musket and handled it better than any soldier. Killed a few of them damn redskins, she did. One with a musket ball, another by clubbing him to death, and a third with the bayonet. That's why they didn't kill her. They was scared of her big medicine." The stranger then added, "They say she come back with a whole bunch of British banknotes sewn into her petticoat. The damn English bastards gave it to the Injuns, who didn't know what it was, so she picked 'em up and hid 'em in her clothes 'til she was rescued."

The overseer seemed to take pride in disproving the rumor. "Well, I don't know about her killing any redskins, but I can tell you for a fact she didn't come wearing any dress with a petticoat. The general brought her here wearin' nothin' but an old Injun sack and a worn out pair of moccasins. Probably suits her better. She may be a pretty little thing, but that's just cause she's been dressed up in a lady's clothes. Someone told me she's just some whore of a camp follower, hanging on to some old army private."

Elizabeth clenched her fists and bit her lip, not sure if she should confront the men or slip away. Mrs. Glasscock had mentioned "stories," but until Elizabeth heard them, they didn't bother her. Now she was bothered. Then the stranger lowered his voice a bit, not wanting any prying ears to hear the salacious tale he was about to relate. "I hear she was the squaw of some old chief named Yellow Hair. Got that name from some yellow-haired scalp he carries around. I hear she even left him a little papoose."

The overseer replied, "Probably won't want no white man after havin' an old wild Injun. Hell, probably had a whole bunch of Injuns. You know how they is; just pass the little squaws around."

For Elizabeth, the idea of quietly slipping away disappeared. Seizing a stout buggy whip that was hanging on the wall next to her, she stormed around the corner, lashing out at the two men, shouting, "How dare you! I'll show you just what sort of woman I am!" The leather end of the whip snapped against the overseer's neck, leaving a bright red welt and causing him to cry out for help. "I am the daughter of a United States Army officer, and I shall not be spoken of in such an insulting manner." The two men retreated into one of the empty stalls, a move they immediately regretted. Cornered, they were forced to endure Elizabeth's stinging whip and lashing tongue. "Never was I inappropriately handled by any Indian, and if you had enough intelligence to count to ten, you would know I wasn't with them long enough to bear anyone a child." The overseer yelped as the whip bit into his leg, while the other man cowered in the corner, his arms covering his face. "And yes, I did kill an Indian or two, and had I a pistol in my hand right now, I should not hesitate to do likewise to you."

Finished with her tirade, she turned around to see two black stable hands standing off to the side, a look of amazement on their faces. As she passed, she calmly handed the whip to one of them. She had often seen the overseer whip his charges, so she told the slave, "Now you can ask him how it feels." As she strode purposely out of the stable, she smiled. They wanted stories? Now they had a good one, and by the end of the week, every slave in the county would have heard it, and by the end of the next week, every white man. She also realized who it was she was so angry with. It was all those uncaring, thoughtless people who spread rumors and lies that eventually led to war.

General Jackson wasn't happy. From where they were positioned, the American cannon could do little more than punch ineffectual craters in the outer walls of Fort Barrancas, walls that would eventually have to be repaired with American taxpayers' money. Unfortunately, the Spanish fortress was surrounded by marshes and swamps, and there simply wasn't any better place to put the guns.

Lieutenant Gadsden thought differently. To the north of the fort was a small dry hill, just big enough for two or three cannon, and perfectly placed to lob cannonballs into the center of the fort. Jackson looked at it and shook his head. It was more or less an island, and all he could see in his mind were gun carriages sunk up to their axles. But so what? He had a thousand men, and at the rate things were going, it would be weeks, if not months, before the Spaniards gave up. "Do it, Lieutenant."

"Forward, march!" It was the happiest order John Stuart had given in his short career as an army officer. The war was over. A day after Lieutenant Gadsden's cannonballs started bouncing around the interior of Fort Barrancas, Governor Masot had given in to the inevitable and accepted General Jackson's terms of surrender. After a short and humiliating ceremony, Masot and most of his men boarded ship and set sail for Havana. Jackson was heading home and taking the bulk of the army with him. He had created a diplomatic mess, but that would be for the politicians in Washington to take care of. Conquerors didn't worry about embarrassing details.

It would take a week or two for the companies of the Fourth Infantry to complete the march to Fort Gaines. Fort Scott, the place so many had suffered and died to defend and keep supplied, was to be shut down and abandoned. With the Seminoles subdued and the Spanish evicted, it was of no further value. The only real threat to peace in the area were the Upper Creeks of Alabama, and it would be years before they recovered enough of their strength to challenge the white man's expansion. For the moment, the future looked secure. Yet something was still nagging at Stuart's mind, and he had no idea whether the future would be a happy one or not.

14

June 29, 1818
Ft. Mitchell,
Alabama Territory

To:
Mr. Robert Vashon
St. Louis, Missouri Terr.

Dearest Robert,

At long last I am to be reunited with my dear Johnny. We received word at Hartford a few days past that the company had arrived at Ft. Gaines, the place which is to be their permanent posting. Johnny said he has secured a small cabin for us to live in and anxiously awaits my return. As you might imagine, I am likewise most anxious to return to him. Although the Glasscocks have been the most hospitable hosts, there is nothing I long for more than to simply be with my dear husband in our own home, as humble as it may be. Yesterday marked the first anniversary of our marriage, and except for those few days we spent together after my rescue, I have been parted from him for nearly that whole time. A year of our life together has been taken by this senseless war, and I do so wish to return to some sort of normalcy and commence the life of a happily married lady.

I write from the Creek Indian Agency at Ft. Mitchell, which is located on the Chattahoochee, about 200 miles north of the line with Florida. Tomorrow morning I board a boat to take me down to Ft. Gaines, which is also on the Chattahoochee, perhaps 80 to 100 miles south of here. There being no coach from Hartford to Ft. Gaines, General Glasscock and I were obliged to come to this place, which is naught but a settlement of a few houses and this post, but there are several Creek villages nearby. It was also convenient for the general, who had business at the Agency. It shall be difficult to say good-bye to the general after all the kindness he and Mrs. Glasscock have shown me. Many were the tears that she and I shed when I left their home. The consideration they showed a complete stranger is most gratifying, and I hope someday to be able to show such hospitality to guests in my own home, after Johnny and I become established.

But I forget myself! The most heartfelt congratulations on the birth of little Amelia. I cannot believe I am an aunt, and do so look forward to the day when I might meet both her and Anna Lynn. It is heartening to hear that Anna Lynn came through the ordeal with no complications, and I know it is a relief to you that the child has "all her glorious little fingers and toes." Your letter containing the news reached us the day before Johnny's letter telling us of his arrival at Ft. Gaines, so you can well imagine my joy for two days straight.

What awaits me at Ft. Gaines I am not sure of, other than the loving embrace of my wonderful husband. In his letter, he did not describe the cabin, so I do not expect much, and would be happy with little more than a large corncrib. At least it will be a home. I know not if it has been well kept or was abandoned and in need of repair, but whatever the condition, a little work shall put it right. We do have some belongings, both our own and Father's, that have been stored since we left Ft. Montgomery, but that was nearly a year ago, and I know not what remains and what condition everything is in.

As for Ft. Gaines itself, there seems little to recommend it at the moment, though many whom I have spoken to believe it to have a fine future. Its location on the Chattahoochee will make it a prime depot for the transport of produce and cotton from southwest Georgia. I hear the area is fast being settled, and already there are a number of large plantations owned by some of the wealthier Creeks, such as MacIntosh, the chief who rescued me from the Seminoles. It may also prove a popular ferry point for those who are entering eastern Alabama. Indeed, "Alabama Fever" appears strong in this part of the Territory, judging from the number of settlers who have crossed the river.

From what I can glean from conversations with those who have been to Ft. Gaines, the town is now larger than the fort, which shows promise.

Since the war, the hostile Creeks have all fled the area, so there is little fear of Indian troubles, which gladdens me much. I have had quite enough of Indian troubles to last me for a lifetime, though as someone who understands their habits, I cannot say I have any special fear or loathing of them, as long as they remain peaceable. Indeed, I have just as much fear of the unprincipled whites who often inhabit the frontier areas. I should feel safer at night in a Seminole village than in many a frontier town.

For now, dear brother, I shall close, but will write again as soon as I am settled. I am sure both Johnny and Jack will have much news to relate of the war and their adventures in Pensacola. I myself long to hear how Johnny fared as an officer. By now I am sure he has returned to his position as a sergeant, but hopefully he has gained much from the experience. Give Anna Lynn a hug from her sister, and a bit of a tickle to your lovely child from her loving aunt.

With deep affection,
Your homeward-bound sister,
Elizabeth

An unexpected feeling of anxiety swept over Elizabeth as she stepped aboard the boat that was to take her to Fort Gaines. The vessel wasn't much different from the one she had been on with Lieutenant Scott, and the river appeared very much the same as the Apalachicola. It was as if she was stepping back in time, to a horrifying experience she very much wanted to forget. Closing her eyes and taking a deep breath, she tried to concentrate on Johnny, hoping to drive the images of the massacre out of her mind. It didn't work. When she looked at the man standing by the tiller, she thought of Scott. When she saw a rather plump woman standing near the front of the vessel, an image of Nellie Crump came to mind, and the burly man handling the lines reminded her of Nellie's husband, Reason. A young woman in a worn-out dress became Annie, and the man by her side looked like Jonathan Driver, the soldier Annie had been with before taking up with Jack. For just a moment, she wanted nothing more than to run screaming from the boat.

Then she remembered the advice her father had once given her when she'd come home crying after being harassed by some older girls. "Don't be afraid. Be angry," he'd said, and the words had served her well throughout the years, especially during her period of captivity. But who should she be angry with now? Certainly no one on this boat. Releasing the breath she'd been holding, she moved to the boat's rail and took a seat. It was time to end the year of fear and anxiety.

Neamathla looked down at the Apalachicola River from the low bluff where a rotting cabin stood. *This was once a good home for another clan,* he thought, *and it shall be a good home for mine.* He missed his home at Fowltown, but knew there was no going back. The whites had burnt it to the ground and would never allow an Indian to reside there again. Still, for some reason, he could not bring himself to take up residence farther south in the peninsula. This land in the north of Florida was his homeland, and he intended to finish out his days here. The Americans had come, had destroyed all they could, but they had left. This was still the land of the Spaniard, and he could live wherever he pleased in it. Would the Americans come back? Of course they would, but he would deal with that when the time came. Right now, his people needed a new home, and this looked like a good place.

There were, unfortunately, far fewer clansmen to provide for. Some had been killed in the war, others had fled farther south, while others had gone to live with the Creeks in the United States. Probably most painful was the loss of Yellow Tom. Upon hearing the fate of his mother, he had simply packed up his few belongings and walked off into the woods. Where he had gone and where he was now, no one seemed to know. Neamathla could understand. Tom had lost a war, his home, his mother, and the woman called Red Bess all in a matter of days. He had a right to give up.

Elizabeth stepped onto the boat landing at Fort Gaines and looked around nervously. When would she see Johnny? Then she heard her name called out and looked to see someone running down the road from the fort, high upon the bluff overlooking the river. Dropping her bag onto the dock, she ran up the road to meet him. When they met, Johnny gathered her in his arms, lifted her off the ground, and spun her around. "Never again will I let you out of my sight," he said, then set her on the ground and took a step back to look at her. "Those are certainly finer clothes than a sergeant's wife would be wearing."

Elizabeth was taken aback. His first comment wasn't how good she looked or how she had changed, but a remark about her dress, as if it wasn't appropriate. "A gift from Mrs. Glasscock," she told him. "She and the general were most generous during my stay with them. A finer gentleman and more lovely lady do not reside in all of Georgia." She then saw Jack walking down the road. Letting go of Johnny's hand, she raced up the road to greet him and gave him a warm embrace.

Johnny walked up and said, "Not so tight, my friend. She's mine, you know."

Elizabeth was excited. "Oh, I have missed you all so much! The other women from the camp—the ones who remained with Major Muhlenberg—are any of them here? I can't wait to see them!"

Jack answered hesitantly, "A few. Between those who were with you, those who were widowed, and those who've moved on, there aren't many left." He saw the look of excitement leave her face as she remembered all the losses from Scott's boat. "But those that remain are most anxious to see you. Your boat has been looked for everyday, none of us knowing when you would arrive. Welcome home."

Then, as all the memories from the past year flooded into her consciousness, Elizabeth began to cry. She reached out and took her husband's hand. "Take me home, Johnny."

The storekeeper wasn't sure what to make of the man who was sitting across the street from his shop, gazing out across St. Augustine harbor, his eyes fixed on the distant horizon. He wasn't even sure what the man was. He was dressed and acted like an Indian, but certainly didn't look like one. *Probably some half-breed,* he thought. The man had come into the store perhaps an hour earlier with a varied assortment of goods to trade. From the look of the stuff, he'd probably salvaged them from some wreck he'd found along the coast. The man had said few words and had taken the money the shopkeeper had offered without haggling, something an Indian never did. The storekeeper had to admit it was one of the most forlorn faces he'd seen in some time.

After leaving the store, the man had taken a seat on a boulder across the street, part of St. Augustine's haphazard seawall. Since then, the man hadn't moved. The storekeeper felt pity for the Indian. *Another refugee from the war,* he thought. *Nobody left, nowhere to go.*

Suddenly the man stood up, turned, walked across the street and back into the store. Setting a pair of Spanish coins on the counter, he said, "Tell me when to stop." He went to a shelf and found a plain white shirt and a simple pair of brown trousers.

The storekeeper shook his head. "Those breeches are too big. Try that other pair." The Indian nodded and did as he was advised, then selected a narrow leather belt. The storekeeper looked at the coins on the counter and said, "That's about it, my friend." The Indian handed him another coin and stepped over to a rack of hats and found one that suited him. The storekeeper smiled. "All you need now is a pair of shoes. The cobbler's one street back." He then had an afterthought and reached under the counter. "Here. You'll need a pair of stockings to go with them shoes." He pointed toward the back of the building, where the storeroom was. "You can change back there, if you like." The man nodded, picked up his new apparel, and walked into the back room.

A few minutes later, a different man walked out. There was a look of purpose and determination on his face. Setting his Seminole longshirt and leggings on the counter, the man spoke in an entirely different voice, saying, "Do with these what you will, sir. I shan't be needing them anymore."

Elizabeth knew something wasn't right the moment she walked into the cabin. As she had assumed, it was a simple one-room structure, the sort commonly found on the frontier. What surprised her was the lack of care that had gone into the preparations for her arrival. She hadn't expected it to be spotless; Johnny wasn't the spotless type. Still, she had expected him to have spent some time getting the place ready for her. Perhaps he would have put the cooking utensils and dishware in the cupboard. As far as she could tell, they were still in the trunk, just as she had packed them when she had left Fort Montgomery.

Most distressing, however, was the bed. She would have expected it to be neatly made, perhaps even with a flower on the pillow. Instead, the sheets were askew, left just as they had been when Johnny had gotten out of bed in the morning. Even in the dim light, she could tell they were filthy, obviously not washed since the day he had moved into the cabin.

Johnny asked, "Well, do you like it? Nothing like the Glasscock's place, I'm sure, but it'll have to do."

Elizabeth pushed her disappointment aside and wrapped her arms around Johnny's neck. "Any place, as long as you're here."

She fully expected Johnny to lead her to the bed, but instead he cheerily said, "Well, I have to get back to the fort. Go ahead and start making the place livable, and I'll be back when I'm off duty." He then leaned over, gave her a kiss on the cheek, and walked out.

She stood there for a moment, stunned. Was it something she had done? How could that be? She'd just arrived. Was it something she *hadn't* done? If so, she had no idea what it was. When they had parted at St. Marks, everything seemed to be fine. They had made love, they had talked, and the future seemed promising. What could have changed in those few months? Had something gone wrong during the expedition to Pensacola? From the few letters she'd received and the reports she'd heard, everything had gone extremely well. Even Johnny's short time as a temporary officer had been praised.

In the end, she blamed it on their long separation and the nervousness both of them were feeling. What else could it be? Stepping out onto the porch, she saw a few other cabins along the dirt road, and at the far end of the street, a modest house. In the other direction, toward the river, was the fort, and to the north, she assumed, was the town itself. She looked down at the trunk one of the soldiers had carried up from the dock. It was time to get out of her fine travelling clothes and into some work clothes.

By the time Johnny came home, the cabin was looking presentable, and a simple meal had been cooked. It wasn't much, but considering how little Elizabeth had to work with, she was proud of what she had accomplished. Johnny was unimpressed. He didn't complain or scold in any way, but neither did he give her any praise. It was simply what he expected.

Andrew Jackson threw down the newspaper, rose from his chair, and began to pace across the floor of the two-story log cabin he called home. "We need a bigger house, Rachel."

Mrs. Jackson looked up from her sewing and smiled. "Not enough room to carry on with your ravings about the goings-on in Washington City? Or is it the Georgia Militia?"

"If I get my hands on that murdering ass, I'll string him up to the nearest tree. And he calls himself a gentleman!"

Rachel smiled. It was the Georgia Militia. She had heard people refer to her husband as an "Indian hater," but she knew better. Above all else, he loved his country, and anyone who stood in the way of the nation's advancement would earn the enmity of Andrew Jackson. It might be the British, the Spanish, or even a New Englander. Unfortunately, on the frontier, it was usually an Indian. At the same time, he held a certain appreciation for the natives. They were generally men of honor, they loved their families, and they respected the land. He had even adopted a young Indian who had been orphaned after the Battle of Horseshoe Bend. People saw her husband the way they wanted to, and it was often one-dimensional. Rachel knew he was much more complicated than that.

At this particular moment, it was Andrew's sense of honor that had been insulted. She knew how strong that was; more than once he'd felt obliged to defend her honor and still carried the scars from one of those duels. On the march down to Florida the army had passed through the friendly Lower Creek village of Chehaw and the elderly headman had been especially gracious in his welcome for the white men. The Indian had given up his cabin for the general's use and the two men had spent hours talking. Andrew had truly liked the man. Then, on their way home from the war, an unruly Georgia Militia company had raided the village, and in the process, the old headman had been killed. Jackson was furious, and had ordered the company's captain arrested. The man had wisely fled the state.

As the general's pacing took him to the far end of the room, he turned around and decided to change the focus of his anger for the return trip. "Damn Henry Clay, up on his high-and-mighty Constitutional podium. How dare he compare me to that damned Bonaparte!"

"Calm down, Napoleon. It's just Congress."

"Damn them! I give them Florida, and what do they do? They go bowing and scraping to the Spaniards and ask to give it back. We should never give it back!"

"Now, Andrew, it's just diplomacy. You did your part, now let Mr. Adams do his. Within a year or two, Florida will be ours, and there'll be no war with Spain or England."

He shouted, "Damn the bloody Redcoats!" then took a seat. Rachel was right, of course. She always was. She knew when to let him rant and rage, and when to cool him down with simple facts. She was certainly right about John Quincy Adams. When the whole matter of the Florida war blew up in Washington, the Secretary of State had been the only member of the Administration to fully back him. That was surprising, for he and Adams were political opposites and had little use for one another. Jackson had expected Treasury Secretary Crawford to come out against him, and he knew he had ruffled Secretary of War Calhoun's feathers by bypassing his authority; that was all politics-as-usual. As for President Monroe, well, he would do all the talking and say very little.

Perhaps he shouldn't have been surprised by Adams's support. Jackson didn't like the man, didn't like his political views, and didn't even like his part of the country, but he had to admit that above all else, Adams was a patriot. The man knew that Florida was vital to the nation's economic interests and also to its security, and would do everything he could to see it become United States territory. Rachel was right: It was time to let Adams do his part.

Jackson went over to his desk and picked up a copy of Adams's reply to the Spanish ambassador's demand for an explanation of why Pensacola and St. Marks had been seized. He smiled. The reply was, indeed, a masterful piece of work. Somehow, when Adams was done, all blame was laid at the feet of Spain or England. About seventy documents were included, nearly all of them letters written by Spanish officers, that damned

Arbuthnot, or American officers. Adams managed to make each one sound like an indictment against the two Old World powers.

In part, Jackson had Lieutenant Gadsden to thank for many of those letters. When the political uproar first broke out, Monroe had written, telling Jackson he needed to produce documentary evidence to back up the need to attack the Spanish posts. Unfortunately, or perhaps conveniently, all the original correspondence Jackson had gathered in Florida had been lost, including a number of letters found on Arbuthnot's boat. As it was, Gadsden had made copies, and proceeded to make another set to send to Washington. If Gadsden happened to embellish certain parts or delete others, well, it was all in a good cause.

Elizabeth was adjusting to her new world, but it was not as satisfying as she had hoped it would be. Try as she might she couldn't quite put her finger on what the problem was. She was feeling slightly trapped, a bit worried, and not very confident. In her mind, she went over everything, yet nothing presented itself as the root cause for her concerns.

Might the problem have something to do with Fort Gaines? No, it was the sort of town she, Johnny, and Jack had often dreamed of. Or at least it promised to be. Jack had already bought some property on Washington Street, though what he intended to do with it had not been decided yet. He had tried to convince Johnny to do the same, but Johnny seemed hesitant. Elizabeth wasn't sure why. It had always been assumed that he and Jack would go into business together when they got out of the army.

Was the cabin the problem? True, it wasn't much, but they had spent quite a bit of time fixing it up and adding nice furnishings. For the moment it suited their needs, and she was perfectly happy with it. She had mentioned to Johnny that they should think about building a house, but he had been noncommittal. He was still in the army, he pointed out, and subject to being transferred at any time. She couldn't argue the point, but it was now November, and the company had been at Fort Gaines for six months. Johnny only had about six months left on his enlistment, so even if they were transferred, they could soon return.

Was it the army? No, she had spent enough time with the army to be used to the sort of life a soldier's family led. If nothing else, duty at Fort Gaines was more like civilian life than any other place she'd known. The garrison was small, Captain Clinch was an easy-going commander, and the local Indians were peaceable. Still, Elizabeth looked forward to the day Johnny's enlistment ran out, and they could begin a normal, settled life. Johnny seemed less excited, but she was sure he was looking forward to it too.

Was it the close proximity of the Indians? The Creeks, though friendly at the moment, could quickly change their mood if the encroaching settlers were not controlled, which was bound to happen sooner or later. Yet for some reason, she wasn't particularly afraid of an Indian uprising. She had lived with the Indians for almost half a year and spoke their language. Perhaps it was a false sense of security, but she felt if she had survived it once, she could survive it again. Indeed, she had a bit of notoriety among the Indians, who called her the "warrior woman" and said she had strong medicine. Some whites called her "the Amazon," but never to her face.

So was Johnny the problem? He had definitely changed since they were first married, but then so had she. She still loved him very much, and it was obvious that he loved her. Why else would he be so protective of her? At times that protectiveness could be annoying, like when he came home in the middle of the day just to check on her. At other times it could be infuriating, like when he forbade her to talk to the Indians. Yet she was willing to forgive his protective nature. After all, hadn't she been stolen from him once already? She believed that sooner or later, as the Indians were pushed farther west, his anxieties would fade, and he would become more confident of her safety.

She was, of course, quite willing to forgive most anything Johnny might do, simply because she loved him. She knew the massacre, her time with the Indians, and even her stay with the Glasscocks had changed her. She also understood that her captivity, the war, and Johnny's brief time as an officer had changed him. They were different people now, but there was no reason they couldn't be happy together. She went out of her way to please him, to show him how much she cared. He had responded in kind, but she had to admit that whenever he gave her a small gift or showed her some special thoughtfulness, he always made her feel obligated in some way, as if it were something he didn't have to do, so she'd better be appreciative. All in all, their love life hadn't suffered, but she had to admit their lovemaking had changed, though not necessarily for the worse. Gone was a certain tenderness and playfulness that had been present when they were first married. It had been replaced by an intensity and aggressiveness that had troubled her at first, but she had gotten used to it after some months and had to admit that it was no less pleasurable.

In the end, she was left with the lingering feeling that *she* might be the problem. Perhaps she hadn't fought hard enough to avoid capture. Perhaps she should have tried to escape. She certainly knew she had come close to taking Yellow Tom as a lover. Maybe she had simply enjoyed herself too much at the Glasscock's. Perhaps an officer's daughter wasn't cut out to be a sergeant's wife. Whatever it was, the only thing she could think to do was try and amend her ways to make herself more pleasing to her husband.

It was a sight John Stuart didn't want to see. There was his wife, standing in the road under a tree covered with the golden leaves of autumn, talking and laughing with an Indian warrior. He was a handsome fellow, with straight black hair and wide, strong shoulders. Worst of all, he could see they were conversing in the warrior's native tongue. Johnny hated that. Why couldn't she just forget it? Did she think she'd be returning to the savages some day?

He had seen her talking to some Indian women occasionally, but had let it go. After all, few of them spoke English, and he didn't feel threatened by the women. To see his wife conversing in such a familiar manner with a warrior was another matter. Although she denied it, he knew the Indian called Yellow Tom had been her lover. He tried to tell himself she'd had no choice, that he'd forced himself upon her, but he just couldn't bring himself to really believe it. And now, to see her so friendly with another of those damned savages . . .

Johnny stood there for some moments, partially hidden by a tree, trying to contain his anger. Every time Elizabeth and the warrior laughed, he grew more enraged. Was she planning some secret meeting with the man? Perhaps a quick romp in the woods while her husband was on duty at the fort? Was he simply watching something that had happened many times before? The more he thought about it, the more convinced he became that she had been willingly unfaithful while in captivity, and might well be now.

That would also explain the way she acted at home. She seemed to be forever going out of her way to please him, as if she were acting out of a guilty conscience. If nothing had happened between her and Yellow Tom, why wouldn't she talk about him? Indeed, she had more or less refused to talk about any aspect of her captivity. Was there something to hide? As far as Johnny was concerned, it was becoming more and more obvious that there certainly was.

Stepping out from under the shade of the tree, Johnny strode purposefully toward Elizabeth and the Indian. The warrior saw the soldier approaching, said a few quick words to Elizabeth, and hurried off. Johnny shouted, "Stay away from my wife, you bloody savage!" Coming up to Elizabeth, he grabbed her by the arm and demanded to know, "What the hell are you doing?"

Infuriated, she tore her arm out of his grip and shouted, "Talking to an old friend! That was Sammy Perry, one of the Creeks who rescued me and brought me back to St. Marks. Don't you remember him? We were joking about General McIntosh and his friend Tom Woodward. Or have you forgotten them too?"

Johnny now realized he did indeed recognize the man, but would not admit it. "They all look the same to me." Knowing he was probably in the wrong put him on the defensive, but he still believed Elizabeth had not been truthful with him since her return. Feeling the need to assert his authority, he told her, "I don't ever want to see you talking to no Indian again, especially in their own language. You're a white woman, damn it. You speak English!"

Elizabeth took a step back. No one, not even an Indian, had ever spoken to her that way. True, Yellow Tom and Conowaw had scolded her occasionally, and her parents certainly had when she was a child, but that had always been with the aim of instruction in mind. This was different. This was an order, and it had nothing to do with her welfare. Her eyes narrowed and she gave Johnny a look he'd never seen before, the same one she'd given Efa-Hadjo when the warrior had threatened her friend Conowaw. In a voice that left no room for argument, she told him, "I'll speak to whomever I care to, in whatever language I care to." Having said what she had to, she turned and stalked back to the cabin. Johnny didn't move. He'd heard the term "righteous anger" before, but now he'd seen it.

For Jack Dill, the future was about to begin. His enlistment was up at the end of 1818, and he could hardly contain his anxiety.

He had plans, but they could not truly begin until he walked out the gates of the fort as a civilian.

There was a reason for Dill's haste to get out of the army. Fort Gaines had one small general store, and the owner, having caught the "Alabama Fever," had put it up for sale. It was an opportunity Dill could not let slip by, and he had taken the plunge. On January first, the store would be his. Ever since he had taken on the position of Camp Sutler at Fort Montgomery, Dill had dreamed of opening a store in some frontier town. Now it was becoming a reality.

Yet the dreams didn't stop there. Growing towns needed other services, and he would keep his eyes open for new business opportunities. Towns also needed leaders, and in future years, as one of the earliest residents of Fort Gaines, he would no doubt be called upon to help steer its course into the future. In his mind he could see streets and houses on land that was still forested, steamboats tied to wharves by the river, and wagon trains lined up for a mile down the road. He would serve the town, and the town would help him thrive. Multiplied thousands of times by thousands of people, that's how the nation would grow.

Of course it was only a dream, and all he had was a little store, but there was no doubt in his mind he could make it work. At the moment there was only one sour note in the great symphony of his plans for the future: He had no one to share it with. Annie was gone, and even though it had been over a year, he still thought of her almost every day. He had also assumed John Stuart would be his partner, but even that part of the dream seemed in jeopardy. Johnny hadn't dismissed the idea, but he also didn't talk about it anymore. While on the trek to Pensacola, Johnny had talked about applying for an officer's commission, and for all Dill knew, that might still be the man's intention. At any rate, Johnny wasn't saying, which meant he was still considering the idea. One thing was obvious: If Johnny did get his commission, it wouldn't be long before he and Elizabeth would be on their way to a new posting. When that happened, Dill would lose the best friends he had ever had.

The young woman looked up from behind the desk in the office of her father's shipyard just outside of Nassau. It was not a position she normally occupied, but her father would be busy all day launching a new boat, so she had come out of the adjacent house to tidy up in his absence. Standing in front of her was a good-looking young man with light hair and a very interesting face. He said, "Good morning, Miss. My name is Thomas Campbell from the trading firm of McKenzie and Gordon. I have come to enquire into the status of the schooner *Desdemona*." It was a strange accent; British, but not quite, and certainly not Bahamian.

She blushed a bit. "Oh, I'm sorry, sir. I don't work here. That's not fit for a lady, you know. My father is Mr. Carney, the owner of the yard, and I was just in here doing a bit of cleaning. He's out in the yard launching a new boat." Then, as an afterthought, she added, "My name's Liz."

Mr. Campbell tipped his hat slightly. "My pleasure, Miss Liz. Most people call me Tom. Is your name short for Elizabeth? I used to have a friend called Elizabeth."

She answered, "So they tell me, but Mum and Dad always just called me Liz or Lizzy." She liked his easy, friendly manner and decided to extend their conversation. "You don't look or sound like you're from around here. Have you been in Nassau long, Mr. Campbell?"

"For several months. But you are right; I am not from this area. I spent a good many years among the Indians of Florida, until the Americans forced me out."

"I used to court a fellow who went to Florida, but he didn't come back when the war ended. Good thing, too, for I would have had nothing to do with him, and neither would anyone else I know. Turns out he spoke against dear old Mr. Arbuthnot and the excellent Mr. Ambrister and got them both killed. To think I had once thought of marrying such a scoundrel!"

Tom knew precisely who she was referring to, but decided not to acknowledge the fact. There was something he liked about the girl. She wasn't what one would call beautiful, especially when compared to the other Elizabeth he'd known, but there was something about her that was appealing. If nothing else, she was easy to talk to.

Liz then asked, "Do you have any family here in the Bahamas, Mr. Campbell?"

"No, I do have some family in England, but have not seen them since I was a child."

She smiled, as if she'd just figured something out. "Are you a half-breed?"

From someone else it might have been insulting, but Tom took it in the friendly manner it was offered, an honest curiosity about his background. "Indeed I am, Miss Liz. Does that lower me in your esteem?"

"Not in the slightest, Mr. Campbell. It just makes you more interesting. Do you ever think of going back to Florida?"

He shook his head. "There is nothing for me there."

It seemed a very direct answer, but she sensed there was more to it. "You want to be there, don't you?"

She had seen right through him. He relaxed a bit and reverted to his normal manner of speaking. Now that she knew his secret, he didn't need to pretend to be a proper Englishman. "It is like the Blue Jay who built his nest in a tree that is then chopped down. There is nothing to do but build a new one in a new tree. I am fortunate in that I can live in either world. My kinsmen cannot, and my heart aches for them."

"Do you still have family in Florida? I should hate to think those awful Americans have driven you from your loved ones."

He nodded, and a sad look came over his face. "There were many people in my clan, but the person most dear to me was my mother. Sadly, she died soon after she was captured by the whites." He then caught himself. "Or should I say the Americans?"

She smiled slyly, as if what she was about to say was a bit naughty. "The *damn* Americans."

He laughed. Perhaps he had found the place to build a new nest.

Elizabeth saw the light snow falling outside the cabin as she placed another log on the fire. January 1819 had arrived, and with it had come the cold weather. Still, this was the South, and whatever snow fell on the ground would soon disappear. She only wished her unhappiness would dissipate as quickly. Maybe there was simply nothing she could do about it. Perhaps this was the way life was supposed to be.

She was starting to feel trapped in her own home. Johnny's protectiveness was turning into possessiveness, and it was becoming stifling. But what could she say? Wasn't that a sign of love? Worst of all was the knowledge that she had let it happen. Afraid of losing her husband, she had decided not to stand her ground when he placed restrictions on her movements. The thought of living without him was worse than living with him.

Not that living with him was all that bad. He was attentive, almost to the point of its being annoying. He was never violent toward her, though she made sure she never gave him cause to be. If nothing else, he was still a good lover. When she looked at what she had, she saw little reason to complain. Besides, things would certainly get better when his enlistment ran out and he went into business with Jack.

Perhaps what she missed the most was having someone to talk to. The only real social life she had was on Mondays, when the women would gather down by the river to do laundry, on Saturdays, which was market day, and Sundays, when everyone gathered at the church. Some of her friends would occasionally have an afternoon get-together and invite her, but she usually declined, knowing Johnny would disapprove. Her friend Sarah Wakefield had even remarked, "You seem to be more of a prisoner here than when the Indians had you." At times, she had to admit that Sarah was right.

Perhaps things would have been better if they'd had a child, but for some reason she was finding it difficult to conceive. She had, early in November, shown the first signs of pregnancy, but had soon lost the child. For several weeks she had been devastated, and had just recently regained her normal mood. Johnny had said he was disappointed, but she hadn't seen it in his demeanor. Indeed, he seemed a bit relieved.

Taking a seat before the fire, she went back to work making a pair of moccasins. She soon heard Johnny's footsteps on the front porch. As he opened the door he was smiling, but then he saw what was in her hands. "What the hell are those?"

"Just a pair of moccasins. These shoes hurt my feet if I wear them all day, and I thought a pair of moccasins would feel good."

With a look of contempt, he said, "What? You miss being an Indian?"

Insulted, Elizabeth shot back, "No, my feet hurt. What of it?"

He didn't answer, but demanded to know, "Where did you get the leather?"

Thinking Johnny was concerned about her spending too much money, she told him, "From one of McIntosh's men as he was passing on his way to town. He didn't even charge me for it."

"Well, you'll not be wearing those in my house," he said, and turned to see what was cooking.

Elizabeth was stunned. He'd spoken to her no differently than if she had been a slave. Getting to her feet, she took a step toward him and declared, "It is *our* house, and I'll wear what I damn well please."

Suddenly his hand lashed out and slapped her face. Moving to within inches of her, he said, "You know I don't like you talking to them Indians." He then stepped back and laughed. "What, does Red Bess miss her redskin lover?" Elizabeth was stunned again. Where had he heard that name? Johnny must have seen it in her face, for he told her, "That Redcoat bastard Ambrister told me all about you and your yellow-haired lover before we shot him."

This time it was Elizabeth's turn to do the face-slapping. Ambrister had saved her life, had been her friend, and had always been the perfect gentleman. How dare Johnny speak of him so callously? She shouted, "He would never have said such a thing! Tom and I were never lovers!"

It may have been a denial, but Johnny saw it as a confirmation of what he had already chosen to believe. "Tom, was it? And how many squaws did old Tom have? Did he do you all the same, or was Red Bess his favorite?"

She slapped him again, but this time he returned the favor with his fist. Elizabeth staggered back and stared at him in disbelief. She tasted blood and spat it out on the floor. "Get out!" she screamed, and looked about for something to defend herself with.

All of a sudden Johnny was afraid. He'd heard the stories, and though they varied, most said that she'd killed at least two or three Indians. He'd never really believed it, but the look on her face made him realize she was certainly capable of doing it.

Then her eyes closed and she shuddered. "Get out! Please!" This time she wasn't threatening, she was pleading. Johnny backed toward the door, turned, and walked out of the cabin.

For a moment, Elizabeth just stood there shaking. Then she stepped over to the table, sat down, and began to cry. What had Ambrister told him? Perhaps he had assumed she and Tom were lovers. But why tell Johnny? Then again, a person might say anything when facing the firing squad. Whatever it was, the damage had certainly been done. She also began to realize just how jealous Johnny had become and how the jealousy was twisting his mind. She didn't know what she could do to make things better, but she did know her husband had just hit her. What might he do the next time something triggered his suspicions?

The thought frightened her, but something else frightened her even more. What might *she* do? When Johnny hit her, she'd instinctively reached for some sort of weapon. Fortunately, nothing had been immediately at hand. She thought of the widow of Soo-Lee Tustennuggee and of Efa-Hadjo. She had killed them both with little hesitation. True, killing the widow had been necessary for her own survival, but what about Efa-Hadjo? That had been pure rage. Could she do the same to Johnny if she felt sufficiently angered? People often wondered what evils they were capable of or what circumstances might make them commit some horrible action. Elizabeth didn't have that problem. She knew full well what she was capable of, and it scared her.

John Stuart left the cabin and charged off into the forest, needing time alone to think about what had just happened. He had hit his wife, something that had always disgusted him when he'd seen other men do it. But why had he done it? He knew what had triggered the confrontation. Earlier that day he'd seen one of the company women flirting with a Creek warrior who was visiting the fort. He couldn't get the image out of his mind, and he had begun to see Elizabeth in the picture, instead of the other woman. Then, to see his wife making a moccasin; it was just too much.

Suddenly he felt angry. She was the one who had been unfaithful. She had slapped him, had provoked him into hitting her. He started to turn around, intent on going back to the cabin and setting the matter straight once and for all. He was the husband; it was time to reassert his authority.

Then the fear swept over him. It wasn't the same fear he'd experienced in the cabin, when he thought she might actually attack him. No, this was a fear of loss. The violent exchange had destroyed something, and he knew it. Never again would she look at him the same. Was he losing her? Would he come home one day and find her gone? He just couldn't let that happen, and he knew that if he confronted her now, he'd only be widening the rift between them. There was also the fear that perhaps it was all his fault, and that he'd gotten it all wrong.

For more than an hour he wandered in the woods, trying to figure it out. What had happened during her captivity to change her so much? Was it the sight of all the slaughter when the boat was attacked? Had she been raped by that Yellow Tom fellow or someone else? Had she been beaten or whipped? Had she been confined or left out in the cold? Had she been threatened with torture? Under what circumstances had she killed those Indians, if indeed she had? She never talked about it, so he just didn't know. Whatever happened, it must have been painful, and it must have left a deep scar in her mind. And now he'd hit her. How stupid could he be? Driven by fear, he began to run back toward the cabin. Would Elizabeth still be there?

She wasn't. Johnny looked around the cabin, trying to figure out where she might have gone. Most of her clothing was missing, so she was off on more than just a walk in the woods. But where had she gone? There were only three possibilities. If it had been a less personal matter, she would have gone to Jack, but not under these circumstances. She might go to Captain Clinch, but only with the complaint, not to stay. The only logical choice was for her to go to Sarah Wakefield's. She was Elizabeth's closest friend, and she had a house with an extra room. Desperate, he began to run toward town. He had to find her.

15

John Stuart stood outside the Wakefield home, trying to decide what he should do. He knew Elizabeth had fled there after he'd hit her, but he had no idea what he would say when they came face to face. Before he could make a decision, Sarah's husband Daniel opened the door and stepped out onto the porch with an awkward smile on his face. "You'd best come on in, John."

Stepping into the parlor, Johnny saw Elizabeth sitting on the sofa, an ugly bruise on her left cheek. Sarah was sitting next to her, and across from them sat Jack Dill. Stuart wondered why he was there. Dill answered the obvious, unasked question. "Sarah sent for me." Dill motioned Johnny toward another chair across from the sofa and assured his friend that, "I'll not take sides, but we all know this cannot happen again." He stood up, saying, "The rest of us will go out on the front porch and let you two sort this out, but the moment we hear a raised voice, we'll be right back in." He may not have been taking sides, but he was certainly protecting Elizabeth.

For the first few minutes, Johnny couldn't look at his wife. He was simply too ashamed by what he'd done. Elizabeth, on the other hand, looked straight at him, but didn't say a thing. She didn't feel it was her place to speak. It was Johnny who needed to explain.

He didn't know where to begin. "Are you all right? I didn't mean to hurt you."

"I've been through worse." It wasn't a joke, and he knew it.

"It'll never happen again, I swear it."

She thought, *It should never have happened the first time.*

He tried to explain, but nothing sounded sufficient. "I love you. I don't know what happened. The thought of you with that redskin . . . it just drives me crazy."

He doesn't believe me, she thought. Then she realized, *No matter how many times I tell him, he'll never believe me.* She wanted things to be better between them, but couldn't imagine how they could do it. If he was always going to be jealous, there was always the chance he would once again become violent. She had seen it all too often with the soldiers and the wives of the company. If it wasn't Yellow Tom he was worried about, someone else would fill his imagination. It might even be Jack. The green-eyed monster was not easily slain.

Johnny was getting desperate, and Elizabeth's silence wasn't helping. What he said next only made matters worse. "Things will be different when I get my commission." He could see the surprise in her eyes, and realized whatever hole he was in had just gotten deeper. He quickly tried to tell her what she should have already been told. "I applied for a Second Lieutenant's commission. Major Wooster endorsed it, General Gaines did too, and even General Jackson. They assure me that all it's waiting on is Congress and the President's signature."

Elizabeth was hurt. "You never told me." Then she was angry. "You never even asked me!"

"I wanted to surprise you." He tried to sound convincing, but knew it wasn't the truth. He had kept the application a secret because he knew she would be opposed to it, and that Jack would be disappointed. His only hope had been that when he finally had the commission in hand, they wouldn't be able to argue the point. He had also known better.

Elizabeth looked him straight in the eye and said, "Don't lie to me. You know I wanted out of the army."

Johnny pointed to the western horizon, begging her to understand. "I want to be out there, Elizabeth. I want to be out there exploring new territory, living in a tent under the big open sky, marching at the head of a company of soldiers into the unknown. It's the future, Elizabeth. It's my dream."

His wife's expression changed to one of disgust and disbelief. "And where do I fit into all this, Johnny? Am I supposed to raise a family in a tent? Or maybe I'm to be left alone at some frontier outpost while you're out there burning with jealousy because you think I've jumped into someone else's bed the moment you marched out. This is your future, Johnny; it isn't mine. I want a home and a place to call home. The army can't give me that."

Johnny didn't have a good answer. He couldn't see that infidelity came in many forms. It was more than simply taking a lover. Fidelity meant trusting your partner and including him or her in your dreams and plans. Johnny had broken faith with Elizabeth just as surely as if he'd been sleeping with another woman. He knew there was no logical argument to defend against what Elizabeth was saying. The best he could come up with was, "I love you. I can't lose you."

A deep sadness came over her, and she closed her eyes. She knew the response, but couldn't bring herself to speak the words. *You already have.*

John and Elizabeth Stuart sat at the table in their cabin and stared at each other. The initial anger had passed, and they both realized their futures would not be settled in one afternoon at the Wakefield's parlor. Emotionally exhausted, they had picked up Elizabeth's hastily packed belongings and walked silently back to their cabin. Now, with a minimal evening meal finished, they tried to imagine what would happen next.

Neither of them wanted to give up on the other, but neither wanted it to go on as it was or as it promised to be. There was no thought of divorce. It simply wasn't done, and the law made it almost impossible. Both of them knew that if they wanted to be happy, it was up to them to find a way to settle their differences.

Oddly enough, the one issue that had been the initial cause of their troubles now seemed insignificant, and even Johnny realized it. "It's me," he began, "I kept thinking you'd been unfaithful, and my imagination just got carried away. I was so afraid I'd lost you." He reached out, took her hand, and squeezed it tightly. "I can't let that happen."

Elizabeth could feel his desperation and commitment, and it worried her. He still needed to control her. If she couldn't be herself, could she truly be happy? She calmly told him, "If you want me to stay, you have to be willing to let me go."

Johnny recoiled at the thought. "That's impossible!"

Elizabeth shook her head and tried to explain. "You don't understand. I'm not saying I *would* go, or that I would even think of it. What I am saying is that I need to know that you trust me not to. I need to know that I can walk out of this house and visit someone it town or talk to an Indian and not feel I'm being watched or that you think I've met some secret lover. I was a captive once. I'll not be a captive again."

He still didn't understand. "I *have* to worry about you."

She smiled and put her other hand over his. "No," she said, "you don't."

There was really no choice but for John and Elizabeth to remain together and try to build a new relationship. Both agreed the past needed to be forgotten. Johnny had never hit her, and she had never walked out. The things that couldn't be forgotten could at least be ignored or not spoken of. They tried to act as if Elizabeth had never been taken captive or that Johnny had ever considered her unfaithful.

If nothing else, they had several months to work things out. Johnny's enlistment wasn't up until May, so no real decisions had to be made until then. At first it was awkward, with both of them trying to make sure they did nothing to upset the other. Things were civil, but they weren't comfortable. After a few weeks a routine settled in, and they began to learn what boundaries couldn't be crossed. Now they were comfortable, but it was still short of optimistic.

Both understood it took time to build trust. Sometimes it was a matter of simple courtesy. If Elizabeth was breaking the routine, she would be sure to tell Johnny, so he wasn't caught by surprise. On the other hand, Elizabeth was not above testing him occasionally. When the Regimental Surgeon was called out to the nearby Creek village to tend to one of the women, he asked Elizabeth to accompany him as an interpreter. She proved such a valuable assistant that he continued to call on her whenever the need arose. Elizabeth knew Johnny didn't like the idea, but she enjoyed the diversion and refused to give it up. She occasionally had to remind him that, "If you want me to stay, you have to be willing to let me go."

At times Johnny felt as if he were the one making all the sacrifices. Elizabeth was the one who visited friends and went to the Indians. He was the one who couldn't question her actions. He complained about it to Jack one time, and his friend reminded him, "You're the one who hit her. You're the one who accused her of being unfaithful. What does she have to prove?"

And yet Elizabeth did have something to prove. In her heart, she knew she had almost slept with Yellow Tom. She also knew that she often stepped beyond the bounds of what a good wife was expected to be. She was a bit too independent and often outspoken. She wore moccasins and was too friendly with the

Indians. She had to prove that her freedom and Johnny's love were not incompatible.

The future, however, was never mentioned, no more than the past. They were trying to make the present work, and if they couldn't do that, the rest didn't matter. Yet the future was what it was all about, and it would soon be upon them. Sooner or later, Johnny would hear if his officer's commission had been granted. For the moment, it was languishing on a desk in Washington, either at the War Department or the president's office. When it arrived, whether approved or disapproved, decisions would have to be made. Someone was going to have to give up their dream.

John Stuart was a man adrift. May had arrived, and his enlistment had run out. He was a free man, a civilian, and he had no idea what to do. Until he received word about his commission, the future was very tentative. How could he and Elizabeth make any plans if they didn't know where they would be in six months?

The simple fact that he was still agonizing over the problem was a problem unto itself. It wasn't like he needed the commission to survive. Jack had managed Captain Vashon's half of the initial investment wisely. In theory, Johnny was either a part owner of Jack's business or had a cash interest in it. He wasn't sure which and was afraid to ask. When and if the commission arrived, he didn't want his financial situation to influence any decision he would have to make.

How to occupy his time in the interim was not a problem. Jack was expanding his store and building an inn across the street. For the moment, Johnny could supervise construction or help run the store. In the future, he and Elizabeth could manage either one. Jack had left all possibilities open and had a few others waiting in the wings. All Johnny needed to do was say what interested him.

And therein lay the true problem. None of the possibilities interested him in the least. All of them required him to settle in and take up roots. He wasn't a shopkeeper or an innkeeper; he was a soldier.

John and Elizabeth sat at the table in their cabin, looking at the future. It lay between them in the form of a curled certificate bearing the signatures of Secretary of War John C. Calhoun and President James Monroe. Next to it was another piece of paper, this one ordering Second Lieutenant John Stuart to report to Fort Crawford, Prairie du Chien, Michigan Territory. Elizabeth asked, "Where is that?"

"Jack said it was way north on the Mississippi, well past St. Louis." He took a pencil and began to draw on the brown wrapping paper that the commission and orders had been sent in. "Here's Lake Michigan . . ."

Elizabeth giggled at the shape he'd just drawn, and then said, "I'm sorry, go on."

"The Michigan Territory extends out a couple of hundred miles on either side of it, east and west. Here's the Mississippi, and right about here is Fort Crawford."

Neither one was sure what to say. Johnny, knowing how Elizabeth would feel about moving to a remote frontier outpost, was doing his best to contain his excitement about the commission and the posting. Elizabeth, sensing Johnny's excitement, was doing her best to contain her disappointment. Both of them were looking at the same crude map, but the visions in their minds were completely different. Johnny saw endless, flowing grasslands, patrols on horseback, and settlers building homes. Elizabeth saw tents on the frozen ground, small boats on the river ferrying troops, and Indians waiting in ambush. He smiled; she shuddered.

It was an awkward silence, the worst they had shared since the day he had hit her and she had walked out. The only good thing was that they were, indeed, sharing it. They weren't arguing, they weren't getting violent, and they weren't storming out the door. They were thinking of each other.

Both of them knew what was at stake. Someone was going to have to give up their dream, someone was going to suffer. Ever since the expedition to Pensacola with General Jackson, Johnny had dreamed of being an officer and exploring the frontier. To please Elizabeth, he would have to resign his commission and settle down in a dreary South Georgia town. No matter how successful they were, he would always feel his life had been wasted.

But there were two people in the room, and ever since Elizabeth had been a child, she had dreamed of a home and a hometown. She had found them both in Fort Gaines. She thought of Jack, the Wakefields, and everyone else she knew in town. She even thought of the friends she'd made at the Creek Indian village nearby. She'd been in Fort Gaines for a year, and she had set down roots. Taking her out to the wilds of the northern prairie would be like sending her into a prolonged exile. Fort Gaines had become as important to her as the army was to him.

Neither one wanted to be the first to break the silence, knowing whatever they said was going to hurt and might lead to harsh words that could not be withdrawn. They kept looking at the papers, picking them up and reading them, looking for something in the words that might lead them out of their dilemma. Both were creating and rearranging sentences in their minds, trying to choose words that could not be misinterpreted. It was not an easy task.

Elizabeth spoke first. "Johnny, I love you, and I'm not going to ask you to give up your commission, but I don't think I can do this. It scares me, it really does." The first words had been chosen carefully, but once she started, the thoughts just began to flow. "All I can see are boats and Indians and snow and desolate landscapes. I don't see a town, I don't see white folks, I don't even see you there. I see you out fighting or exploring and me by myself in the loneliest place on earth. I may have it all wrong, Johnny, but it scares me." There weren't many things that frightened Elizabeth, but the thought of being isolated deep in hostile Indian territory was certainly one of them. True, Fort Gaines was on the frontier, but not for long, and nothing like the old Northwest. The Indians in Georgia and Alabama were partly civilized, and Elizabeth was comfortable with them. From what she'd heard, the ones on the northern plains were still wild savages.

Johnny took a deep breath, held it for a moment, then let it out. He couldn't throw away his commission. He wanted it too much. He said, "You know, maybe you could go out to St. Louis and live with Robert. I'm sure I could get down to see you a few times a year. It's not that far, and right down the Mississippi."

Elizabeth knew it wouldn't work, but didn't want to dismiss the notion completely. Johnny was always optimistic and knew things would work out. It was one of the things she loved about him. It was she who usually saw the difficulties. "I don't know. . . I would hate to impose upon Robert in such a way. He has Anna Lynn and the baby to support. He doesn't need me there too. Besides, you saw his last letter: If Uncle Paul's health doesn't improve, he'll have to move back to New Orleans."

Johnny began to feel cornered. "You don't want me to go, do you?"

She wasn't sure how to take the question. Was he happy she felt that way, or was he trying to shift the entire burden of decision onto her shoulders? She wasn't going to have it that way; it was going to be a joint decision. "No, I don't want you to go, but I would never tell you not to. I know how much this means to you."

He didn't want to have to choose, and he didn't want to be told how to live the rest of his life. More than anything, he wanted to get out of Fort Gaines and start his military career. He was getting frustrated, and the emotion came out in his words. "So this rotten little shack is more important to you than I am."

This time there was no mistaking the meaning of his comment. Elizabeth's eyes narrowed, her voice rose, and she came to her feet. "The only thing more important to me is *us*, and Fort Gaines is *our* home." Just in case he didn't understand her, she put it another way: "I mean to have a home, a place that I am a part of, and this is it." She'd been with the army long enough to know that for a soldier, "home" was always where you weren't. She remembered how her parents felt about Baton Rouge, and how Yellow Tom and Conowaw had spoken about Fowltown. Perhaps her captivity had made such things seem more important, but "home" was something she desperately needed, and she was not going to be made to feel guilty about it. "So I guess the army is more important to you than I am."

Johnny also came to his feet, anger in his eyes. "So it's all on me, is it? Just load up my trunk and go. Is that what you want? Is there someone else going to keep you warm while I'm away? Maybe Jack? Or maybe you'll run back to the Indians."

She could have slapped him, she could have told him she'd done without a man for months at a time and could do it again, or she could have cried. Instead, she calmly told him, "I can go to Sarah's or you can go to Jack's, but I'll not spend another minute with you until you apologize."

Johnny sat back down and lowered his head. He'd done it again. He looked up, pleading in his eyes, and asked, "What should I do, Elizabeth? If I go out west, you're all I'll think about. I can't help it. You're mine; I can't let anyone else have you."

She reached down and held his hand. "No one ever has." She had known the answer to their problem all along. Now she had to bring him to the same conclusion. She sat down and gave him the most tender look she ever had. "Go. Follow your dream. Think about me until it drives you crazy, or you drive it out of your head. There's nothing else for it. When you sort it out, let me know. I'll be here waiting."

Three days later, Second Lieutenant John Stuart went down to the dock below Fort Gaines and boarded a boat that would take him down the Chattahoochee toward the Gulf of Mexico. As the boat moved into the current, he looked back at the pier and at the small group of friends who had come to see him off. At the center stood Elizabeth, who wiped a tear from her eye and tried to smile. Next to her was Sarah Wakefield, a protective arm around Elizabeth's shoulder. On Elizabeth's other side was Jack, who smiled and gave him a thumbs-up for encouragement. He had disappointed those he loved the most, yet as true friends, they were wishing him the best.

Later that day the boat came to the confluence with the Flint River, where the waterway changed its name to the Apalachicola and entered Florida. About a mile further down, they came to a bend in the river. Stuart knew the spot well. It was the place where he had lost his wife.

* * *

Elizabeth glanced into the mirror and shifted a lock of hair back into place. Leaning slightly toward the mirror, she noticed a few white hairs intertwined among the bright red strands. She sighed. *They could have waited two more years,* she thought, *at least until I turned forty*. Then a soft smile formed on her lips. A picture came to mind of her friend Sarah Wakefield. *I'll not complain. Sarah was near white-headed by the time she was my age*. She turned at the sound of the back door slamming and footsteps running through the back storeroom. *How many times must I tell that girl not to slam the door? I'd give her a thorough whipping, if I thought it would do any good.*

Into the hallway ran a young black girl, carrying a small package and a number of letters. "I gots the mail from the post office, Missy Lizbith."

"Thank you, Junie. Now run upstairs and check the chamber pots in all the rooms. I do not want our guests returning to foul-smelling rooms again. Another such complaint and I shall have the General give you a sound whipping."

"Yes, Ma'am, Missy Lizbith. Right away," Junie promised as she ran up the staircase. Elizabeth shook her head slightly and smiled. She threatened to whip the young slave at least twice a day, but never actually did. Junie was a bright girl and knew precisely how much she could get away with.

Looking down, Elizabeth thumbed through the stack of letters. They were all addressed to guests of the hotel, so she set them on the small credenza that stood against the wall. The parcel, however, was addressed to her and her husband. The sender's name and address were a complete mystery. Entering the parlor, she took a seat on the sofa and began to remove the wrapping paper. Inside was a small box covered in another layer of wrapping paper, and tied over it was a letter. She set the parcel down and opened the letter.

December 9, 1838
Fort Gibson
Indian Territory

Genl. and Mrs. Dill,

It is with deep regret that I must inform you of the passing of Capt. John Stuart in his sleep last night from a cancerous growth within his abdomen. Although he had been ill for some time, the Captain was spared any severe pain for all but his final few days here on Earth. I can truly say that in the short time in which I have been privileged to serve under him, it has been a pleasure to be in his company. The regiment has indeed lost one of its finest officers.

Enclosed you will find several small items from his estate that he has bequeathed to you. Other belongings, such as his sword and pistols, will be personally delivered by the first officer passing from here to the east by way of Ft. Gaines. Enclosed is a draft for $143, the sum total of his wealth, less the expense of a keg of whiskey he instructed me to purchase for a wake to be held in his honor. I can assure you the toasts will be most heartfelt. You *will also find a silver pocketwatch, perhaps his most prized possession. The final item is a gold locket containing a curl of the most lustrous red hair. I saw him gazing upon it most wistfully yesterday morning, and heard him whisper "Farewell, Elizabeth" as he closed it. In instructing me as to the disposition of his estate, he said that you two were the only real family he had ever had.*

Again, I convey my deepest sympathies for your loss. From his words and actions, I can say with complete sincerity that he loved you both very deeply.

You Most Obedient Servant,
Joseph E. Johnston,
Lt., U. S. Army

Folded in with Johnston's letter was another, and Elizabeth trembled as she unfolded it. Memories came flooding back, some of them wonderful, some of them painful. She saw Johnny's face a half-dozen ways. She remembered how excited he'd looked when they'd first met after the Battle of New Orleans, and the sympathy he'd shown her after her mother's death. She recalled the sheer joy on his face when they were married, and the mixed emotions when she returned after her captivity, thankful to see her but knowing she would soon find out her father was dying. She even remembered the anger in his eyes when he'd hit her, and the tear that ran down his cheek as he stepped aboard the boat when he'd left her.

8 December 1838
Fort Gibson
Indian Territory

To:
Genl. and Mrs. Dill
Ft. Gaines, Georgia

Dear Jack and Elizabeth:

Please excuse this intrusion from a spectre of your past. You have been much in my thoughts of late, a result, no doubt, of the good Doctor informing me that my time on this Earth is short, due to some malignancy that is beyond his curative powers. Alas, his standard cure for everything is amputation, and the defect being deep within my bowels, such a remedy seems unlikely. Better if it had been in my head—he could have removed that organ with little loss to my usefulness to the Army.

I have asked Lt. Johnston to send Capt. Vashon's pocketwatch as a remembrance for Jack, and the locket is, of course, for you, Elizabeth. They have both served to keep the memory of you two and the Capt. alive in my mind, and I hope they do the same for me in your minds.

Although we parted on not the best of terms, never have I thought ill of either of you. Our choices were the best for all of us, and none can be held at blame.

My life in the twenty years since I have last seen you has been what I hoped it would be and, probably, dear Elizabeth, what you feared. The Army has treated me as well as the Army treats any officer, the meager pay and infrequent promotions notwithstanding. I have had numerous postings throughout the frontier and have finally arrived here, at my last, in the Indian Territory. I actually deem it fortunate that I have fallen ill out here. Had I remained healthy, they might well have sent me to fight that horrid war in Florida. Once was enough.

I have often thought about our time together and wondered what it would have been like had Lt. Scott's boat not been attacked. I suppose there would now be a pair of identical houses sitting next to each other in Ft. Gaines or some similar town, with Jack and Annie in one, and Elizabeth and me in the other. Captain Vashon, surely a general by now, would be living upstairs, and a dozen children would be running all about. That was the dream, but alas, dreams never come out the way we think they will. Do they ever, and would we really want them to? The unknown, though sometimes frightening, is much more exciting.

When I applied for my commission, I envisioned all the glories of the

West, but nothing is as I foresaw it. Some of it is grander than you could imagine, while other parts are horribly commonplace. So it is with the expectations of my life. I saw myself boldly exploring the great Missouri River, but in truth, it was nothing more than just another river flowing across a relatively flat landscape. Oh, but what a beautiful landscape, the most glorious scenery God has ever created. I suppose I could tell you that I conquered the fiercest tribes of savages in the west, but no, all I did was come to appreciate that they love the land as much as I do. No, it is not what I expected, but I have enjoyed every minute of it.

How often do we see not what is there, but only what we want to see? When we were in Florida, I saw the Seminoles as my deadly enemy, somehow out to destroy me personally. Yet were they doing anything more than defending their homes? Back then, I saw General Jackson as an avenging angel, driving the bloodthirsty savages before him. Now, as I meet the wretched Seminoles that he has forced from their homes in the lush forests of Florida to this cold and barren land, I see him as little more than a vindictive demon. I cannot say I was blind, I just wasn't looking.

Most painfully, I now realize that I wasn't looking at you, dear Elizabeth. From the moment I first cast my eyes upon you, I saw what I wanted to, and in the beginning, you were precisely what I imagined you would be. The war changed all that. In my mind, I began to see you with other men, even though there weren't any. When you came back to me after your captivity, I still saw you as the girl I had fallen in love with, not the woman who had lived through Hell and come back stronger for it. Worst of all, I began to see you as a possession, not a person. If only I had seen the truth.

There is so much more I have to tell you, but I grow weak and the hospital orderly tells me I must retire. Perhaps I shall write more when I awake. If perchance my hour has come and I do not awake, please know that I send you both all the love that I have. I truly believe things have turned out for the best.

Johnny

Focused on the letter, Elizabeth didn't notice her husband enter the room. He stood motionless for a moment, curious as to why she should be crying. Then he stepped forward and took a seat next to his wife. Still weeping, she handed him the letter.

Nearly twenty years had passed since Johnny had left Fort Gaines. It had been a quiet and civil farewell, with more regret than rancor, as much laughter as there were tears. John Stuart simply walked down to the river, stepped aboard a boat, and was gone from their lives forever.

There had been a regular exchange of letters at first, as frequent as mail could be between two remote corners of the nation. Elizabeth wrote about how much Fort Gaines was growing and how well Jack was doing. She tried not to sound like she was begging him to come home, but she wanted to let him know that if and when he did return, a prosperous life awaited him. Johnny wrote about the excitement of the frontier, his fellow officers, and the pleasures of military life. He never asked Elizabeth to join him, but always hinted that she'd love it out there, even though he failed to explain exactly why. Neither one ever acknowledged the invitations.

Then, in early 1821, came the most soul-searching letter Johnny had ever written. He was going even further west, joining an expedition to the Yellowstone River. He didn't know when he'd be back or even when he'd be able to send a letter. He told Elizabeth he still loved her but knew things could never go back to the way they were before the Florida War. Both of them had been changed by the experience, and no one was to blame. He acknowledged that he would probably never return to Fort Gaines, and saw no reason why she should ever leave it. He then asked her to begin divorce proceedings on the grounds that he had abandoned her. Elizabeth was stunned and saddened, but relieved.

Initially, the divorce meant little to Elizabeth. She had been running Jack's little four-room inn since it had been finished, and intended to continue doing so. Jack certainly had no time for it. The store was prospering, and he had also opened a saddlery and leather shop, though he would be the first person to admit that he didn't know the first thing about leather work. Instead, he had purchased a slave who was an excellent craftsman and had set the man up in his own shop with the promise that he could eventually buy his freedom. He had also teamed up with a friend, John Sutlive, and the pair were about to open a brickyard. Florida had become a United States Territory in 1821, and the Apalachicola now ran freely to the Gulf without interference from Seminoles or Spaniards. Fort Gaines was becoming a major port, sending cotton and produce from all of southwest Georgia to the world. As Jack had foreseen, the town was growing, and his fortunes were growing with it. There was even talk of expanding the inn and making it a twelve-room hotel.

The divorce did change the relationship between Jack and Elizabeth, though they were perhaps the last to acknowledge it. They were, of course, still the closest of friends, but their relationship revolved around the business. Jack lived for his work, and as far as Elizabeth was concerned, the guests and the slaves who worked at the inn were her family. As long as she was married to Johnny, even while the divorce was pending, she intended things to stay that way. There were, of course, the town gossips, but neither he nor she paid any attention to them. After the divorce, the wagging tongues shifted from talking about Jack and Elizabeth secretly getting together at night to wondering when they would get married.

It took awhile, but both began to see each other in a different way. Jack was hesitant, wondering if he could possibly take Johnny's place in her heart. He had to admit that he'd grown to love Elizabeth, but certainly not with the intensity Johnny had. If that was the sort of man she expected, he might be a disappointment to her. Jack was also still haunted by the loss of Annie. The sight of her bloody face had not faded from his memory, and he swore he would never let it. Deep inside, he feared what would happen if he were married to Elizabeth and somehow lost her, just as he'd lost Annie. His friend John Sutlive dismissed the idea, telling him, "You're a damn fool, Jack. If the good Lord took her tomorrow, would the loss be any greater if she were your wife?" Jack couldn't disagree, but still found it hard to broach the subject to Elizabeth.

Elizabeth had her own reasons to be hesitant. Even though Jack was her best friend and employer, she still felt herself to be an independent woman. Freedom was important to her. She had been a prisoner of the Indians and had been married to a jealous, possessive husband. She would not let it happen again. Besides, she wasn't sure of her own feelings. Johnny had excited her in a very animal way. The attraction to Jack was more comfortable and practical, and she wasn't sure what to make of it. Anyway, the present situation seemed to suit them both. Why rock a boat that was sailing smoothly? Her friend Sarah Wakefield couldn't understand it. "You're a damn fool, Elizabeth. You got too close to the fire last time. Now's the time to sit back and enjoy the warmth."

In the end, it was Elizabeth who gave in to what everyone else saw as inevitable. As happened occasionally, she had woken up in the middle of the night to an empty hotel. There were no guests that night, and lacking the usual evening conversation or game of cards, she had gone to bed early. She tossed and turned for awhile, trying to go back to sleep, but couldn't. She got up, put on her dressing gown, and walked about the hotel, looking for something that wasn't there. Finally, she said, "Oh, this is ridiculous!" and walked out the front door. Crossing the street, she knocked on Jack's door.

Jack came to the door, a candle in hand and a worried look on his face. "What's the matter? Is everything all right?"

"I have absolutely no problem with you calling your hotel 'The Dill House,' but I am getting very tired of explaining to all the guests that I am not Mrs. Dill." The wedding, the biggest Fort Gaines had ever seen, was held two weeks later.

It had been a good seventeen years. Jack's businesses thrived as the town grew, and Elizabeth was happy running the expanded hotel. He dabbled in local politics and served in some minor elected offices, becoming a prominent man both locally and within the state.

Even Jack's military experience proved useful. The Creek Indians might have been subdued after the war in Florida, but tensions inevitably arose as white settlers pushed into areas that had once been Creek land. A local militia unit was formed, and Jack was elected its captain. He steadily rose in rank, eventually being appointed a general in the Georgia Militia and even finding himself called to Florida in 1836 to once again fight the Seminoles, who were resisting deportation to the west. It had been an awkward experience, finding himself a superior officer to his old commander, Major Wooster, who had risen to the rank of colonel in the regular army.

For her part, Elizabeth enjoyed meeting the guests who stayed at the hotel, and prided herself on being the finest hostess in Fort Gaines. She worked to make the community a better place to live in, and could always be counted on to help in times of need. She had once told Johnny that all she wanted was a place to call home. Jack had given her that, and she loved him for it.

The one thing she never spoke of was her time as a captive among the Indians. She was still haunted by the occasional nightmare, and once in a while she thought of Yellow Tom, but only as a fond memory. She still spoke to the local Indians in their own language, yet if a curious stranger asked her about the massacre or her captivity, she would politely but firmly say, "I'm sorry, that was Elizabeth Stuart. I'm Elizabeth Dill," as if those events had happened to someone else. But she still wore moccasins when she walked around the house and kept an Indian war club by the door, next to her father's sword.

The History Behind the Story

This novel is the result of a quest to identify a group of fallen heroes from the First Seminole War, the victims of the Scott Massacre of November 30, 1817. Although unknown to most Americans, the Scott Massacre was an important historical event. Like Pearl Harbor or the attack on the World Trade Center, it forced the nation into war. The First Seminole War was a short affair, lasting only about six months, but it helped lead to the acquisition of Florida and served to cement Andrew Jackson's popularity and reputation.

Over forty people died in the ambush, and we wondered who they were. It bothered us that, in a nation capable of building a memorial displaying the name of every soldier lost in the Vietnam War, there was no casualty report or any letter from a commanding officer listing those slain on the Apalachicola River. The army has always been obsessed with paperwork and reports, and it just didn't seem possible that no list existed. Unable to find one, we decided to compile the list ourselves.

It was not a simple task. There were names we had no hope of finding, such as the women who were killed or any Indians slain in the battle. Compiling the list took years, with countless hours spent searching through muster rolls, the Register of Enlistments, and other literature of the period. Although we couldn't find every name, we did come up with a fairly complete list. Having discovered their identities and learned something about these unfortunate people, we were determined to tell their story.

But why a novel? One answer is that we felt there were not enough facts concerning the battle to do a proper history that would be published by a university press. We tried, but the result was not pleasing. In order to fill pages, we wasted too much time on unnecessary background information. A lack of hard facts also led to too much speculation. If we were going to speculate, we might as well move from nonfiction to fiction. We'd done it before.

Our first book was a scholarly history of the Seminole Wars. We later wrote *Hollow Victory*, a novel about the Second Seminole War. We enjoy doing both, and in this case, a novel with the factual history included at the end seemed more appropriate.

Another reason for telling the story as a novel cropped up while doing our research. The only person taken captive in the attack was Elizabeth Stuart, wife of Sergeant John Stuart. She was reportedly held captive by a warrior named Yellow Hair. After the war, she and Stuart separated, and she later married John Dill, who had been another sergeant from the same company. Elizabeth's experience was certainly a story with an abundance of human drama, but with no real facts as to everyone's true relationships, anything we wrote would be pure speculation and better left to the realm of fiction.

A final reason for writing a novel was to make it a "prequel" to our first novel. The major connection between these two works is the character of Major Wooster, who is one of the protagonists of *Hollow Victory*. When we wrote the first novel, there was no plan for another along the same lines, and no thought of a series. There were, however, three Seminole wars, so a trilogy now seemed the natural thing to do.

As in all works "based on a true story," the reader is cautioned not to consider the events in this book as historically accurate. The general course of events we give for the First Seminole War is very close to what transpired, though we have often simplified things to allow the work to flow more smoothly. We also had no hesitation in applying literary license to time, place, or other facts if reality did not mesh with the story we wanted to tell.

Any reader of historical fiction will always wonder where the truth ends and the imagined tale begins. To that end, we've included a short history of the Scott Massacre and the First

Seminole War, with emphasis on events portrayed in the novel. Before getting into the history, there are a few points the reader might find interesting:

Letters: The letters that begin each chapter are entirely from our imaginations, with the following exceptions: The note from Lieutenant Scott to General Gaines in Chapter Seven is very close to the original. Gaines's letter to Acting Secretary Graham in Chapter Eight is modeled after several letters he sent on December 2, after the survivors reached Fort Scott. The letter from Andrew Jackson to President Monroe in Chapter Nine is fictitious, but Jackson did write something similar, offering to take Florida from Spain and telling the president to respond through Mr. Rhea. Historians are still debating whether or not Monroe responded, and in what manner.[1]

Muhlenberg's voyage: One of the historical mysteries of the Scott Massacre is why Major Muhlenberg's convoy was so late arriving at Fort Scott. Had he shown up when expected, none of this would have happened. No letter giving an explanation has been found, which is a disappointment. We know that a letter from Muhlenberg to Gaines was included with the note Scott sent to Gaines from Spanish Bluff the day before the attack, but it appears lost. Having no good information about the delay, we were forced to come up with all sorts of nautical mishaps to delay his passage. Whatever the true causes, they were probably just as frustrating for the real Muhlenberg as the fictional ones were for ours.

Children on the boat: For us, one of the most controversial questions about the Scott Massacre was whether or not there were children on the boat. Peter Cook, the young Bahamian who testified against Alexander Arbuthnot, stated in a letter to Elizabeth Carney of Nassau that the Indians had taken the

---

1 James Schouler, "Monroe and the Rhea Letter," *The Magazine of American History,* 12, no. 4 (October, 1884): 308-322.

children by their ankles and smashed their heads against the side of the boat. Unfortunately, Cook is anything but a reliable source. He wasn't at the attack, was writing to what we assume was a love interest (and therefore might be prone to exaggeration), and the original letter is lost. All we have is a copy of a copy made by Lt. James Gadsden, Jackson's aide, after the originals were lost in the mail. Considering that Cook was more or less at the mercy of the Americans who had captured him, and that Jackson had been told by the Administration to provide evidence to back up his actions against the English and Spanish, we cannot accept Cook's testimony or the letter as fact. That's not to say they weren't, but until a more reliable source was found, we were forced to view the tale with suspicion. It is also interesting to note that Cook did enlist in the American army, apparently against his will.[2]

On the other side of the coin, various letters from General Gaines that were written immediately after interviewing the six survivors who reached Fort Scott make no mention of children. He mentions the forty soldiers, the seven women, and what stores the boat was carrying, but says nothing about children. Unfortunately, like Cook's letter, it didn't settle the issue. Just because he doesn't say anything about children doesn't mean they weren't there. Let's face it: If there were army wives in Muhlenberg's convoy, there were certainly army children. What we don't know is who was selected to be on Scott's boat and for what reasons.

For us, the matter was finally settled when we read Dale Cox's book *The Scott Massacre of 1817*. His research had turned up almost precisely the same sources as we did, but he had an additional letter, written by Major Clinton Wright to Major

2 Peter B. Cook to Elizabeth A. Carney, 19 January 1818, *American State Papers: Foreign Relations* (hereinafter cited as *ASP:FR*), 6 vols. (Washington, D.C.: Gales and Seaton, 1832-1861), 4:605; *United States Registers of Enlistments in the U.S. Army, 1798-1914* (hereinafter cited as *Register of Enlistments*), Microcopy M 233, National Archives Records Administration (hereinafter cited as NA).

Muhlenberg from Fort Scott on the same day as Gaines wrote his, but in Wright's letter, he mentions children. Having already completed the novel, we decided to leave the children off the boat, as it makes little difference to the complete narrative.[3]

The trial: The trial of Ambrister and Arbuthnot was, of course, more thorough and longer than we have depicted, but the outcome was the same. The reaction from London was much as we have stated. While incensed that Jackson would do such a thing, England had no wish to go to war with one of its major trading partners. Having just finished the costly Napoleonic Wars and deeply in debt, England simply couldn't afford another war.[4]

Major characters: With the exception of Major Wooster, most of the major characters are real persons. Their personalities, however, are our creations. Having no idea what they were really like, we molded them to suit our story. The exceptions might be Andrew Jackson and John Quincy Adams. The personalities we've given them are based upon the impressions we've gotten from the historical record. It may not be accurate, but it's what they've left us.

The relationship we present between Elizabeth and the men in her life is entirely made up. The truth may well have been more interesting and salacious than the version we tell, and we could certainly have made the story more violent and sexual, but that wasn't the path we wanted to go down.

Because the story is based on four real people, we thought it proper to relate what facts we have been able to discover about their lives.

Elizabeth: Census records indicate Elizabeth Stuart was seventeen at the time of her abduction, but we don't know her

---

3 Dale Cox, *The Scott Massacre of 1817,* (CreateSpace Independent Publishing Platform, 2013), 71.

4 Minutes of the Proceedings of a Special Court, 26 April 1818, *American State Papers: Military Affairs* (hereinafter cited as *ASP:MA),* 7 vols. (Washington, D.C.: Gales and Seaton, 1832-1861), 1:721-734.

maiden name or who her parents were. Was she Captain Vashon's daughter? It is interesting to note they were both born in Maryland, and that John Stuart and John Dill were both sergeants in Vashon's company during the war, but there is no proof or indication of her being his daughter. Legend has it that she had red hair, so we incorporated that into our story. Legend also tells of her pinning bank notes to her petticoat while in captivity. The first legend is possible; the second seems highly unlikely. There is no indication that she killed any Indians.[5]

One of the few sources for information about the Scott Massacre is Thomas Woodward, a white man living among the Creeks who fought in the First Seminole War and helped rescue Elizabeth. In his reminiscences, Woodward gives an account of Elizabeth's capture and rescue:

> Mrs. Stuart was taken almost lifeless as well as senseless. … After taking her from the boat, they [the Indians] differed among themselves as to whose slave or servant she should be. An Indian by the name of Yellow Hair said he had many years before been sick at or near St. Mary's and that he felt it a duty to take the woman and treat her kindly, as he was treated so by a white woman when he was among the whites. The matter was left to an old Indian by the name of Bear Head, who decided in favor of Yellow Hair. I was told by the Indians that Yellow Hair treated her with great kindness and respect. I never asked her any questions as to her treatment, and presume she never knew me from any other Indian, as Brown and myself were both dressed as Indians. We knew long before we re-captured her what band she was with, and had tried to come up with them before.
>
> Shortly after the firing commenced, we could hear a female voice in the English language calling for help, but she

5 1820 U. S. Federal Census, Early County, Georgia.

was concealed from our view. The hostile Indians, though greatly inferior in number to our whole force, had the advantage of the ground, it being a dense thicket, and kept the party that first attacked at bay until Gen. McIntosh arrived with the main force. McIntosh, though raised among savages, was a General; yes, he was one of God's make of Generals. I could hear his voice above the din of firearms—"Save the white woman! Save the Indian women and children!" All this time Mrs. Stuart was between the fires of the combatants. McIntosh said to me, "Chulatarla Emathla, you, Brown and Mitchell, go to that woman." (Chulatarla Emathla was the name I was known by among the Indians.) ... I can see her now, squatted in the saw palmetto, among a few dwarf cabbage trees, surrounded by a group of Indian women. There I saw Brown kill an Indian, and I got my rifle-stock shot off just back of the lock. Old Jack Carter came up with my horse shortly after we cut off the woman from the warriors. I got his musket and used it until the fight ended. You saw her (Mrs. Stuart) when she reached the camp, and recollect her appearance better than I can describe it.[6]

William McIntosh, the Creek leader, made the following report after her rescue: "There was among the Hostiles a woman that was in the boat when our friends the white people were killed on the River below Fort Scott. We gave her to her friends. Her Husband and Father are with Genl. Jackson."[7]

---

6 Thomas S. Woodward, *Woodward's Reminiscences of the Creek, or Muscogee Indians, Contained in Letters to Friends in Georgia and Alabama,* (Montgomery, AL: Barrett & Wimbish, 1859), 53-54.

7 Brig. Genl. William McIntosh to David B. Mitchell, 13 April 1818, Hargrett Rare Book and Manuscript Library, Telamon Cuyler Collection, The University of Georgia Libraries, presented by the Digital Library of Georgia, Document TCC921.

Exactly what happened in Elizabeth's life between 1818 and 1821 is open for speculation. Stuart was discharged from the army at Fort Scott, and the couple may have moved to nearby Fort Gaines, where a new community was growing. Sometime in that period, she and John Stuart separated. Divorce was difficult at the time, requiring an act of the state legislature and the governor's signature, and there is always the possibility they had never been legally married. Among those settling in Fort Gaines was Stuart's fellow sergeant John Dill, and on September 25, 1821, Elizabeth and John Dill were married. Whether she and Dill were together before the marriage is unknown. The 1820 census lists one white female between the ages of ten and forty-five living in the John Dill household (along with a number of other people), but that person's name is not given.[8]

We don't know much about the Dills' domestic life. They had one child, John P. M. Dill, who was born in May of 1832 and died a little over five years later. The couple remained in Fort Gaines for the rest of their lives. John died in 1856, and in 1860 her assets were listed as approximately $5,000, a considerable sum at the time. Yet in 1858 Woodward had commented to a friend, "I am sorry that one who in early life witnessed so many horrors, should in old age be reduced to destitution." When Elizabeth died on September 5, 1864, her estate was listed as a watch, a wardrobe, and a slave named June. As far as we can tell, she left no record of the massacre or her time in captivity, either in a diary or an interview. Her experience was no doubt very different from what we have portrayed in this novel, and it may have been something she didn't want to talk about.[9]

All this information gives us a timeline, but none of it tells us about her personality or appearance. We have no idea of her upbringing, attitudes, or education. Historically, it's a pity, but for

---

8 Early County, GA, Marriage Book I (1820-1833), 5.

a writer, it's a blessing. It allowed us to create our fictional Elizabeth as we wanted her to be.

John Stuart: According to Woodward, Stuart was "a fine looking man." John's enlistment ended in 1819, but soon after being discharged he received a commission as a Second Lieutenant, an unusual occurrence in those days. In an Inspector General's Report from 1820, while he was stationed at Fort Scott, Stuart is described as "sober, active, and industrious ... careful to acquire knowledge and communicate" and considered a "valuable" officer. By the 1830s John Stuart was a captain serving in the Indian Territory (Oklahoma), helping in the re-settlement of some of the same Indians he had fought against in 1818. His letters indicate that he had taken an interest in his charges and had learned to respect them. He died while on duty on December 8, 1838.[10]

As might be expected, Stuart's surname is often spelled "Stewart" in the historical records. For some time we were unsure

---

9 Grave marker for John P. M. Dill, Old Pioneer Cemetery, Fort Gaines, GA; grave marker for John Dill, Old Pioneer Cemetery, Fort Gaines, GA; obituary of John Dill in *Columbus (GA) Enquirer, 8* July 1856; 1860 U. S. Federal Census, Clay County, GA; Woodward, *Reminiscences,* 81; "Ancestral File" database, *FamilySearch* (https://familysearch.org); Last Will of Elizabeth Dill, 5 September 1864, Clay County, GA Probate Court.

10 Woodward, *Reminiscences,* 53; Morris Davis to Daniel Parker, 30 June 1820, Inspection Reports of the Office of the Inspector General, 1814-1842, Microcopy M 624, Roll 1, Record Group 159: Records of the Inspector General, NA; Grant Foreman, "Captain John Stuart's Sketch of the Indians," *Chronicles of Oklahoma,* 11, no. 1 (March 1933), 667; Capt. John Stuart to Genl. R. Jones, 15 January 1837, Oklahoma Historical Society, Grant Foreman Collection, mss#83.229, Box 37, Folder 20 John Stuart; *Arkansas Gazette, 2* January 1839; *Army and Navy Chronicle,* 31 January 1839, *Niles' National Register (Washington, D.C.),* 16 February 1839; Francis B. Heitman, *Historical Register and Dictionary of the United States Army, from Its Organization, September 29, 1789 to March 2, 1903,* 2 vols. (Washington, D.C.: Government Printing Office, 1903), 1:925.

as to which was correct, until we found a letter he had written shortly before he died, in which he signed it "John Stuart."[11]

John Dill: As mentioned earlier, his real name was John, but having two main characters with the same name would have been unwieldy, so we used the common nickname of Jack. After leaving the army, Dill became a prominent man in Fort Gaines and was appointed the first tax receiver when Early County was formed in 1820. Besides marrying Elizabeth in 1821, he formed a partnership with John Sutlive, which led to several successful business ventures, including a tannery that was known for fine quality shoes, boots, and saddles, all crafted by highly skilled slaves. They also opened a brickyard, and some of the oldest buildings in today's Fort Gaines were built using those bricks. Dill also served as a town commissioner and rose to the rank of brigadier general in the state militia. We found no record of his having served in Florida during the Second Seminole War. In 1827, John and Elizabeth built a fine two-story home and later expanded it into a large hotel, which until recently was operated as a bed and breakfast. During our research at Fort Gaines, it was a thrill to have slept in what may have been Elizabeth's bedroom.[12]

The fact that John Stuart became an officer and John Dill rose to prominence in civilian life showed them both to be educated, intelligent, and ambitious men. They certainly didn't fit the

---

11 Capt. John Stuart to Gen. R. Jones, 9 June 1838, Oklahoma Historical Society, Grant Foreman Collection, mss#83.229, Box 37, Folder 20 John Stuart.

12 Early County State Historical Marker at the Early County Courthouse, Blakely, GA; *Columbus (GA) Enquirer,* 16 March 1833; John Rutherford, comp., *Acts of the General Assembly of the State of Georgia, Passed in Milledgeville, at a Biennial Session, 1853-1854,* (Savannah: Samuel T. Chapman State Printer, 1854), 193-195, 435-437; Colonel E. A. Greene, *History of Fort Gaines and Clay County, Georgia,* (Georgia Historical Society, 1939), 4-19; Mrs. Donald (Priscilla Neves) Todd, *The History of Clay County, GA,* (compiled at the Clay County Library, Fort Gaines, GA, 1976), 2-9, 88, 173.

stereotypical profile of the common enlisted man of the time, who was often illiterate, an alcoholic, a social misfit, or foreign born. This knowledge helped inform the type of characters we developed.

Yellow Tom: Little, if anything, is known about the real Yellow Hair, and none of it suited the type of character we needed for a possible love-interest for Elizabeth. Woodward's description indicated a person who was thoughtful and compassionate, and definitely not a "bloodthirsty savage." His name indicates he was possibly of mixed-blood heritage, so we decided to expand upon that. We also wanted someone who could articulate the realities of Indian life to a white person, and giving him a wider cultural background allowed us to do that. To add to the confusion, there was a chief with the same name who lived in the vicinity of the massacre, but was friendly to the Americans and may have aided the six survivors of the attack.

Minor Characters: Because the main thrust of our research into the Scott Massacre had been to find the names of the people who were victims of the attack, it seemed fitting that any non-historical character we created bear the name of one of those victims. Most of those characters were in fact victims of the massacre, so their inclusion is appropriate. On the other hand, if we knew the name of a real person tied to the events, we used it, such as Mr. Tankersley, an agent in Mobile who was mentioned in an official letter. Others include Hambly and Doyle, who managed the Forbes & Company store at Spanish Bluff on the Apalachicola.

One of the most interesting of the minor characters is Milly Francis, daughter of Hillis Hadjo, the Red Stick Prophet. In March 1818, Private Duncan McKrimmon of the Georgia Militia wandered away from camp and was captured by a party of Red Sticks. Taken back to the Indian camp, he was to be tortured and executed. Milly, then fifteen years old, took pity on the soldier and begged her captor to spare his life. The warrior, who was seeking revenge for two sisters slain in the Creek War, relented, and

McKrimmon was taken to St. Marks, where he was later rescued when Jackson took the Spanish fort. After the war, McKrimmon located Milly and offered to marry her, but she refused, wishing to stay with her people. Later in life, destitute and living in the Indian Territory, she was found by an army officer, Lt. Col. Ethan Allan Hitchcock, who petitioned Congress to provide relief for the woman. Congress awarded her a small pension and a medal, but Milly died before she received them.[13]

---

13 T. Frederick Davis, "Milly Francis and Duncan McKrimmon: an Authentic Florida Pocahontas," *Florida Historical Quarterly,* 21, no. 3 (January 1943): 254-265 .

The History of the Scott Massacre

Animosity between the Indians of Florida and the Americans to their north existed long before the First Seminole War. During what was known as the Patriot War of 1812 (an abortive attempt by the United States to seize Spanish East Florida) the Seminoles had sided with the Spanish government and helped disrupt supply lines to American forces outside St. Augustine. In consequence, Georgia Militia forces attacked the main Seminole villages in the Alachua area, and in the ensuing battle Seminole leader King Payne was mortally wounded.[1]

The Seminoles of the time were a poorly defined tribe lacking the identity they enjoy today. By the late seventeenth century, the indigenous tribes that had populated the peninsula when the Spanish arrived had been nearly eradicated by disease, warfare, and enslavement, leaving a land ripe for settlement by other native groups. During the 1700s, Creek Indians from what is now Georgia and Alabama came to Florida for a variety of reasons. Some were fleeing white encroachment, others were looking for new hunting grounds, while still others left their homelands because of political and personal differences within the tribe. Having found new homes, they grew to consider themselves separate from the Creek tribes they had left.

One of the main groups were the Alachuas, who resided around the Alachua Prairie near what is now Gainesville. This was prime grazing land and the Indians soon possessed large herds of cattle. Another significant group were the Mikasuki, who lived in the area of Lake Miccosukee, northeast of present-day Tallahassee. Other, smaller bands lived either in proximity to the larger groups or in towns of their own. Whites, not understanding the

---

1 James G. Cusick, *The Other War of 1812: The Patriot War and the American Invasion of Spanish East Florida,* (Gainesville: University Press of Florida, 2003), 241.

relationships between all these tribes, applied the term "Seminole" to any Indian living in Florida.

Another population living among the Seminoles were runaway slaves and their descendants. Spain had welcomed runaways from the English colonies, and many of those blacks had taken up residence among the Indians. The Indians also purchased slaves, but allowed them a substantial amount of freedom and treated them much better than plantation slaves. When the wars came, blacks fought as hard as any Seminole to protect their way of life.

Another part of the mix were Creek Indians from Georgia and Alabama who had been forced into Florida at the end of the Creek Civil War of 1813-1814. The Creeks had split into two factions, Lower Creeks living primarily in southern Georgia, and Upper Creeks, known as Red Sticks, living in Eastern Alabama. Lower Creeks were beginning to assimilate into white culture, while the Upper Creeks were steadfastly opposed to it. When war broke out between the two groups, forces under Andrew Jackson were sent in to quell the uprising. At the Battle of Horseshoe Bend in March 1814, Jackson destroyed the Red Sticks, causing many to flee to safety in Spanish Florida. In the treaty that ended the war, Jackson forced the cession of large amounts of land from both groups, even the friendly Lower Creeks.

Although all these groups had come from different backgrounds, were often rivals, and did not even possess a common language, they all came together to fight their common American enemy.

After the War of 1812, it was the issue of runaway slaves that brought American forces into Florida. During the war, the English had come to Florida hoping to recruit the runaways and disgruntled Creeks into the war against the Americans. As part of the effort, they erected a large fortification on the Apalachicola

River, about twenty-five miles above the Gulf of Mexico. At war's end they abandoned the fort, but left it well stocked with weapons and ammunition. The local Indians had little use for the fort, but the runaways saw it as a point of refuge and built a settlement around it. American slave owners began to call it "The Negro Fort," and saw it as a beacon for runaways and a possible rallying point for those who might wish to incite a slave rebellion. Pressure was applied in Washington to do away with the settlement.

Although the fort was in Spanish territory, Spain was in no position to do anything about the Negro Fort. Still devastated from the Napoleonic Wars and facing revolutions throughout the Western Hemisphere, Spain simply didn't have the resources to police or defend the unprofitable Florida colonies. In light of this, President James Madison ordered Maj. Gen. Andrew Jackson, in command of the Southern Division of the Army, to destroy the fort, capture its inhabitants, and return them to bondage. Jackson passed the order on to his second-in-command, Maj. Gen. Edmund Gaines, telling him, "It ought to be blown up regardless of the ground it stands on, and from the facts and knowledge you possess regarding this negro fort, if your mind should have formed the same conclusion, destroy it and restore the stolen negroes and property to their rightful owners."[2]

Needing a pretext for launching an attack, Gaines ordered Col. Duncan Clinch to erect Camp Crawford on the Flint River, about seven miles north of the Florida-Georgia line. The site would later be renamed Fort Scott. Gaines intended to supply the fort via the Apalachicola, in hopes the supply vessels would be fired upon, thereby providing the excuse he needed to destroy the fort. Gaines ordered two supply ships to ascend the Apalachicola,

2 Secretary William Crawford to General Andrew Jackson, 15 March 1816, John Spencer Bassett, *Correspondence of Andrew Jackson,* 7 vols. (Washington, D.C.: Carnegie Institute of Washington, 1926-1835), 2: 236-237; Jackson to Brig. General Edmund P. Gaines, 8 April 1816, Bassett, *Correspondence of Jackson,* 2: 238-239.

escorted by two navy gunboats, which were to cooperate with a ground force led by Col. Clinch. On 10 July 1816 the ships arrived at Apalachicola Bay. A week later, shortly before dawn, Loomis dispatched a Midshipman Luffborough and four crewmembers in search of fresh water. While pulling their boat ashore, the men were attacked, resulting in the deaths of Luffborough, Robert Maitland, and John Burgess. John Lopez managed to dive overboard and swim to a nearby sandbar, while Edward Daniels was taken prisoner and later executed.[3]

After receiving news of Loomis's arrival at the mouth of the Apalachicola, Clinch took 116 men from the 4th Infantry and descended the river with merchant William Hambly as their guide. During the evening they were joined by Chief William McIntosh and 150 friendly Creeks, and the next day by another large body of Indians. Around 2:00 a.m. on 20 July Clinch arrived about a mile north of the Negro Fort and sent one of his men and two Indians to notify the gunboats of his arrival. Three days later, an allied Creek entered the fort under a white flag. Former slave Garçon, in command of the fort, refused to surrender, warning that "he would sink any American vessels that should attempt to pass it, and blow up the fort if he could not defend it."[4]

Later that day, messengers from Clinch met up with Sailing Master Jarius Loomis of the navy and presented him with verbal

---

3 Gaines to Colonel D. L. Clinch, 23 May 1816, *ASP:FR*, 4: 558; Gaines to Commodore Daniel T. Patterson, 22 May 1816, *ASP:FR* 4: 558-559; J. Loomis to Patterson, 13 August 1816, *ASP:FR*, 4: 559-560; Reports of the Army's use of Fort Scott from Daniel Parker, 28 January 1819, Robert L. Meriwether, ed. *The Papers of John C. Calhoun*, 28 vols. (Columbus: University of South Carolina Press, 1959), 3: 525.

4 Extract of a letter to a gentleman in Charleston, 4 August 1816, *The National Register*, September 1816, 2:32; Rembert W. Patrick, *Aristocrat in Uniform: General Duncan L. Clinch*, (Gainesville: University of Florida Press, 1963), 29; J. Loomis to Patterson, 13 August 1816, *ASP:FR*, 4: 559-560; Clinch to Col. R. Butler, 2 August 1816, *Niles' Register*, 20 November 1819, 17:186-188.

instructions to ascend the river and wait for Clinch at Dueling Bluff, about four miles below the fort. Concerned that it might be a trick to lure him into another ambush, Loomis refused the order and sent one of the Indians back with a message for Clinch to send written communications through an officer. Clinch complied, and the gunboats, followed by the two supply ships, arrived below the fort and met up with Clinch on 25 July. After searching the area for a suitable spot to erect a small battery of two eighteen-pounders, Loomis and Clinch got into an argument over the placement of the guns. Frustrated, Loomis told Clinch he would attempt the passage without the army's help.[5]

On 27 July, just before dawn, the gunboats came within range of the fort. True to his promise, Garçon and the occupants of the Negro Fort opened fire. After securing the gunboats to the opposite riverbank, the sailors began to return fire, refining their aim with each shot fired at the fort. By the eighth round, they had found their target. Inside an oven on the deck of Gunboat 154 a fire had been built, and within the glowing coals a cannon ball had been placed. When it reached the point where it was glowing red-hot, it was carefully carried to the waiting cannon and loaded into the muzzle of the weapon. The "hot shot" landed squarely in the fort's powder magazine. In one horrific flash, the powder exploded, instantly killing nearly three hundred of the men, women, and children who had taken refuge in the fort. The Negro Fort had been reduced to splinters, ashes, and torn bodies.[6]

After the destruction of the Negro Fort, the War Department felt Indian troubles would end along the Florida-Georgia border

---

5 J. Loomis to Patterson, 13 August 1816, *ASP:FR*, 4:559-560.

6 *Ibid;* Clinch to Butler, 2 August 1816, *Niles' Register*, 20 November 1819; Patterson to Benjamin W. Crowninshield, 15 August 1816, *ASP:FR*, 4:561.

and closed Camp Crawford. In January 1817 hostile Creeks ran off the Indian caretaker and set fire to the unoccupied buildings. Unconvinced that peace would prevail, Georgia Governor David Mitchell complained to the War Department, asking that the fort be reopened. He had cause to worry. In retaliation for attacks by outlaws from Georgia, a party of about fifteen Indians attacked the home of Obadiah Garrett near St. Marys, Georgia. In his absence, the Indians killed Garrett's wife and two small children; one, an infant, the other, a toddler. Mrs. Garrett had been shot twice, stabbed, and scalped. The oldest child had also been scalped.[7]

Meanwhile, in West Florida, the Bahamian trader Alexander Arbuthnot had arrived near the Apalachicola River and established a trading post at Ochlochnee Sound. Carrying a letter of support from Bahamian Governor Charles Cameron, Arbuthnot met with several chiefs and then forwarded their complaints and his observations to the British Ambassador in Washington, Charles Bagot. Believing illegal squatters were the root cause of problems along the frontier, Arbuthnot commented, "It is persons in the back settlements of Georgia who enter the Seminole territory in large parties to steal cattle, which they frequently drive off in gangs of 50 and 100 at a time, and if in these excursions the Indians meet them and oppose these predatory plunders, blood sometimes has been spilt." Arbuthnot had sympathy for the Indians and was not pleased with his own government's actions toward them, writing, "I say the English ill-treat them: after making them parties in the war with America, they leave them without a pilot, to be robbed and ill-treated by their natural and sworn enemies, the Americans."[8]

Also in Florida was Robert Chrystie Ambrister, a young man looking for adventure. He had served as a midshipman in the

---

7 R. Sands to the Officer at Fort Hawkins, 2 February 1817, *ASP:MA*, 1:681; Intendant Archibald Clarke to Gaines, 26 February 1817, *ASP:MA*, 1:682.

Royal Navy during the Napoleonic Wars but had been discharged in 1813, supposedly for illegal dueling. Still, as son of the commander of the New Providence Militia and nephew of Governor Cameron, he had high hopes of obtaining a military position. Those connections worked, and on 25 July 1814 Ambrister was appointed auxiliary second lieutenant in the colonial marines.[9]

During the War of 1812, in conjunction with Col. Edward Nicolls and Capt. George Woodbine, Ambrister had been in charge of training and arming the Indians and blacks who would serve with the colonial marines during the failed expedition to capture New Orleans. Following the war, Ambrister returned to New Providence in hopes of obtaining a permanent commission in one of the colonial regiments. Two years later he was enticed by Woodbine to return to Florida to make contact with the Indians for unspecified reasons. Woodbine seemed to have designs on Florida, but no one was sure what they were.[10]

In the summer of 1815 the Red Stick Prophet Josiah Francis, also known as Hillis Hadjo, had been taken to England by Col. Nicolls, who was supportive of the Seminole and Creek cause. After nearly two years travelling and waiting for an audience with the Foreign Office, Francis returned home in the spring of 1817

---

8 R. Arbuthnot to the Officer Commanding at Fort Gaines, 3 March 1817, *ASP:MA* 1:682; Alexander Arbuthnot to Charles Babot, [no date], *ASP:FR*, 4:606-607; Alexander Arbuthnot's journal entry of November 10, 1817 found among his papers, *ASP:FR*, 4:609-610.

9 Frank L. Owsley, Jr., "Ambrister and Arbuthnot: Adventurers or Martyrs for British Honor?," *Journal of the Early Republic*, 5 (Fall 1985): 299, 305; Robert C. Ambrister's Memorial to Frederick, Duke of York, *ASP:FR,* 4:604-605; Robert C. Ambrister's commission as auxiliary second lieutenant from Alexander Cochrane, 25 July 1814, *ASP:FR*, 4:605.

10 Ambrister's memorial to Frederick, Duke of York, *ASP:FR*, 4:604-605; Ambrister's commission from Cochrane, 25 July 1814, *ASP:FR*, 4:605; Owsley, Jr., "Ambrister and Arbuthnot," 299, 304-305, 308.

empty handed. The British government was turning its back on the people they had promised to help. In June 1817, Alexander Arbuthnot gained Power of Attorney from a dozen Seminole and Red Stick leaders, including Peter McQueen and Josiah Francis.[11]

While at Camp Montgomery, Gaines received a letter from Mikasuki chief Chappachimico promising to attend a meeting and resolve the matter of surrendering the Garrett murderers. The following day, Gaines forwarded the letter to Jackson, commenting that "the chief, as was to be expected, appears to have taken the advice of the man who calls himself A. Arbuthnot. ... This British agent then it seems, may be considered as the prime director on the part of the Seminola Indians in the adjustment of our affairs, and thereby endeavor to put off the dreaded hour of just retribution." If Gaines failed to receive "satisfactory assurance [of] a determination on the part of the chiefs to comply with the demand ... I shall then try the effect of force."[12]

During mid-July, Gaines prepared to reactivate Camp Crawford on the Flint River, now renamed Fort Scott. Major David Twiggs, in command of the 7th Infantry at Camp Montgomery (near Mobile), was ordered to march overland with his troops and garrison the newly reactivated fort. Shortly after their arrival at the end of July, Twiggs sent runners to nearby Indian villages inviting them to meet with him on 4 August. On the day appointed, six chiefs showed up and agreed to concessions made by the other chiefs during their meeting with Indian Agent (and former governor) David Mitchell the previous month. Twiggs then read a message from Gaines informing the chiefs that the President was aware of "murders and thefts committed by hostile Indians" and had authorized General Jackson to "arrest the offenders, and cause

---

11 Power of attorney from the Indian chiefs to Arbuthnot, 17 June 1817, *ASP:FR*, 4:589.

12 Gaines to Jackson, 10 July 1817, Bassett, *Correspondence of Jackson,* 2:305-307.

justice to be done." Gaines's letter warned, "They have been at war against helpless women and children, let them now calculate upon fighting men." He also warned them of false promises made by the British. "The hostile party pretend to calculate upon help from the British! They may as well look for soldiers from the moon to help them. Their warriors were beaten, and driven from our country by American troops. The English are not able to help themselves; how, then, should they help the old 'Red Sticks,' whom they have ruined by pretended friendship."[13]

Most of the chiefs had been conciliatory and respectful toward Twiggs and the message he brought, and promised to give him their answer in ten days. The one exception was Neamathla, headman of Fowltown, located a few miles upriver from Fort Scott on the opposite (east) bank. The chief told Twiggs that the Flint River was the line between them and warned that the soldiers "must not cut another stick of timber" on the Indian side of the river. The land was his, he said, and he had been "directed by the Powers above to protect and defend it." He intended to do so, he told Twiggs, and the Americans would see that "talking could not frighten him."[14]

Back in the Bahamas, Alexander Arbuthnot wrote a letter to his old friend Edward Nicolls, the self-styled Seminole agent who was now in London. "I sincerely trust, sir, you will use the powers you are vested with for the service and protection of these

---

13 David S. Heidler and Jeanne T. Heidler, *Old Hickory's War: Andrew Jackson and the Quest for Empire,* (Mechanicsburg, PA: Stackpole Books, 1996), 98; Major D. E. Twiggs to David B. Mitchell, 4 August 1817, *ASP:MA,* 1: 750; Gaines to Chiefs and Warriors, [no date], *ASP:MA,* 1: 688; Twiggs to Gaines, 17 September 1817, *American State Papers: Indian Affairs,* (hereinafter cited as *ASP:IA*) , 2 vols. (Washington, D.C.: Gales and Seaton, 1834), 2:158; Gaines to Chiefs and Warriors, [no date], *ASP:MA*, 1:688; Gaines to the Secretary of War with a Talk to the Chiefs and Warriors, 2 December 1817, *ASP:FR*, 4:598.

14 Gaines to Jackson, 31 August 1817, Bassett, *Correspondence of Jackson,* 2:323-324.

unfortunate people, who look up to you as their savior." Believing the problems between the whites and Indians were primarily caused by "back-woods Georgians" and exaggerated newspaper reports of Seminole atrocities, Arbuthnot asked Nicolls to present his letter to British authorities, hoping an agent would be appointed to correspond with British Ambassador Bagot, so "his eyes will then be open as to the motives that influence American individuals, as well as the Government, in vilifying the Indians." Warning of the consequences, Arbuthnot remarked, "Against such oppressions the American Government must use not only all their influence, but, if necessary, force, or their names be handed down to posterity as a nation more cruel and savage to the unfortunate aborigines of this country than ever were the Spaniards, in more dark ages, to the nations of South America."[15]

Besides Indian problems, the United States was also concerned about continued foreign influence in Florida. Starting in March, the situation in and around East Florida had become potentially dangerous. Adventurer Gregor MacGregor had arrived at Amelia Island after receiving financial backing from influential citizens in the northeast United States, and he seized the island as an operational base for Venezuelan privateers. Plagued by a lack of funds and desertions among his followers, MacGregor met with George Woodbine, the former British officer living in the Bahamas who also had designs on Florida. No sooner had MacGregor gone to Nassau to finalize plans with Woodbine, then French pirate Luis-Michel Aury arrived at Amelia Island and took control in MacGregor's absence. Claiming to be serving the revolutionary governments of Latin America, the pirates seized the island for the Republic of Mexico and began smuggling slaves into the United States.[16]

---

15 Arbuthnot to Lieutenant Colonel Nicolls, 26 August 1817, *ASP:FR*, 4:578-579; Arbuthnot, "Note of Indian talks," [no date], *ASP:FR*, 4:586.

On 18 September 1817 the Indians delivered a written response to Gaines's demands to Major Twiggs at Fort Scott. In it, the headmen of ten towns declared:

> This is now three years since the white people killed three Indians. Since that, they have killed three other Indians … and this summer they killed three more; and very lately they killed one more. … The white people killed our people first; the Indians then took satisfaction. There are yet three men that the red people have never taken satisfaction for. … On that side of the river, the white people have killed five Indians; but there is nothing said about that; and all that the Indians have done is brought up. … It appears that all the mischief is laid on this town; but all the mischief that has been done by this town, is two horses; one of them is dead, and the other was sent back. The cattle that we are accused of taking, were cattle that the white people took from us; our young men went and brought them back, with the same marks and brands.

Describing the cause of the Garrett murders, the chief explained, "There was some of our young men out hunting, and they were killed; others went to take satisfaction, and the kettle of one of the men that was killed was found in the house where the woman and two children were killed; and they supposed it had been her husband who had killed the Indians, and took their satisfaction there." Twiggs forwarded a copy of the letter to Gaines.[17]

---

16 Thomas Wayne, Esq. to Benjamin Homans, 27 September 1817; Extracts of letter to the Secretary of State from [unknown], 24 December 1817; Instructions for sailing in Tampa bay in MacGregor's handwriting, enclosed in 24 December 1817 letter; extracts of letter to a gentleman in the District of Columbia, 30 July 1817; G. MacGregor's response to previous letter, 27 December 1817, all in *ASP:FR*, 4:603-604.

Gaines began to reposition his men. On 11 October he issued orders to Major Peter Muhlenberg at Camp Montgomery to obtain provisions from Mobile and transport part of the troops by water to the mouth of the Apalachicola River and from there to Fort Scott on the Flint River. The remainder of the force would make their way through the woods.[18]

On 30 October Acting Secretary of War George Graham wrote to Gaines that President Monroe had approved the "movement of troops from Fort Montgomery to Fort Scott," believing it "will at least have the effect of restraining the Seminoles from committing further depredations, and perhaps of inducing them to make reparation for the murders which they have committed." If they refused, "it is the wish of the President that you should not, on that account, pass the line, and make an attack upon them within the limits of Florida, until you shall have received instructions from this department." Authorization was given to "remove the Indians still remaining on the lands ceded," with exception of those that had been granted reservations in the treaty, and Graham suggested, "it may be proper to retain some of them as hostages until reparation may have been made for the depredations which have been committed." With regards to the matter and manner of removing them, Graham told Gaines, "you will exercise your discretion."[19]

In the meantime, the administration had decided to act against the pirate's nest on Amelia Island. Following proper

---

17 Indians to the Commanding Officer at Fort Hawkins, 11 September 1817, *ASP:MA*, 1:685; Twiggs to Gaines, 18 September 1817, *ASP:IA*, 2:159.

18 *Niles' Register,* 4 October 1817; Gaines to Major Peter Muhlenberg, 11 October 1817, Letters Received by the Office of the Adjutant General (main series), 1805-1821, Microcopy M 566, Record Group 94: Records of the Adjutant General's Office, Microfilm Publication, NA.

19 George Graham, Acting Secretary of War, to Gaines, 30 October 1817, *ASP:MA*, 1:685-686 and *ASP:IA*, 4:159.

procedure, Monroe asked Congress for authorization to enter foreign territory. Congress concurred, and the army and navy began to make plans to evict Luis-Michel Aury and his band of smugglers from Florida.[20]

Also on 20 October, troops of the 4th and 7th Infantries, in command of Lt. Col. Matthew Arbuckle, departed from Forts Montpelier and Camp Montgomery and headed toward Fort Crawford, above Pensacola. After being joined by Capt. George Vashon's command, the troops proceeded along the newly constructed military road to Fort Gaines. From there they would proceed by boat to Fort Scott. Also that day "three vessels laden with ordnance stores, Baggage and provisions, with eighty men under the command of Maj. Muhlenberg were detached by water" from Mobile, underway for the Apalachicola.[21]

Three days later, Gaines informed Jackson that he had transferred troops to the "troubled area," but that his entire effective force would be "not more than 800 men." Delaying his departure until rumors were confirmed that "500 Indians had gone to Pensacola because their towns were preparing for war," Gaines told Jackson if the reports were confirmed, he would order a few companies of Georgia militia to the area until the second brigade arrived. In the meantime, he anticipated meeting Muhlenberg with the transports and supplies on 6 November or, at the latest, 10 November. Upon arriving at Fort Scott on 17 November, Gaines was surprised to learn that Muhlenberg had yet to arrive with the reinforcements and provisions.[22]

---

20 Heidler and Heidler, 102; Frank L. Owsley, Jr. and Gene A. Smith, *Filibusters and Expansionists: Jeffersonian Manifest Destiny, 1800-1821,* (Tuscaloosa: University of Alabama Press, 1997), 140.

21 Gaines to Muhlenberg, 11 October 1817, Letters Received by the Office of the Adjutant General (main series), 1805-1821, M 566, RG 94, NA; Annie Waters, "A Documentary History of Fort Crawford, Located in West Brewton, Escambia County, Alabama," *Escambia County Historical Quarterly,* 3 (September 1975): 10.

Gaines's first priority, however, was to deal with the hostile Indians on the opposite side of the Flint River. That same day, Gaines dispatched an Indian runner to Fowltown in order to determine Neamathla's temperament and to request that the chief return with the runner to meet with him. Additional troops arrived at Fort Scott the next day, and Gaines could only hope that Muhlenberg would arrive shortly with the much-needed supplies. Sometime during the day, the Indian runner returned with a message from Neamathla: The chief had said all that he had to say to the commanding officer at Fort Scott and would not meet with Gaines. The general then ordered Twiggs to assemble 250 men and issued instructions to bring the recalcitrant chief in:

> The hostile character and conduct of the Indians of the fowl Town ... rendering it absolutely necessary, that they should be removed, you will proceed to the town with the detachment assigned you, and remove them. You will arrest and bring the chiefs and Warriors to this place, but should they oppose you, or attempt to escape, you will in that event treat them as enemies. Your men are to be strictly prohibited, in any event, from firing upon, or otherwise injuring women and children. You will return to this place with your command, as soon as practicable.[23]

After marching all night, Twiggs and his detachment reached Fowltown at daylight on the 21st. Once the troops were in battle formation, Twiggs ordered his men to surround the town, avoid bloodshed, and take the warriors by surprise.

---

22 Waters, "Fort Crawford," 10; *Augusta Chronicle,* 13 December 1817; Gaines to John C. Calhoun, Secretary of War, 2 December 1817, *ASP:MA,* 1:687.

23 *Augusta Chronicle,* 13 December 1817; Gaines to Jackson, 21 November 1817, *ASP:MA*, 1:686; *ASP:IA*, 4:160; and Bassett, *Correspondence of Jackson,* 2:334.

The plan almost succeeded. Before the trap could be sprung, the villagers realized their predicament and fled from the two companies approaching on their right, then fired on the two companies approaching from the left. Twiggs ordered a pursuit and his men returned fire, killing four warriors and one woman before the Indians fled into a nearby swamp. The troops remained in possession of the town until sunset, and then marched back to Fort Scott without destroying the town. With the exception of a few head of cattle and some horses, Twiggs returned to Fort Scott empty handed.[24]

In a letter to Jackson, Gaines explained that the Indian woman had been shot accidentally and that a British uniform with a pair of gold epaulettes and a certificate had been discovered in Neamathla's house. The certificate, signed by Robert White in the absence of Colonel Nicolls, stated that the chief had always been a true and faithful friend to the British.[25]

The next day, Gaines ordered Colonel Arbuckle to assemble three hundred men and reconnoiter the vicinity of Fowltown to determine the strength of the hostile Indians. Hidden in a nearby swamp, about sixty warriors commenced firing on the troops as they approached the town. The fire was quickly returned and continued for about twenty minutes before the Indians again disappeared into the swamp with a loss of six to eight killed and a greater number wounded. Arbuckle had one man killed and another wounded.[26]

Meanwhile, Gaines was still waiting on Muhlenberg. The general had been specific as to what was to be taken on board the

---

24 Gaines to Jackson, 21 November 1817, *ASP:MA,* 1:686; *ASP:IA*, 4:160; and Bassett, *Correspondence of Jackson,* 2 :334.

25 *Ibid.*

26 Gaines to Graham, 26 November 1817, *ASP:MA*, 1:686.

vessels. The highest priority items were the ordnance stores and the baggage of the troops, followed by, "such contractors stores as Mr. R. Tankersley the principle agent of Mobile may put on board to complete the cargo of each vessel." The items were to consist mainly of "salted pork together with vinegar, soap and candles," and were part of a previous order that had yet to be delivered. Once everything was ready "You will embark ... as soon as they [the ships] shall be ready for your reception and repair to Fort Scott upon the Flint River."[27]

Gaines had taken pains to warn Muhlenberg of the dangers he might encounter along the way. "The unfriendly character of the Seminole Indians and other persons inhabiting the country south and east of Fort Scott and the possibility of your falling in with some of the pirates with which the coast of the Gulf of Mexico has been infested render it proper that your men should be kept upon the ... alert and always ready for action in defense of the vessels and cargo." He also told Muhlenberg to "calculate upon meeting some boats below Fort Scott to assist you in ascending the river." Gaines emphasized the need to move swiftly: "Your vessels being employed by the day and at a high rate, no time should be lost upon the passage."[28]

Upon his arrival at Mobile, Muhlenberg ran into his first delay. One of the vessels he would need, the Sloop *Phoebe Ann*, was at Blakeley, on the Tensaw River, about thirty miles to the

---

27 Gaines to Muhlenberg, 11 October 1817, Letters Received by the Office of the Adjutant General (main series), 1805-1821, M 566, RG 94, NA.

28 *Ibid;* Major Muhlenberg was the son of Peter Muhlenberg, a well-known General in the Revolutionary War, the younger Muhlenberg had joined the army in 1808 as a lst Lieutenant in the 6th Infantry. Two years later he was promoted to Captain, and in 1814 was promoted to Brevet Major of the 31st Infantry. Six months after the close of the war with England, Muhlenberg left the service, but was reinstated as a Captain of the 4th Infantry on January 1, 1816, retaining his brevet as a major; Heitman, *Register and Dictionary of the U.S. Army,* 1:734.

northeast. Men from the 4th Infantry were sent to bring her down, and when she arrived the soldiers commenced loading nearly four thousand rations, military clothing, and a large quantity of goods belonging to the sutler. Also on board were, "the greater part of the command including all the sick," and an unknown number of the men's family members.[29]

The three-ship fleet departed Mobile Bay on 2 November. As night fell over the Gulf, the ships lost sight of each other and did not regroup until 20 November. Muhlenberg did not explain why it took so long to make the trip. With a moderate breeze, the distance could normally be covered in about three days, though in the age of sail travel times were subject to the whims of the wind.[30]

To ascertain Muhlenberg's whereabouts, Gaines ordered Lieutenant Richard W. Scott to take forty men from the 4th and 7th Infantries and go downriver to assist the major in bringing the vessels up to Fort Scott. For some unknown reason, perhaps in haste or believing he was in no danger while descending the river, Scott did not bother to place a protective wooden covering over the boat. It was an omission he would later regret.[31]

In a day or two Scott met up with Muhlenberg near the mouth of the Apalachicola River. Muhlenberg had other problems besides navigating the Apalachicola. A number of his men were in need of medical attention and the nearest doctors were at Fort Scott. Muhlenberg decided to retain half of Scott's forty men and "in their place, put a like number of sick, with the women, and some regimental clothing." If either man was concerned over the chance of Indian attack, they didn't show it. Scott had reached the Gulf unmolested, so the two officers may have felt the return trip

---

29 Muhlenberg to Gaines, 25 March 1818, Letters Received by the Office of the Adjutant General (main series), 1805-1821, M 566, RG 94, NA.
30 *Ibid.*
31 Gaines to Graham, 2 December 1817, *ASP:MA,* 1:687.

would be just as uneventful. They had no way of knowing what was happening at Fowltown.[32]

For nearly a week, Scott's boat moved steadily against the current of the Apalachicola River. Although the exact design of the boat is unknown, it may well have been a type of flatboat. This type of vessel had a flat bottom, may or may not have been equipped with oars, and was designed more to move with the current than against it. Generally uncovered and with a small cabin, such vessels offered little protection from the elements or from Indian attack. When the river was shallow enough, the men used long poles to push the boat forward. When the depth increased, they were forced to throw anchor lines ahead of them and pull against the current in a process known as "warping." With only about twenty healthy men on board, progress would have been slow.

On 28 November Scott and his crew reached Spanish Bluff, where the trading post of Forbes and Company was located. From proprietor William Hambly, Scott learned distressing news: The Indians were upset about something and were gathering along the Apalachicola near the Florida-Georgia border. If the news were true, Scott would have to pass right by them.[33]

As Muhlenberg had instructed, Scott dispatched a runner to Fort Scott with Muhlenberg's message to Gaines. He also included a letter of his own:

> Enclosed you will receive Major Muhlenberg's communication, which he directs me to forward to you by express from this place. Mr. Hambly informs me that Indians are assembling at the junction of the river, where they intend

32 Muhlenberg to Gaines, 25 March 1818, Letters Received by the Office of the Adjutant General (main series), 1805-1821, M 566, RG 94, NA; Gaines to Graham, 2 December 1817, *ASP:MA*, 1:687.

33 Lieutenant R. W. Scott to Gaines, 28 November 1817, *ASP:MA*, 1:688.

to make a stand against those vessels coming up the river; should this be the case, I am not able to make a stand against them. My command does not exceed forty men, and one half sick, and without arms. I leave this [place] immediately.

I am, respectfully,
your obedient servant,
R. W. Scott, Lieut. 7th Infantry,
Commanding Detachment

Note: The bearer of this is entitled to three dollars on delivering this letter. The Indians have a report here that the Indians have beaten the white people."[34]

Gaines received Scott's letter at 11:00 a.m. on 30 November. After reading the correspondence, Gaines summoned Captain Joseph Clinch (brother of Col. Duncan Clinch) and ordered him to prepare to assist Lieutenant Scott. Gaines's orders to Captain Clinch revealed a sense of urgency. "You will embark with the party assigned you on board the two covered boats; descend the river until you meet with Lieutenant Scott; deliver to him a cover for his boat, and give him such assistance as, in your judgment, shall be necessary to secure his party, and expedite his movement to this place." After attending to Scott's needs, Gaines ordered that, "You will then proceed, with the residue of your command, down the river, until you meet with Major Muhlenberg; report to him, and act under his orders."[35]

After fitting two boats with wooden covers with portholes for defense, Captain Clinch, one other officer, and forty men left Fort Scott during the evening of the 30th in search of Scott's boat. Although visibility was minimal, Clinch was reminded of Gaines's

34 *Ibid.*
35 Gaines to Captain Joseph Clinch, 30 November 1817, *ASP:FR*, 4:599.

instructions: "You will, in no case, put your command in the power of the Indians near the shore. Be constantly on the alert. Remember that United States troops can never be surprised by Indians without a loss of honor, to say nothing of the loss of strength that might ensue." It was dark by the time they reached the junction of the river. As the current carried them down the Apalachicola, the men kept their eyes focused in front of them, searching for Scott's boat. After passing Spanish Bluff, Clinch must have known something had not gone according to plan. As instructed, he continued towards the Gulf and Major Muhlenberg.[36]

Today there is a dam at the confluence of the Chattahoochee and Flint Rivers, and behind it has risen the aptly named Lake Seminole. About a mile below the dam is a slight bend in the river. It's a lovely spot, a small county park with a boat ramp, picnic tables, and a playground. You can sit there and imagine that the dam is gone and the river is flowing freely, its current strong, carrying water that has come all the way from the mountains of northern Georgia. As the river curves toward the east, the swift current would have driven an oncoming boat right toward you. This is the place where it happened.

Even though Scott and his men were aware of the danger, the attack still came as a surprise. The Seminoles had known the current would drive the boat toward shore and had patiently waited, well hidden in the densely forested riverbank. When the boat was closest to them, they rose and fired a murderous volley, which must have thrown the boat's crew into a panic. The warp lines would have been lost and the rudder unmanned. Adrift, the boat would have been pushed towards shore by the current, the uninjured soldiers powerless to stop it. If the Indians had time to fire a second volley, more of the boat's occupants would have

---

36 Gaines to Graham, 2 December 1817, *ASP:FR,* 4:598; Gaines to Captain Clinch, 30 November 1817, *ASP:FR,* 4: 599.

fallen. As the boat neared shore, some Indians would have entered the water and pulled it toward the bank while others climbed aboard and commenced the slaughter.

At close quarters, it would have been tomahawk and knife against bayonets and swinging rifle butts. It would have been a short battle, blood flowing down the deck of the boat and into the water. The soldiers no doubt fought valiantly, but they were few in number, powerless to stop hundreds of warriors bent on revenge for the insult received at Fowltown. Of the forty-one soldiers, only six or seven managed to escape the boat and swim to safety on the opposite shore. We don't know how the women died. All we know for sure is that six of them were killed and one, seventeen-year-old Elizabeth Stuart, taken prisoner.

Aided by friendly Indians, the six survivors found their way through miles of wilderness to the safety of Fort Scott. It took two days, travelling warily, hoping to avoid contact with any hostile war parties. The presence of the wounded would have slowed them down, and some of them may have been very ill. After all, half the boat's crew had been invalids. At some point, it would have been necessary to cross the Chattahoochee River and probably a number of smaller streams.[37]

The survivors arrived at Fort Scott on 2 December. The tale of their ordeal must have sent a shock wave through the fort's garrison. The news that thirty-five of their friends and comrades had been killed would have touched everyone at the post. For a number of men, the loss would have been heart-wrenching: Their wives had been on that boat. The survivors had not taken time to sit on the opposite riverbank and note who had lived and died. They could only report that the seven women were either killed or taken prisoner.[38]

---

37 William James's pension, Old War File #28575, NA.

38 Gaines to Graham, 2 December 1817, *ASP:MA,* 1:687.

After interviewing the survivors, Gaines prepared an official report, copies of which he transmitted to the War Department, Andrew Jackson, Governor Rabun, and Creek Agent Mitchell. The wording was slightly different in each letter, but the message was the same:

> It is now my painful duty to report an affair of a more serious and decisive nature than has heretofore occurred, and which leaves no doubt of the necessity of an immediate application of force and active measures on our part. A large party of Seminole Indians, on the 30th ultimo, formed an ambuscade, upon the Apalachicola river, a mile below the junction of the Flint and Chattahoochee, attacked one of our boats, ascending the river near the shore, and killed, wounded, and took, the greater part of the detachment, consisting of forty men, commanded by Lieutenant R. W. Scott of the 7th Infantry. There were also on board, killed or taken, seven women, the wives of soldiers. Six men of the detachment only escaped, four of whom were wounded. I shall immediately strengthen the detachment under Major Muhlenberg with another boat secured against the enemy's fire. He will, therefore, move up with safety, keeping near the middle of the river; I shall, moreover, take a position, with my principal force, at the junction of the rivers, near the line; and shall attack any force that may attempt to intercept our vessels and supplies below.[39]

If Gaines had been looking for an excuse to enter Spanish Florida, the Scott Massacre provided him with one. "I feel persuaded the order of the President, prohibiting an attack upon the Indians, below the line, has reference only to the past, and not

39 *Ibid.*

to the present or future outrages, such as the one just now perpetrated and such as shall place our troops strictly within the pale of natural law, when self defence is sanctioned by the privilege of self preservation."[40]

Estimating the number of hostile Indians in the area, Gaines reported, "The wounded men who made their escape concur in the opinion, that they had seen upwards of five hundred hostile Indian warriors at different places, below the point of attack; of the force engaged, they differ in opinion, but all agree that the number was very considerable, extending about one hundred and fifty yards along the shore, in the edge of a swamp or thick woods." Three days later, Gaines turned command of Fort Scott over to Arbuckle and headed for Fort Hawkins "to hasten the movement of troops from Georgia."[41]

On 8 December John C. Calhoun became Secretary of War, replacing Acting Secretary Graham. Prior to leaving office, Graham responded to Gaines's letter of 21 November, commenting on the attack on Fowltown. "Although the necessity of this attack, and the consequent effusion of blood, is exceedingly to be regretted, yet it is hoped that the prompt measures which were taken by you on your arrival at Fort Scott, and the display of such an efficient force in that quarter, will induce the Indians to abstain from further depredations, and sue for peace."[42]

As much as Graham may have hoped for peace, he also knew the attack on Fowltown had changed the status quo. Bowing to that reality, he gave Gaines limited permission to cross the Florida line: "Should the Indians, however, assemble in force on the

---

40 *Ibid.*

41 *Ibid;* Lt. Col. Mathew Arbuckle to Graham, 19 December 1817, Meriwether, *Papers of John C. Calhoun,* 2:28.

42 Graham to Gaines, 9 December 1817, *ASP:MA,* 1:688.

Spanish side of the line, and persevere in committing hostilities within the limits of the United States, you will, in that event, exercise a sound discretion as to the propriety of crossing the line for the purpose of attacking them, and breaking up their town."[43]

As if the situation on the Apalachicola wasn't enough, incoming secretary Calhoun was faced with the task of removing Luis Aury and his pirates from Amelia Island. Unaware of the Scott Massacre, the War Department ordered all disposable troops from the Carolina and Georgia coastlines to gather at the St. Mary's River and sent orders for Gaines to take command of the campaign against the pirates.[44]

While all these preparations for war were getting underway, Creek Agent Mitchell was attempting to negotiate a peace. In a letter to Gov. William Bibb of the Alabama Territory, Mitchell expressed his regrets that Gaines had deemed it necessary to use force against the Fowltown Indians, who had remained neutral during the Creek War and had recently expressed a desire to be on friendly terms with the United States. "The rupture with them has precipitated the General into a state of open and declared war, before he was fully prepared."[45]

On 15 December, two days after arriving at Fort Hawkins, Gaines received the order to report to Amelia Island. Writing to Secretary Calhoun, Gaines said, "You can more readily conceive then I can describe the mortification and disappointment I have experienced in being compelled to suspend or abandon my measures at a moment when the loss of Lieutenant Scott and his party had given the enemy an occasion of triumph, and a certain

---

43 *Ibid.*

44 Calhoun to Gaines, 26 December 1817, Meriwether, *Papers of John C. Calhoun,* 2:38-39; *ASP:MA,* 1:689-690.

45 David B. Mitchell to Governor William W. Bibb, 15 December 1817, Clarence E. Carter, *The Territorial Papers of the United States,* 28 vols. (Washington, D.C.: United States Government Printing Office, 1934), 18: 215-216.

prospect of increasing his strength, by enlisting against us all who had before wavered or hesitated."[46]

Gaines was also concerned about obeying the President's orders to discharge the Georgia militia, fearing it would jeopardize the safety of frontier settlements. Pointing out the consequences, Gaines explained, "The Seminole Indians, however strange and absurd it may appear to those who understand little of their real character and extreme ignorance, entertain a notion that they cannot be beaten by our troops. They confidently assert that we never have beaten them, or any of their people, except when we have been assisted by 'red people' … they have little or no means of knowing the strength and resources of our country … I feel warranted, from all I know of these savages, in saying they do not believe we can beat them." Feeling compelled to "adopt the only measures which has proved to put a stop to the outrages," Gaines asked permission to return to Fort Scott. "There is little ground to apprehend that we shall find it necessary to follow the Indians far beyond the national boundary." Unfortunately, the orders had been issued and received. He would have to obey them and proceed to Amelia Island, where he would await orders to return to Fort Scott.[47]

The following day, still unaware of what had happened on the Apalachicola but anticipating Gaines's eventual return to Fort Scott, Calhoun wrote to the general, authorizing him to cross the Florida line if the Seminoles still refused to "make reparation for their outrages and depredations" on American citizens. "It is the wish of the President that you consider yourself at liberty to march across the Florida line and to attack them within its limits, should it be found necessary, unless they should shelter themselves under a Spanish post. In the last event, you will immediately notify this Department." The administration wanted to be absolutely certain

46 Gaines to Calhoun, 15 December 1817, *ASP:MA,* 1:689.

47 *Ibid.*

that any efforts to chastise the hostile Indians in foreign territory did not appear to be an act of aggression towards Spain. The risk of war and the price of terminating the negotiations for Florida were too high.[48]

On 13 December the Mikasukis abducted William Hambly and Edmund Doyle from their store on Spanish Bluff. Two days later Muhlenberg's supply vessels were attacked by an estimated 1,000 hostile Indians thirty miles below Fort Scott. Forced to stop, Muhlenberg ordered Captain Clinch to take a keelboat and carry a message to Fort Scott, reporting the attacks and requesting assistance. Two of Muhlenberg's men had been killed and another thirteen had been wounded during the attack:

> We are now compelled to remain here, as it is impossible for us to carry out a warp, as a man cannot show himself above the bulwark without being fired on. I can assure you that our present situation is not the most pleasant, not knowing how soon, or whether, we are to receive succor from above. The wounded are in but a bad situation, owing to the vessels being much crowded, and it is impossible to make them any ways comfortable on board.[49]

Muhlenberg had reason to be concerned. Six weeks after leaving Mobile the 4,000 rations that had been intended for Fort Scott were nearly exhausted. His men had been on half rations for some time and they had but a few days' provisions remaining. For the next four days, the hostile Indians kept the vessels under constant siege.[50]

In response to Muhlenberg's request, Arbuckle dispatched an armed boat with fifteen days' rations under the command of Capt.

48 Calhoun to Gaines, 16 December 1817, *ASP:MA,* 1:689.
49 Muhlenburg to Arbuckle, 16 December 1817, *ASP:MA,* 1:691.
50 Muhlenburg to Arbuckle, 16 and 19 December 1817, *ASP:MA,* 1:691.

Thomas Blackstone. Acknowledging receipt of the supplies, a frustrated Muhlenberg dispatched a message to Arbuckle the following day, alerting him to his dire need for reinforcements which, if not received in a timely manner, would force him to return to Apalachicola Bay. "I shall now dispatch the keel-boat under the command of Lieutenant Gray, and try to retain our present position until the night of the 21st."[51]

The day after sending Capt. Blackstone downriver, Arbuckle wrote to Gaines, informing him of Muhlenberg's situation and of news that Fort Hughes, at Bainbridge, Georgia, was under attack. He also expressed fears that Hambly and Doyle had been killed by their captors. Before Arbuckle could post the letter, a keelboat bearing some of the wounded arrived from Muhlenberg's convoy. Arbuckle told Gaines he would immediately dispatch a force downriver under Maj. Twiggs and anticipated their reaching Muhlenberg by sundown "provided it is not interrupted in its descent." Explaining the critical situation at Fort Scott, Arbuckle remarked, "Men and means of every description are greatly wanted here, and should any misfortune happen to the vessels we have not half a supply of ammunition, and not a single stand of spare arms."[52]

On 23 December, after several unsuccessful attempts to dispatch messages to Arbuckle, Capt. Robert Irvin at Fort Gaines reported that there was considerable confusion amongst the militia and friendly Indians about the coming campaign. After arriving at Fort Hawkins, McIntosh and the allied Creeks had been instructed to return home. In an attempt to mollify the unhappy Indians, Agent Mitchell told them that, "General Gaines had no business to go to the Indian towns and fire on them in the night; that he had acted like the Indians themselves in doing so." Irvin

51 Muhlenburg to Arbuckle, 19 December 1817, *ASP:MA,* 1:691.
52 Arbuckle to Gaines, 20 and 21 December 1817, *ASP:MA,* 1:690-691.

also reported rumors that Arbuthnot's son John was responsible for having Hambly and Doyle captured.[53]

To the east, an invasion of another sort was already taking place. On the same day that Irvin was writing to Arbuckle, American forces landed at Amelia Island, forced Luis Aury and his pirates to flee, and took possession of the island for the United States.[54]

On 16 December, still unaware of the Scott Massacre and of Calhoun's appointment, Andrew Jackson wrote to Acting Secretary Graham about the worsening situation in Florida. "The protection of our citizens will require that the wolf be struck in his den; for, rest assured, if ever the Indians find out that the territorial boundary of Spain is to be a sanctuary, their murders will be multiplied to a degree that our citizens on the southern frontier cannot bear." Pointing out that Spain was bound by treaties to restrain hostile Indians from committing hostilities on the United States, Jackson added, "Having failed to do this, necessity will justify the measure, after giving her due notice, to follow the marauders and punish them in their retreat. The war hatchet having been raised, unless the Indians sue for peace, your frontier cannot be protected without entering their country; from long experience, this result has been fully established."[55]

On 26 December, Secretary Calhoun wrote to Gaines acknowledging receipt of his letters dated 26 November, 2 December, and 3 December. Expressing regrets for the fate of Lieutenant Scott and his detachment, Calhoun assured Gaines that "no blame can attach to yourself or the officers immediately concerned." Calhoun then informed Gaines that Andrew Jackson

---

53 Captain Robert Irvin to Arbuckle, 23 December 1817, *ASP:MA,* 1:692.

54 Calhoun to Major James Bankhead, 12 December 1817; Bankhead to Graham, 20 December 1817; Calhoun to Bankhead, 16 December 1817, Meriwether, *Papers of John C. Calhoun,* 2:11, 20, 29.

55 Jackson to Graham, 16 December 1817, *ASP:MA,* 1:689.

had been ordered to take command at Fort Scott and would lead the American offensive. Hoping the situation at Amelia Island had been settled, Calhoun instructed Gaines to return to Fort Scott and assume command until Jackson arrived.[56]

Calhoun next issued orders to Jackson, telling the general to "repair, with as little delay as practicable, to Fort Scott, and assume the immediate command of the forces in that section of the southern division." Calhoun enclosed copies of previous correspondence to Gaines, making Jackson aware of the administration's restrictions with regard to the Spanish posts. Informing Jackson that his force would consist of 800 regulars and 1,000 Georgia Militia, the secretary went on to estimate the hostile force in Florida at 2,700 men. He also gave Jackson authority to call on the adjacent states for additional militia as needed.[57]

Although the American offensive had yet to begin, for some men, there was little doubt as to the outcome. While Andrew Jackson was busy gathering his army, his nephew John Donnelson was in Pensacola purchasing property for a number of the general's acquaintances.[58]

Although Edmund Gaines was an extremely competent, experienced officer, there were several good reasons for Secretary Calhoun to place Andrew Jackson in command of the Seminole War. The first reason was fundamentally bureaucratic: Jackson was in command of the Southern Military District. The second reason was more practical: No one could raise large numbers of volunteer soldiers better than the Hero of New Orleans. The third reason for putting Jackson in charge was less obvious. Either Gaines or Jackson could accomplish the task of punishing the

---

56 Calhoun to Gaines, 26 December 1817, *ASP:MA,* 1:689-690.
57 Calhoun to Jackson, 26 December 1817, *ASP:MA,* 1:690.
58 Statement of John H. Eaton, [no date], *ASP:MA,* 1:751.

Seminoles, but Jackson would do it quicker and more permanently. Gaines would punish the Indians and drive them from the borderlands. Jackson would drive the Seminoles from north Florida and leave them devastated.

There were, of course, good reasons for *not* placing Jackson in command. The first was his health. Jackson was only fifty years old, but those had been an extremely hard fifty years. At age fourteen, Jackson had contracted smallpox while being held captive by British soldiers during the Revolutionary War. He also carried a scar on his scalp from the blow of a British sword. Twenty-five years later he suffered a bullet wound to the chest during a duel with Charles Dickson. The bullet shattered his ribs and buried itself near his heart, remaining there for the rest of his life. Shot in the left shoulder during a brawl with the Benton brothers in downtown Nashville seven years later, Jackson refused to have his arm amputated, and was confined to his bed for three weeks. A month later he was commanding troops in the field. Contracting chronic dysentery during the Creek War, Jackson "sometimes subsisted on nothing more than diluted gin" and by then his health had been "permanently broken." Andrew Jackson was not a healthy man, but unless his condition was terminal, he was not going to be stopped.[59]

Then there was the matter of Jackson's temperament. He was an obsessively determined man who had little respect for anyone else's point of view. For him, the end always justified the means, and expediency was considered a virtue. Put in command of a large force, Jackson might do whatever he pleased, whether it was what the administration wanted or not. The only authority Andrew Jackson truly respected was Andrew Jackson.

---

59 Robert V. Remini, *The Life of Andrew Jackson*, (New York: Harper & Row), 1988), 8-9, 54, 70; James Marquis, *The Life of Andrew Jackson,* (Indianapolis, IN: Bobbs-Merrill, 1938), 157; Sean Wilentz, *Andrew Jackson,* (New York: Henry Holt, 2005), 26-27.

The idea that Jackson might do as he pleased was not mere speculation. The general had challenged the administration's orders to Gaines before taking command of the Seminole War, especially the part that prohibited the army from pursuing hostile Indians who took refuge in Spanish posts. "The arms of the United States must be carried to any post within the limits of East Florida, where an Enemy is permitted and protected," he told Calhoun. The notion of having to wait for permission from Washington before attacking a Spanish post was unthinkable to Jackson.[60]

In order to carry the war into Florida, Jackson first had to do two things: Gather an army and see that it was well supplied. He would find it much easier to raise the army than to feed it. Bypassing the Governor of Tennessee, whose responsibility it was to call out the volunteers, Jackson sent a circular to his former officers on 11 January 1818, requesting they raise 1,000 volunteers from West Tennessee. "The Seminole Indians have raised the war hatchet. They have stained our land with the blood of our citizens; their war spirit must be put down, and they taught to know that their safety depends upon the friendship and protection of the United States." Jackson gave the officers five days to notify him of their ability to recruit, arm, and equip the volunteers, then asked them to meet with him in Nashville on 19 January.[61]

While Jackson was gathering his forces, General Gaines was desperately trying to keep the men at Fort Scott from starving. For over a month, Gaines had been diligently requesting supplies and reinforcements from his temporary headquarters at Hartford, Georgia. Although an advance of $2,000 had been sent to the contractor, supplies had not been received and Muhlenberg's vessels had yet to arrive at Fort Scott. Indeed, with Muhlenberg's men having eaten most of the rations on their vessels, there was

---

60 Jackson to President James Monroe, 6 January 1818, Bassett, *Correspondence of Jackson,* 2:345-346.

61 Jackson's Circular, 11 January 1819, *ASP:MA,* 1:767.

the real possibility that the ships would have to return to Mobile, taking the much needed munitions and military stores with them.[62]

After struggling for well over a month to ascend the Apalachicola, Muhlenberg finally arrived at Fort Scott in mid-January, only to find that several officers had resigned, reinforcements had not arrived, and the men were almost out of food. Having consumed nearly all the rations on board their boats, Muhlenberg's reinforcements only added to the hunger at Fort Scott. Colonel Arbuckle, in command at Fort Scott, wrote to Jackson about the critical situation he was now faced with. Although part of Arbuckle's command had gone to Fowltown, burned the deserted village, and driven back a number of cattle, he was still critically short of food. With only two days' worth of meat left and about a month's supply of flour, Arbuckle told Jackson he would do his best to maintain his position but doubted his ability to remain at Fort Scott.[63]

South of the border, the Indians' British friends were attempting to forestall the impending disaster. Still believing that the land taken from the Creeks by Andrew Jackson in 1814 should be returned to them, Alexander Arbuthnot wrote to Agent Mitchell on 19 January 1818, arguing that nothing had been done to prohibit the influx of settlers onto Indian lands. "Far from any stop being put to their inroads and encroachments, they are pouring in by hundreds at a time, not only from land side, but both troops and settlers ascending the Apalachicola river in vessel-loads." Accusing Forbes & Company merchants Hambly and Doyle of instigating the troubles, Arbuthnot told Mitchell the pair had been seized for selling Indian land to the whites without the Indians' knowledge or consent, and that he wished to see "an

62 Gaines to Calhoun, 9 and 30 January 1818, *ASP:MA,* 1:690 and 694.

63 Arbuckle to Jackson, 12 January 1818, *ASP:MA,* 1:695.

end to a war" which he thought would eventually ruin the Indians.[64]

That same day, at the Suwannee River, Arbuthnot's clerk Peter B. Cook wrote to Elizabeth Carney of New Providence, Nassau, describing the situation in Spanish Florida. "We are threatened every day by the d—d Americans; not threatened only, but they have made an attempt, which we have stopped. On 1st December I marched with thirty men to go against them." Describing the attack on Fort Hughes a week later, Cook said, "The balls flew like hail-stones; there was a ball that had like to have done my job; it just cleared my breast. For six days and six nights we had to encamp in the wild woods, and it was constantly raining night and day; and as for the cold, I suffered very much by it; in the morning the water would be frozen about an inch thick." Informing her of the attack on Lieutenant Scott, Cook added, "There was a boat that was taken by the Indians, that had in it thirty men, seven women, and four small children; there were six of the men got clear and one woman saved, and all the rest of them got killed; the children were taken by the heels, and their brains dashed out against the boat."[65]

Blaming the storekeepers for causing the turmoil, Cook said, "We have got Mr. Hambly and Doyle prisoners, and we are going to send them to Nassau to stand their trial, as they have caused all this disturbance." Aware that the Americans intended "to take possession of the nation in March," Cook informed her that she might see him sooner than expected, especially if the Americans came while their vessels were away, forcing them to flee in Indian canoes. Even though he agreed with Arbuthnot as to the mistreatment of the Indians, Cook was not on good terms with his employer, who had threatened his life several times. For that

64 Arbuthnot to David Mitchell, 19 January 1818, *ASP:FR,* 4:611.

65 Peter B. Cook to Elizabeth A. Carney, 19 January 1818, *ASP:FR,* 4:605.

reason Cook also intended to "punish him by the law" when they returned to Nassau.[66]

Jackson arrived at Fort Hawkins on 9 February. What he found was not encouraging. General Glasscock's Georgia militiamen had returned to their homes after their terms of enlistment had expired, leaving the frontier exposed. Fort Scott was without provisions and the likelihood of obtaining rations seemed dismal. Lt. Col. William Trimble had written from New Orleans, concerned that supplies would be intercepted before reaching Fort Scott, and those ordered by General Gaines had yet to arrive. Prior to leaving, Jackson reported the situation to Calhoun, then headed for Gaines's temporary headquarters at Hartford.[67]

Running critically low on supplies, Arbuckle was finding it difficult to maintain his position at Fort Scott. Occasionally he would send a boat downriver in an attempt to ascertain the strength of the enemy. On one such trip, the boat's commander reported a grisly discovery: "Come to a little before sunset about one mile above the Styx, near to a pile of driftwood on which we saw the bodies of some of our slaughtered soldiers who were massacred with Lt. Scott."[68]

On the evening of 19 February Gaines received an alarming message from Arbuckle, threatening to abandon Fort Scott if supplies did not arrive soon. Unwilling to allow such an action,

66 *Ibid;* John W. Griffin, ed. *Narrative of a Voyage to the Spanish Main, in the Ship "Two Friends,"* a Facsimile Reproduction of the 1819 Edition, with an Introduction and Index by John W. Griffin, (Gainesville: University Presses of Florida, 1978), 215-216.

67 Jackson to Calhoun, *ASP:MA,* 1:697; Lt. Col. William A. Trimble to Jackson, 12 February 1818, Meriwether, *Papers of John C. Calhoun,* 2:136; Gibson to Jackson, 12 February 1818, Bassett, *Correspondence of Jackson,* 2:354.

68 Lieutenant Edward Randolph's diary entry of 15 February 1818, in the Edward Brett Randolph Diary, #619-z, Southern Historical Collection, The Wilson Library, University of North Carolina at Chapel Hill.

Gaines and a small party boarded a boat and headed down the Flint River for Fort Scott. Forty miles downstream the boat capsized, killing everyone except Gaines and one other soldier. Nearly starved after wandering through the woods for almost a week, Gaines finally reached the safety of Fort Scott on 26 February.[69]

Jackson arrived at Fort Scott on the evening of 9 March and found the post critically short of provisions. Those that the Tennessee Volunteers had brought with them were nearly exhausted. Something needed to be done, and very soon. Fearing the supply vessels coming from New Orleans would have just as much difficulty ascending the Apalachicola as Muhlenberg's convoy had, Jackson decided to go on the march. If the food couldn't reach him, he'd go to the food. On the morning of the 11th, Jackson and his soldiers left Fort Scott, crossed the Flint, and headed south toward the Florida border. It was no small army. Jackson's force would eventually consist of about 1,000 Tennessee volunteers, a like number of Georgia militia, and around 800 regulars. Accompanying the white force was a contingent of around 2,000 Lower Creek allies.[70]

Five days after leaving Fort Scott, Jackson and his troops arrived at the former site of the Negro Fort. He immediately ordered the construction of a new, smaller fort over the remains of

---

69 Jackson to Calhoun, 25 March 1818, *ASP:MA,* 1:698-699; Jackson to Calhoun, 25 March 1818, *ASP:FR,* 4:572-573; Heitman, *Register and Dictionary of the U.S. Army,* 1: 205; Heidler and Heidler, *Old Hickory's War,* 131.

70 Jackson to Calhoun, 25 March 1818, *ASP:FR,* 4:572-573; John Banks, *A Short Biographical Sketch of the Undersigned by Himself,* (Austell, GA: Privately Printed, 1936), 9, 11; Calhoun to Jackson, 26 December 1817, *ASP:MA,* 1:690; Jackson to Calhoun, 12 January 1818, *ASP:MA, 1:690*; Meriwether, *Papers of John C. Calhoun,* 2:347; *Niles Register,* 14 February and April 25, 1818; *The Reflector,* 21 March and 14 April, 1818; Extract of letter from Ft. Hawkins in the *National Intelligencer,* 18 December 1818.

the old one. The fortification was named Fort Gadsden in honor of Jackson's aide-de-camp, Lt. James Gadsden, who was in charge of construction. After receiving word that a vessel had been seen approaching the bay, Jackson dispatched a boat down the Apalachicola and ordered Quartermaster George Gibson to wait at the bay for the arrival of the other vessels from New Orleans. Three days later, Gibson reported to Jackson that the flotilla had not been sighted since it passed Fort Bowyer at Mobile.[71]

Until such time as supplies arrived, Jackson put his men on half rations and kept them busy working on the fort. The structure would be needed to protect any supplies that arrived after Jackson and his army departed. Fully equipped or not, Jackson was determined to begin his campaign. On 24 March the supply vessels arrived on scene, allowing Jackson to provide his men with adequate provisions for the march.[72]

After packing rations sufficient to last eight days, Jackson and his troops left Fort Gadsden on 25 March and headed northeast towards the Mikasuki towns around Lake Miccosukee, north of present-day Tallahassee. After crossing the Ochlockonee River and setting up camp on the evening of the 30th, Jackson ordered Major Twiggs to take one company of the 7th Infantry and about two hundred allied Creeks and advance on the Indian town of Tallahassie.[73]

The next morning Twiggs discovered the town deserted, ordered it burned, then set up camp and waited for Jackson. Reinforced by Tennessee volunteers and allied Creeks, Jackson quickly ordered an advance. Within a few miles of Chief

---

71 Jackson to Calhoun, 25 March 1818, *ASP:MA,* 1:698-699; Banks, *Biographical Sketch,* 12.

72 Calhoun to Jackson, 26 December 1818, *ASP:MA,* 1:698-699; *Ibid.*

73 Jackson to Calhoun, 8 April 1818, *ASP:MA,* 1:699-700; Robert Butler to Brig. Genl. Daniel Parker, 3 May 1818, *ASP:MA,* 1:703-704; Banks, *Biographical Sketch,* 12.

Kenhagee's town, the troops noticed a number of Indians herding cattle near a large pond. To cut off the enemy's retreat, Jackson ordered the right and left columns to advance.[74]

Unable to hold their ground against an army the size of Jackson's, nearly three hundred warriors briskly exchanged fire with the Americans, and then fled the field. The sudden appearance of a number of Jackson's allied Creeks caused some confusion, and the soldiers, thinking the Seminoles were friendly Creeks, ceased fire, giving the Seminoles time to escape. At the end of the day, there were fourteen Indians killed, several wounded, and four women taken prisoner.[75]

During their search of the Miccosukee towns, "more than fifty fresh scalps" were discovered in the council houses. In the center of the public square, an "old Red Stick's standard" (red pole) was erected, reportedly "crowned with the scalps, recognized by the hair, as torn from the heads of the unfortunate companions of Scott." Prior to leaving, the troops burned nearly three hundred homes and confiscated thousands of bushels of corn and hundreds of cattle.[76]

To the south, the navy was doing its part. On 1 April Lieutenant McKeever's ship arrived at the Bay of St. Marks, but instead of hoisting the American flag, he displayed the British Union Jack. The next day, out of curiosity, a Spanish lieutenant from St. Marks came on board, inquiring as to the nature of McKeever's business and whether he had authority from the Captain General of Cuba to enter Spanish territory. Posing as a British officer, McKeever told the lieutenant that he would explain the nature of his business after Woodbine arrived, indicating that

---

74 *Ibid.*

75 Butler to Parker, 3 May 1818, *ASP:MA,* 1:703-704.

76 *Ibid;* Jackson to Calhoun, 8 April 1818, *ASP:FR,* 4:574-575; Banks, *Biographical Sketch,* 13; Butler to Parker, 3 May 1818, *ASP:MA,* 1:703-704.

the supplies were intended to aid Prophet Francis and his warriors in their present distress. Replying that Woodbine, Prophet Francis, and Arbuthnot were friends of the Spanish commandant at St. Marks, the lieutenant told McKeever that Arbuthnot was still at St. Marks and that he should expect a visit from Prophet Francis shortly.[77]

That same day, Arbuthnot forwarded a message to his son John at the store on the Suwannee River, informing him of Jackson's movements and telling him to urge Chief Boleck (Bowlegs) to move to the opposite side of the Suwannee for safety. Estimating Jackson's army to be about 3,000 strong and with eighteen vessels anchored off Apalachicola, Arbuthnot told his son that he expected the Americans to leave after destroying the settlements but would know more once the Spanish commandant determined their motives. Concerned for their trade goods, he added, "If the schooner is returned, get all the goods on board of her, and let her start off for Manatee creek, in the bottom of Cedar Key bay."[78]

The next day, the Red Stick Prophet Francis and the chief Homathlemico arrived at St. Marks and took a canoe out to McKeever's vessel, which was still flying the British flag. Instead of being welcomed by their English friends, the pair was immediately slapped in irons.[79]

After instructing the volunteers to scour the countryside around Lake Miccosukee for any hidden Indians, Jackson and the regulars commenced marching toward St. Marks on 5 April, convinced the Mikasuki and their allies had fled in that direction. Shortly after setting up camp the following day, Jackson

---

77 Lt. Isaac McKeever's Statement, 5 June 1819, *ASP:MA,* 1:763; Jackson to Calhoun, 8 April 1818, *ASP:FR,* 4:574-575.

78 Arbuthnot to son John Arbuthnot, 2 April 1818, *ASP:FR,* 1:584.

79 Jackson to Calhoun, 8 April 1818, *ASP:MA* 1: 699-700; Butler to Parker, 3 May 1818, *ASP:MA,* 1:703-704; Banks, *Biographical Sketch,* 13.

dispatched a message to Commanding Officer Francisco Caso y Luengo at St. Marks, informing him that President Monroe had authorized his movement into Florida to chastise the Seminoles and blacks accused of carrying on a "cruel and unprovoked war" with citizens of the United States.[80]

Citing threats by the hostile Indians to take possession of St. Marks, Jackson told Luengo it would be expedient to garrison the post with American troops until the war ended. Assuring Luengo he had come as a friend, Jackson promised to respect the Spaniards' rights and properties and would refer the subject of taking possession of the garrison to their respective governments for amicable adjustment. Luengo congratulated Jackson on his success against the Mikasuki Indians but denied accusations that the hostile Indians had been supplied with war materials at St. Marks and of his having violated the law of neutrality. Although he promised to show good faith toward any troops who would assist in its defense, Luengo explained that he was not authorized to allow American troops to garrison St. Marks until he received orders from his government. Unfazed by Luengo's logic, Jackson explained, "The occupation of St. Marks is essential to the accomplishment of my campaign."[81]

Without waiting for Luengo's response, Jackson ordered Major Twiggs to take possession of Fort St. Marks on the morning of 7 April. Accompanied by three companies of the 7th Infantry and one from the 4th, Twiggs marched through the open gates, taking the Spaniards by complete surprise. After appointing Captain George Vashon of the 4th Infantry as commanding officer, Jackson ordered an inventory to be

---

80 Butler to Parker, 3 May 1818, *ASP:MA,* 1:703-704; Banks, *Biographical Sketch,* 13.

81 Jackson to Francisco Caso Luengo, 6 April 1818, *ASP:MA,* 1:704-705; Luengo to Jackson, 7 April 1818, *ASP:MA,* 1:705; Jackson to Luengo, 7 April 1818, *ASP:MA,* 1:705.

taken. One of the items found and placed under lock and key was the person of Alexander Arbuthnot, who had taken refuge in the post as a guest of the commanding officer.[82]

On the morning of the 8th Prophet Francis and Homathlemico were brought ashore and immediately hung. Jackson forwarded the news to Calhoun the following day, commenting that Homathlemico had been in command of the party who, "so inhumanly sacrificed Scott and his companions." He also reported that Arbuthnot was being held in confinement until evidence could be gathered confirming his guilt. It was doubtful that anyone would be looking for evidence to confirm his innocence.[83]

After scouring the countryside near the Mikasuki towns, the Tennessee volunteers and allied Creeks reunited with Jackson's regulars at his camp near St. Marks, then headed southeast towards the Suwannee River. On the morning of the 12th Major Kinnard, a mixed-blood in command of a detachment of allied Creeks, and Captain Bell with fifty Tennessee volunteers, surprised Red Stick chief Peter McQueen's band near Econfina Creek. Following an hour-long fight in the swamp, the Indians fled and were pursued for three miles, after which they fought for several more hours, resulting in approximately thirty-seven warriors being killed and ninety-eight women and children taken prisoner. McQueen and nearly two hundred warriors managed to escape.[84]

---

82 Jackson to Calhoun, 8 April 1818, *ASP:MA,* 1:699-700; Butler to Parker, 3 May 1818, *ASP:MA,* 1:703-704; Banks, *Biographical Sketch,* 13.

83 McKeever's Statement, 5 June 1818, *ASP:MA,* 1:763; Jackson to Calhoun, 8 April 1818, *ASP:MA,* 1:699-700; Jackson to his wife Rachael, 8 April 1818, Bassett, *Correspondence of Jackson,* 2:357-358; Butler to Parker, 3 May 1818, *ASP:MA,* 1:703-704; Banks, *Biographical Sketch,* 13.

Reporting news of the battle to Agent Mitchell, Chief McIntosh said, "There was among the Hostiles a woman that was in the boat when our friends the white people were killed on the River below Fort Scott. We gave her to her friends. Her Husband and Father are with Genl. Jackson. Major Kinnard took her himself." Elizabeth Stuart had been rescued. The next day, the Creeks reunited with the main body of Jackson's army and proceeded towards the Suwannee River.[85]

After marching for three days, Jackson and his troops arrived at the Suwannee River on the morning of 16 April. Following a short rest, the army marched six more miles before reaching Bowlegs's Town in midafternoon, where Jackson ordered the men into battle formation.[86]

Jackson had hoped to surround the enemy, but the left flank of Tennessee volunteers and allied Creeks engaged the Seminoles and their black allies before the right flank could get into position to prevent their escape. As a consequence nearly three hundred Indians and blacks escaped across the river, fleeing to the black villages south of the Suwannee. Although he was no doubt disappointed for not having killed or taken a large number of Indians or runaway slaves, Andrew Jackson had accomplished his primary mission: The Seminoles had been driven far from the border with Georgia, their homes were in ashes, most of their livestock was slaughtered or taken, and a good portion of their crops were destroyed.

---

84 Jackson to Calhoun, 8 and 20 April 1818, 5 May 1818, *ASP:MA,* 1:699-701, 703-704; Banks, *Biographical Sketch,* 14.

85 McIntosh to Mitchell, 13 April 1818, Hargrett Rare Book and Manuscript Library, Telamon Cuyler Collection, The University of Georgia Libraries, presented by the Digital Library of Georgia, Document TCC921; Banks, *Biographical Sketch,* 14.

86 Jackson to Calhoun, 20 April 1818, *ASP:MA,* 1:700-701; Banks, *Biographical Sketch,* 14.

Whatever prosperity the Seminoles of north Florida had enjoyed was gone.[87]

The next morning Jackson dispatched foraging parties into the surrounding countryside. After burning nearly thirty houses, they returned with several thousand bushels of corn and ninety head of cattle. The following evening, hoping to obtain provisions at Bowlegs's town, former Royal Marine officer Robert Ambrister and Peter Cook, Arbuthnot's clerk, unsuspectingly walked into the army camp and were taken prisoner. After Jackson was told that Arbuthnot's schooner was anchored in the bay, he ordered Lieutenant Gadsden to descend the river and capture the vessel.[88]

Having taken possession of St. Marks, destroyed Bowlegs's Town, and captured Arbuthnot and Ambrister, Jackson wrote to Calhoun that he believed the war was at an end. Just in case, the positions at St. Marks and Ft. Gadsden would be held, which would enable any further hostilities to be dealt with quickly. Once those positions were well garrisoned and "security given to the southern frontier," Jackson would return to Nashville. In the meantime, the general planned a reconnaissance in the area around Pensacola. Intelligence had informed him that several hundred hostiles were near the capital, being fed and supplied by Governor José Masot.[89]

As Jackson and his army left the Suwannee, it appeared as if the war were over. General Glasscock was ordered to march the Georgia Militia to Hartford and muster them out of service, while Chief McIntosh was instructed to discharge the allied Creeks from Fort Scott. The sick and wounded were put aboard Arbuthnot's schooner to be transported to St. Marks, while Jackson prepared to return overland with the remaining troops. On 25 April, the

---

87 Jackson to Calhoun, 20 April 1818, *ASP:MA,* 1:700-701.

88 *Ibid.*

89 *Ibid.*

schooner, the troops, and General Jackson all arrived back at St. Marks.[90]

The next day Jackson sent another letter to Secretary Calhoun informing him of their arrival at St. Marks and noting that he had confiscated correspondence on board Arbuthnot's schooner "all pointing out the instigators of this savage war." Assuring Calhoun of their defeat, Jackson remarked, "The Indian forces have been divided and scattered, and cut off from all communication with those unprincipled agents of foreign nations who have deluded them to ruin; they have not the power, if the will remain, of again annoying our frontier." What Jackson did not tell Calhoun was that Arbuthnot and Ambrister were going to be tried that day before a hastily convened military tribunal.[91]

At noon, General Gaines, as presiding officer, called the military court of justice to order. Twelve officers stood in judgment. William Hambly, Edmund Doyle, and Arbuthnot's clerk Peter Cook testified against the two British subjects. No one questioned the court's legality or right of jurisdiction.[92]

After presenting evidence against the two men, the court charged Arbuthnot with inciting the Creeks to make war against the United States and her citizens; acting as a spy; aiding, abetting, and comforting the enemy; supplying the Indians with means of war; and inciting the Indians to capture Hambly and Doyle with the intent of condemning them to death. Ambrister was charged with aiding, abetting, and comforting the enemy; supplying them with the means of war; and leading the Lower Creeks in war with the United States.[93]

---

90 *Ibid.*

91 *Ibid.*

92 General Order by Jackson, 26 April 1818, *ASP:MA,* 1:721; Griffin, *Voyage to the Spanish Main,* 214-216.

93 *Ibid;* Charges against Robert C. Ambrister, 27 April 1818, *ASP:MA,* 1:731; Griffin, *Voyage to the Spanish Main,* 252-253, 264-265.

The court found Arbuthnot guilty of all charges with the exception of acting as a spy and sentenced him to be hanged. Ambrister was found guilty of all charges and sentenced to be shot, presumably out of respect for his military background. Ambrister begged the court's mercy and actually received it. Perhaps taking into account that the young man could be considered a British prisoner of war, the court changed the punishment to fifty lashes on his bare back and confinement for one year at hard labor. Jackson, always one to interpret the rules the way he cared to, overturned the court's decision, ordering Ambrister to be shot on the basis of, "an established principle of the laws of nations" arguing that "any individual of a nation making war against the citizens of another nation, they being at peace, forfeits his allegiance, and becomes an outlaw and pirate." By those same standards, Jackson himself could have been considered an "outlaw and pirate" for his actions against the Spaniards. On 29 April seventy-year-old Alexander Arbuthnot was hung from the mast of his schooner *Chance*. Robert Chrystie Ambrister, soldier of fortune, was shot to death by firing squad.[94]

At the end of the trial, but before the executions took place, Jackson, the Tennessee Volunteers, and the regulars headed for Fort Gadsden. Soon after their arrival on 2 May, Jackson began soliciting affidavits attesting to the presence of hostile Indians at Pensacola. Two days later, he wrote to Col. William Davenport, announcing, "a large assemblage of Indian Warriors, has collected at Pensacola (five hundred in number) who are fed and countenanced by the Governor." Once the Governor was either "punished or shipped as Circumstances may require," Jackson felt confident the southern frontier would be safe and peaceful.[95]

---

94 Calhoun to Jackson, 14 August 1818, *ASP:MA,* 1:734-735; Griffin, *Voyage to the Spanish Main,* 265-272.

95 Jackson to William Davenport, 4 May 1818, Bassett, *Correspondence of Jackson,* 2:364-365; Depositions, 3-18 September, 1818, *ASP:MA,* 1:716-717, 762-763.

After submitting his official report to Calhoun, Jackson and the troops left Fort Gadsden and began the one-hundred-mile trek to Pensacola, arriving at the Escambia River on 20 May. Aware of their movements through West Florida, Governor Masot dispatched a letter of protest to Jackson, demanding that he leave the territory. "If you do not, and continue your aggressions, I shall repel force by force. The consequence in this case will, doubtless, be the effusion of blood, and also an interruption of the harmony which has hitherto reigned between our respective nations; but, as the repeller [*sic*] of an insult has never been deemed the aggressor, you will be responsible, both of God and man, for all the fatal consequences which may result."[96]

Jackson brushed off the threats and replied that he took Masot's remarks as "an open indication of hostile feelings." Justifying his actions, Jackson remarked, "I deem it politic and necessary to occupy Pensacola and the Barrancas with an American garrison" to be held "until Spain has the power or will to maintain her neutrality. This is justifiable on the immutable principles of self-defense." If Masot refused to surrender the capital, Jackson warned he would "enter Pensacola by violence, and assume the Government until the transaction can be amicably adjusted by the two Governments."[97]

On 21 May Jackson and over 1,000 troops entered Pensacola and captured the town with little resistance. Masot had fled the city and taken refuge in Fort Barrancas. Four days later, Jackson took up position before Fort Barrancas and the Spaniards opened fire on the American troops. After two days of sporadic firing, the governor agreed to suspend hostilities and a capitulation was signed on 28 May.[98]

---

96 Governor Jose Masot to Jackson, 23 May 1818, *ASP:MA,* 1:712.

97 Jackson to Masot, 23 May 1818, *ASP:MA,* 1:712-713.

98 Jackson to Calhoun, 2 June 1818, *ASP:MA,* 1:708-709.

After leaving American troops in charge at St. Marks and Pensacola and with strong garrisons stationed at Fort Gadsden and Fort Scott, Andrew Jackson left Pensacola and arrived at Camp Montgomery, above Mobile, on 1 June 1818. The next day he sent a letter to Secretary Calhoun announcing the end of the war. "The Seminole War may now be considered at a close, tranquility again restored to the southern frontier of the United States."[99]

99 *Ibid;* Jackson to Calhoun, 2 June 1818, *ASP:FR,* 4:602-603; Jackson to President James Monroe, (private), 2 June 1818, Bassett, *Correspondence of Jackson,* 2:376-378.

The Crew of Lieutenant Scott's Boat

Who were the people slain in the attack on Lieutenant Scott's boat? In order to find out, we needed a list of passengers. Knowing the army's penchant for record keeping, we attempted to find a casualty report. Much to our surprise, we couldn't find one. This doesn't mean it doesn't exist; heaven knows there were plenty of opportunities in the past two centuries for it to get misplaced. There is also the possibility we haven't looked in the right place. At any rate, curiosity turned into an obsession. We *had* to know who those people were, and we wanted to tell their story.

The only thing we really knew was that they were from the Fourth and Seventh Infantry Regiments. After consulting with the helpful research staff at the National Archives, it was decided that the best way to compile a list of the deceased would be to review the monthly muster rolls for those two regiments. A muster roll is a preprinted form, about 24″ x 36″, that each company commander was required to submit to the war department on a monthly basis. Its purpose was to record the status of each man in the company, whether he was present, sick, or absent, and for what reason. Each regiment might be made up of eight or ten companies, and each company was supposedly made up of fifty men, though the number was often less. Going through the rolls was a time consuming process, but fascinating nonetheless.

Our method was to look at the rolls from October to December 1817 and January and February 1818. Any change in the makeup of a company should have been noted somewhere in the reports. One can easily imagine our excitement the first time we came across that fateful notation: "Killed in action on the Apalachicola River, November 30, 1817." After several days' work, we had gone through all the available muster rolls for those two regiments and had compiled a list of twenty-six men (twenty-five enlisted and one officer) who had died that day.

We were thrilled at the accomplishment, but there was a problem: There were supposedly forty-one soldiers on the boat. Who were the other fifteen? We knew that six had escaped and found their way to Fort Scott. Lucky for them, but unfortunate for us, as only those "killed in action" had a notation on the muster rolls. There were any number of men listed as being on the sick list, but it was impossible to tell if they were one of the four wounded or simply victims of disease. It looked as if the survivors' names would remain a mystery.

Fortunately, the Register of Enlistments, which covered all soldiers from the 1790s to the early 1900s, was on microfilm and could be ordered through the Family History Center at the local Mormon Church. It was also fortunate that the records were broken down into time periods. We certainly didn't care to go through the names of everyone who had served in the Civil War. The bad part was that we did have to go through the names of everyone who had served in the War of 1812, of which there were many thousands.

It was a slow process, but we were in no particular hurry. Mary Lou would order a microfilm, a few weeks later the church would call to tell her it was in, and she would go down during lunch hour or after work and look it over. One advantage of going through the Register of Enlistments was that it provided a cross-check of our muster roll search. If the twenty-five enlisted men we had found were on one list, they ought to be on the other. As it turned out, they were. The Register of Enlistments also provided physical descriptions, occupations, and places of birth. Also included was information concerning promotions, demotions, and disciplinary actions. Our twenty-five soldiers began to take on personalities.

Thomas Woodward, who had related the details of Elizabeth's capture and rescue, also provided two other names. One was Sgt. Frederick McIntosh, the Scotsman who had supposedly fired the small cannon during the attack. Woodward also mentioned someone named Gray, who had managed to escape. After looking through the register, process of elimination left us with Private John Gray of Virginia.

While doing other research into the massacre we were able to add one other name to the list. A search through the correspondence of John C. Calhoun revealed a letter from General Gaines attesting to the veracity of a pension claim by one William James, who had been wounded on 30 November 1817 during the war with the Seminoles. He had lost some fingers.[1]

One name on the list that proved questionable was Private James Shirley. The Register of Enlistments said he was killed in action either 30 November or 15 December 1817. Major Muhlenberg's vessels were, in fact, attacked on 15 December, leaving two men dead. In the end, there was a fifty percent chance of his being on Scott's boat, so we couldn't leave him off the list.[2]

So who were the other nine men? We had no idea. There were a few muster rolls missing, but one would think we'd have found any missing names while going through the Register of Enlistments. We didn't.

The matter rested there for several years. Then Mary Lou discovered the Register of Enlistments was available on-line, from Ancestry.com. She could now go through it at home at a leisurely pace, instead of rushing through a microfilm on her lunch hour. To our surprise, her efforts paid off. Overlooked had been James Thompson, Nathan Gorman, and Joseph Wheadon, the last two being in companies from the 2nd Artillery.

We also added David Brewer, Wilson Wall, and Banister Young, who were reported killed in action on 1 December 1817,

1 Gaines to Calhoun, 31 July 1818, W. Edwin Hemphill, ed., *The Papers of John C. Calhoun,* 28 vols. (Columbia: University of South Carolina Press for the Southern Caroliniana Society, 1963), 2:445.

2 Adjutant General's Office, Muster Rolls, Orders and Returns of the Regular Army Organizations, 1780s to 1917, RG 94: Records of the Adjutant General's Office, NA; *Register of Enlistments,* NA.

and William Desern, slain either on 1 or 2 December 1817. Since there were no other battles reported for those dates and they were so close to the Scott Massacre, we thought it possible those men were on the boat. After all, muster rolls and monthly post returns were often filled out well after the fact, especially during wartime, and the person filling them out may not have known the exact date of the attack.

Will the list ever be complete? Probably not. We're still two names short. Also, as mentioned above, some of those men may not actually have been on the boat. Then again, perhaps there were not a total of forty-one men on board. Reports indicated that Lt. Scott had substituted "about" twenty men before proceeding back to Fort Scott. Also, in the message he sent from Spanish Bluff, Scott said his command "did not exceed" forty men, meaning it could have been less.

There are a few other factors that need to be taken into consideration. The two men who do not have physical descriptions in their enlistment records (Frederick McIntosh and David Brewer) enlisted after the War of 1812 had ended. As the army downsized, record keeping and enlistment standards may have suffered. A notation in McIntosh's record also provides another clue: He had enlisted as a substitute for a man named Youngblood. The army wanted men, and they often didn't care what their names were or how they came by the men's services. If a soldier could find some willing soul to finish out the term of his enlistment, the commanding officer might be happy to let him go, especially if that person were a disciplinary problem. Another possibility is that one or more of the invalids may have been seamen from the transport vessels. Without an official list specifically naming the casualties, we can never know for sure who these unfortunate people were.

Given below is our list of the passengers we believe were or may have been on Lieutenant Scott's vessel, along with any information we have been able to glean from muster rolls, enlistment records, or other sources.

Lt. Richard W. Scott, 7th Infantry, Co C. (commanded by Capt. George Birch). Scott was born in Virginia but his vital statistics are not recorded. He was commissioned an Ensign in the 35th Infantry on 31 March 1813. A year later he was promoted to 3rd Lieutenant, then to 2nd Lieutenant on the first of October 1814. In the downsizing and reorganization of the army after the War of 1812, he was transferred to the 7th Infantry and promoted to 1st Lieutenant on 30 April 1817. At a 4 July 1818 celebration at Fort Hawkins, an officer offered a toast to Lt. Scott and other fallen comrades "who were so unfortunately sacrificed" in the conflict with the Seminoles, "Nature had molded them for nobler services, but fate decreed their destiny. Let us treasure the memory of those whom we so much lamented to have lost."[3]

Private John Asbury (age 22), 7th Infantry, Co. B (Capt. David E. Twiggs). Asbury was born in Henry County, Virginia, in 1795 and enlisted on 3 November 1813. He was a 5′ 10-11″ farmer with dark complexion, dark hair, and grey or dark eyes.

Sergeant David Brewer, 4th Infantry, Co. D (Capt. James E. Dinkins). Brewer's vital statistics and military career were not recorded in the enlistment records.

Private David Brooks (age 37), 7th Infantry, Co. B (Capt. David E. Twiggs). Brooks was born in Amelia County, Virginia, in 1776 and enlisted on 25 September 1813. He was a 5′ 11″ farmer with dark complexion, light hair, and blue eyes.

---

3 *The Reflector*, 7 July and 4 August 1818.

Private Charles Craft (age 34-36), 7th Infantry, Co. E (Capt. John Corbally). Craft was born in North Carolina in either 1781 or 1783 and enlisted on 26 June 1813. He was a 5′ 10½″ farmer with fair complexion, light hair, and blue eyes. On 31 January 1813, he was promoted to corporal but reduced to private on 31 May 1817.

Private Reason Crump (age 42), 7th Infantry, Co. I (Capt. Elijah Montgomery). Crump was born in Abbeville, South Carolina, in 1775 and enlisted on 13 or 16 December 1813. He was a 5′ 11″ farmer with light complexion, light or dark hair, and dark eyes.

Private William Darbey (age 29), 7th Infantry, Co. C (Capt. George Birch). Darbey was born in Spartanburgh, South Carolina, in 1788 and enlisted on 8 September 1814. He was a 6′ ½″ farmer with dark complexion, light hair, and dark eyes.

Corporal Archbald Davis (age 20), 7th Infantry, Co. B (Capt. David E. Twiggs). Davis was born in Blount, Tennessee, in 1797 and enlisted on 10 September 1814. He was a 5′ 9″ farmer with fair complexion, light hair, and blue eyes. He was promoted to corporal on 28 December 1814, confined for desertion 10 June 1816, promoted to sergeant 25 February 1817, and reduced to corporal 11 September 1817.

Private Edward Deserne (age 21), 4th Infantry, Co. C (Capt. Peter Muhlenberg). Deserne was born in Surrey County, North Carolina, in 1796 and enlisted on 18 or 19 October 1813. He was a 5′ 1″ farmer with fair/dark complexion, light brown hair, and blue/grey eyes. On 21 April 1817 he was promoted to corporal then reduced to private 17 July 1817.

Private Jonathan Driver (age 25), 7th Infantry, Co. C (Capt. George Birch). Driver was born in South Carolina in 1792 and enlisted on 22 October 1813. He was a 5′ 11″ farmer with fair complexion, fair hair, and blue eyes.

Corporal James Edwards (age 24), 7th Infantry, Co. B (Capt. David E. Twiggs). Edwards was born in Gloucester, Virginia, in 1793 and enlisted between 9 and 14 December 1814. He was a 5′ 8-10″ farmer with fair skin, light/dark hair, and blue eyes. He was promoted to corporal on 22 April 1816, reduced to private 12 July 1816, and again promoted to corporal 25 February 1817.

Private James Fail (Failes) (age 29 or 31), 7th Infantry, Co. E. (Capt. John Corbally). Fail (Failes) was born in Georgia in either 1788 or 1786 and enlisted on 8 May 1813. He was a 5′ 4¾″ farmer with dark complexion, dark hair, and grey eyes.

Private Nathan Gorman (age 21), 2nd Artillery, Co. E (Capt. Sanders Donoho). Gorman was born in Rockingham County, North Carolina, in 1796 and enlisted on 3 November 1814. He was a 5′ 7″ farmer with dark complexion, dark hair, and grey eyes. He deserted from Fort Johnson on 6 August 1816.

Private John Gravit (age 41), 7th Infantry, Co. A (Capt. William Bee). Gravit was born in Franklin, Virginia, in 1776 and enlisted on 20 August 1814. He was a 5′ 6″ farmer with dark/fair complexion, dark hair, and blue eyes. He was put in confinement on 31 December 1815.

Private John Gray (age 35, survivor), 4th Infantry, Co. K (Capt. James H. Hook). Gray was born in Rupert, Bennington County, Vermont in 1782 and enlisted on 31 December 1812. He was a 5′ 9″

farmer with light complexion, light hair, and blue eyes. He was discharged on 31 December 1817 at Fort Scott, his term expired.

Private Jesse Greenlee (age 25), 7th Infantry, Co. A (Capt. William Bee). Greenlee was born in Virginia in 1792 and enlisted on 12 August 1814. He was a 5′ 7″ farmer with fair complexion, dark hair, and blue eyes.

Private John Henderson (age 22), 7th Infantry, Co. B (Capt. David E. Twiggs). Henderson was born in either North Carolina or Virginia in 1795 and enlisted on either 15 September or 16 October 1814. He was a 6′ farmer with fair skin, dark hair, and grey eyes.

Private James Holley (age 26), 7th Infantry, Co. C (Capt. George Birch). Holley was born in Burke County, Georgia, in 1791 and enlisted on 10 October 1813. He was a 5′ 6¾″ farmer with fair complexion, dark hair, and blue eyes.

Private Smith Irvin (age 22), 7th Infantry, Co. B (Capt. David E. Twiggs). Irvin was born in Oglethorpe, Georgia, in 1795 and enlisted on 2 June 1814. He was a 5′ 10″ farmer with fair complexion, dark hair, and blue eyes. On 26 January 1815 he was promoted to corporal, reduced to private 18 November 1815, promoted to corporal 6 April 1816, promoted to sergeant 12 May 1816, reduced to private 18 May 1816, promoted to sergeant 24 May 1816, reduced to private 20 February 1817. Four months later he was tried by Court Martial at Camp Montgomery on 30 June for the theft of a hog and sentenced to pay for the hog.

Corporal William James (age 23 or 24, survivor), 7th Infantry, Co. B (Capt. David E. Twiggs). James was born in Franklin County, North Carolina, in either 1793 or 1794 and enlisted on 8

November 1814. He was a 5′ 8½-10″ farmer with dark/fair complexion, dark hair, and grey/blue eyes. He was listed as a corporal 31 December 1815, wounded in action near Fort Apalachicola 30 November 1817, on sick list 28 February 1818, reduced to private 4 April 1818, and discharged at Fort Gadsden on surgeon's certificate 22 May 1818. He was disabled when his left thumb, fore- and middle fingers were shot off. His right hand was also badly injured. After being discharged he returned to Charlotte, North Carolina, where he taught school for twelve years, then became a merchant.

Private Samuel McDonald (age 20), 7th Infantry, Co. B (Capt. David E. Twiggs). McDonald was born in Edgefield, South Carolina, in 1797 and enlisted on 24 July 1814. He was a 5′ 6″ farmer with fair complexion, light hair, and grey eyes.

Sergeant Frederick McIntosh, 7th Infantry, Co. B (Capt. David E. Twiggs). McIntosh's vital statistics were not listed in the enlistment records. They note that he enlisted on 5 March 1817 as a substitute for William Youngblood. Thomas Woodward recalled that, "There was a Sergeant named McIntosh, a Scotchman, on board, whom I knew well. He was with Colonel, afterwards Gen. Thomas A. Smith, before St. Augustine, Fla. in 1812, and a Sergeant in Capt. Woodruff's company, at the beginning of the war of 1812, and was a favorite among officers and soldiers. He was an own cousin of the Indian General McIntosh you knew, whose grave you say you not long since visited. Sergeant McIntosh was a man of giant size, and perhaps more bodily strength than any man I have known in our service. When he found all on the boat were lost, and nothing more could be done, he went into a little kind of cabin that the Lieutenant had occupied as his quarters, in which was a swivel or small cannon; loaded it, took it on deck, and resting the swivel on one arm ranged it as well as he could, and (the Indians by this time were boarding the boat) with a firebrand, he set off the swivel, which cleared the boat for a few minutes of Indians. At the firing of the swivel he was thrown overboard and drowned, and this clearing of the Indians from the boat for a short time gave Gray a chance to escape."[4]

Private Henry Moore (age 25), 7th Infantry, Co. B (Capt. David E. Twiggs). Moore was born in Richmond, North Carolina, in 1792 and enlisted on 15 November 1814. He was a 5′ 8″ farmer with fair complexion, fair hair, and blue eyes.

Private George Mullis (age 23), 7th Infantry, Co. B (Capt. David E. Twiggs). Mullis was born in Wilkes County, North Carolina, in 1784 and enlisted on either 27 or 29 July 1814. He was a 5′ 8″ farmer with light complexion, light hair, and blue eyes.

Private James O'Neal (age 27), 7th Infantry, Co. I (Capt. Elijah Montgomery). O'Neal was born in Rockbridge, Virginia, in 1791 and enlisted on 17 September 1814. He was a 6′ farmer with light complexion, light hair, and grey eyes. He was listed as a sergeant on 28 February 1815 and reduced to a private 15 March 1815.

Private Jackson Scarborough (age 30), 7th Infantry, Co. I (Capt. Elijah Montgomery). Scarborough was born in Edgecomb, North Carolina, in 1787 and enlisted on 2 October 1814. He was a 5′ 8″ farmer with dark complexion, dark hair, and dark eyes.

Private James Shirley (age 21), 7th Infantry, Co. H (Capt. Thomas Blackstone). Shirley was born in Tennessee in 1796 and enlisted on 17 September 1814. He was a 5′ 7″ farmer with fair complexion, fair hair, and dark eyes.

---

4 Woodward, *Reminiscences*, 53-54.

Private Alfred Simmons (age 19), 7th Infantry, Co. A (Capt. William Bee). Simmons was born in Claiborne, Tennessee, in 1798 and enlisted between 22-27 October 1814. He was a 5′ 7″ farmer with fair complexion, light hair, and blue eyes.

Corporal William P. Sissom (age 27), 7th Infantry, Co. I (Capt. Elijah Montgomery). Sissom was born in Edgefield, South Carolina, in 1790, and the enlistment records state he enlisted on either 7 September or 2 November or July 1814. His occupation was a shoemaker, and he was 5′ 8″ with fair complexion, light hair, and blue eyes. He was promoted to corporal on 31 August 1817.

Private James Thompson (age 35), 7th Infantry, Co. K (Capt. J. S. Allison). Thompson was born in Georgia in 1782 and enlisted on 6 January 1814. He was a 5′ 8″ farmer with light complexion and had dark hair and eyes.

Private Wilson Wall (age 20) 4th Infantry, Capt.William Neilson's company. Wall was born in Montgomery County, North Carolina, in 1797 and enlisted on 10 September 1813. He was a 5′ 7¼″ farmer with fair complexion, light hair, and blue eyes. He was promoted to corporal on 7 November 1816, suspended for one month from 20 June 1817, and reduced to private on 1 August 1817.

Private Joseph Wheadon (age 37), 2nd Artillery, Co. E (Capt. Sanders Donoho). Wheadon was born in Newport, Rhode Island, in 1780 and enlisted on either 4 or 5 August 1814. He was a 5′ 8″ farmer with fair complexion, brown hair, and blue eyes.

Private Henry Williams (age 20), 7th Infantry, Co. A (Capt. William Bee). Williams was born in Virginia in 1797 and enlisted on 21 April 1814. He was a 5′ 3″ farmer with dark/fair complexion, dark brown hair, and brown eyes.

Private Banister Young (age 27), 4th Infantry, Co. D (Capt. James E. Dinkins). Young was born in North Carolina in 1790 and enlisted on 9 October 1813. He was a 5′ 6″ farmer with dark complexion, light hair, and white eyes. He was promoted to corporal on 19 August 1816 and reduced to private 20 November 1816.

Other Military Records

Sergeant John Dill, 7th Infantry, Co. G, (Capt. George Vashon). Dill was born in Darlington County, South Carolina, in 1788 and enlisted on 26 September 1814. He was a 5′ 9½″ farmer with fair complexion, fair hair, and blue eyes. He is listed as a sergeant, 39th Infantry (30 June 1815), transferred to Captain Vashon's company (30 November 1815), reduced from sergeant (14 December 1814), promoted to corporal (1 March 1816), promoted to Sergeant Major (1 April 1818), and discharged at Fort Scott 20 September 1819, term expired.

Sergeant John Stuart (Stewart), 7th Infantry, Co. G (Capt. George Vashon). Stuart was born in Bourbon, Kentucky, in 1794. His occupation is unknown, and he enlisted as a private in the 39th Infantry on 20 July 1814. He was 5′ 7½″ with fair complexion, red hair, and grey eyes. He is listed as a sergeant in the 7th Infantry (June 1815), transferred to Captain Vashon's company (November 1815), and discharged at Fort Scott 19 July 1819 when his term expired. On 13 August 1819 he was commissioned 2nd Lieutenant in the 7th Infantry; promoted to 1st Lieutenant (6 October 1822), on duty at Fort Smith, Arkansas (1822); on duty at Fort Gibson, Indian Territory, (1824); promoted to Captain, Co. C, 7th Infantry (30 June 1828); established Fort Coffee, Indian Territory (1834) and Fort Wayne, Indian Territory (1838), where he died on 8 December of that year.[1]

Captain George Vashon, commanding Co. G, 7th Infantry. Vashon was born in Maryland and resided in Virginia when

1 Obituary, *Western Weekly Review (Franklin, Tennessee)*, 18 January 1839.

he joined the U. S. Army. He was a 1st Lt., 10th Infantry (12 March 1812); adjutant (April to November 1813); Captain (29 November 1813); transferred to 7th Infantry (17 May 1815); and resigned (31 December 1819). He was later appointed Agent then Sub-Agent to the Cherokee residing in Arkansas until his death at the Seneca Agency on 31 December 1835.[2]

Peter B. Cook was born in New Providence, Nassau, where he was a "collector of vendue accounts" and lived with an employer in that line of business until he was discharged after stealing a "considerable sum" from him. He was later hired by Alexander Arbuthnot, who overlooked his first offense, and served as a clerk in Arbuthnot's store in Florida. Shortly after that he was accused of stealing from Arbuthnot who turned him over to the Spanish commandant at St. Marks to be "dealt with according to law." Cook was not on good terms with his employer, who threatened his life several times. For that reason Cook also intended to "punish him by the law" when they returned to Nassau. Three months later Cook testified against his former employer in Arbuthnot and Ambrister's trial. He enlisted as a private in Co. H, 7th Infantry on 13 May 1818 for five years. The Monthly Returns indicate he was at Fort Gadsden on the 31st then deserted on 10 July 1818. He was tried before a General Court Martial on 1 October 1818 at Fort Gadsden before Major D. E. Twiggs, appointed President, and three other officers. He was charged with "deserting with an intention of joining the enemy" and endeavoring to get to the Suwannee where "the Indians and Negroes (who are in arms against the United States)" were said to be assembled. In his defense, Cook wrote, "I was Enlisted entirely against my own will, not voluntarily Enlisted as a Soldier, but

---

2 Heitman, *Register and Dictionary of the U.S. Army*, 1:985; *Army and Navy Chronicle,* 2, no. 5 (4 February 1836): 70.

compelled if I did not Enlist that I should have the same fate of Ambrister and others and that it was not my inclination or desire to enlist at all and my feelings were almost much in despair, although I was under obligations to do that which was entirely against my own will and person. …" After deliberation, the Court found him guilty and sentenced him "to be shot to death," but on 22 December 1818 Cook was granted a full pardon by President James Monroe. He continued to serve the U. S. Army until 30 June 1820 when he furnished a substitute and was discharged.[3]

---

3 Griffin, *Voyage to the Spanish Main*, 215-216; Peter B. Cook to Elizabeth A. Carney, 19 January 1818, *ASP:FR,* 4:605; *Register of Enlistments,* NA; Peter B. Cook & Others (9 September to 10 October 1818), Record Group 153: Records of the Judge Advocate General's Office (Army), Entry 15: Court-Martial Case Files, 1809-94, 7E3: 13/11/4, Box #34, File #S-8, NA.

John and Elizabeth Dill Census Records

1820, Early County, Georgia. John Dill, page 61: 2 males (ages 20-45); 6 males (ages 45+); 1 female (10-45); 10 slaves.

1830, Early County, Georgia. John Dill, page 98: 3 males (ages 20-30); 2 males ages (40-50); 1 female (ages 20-30); 1 male slave (ages 10-24); 1 male slave (ages 24-36); 1 female slave (under 10); 2 females slaves (ages 35-55).

1840, Early County, Georgia. John Dill, sheet 113, page 3: 1 male (ages 15-20); 2 males (ages 20-30); 2 males (ages 30-40); 1 male (ages 50-60); 1 female (ages 40-50); 1 slave (ages 24-36).

1850, Early County, Georgia, page 303A: Dill, John, age 62, merchant, worth: $10,000, born South Carolina. Dill, Elizabeth A., age 39 (error?), born Maryland.

1860, Early County, Georgia: Elizabeth Dill, age 60, property: $5,000, born Maryland. Living with James and Sarah Touson.

Further Reading

For those who would like to explore the events covered in this book deeper, we would recommend the following titles:

A more detailed history of the Scott Massacre is *The Scott Massacre of 1817,* by Dale Cox, (CreateSpace Independent Publishing Platform, 2013, available through amazon.com).

The best history of the First Seminole War is *Old Hickory's War: Andrew Jackson and the Quest for Empire,* by David S. and Jeanne T. Heidler, (Stackpole Books, 1996).

To learn about the Seminole Wars in general, see *The Seminole Wars: America's Longest Indian Conflict,* by John and Mary Lou Missall, (University Press of Florida, 2004).

For those interested in learning about the Patriot War of 1812, we suggest *The Other War of 1812: The Patriot War and the American Invasion of Spanish East Florida,* by James G. Cusick, (University of Georgia Press, 2007).

Acknowledgements

There have been numerous individuals who have helped us in our search for victims of the Scott Massacre. First and foremost are our good friends Dr. Joe Knetsch, who supplied countless pieces of research material, and Earl, Bettie, and Jeremy DeBary, who offered constant encouragement throughout the years. Special thanks go to Dale Cox, who has also investigated the Scott Massacre and has graciously shared much of his research material. We'd also like to thank our good friend and artist Jackson Walker for the cover art on this as well as other works we've done. We also express appreciation to the many librarians and staff members of the Lee County, Florida, Library System, the National Archives, and the Family History Center at the Church of the Latter Day Saints who aided us in our research. We would especially like to thank Carol Hoyt for allowing us to stay the night in Elizabeth's bedroom at the Dill House in Fort Gaines.

Thanks also go to the following people who assisted us in our endeavors to find material relating to Elizabeth Stuart, John Stuart, John Dill, and the men of Lieutenant Scott's command: James E. Coleman of Fort Gaines, Georgia; Jennifer Silvers, Manuscript Archivist at the Oklahoma Historical Society; Stephanie Hanks of the Early County, Georgia, Probate Court; and Melissa Shriver of the Clay County, Georgia, Probate Court.

Finally we would like to thank those family members and friends who have probably heard the story of the Scott Massacre and Elizabeth Stuart more times than they've really cared to. We hope that after reading this, they will think that it was all worthwhile.

Other Works by John and Mary Lou Missall

Hollow Victory: A Novel of the Second Seminole War, Florida Historical Society Press, 2010.

The Seminole Wars: America's Longest Indian Conflict, University Press of Florida, 2004.

This Miserable Pride of a Soldier: The Letters and Journals of Col. William S. Foster in the Second Seminole War, University of Tampa Press, 2005.

This Torn Land: Poetry of the Second Seminole War, Seminole Wars Foundation Press, 2009.

Just Havin' Fun: Adventures of an Oil Well Firefighter, with Boots Hansen, Middle River Press, 2011